LIGHTNING *in a* SHOT GLASS

a novel

PRAISE FOR *LIGHTNING IN A SHOT GLASS*

'Absolutely top-tier Indian contemporary fiction. Empathetic, smart, layered, sharp, funny, honest, authentic and complex. Loved it.'

—Samit Basu

'Wickedly funny, wildly unserious about serious things, while simultaneously being whip-smart, *Lighting in a Shot Glass* is the kind of book you'll breeze through with a grin on your face.'

—Aditi Mittal

'A vibrant story of friendship and affinity, saturated with the exuberance of Mumbai.'

—Mahesh Rao

'*Lightning in a Shot Glass* manages to be witty and breezy while also forcing you to face discomfort. Deepanjana Pal's lightness of touch makes you feel like you're sitting with your cleverest friends.'

—Diksha Basu

'Bombay gets a rom-com it deserves—as irrepressible and heartfelt as itself; a book that allows women to read for pleasure without any guilty-shilty added on.'

—Paromita Vohra

LIGHTNING *in a* SHOT GLASS

a novel

DEEPANJANA PAL

HarperCollins *Publishers* India

First published in India by HarperCollins *Publishers* 2025
HarperCollins *Publishers* India, Cyber City, Building 10-A, Gurugram, Haryana-122002, India
www.harpercollins.co.in

2 4 6 8 10 9 7 5 3 1

P-ISBN: 978-93-7307-986-8
E-ISBN: 978-93-7307-876-2

Typeset in 11.5/15.2 Adobe Caslon Pro
by HarperCollins *Publishers* India Pvt. Ltd

Printed and bound at
Thomson Press (India) Ltd

MIX
Paper | Supporting responsible forestry
FSC® C010615

This book is produced from independently certified FSC® paper to ensure responsible forest management.

*

HarperCollins *Publishers*, Macken House, 39/40 Mayor Street Upper, Dublin 1, D01 C9W8, Ireland

Does it shine? Does it sing?
Does it spark and crackle? Does it sting?
Does it scan? Does it rhyme?

Does it make sense;
and, if it does, what does it mean?
Ask yourself,

Will it fit in with the rest?
Is this precisely the twig you need for your nest
at precisely this moment?

—'To a Crow', Arun Kolatkar

1

One divorce, two long-term relationships and multiple one-night stands later, Meera was on a train to Kandivali, standing at the doorway of a general compartment, clutching like a nervous stripper the steel pole that usually anchors commuters in the face of waves of incoming and exiting crowds. It was 12.45 a.m., there were barely ten people sitting in the compartment, and standing next to her was Jeet, the Kandivali resident who was definitely in his twenties, had been her junior for the past two years that he'd worked at the same newspaper, and whose home she was going to with the intention of having sex. At least that's what Meera thought she was doing. Surely no one travels an hour by local train to just make out? Turning her back on the blazing blue neon inside the train compartment, Meera looked out and tried not to think about how much older than Jeet she was. Not that she knew his age exactly. She really didn't know much about him, except for the fact that he had skin that felt like polished cotton.

The train hurtled past neighbourhoods she just about recognized despite fifteen years spent in the city. Meera could see squares and flashes of light, silhouettes framed against windows, and darkness. She felt Jeet move to stand beside her.

He was tall, Meera thought to herself, taller than he'd felt an hour ago when he'd been sitting by her side during the farewell dinner her colleagues had thrown for her. Colleagues including him. She reminded herself that they weren't colleagues anymore. Today had been her last day. Jeet's hand tentatively curved around her waist; a couple of fingers on the edge of her blouse, so close to the underside of her breast; the other fingers touching her skin.

It was when the train rushed past Goregaon station that Meera, aged forty years and four months, clutching a steel pole and pressed against the erection of a man whose age she didn't know and whose article she'd corrected last week, faced up to the fact that she was going through a mid-life crisis.

Jeet's flat was a ten-minute auto ride from the station. Inside the rattling three-wheeler, he put his arm around Meera and pulled her close to him. Meera looked at the reflection in the rearview mirror. The two of them were in shadow. Occasionally, the yellow of streetlights slashed the darkness and she could see Jeet's eyes, the sharp line of his nose, his lips pressed close together. She turned his face towards her own and, closing her eyes, kissed him, once, twice; the third time, she touched her tongue to the seam of his lips. His hand around her shoulder tightened. They opened their eyes at the same time. Jeet darted a glance at the driver.

The man was looking ahead with the studiousness of someone determined to not acknowledge that a middle-aged woman and a man in his twenties were making out at the back of his vehicle. Jeet's nervous face broke into a quiet little laugh. His teeth were starry white. A small puff of his breath settled on Meera's skin. She smelt the cheap rum he'd been drinking. She'd drunk vodka with tonic. She wondered if her breath smelt sour. Jeet held her face in his hands and whispered, 'I can't believe I'm doing this in an auto, but what the hell. Open your mouth.' And as he kissed her with intent and tongue, Meera melted, and in a far corner of her brain, the few cells that were still functional crossed their fingers in the hope that there wouldn't be a wet patch on her sari when they got out of the auto.

The guard did a double take when he saw Jeet and Meera enter the building premises. The silver lining, Meera told herself, was that clearly Jeet didn't bring too many women home at 1.30 a.m.

'Hello Pandeyji,' Jeet said warmly to the guard. 'All good?'

Meera realized she would probably have sex with Jeet soon. Except she didn't have a condom. What if he didn't have one? What if he didn't use one? She started when she felt a hand at the small of her back.

'The lift is over there,' Jeet said to her. She smiled brightly at him. He lived on the tenth floor. In the lift, he stood a short distance away.

Meera saw the camera in one corner. She wondered if he lived with a flatmate. What if the flatmate was awake? What if he was a journalist? The doors of the lift opened, and Jeet walked out. 'This way,' he said. Meera saw beads of sweat at the corner of his brow. Outside his door—dark wooden finish; small window with a grille at the centre; a Ganesha on the doorframe—he fumbled with the keys. He was tense, Meera could tell. Of course he was. She was like his boss. Had been. She had been like his boss.

The sound of the lock slipping back was loud in the late-night stillness inside the building. Jeet opened the door, stepped in and vaguely flapped his arm to usher her inside. Meera walked in and the still-active brain cells reminded her that in women, sexual desire led to a surge of testosterone rather than oestrogen. She felt her testosterone recede and panic rise, like a tsunami wave. Jeet pushed the door shut behind her and moved closer. She took a step back. Behind her was the solid flatness of the door; in front of her, a few breathless inches away was all of Jeet. He leaned forward a little, his palms flat on either side of her head. She put her hands on his chest. Under her palm, his heart juddered. He was warm. One of her hands moved to slip a finger through the gap between two of his buttons. His skin was smooth and the body hair reminded her of the veins on a new leaf. He lowered his head and pressed a kiss on the skin behind her ear, another one on her neck and then another, lower, near her collarbone.

He really was tall. She could feel how much he was bending. Meera rose on her tiptoes, making it a little easier for him to fit his face against the curve of her neck. He opened his mouth. The warmth of his tongue and edge of his teeth made her catch her breath. She could just about see over his shoulder into the room. The mattress on the floor had a mirror-work bedcover. There was a table lamp next to it. On the wall was a poster of Quentin Tarantino's *Pulp Fiction*. A bookshelf that looked strangely precarious was crammed with books and festooned with fairy lights. On top of it were little action figures. One of them was definitely a miniature Hulk. In the middle of the room was a low table, its surface covered with glasses, an almost-overflowing ashtray, and used plates. There was a chair with a towel draped on the armrest. The air in the room had the faint bitter burn of cigarettes smoked hours ago.

Everything about the room screamed youth. Meera found herself remembering her hostel room from twenty years ago, even as her hands untucked Jeet's shirt and slipped under to feel his skin. His waist had a gentle dip, and his stomach clenched when her fingers wandered from back to front. No washboard abs, but the firm yet soft tautness of someone whose body hasn't slackened. Meera didn't hear the sweet nothings he mumbled against her skin. All she could think of was that she was practically forty-one and Jeet was a boy. He lived far out in the suburbs, in a flat that didn't even have a sofa. His bookshelf had a Hulk on it. If she looked at the books on that shelf, maybe she'd find Paulo Coelho and Chetan Bhagat. Worse, Ayn Rand. She'd kept *Atlas Shrugged* in plain sight in her bookshelf for years, when she was in her early twenties. She didn't know better. Maybe neither did Jeet—not just about what was on his bookshelf, but what he was doing now. With an older woman in his arms and cheap rum on his tongue. Jeet's hand cupped Meera's breast over the sari and blouse. The tip of a finger—did he have big hands or were blouses excessively low-cut?—touched the skin at the blouse's neckline.

Meera pulled her hands out from under Jeet's shirt and pushed at him. 'I'm sorry, I can't do this,' she said, her eyes squeezed tightly shut.

Jeet stopped and moved away immediately. He looked confused. Meera searched his face for signs of anger or discontent, but didn't see any. His shirt was rumpled and a wedge of his chest was visible because she'd unfastened the top three buttons. She remembered doing that. That part of him did not look like a boy and for a long, uncomfortable moment, Meera's brain struggled to reason with the messages being sent by her hormones.

'I'm not sure …'

'I should get a cab to go home,' Meera interrupted Jeet and reached into her bag for her phone. She opened the taxi app and held her phone out to him. 'This is your address, right?' she asked.

Jeet stared at her for a moment and then took the phone. He nodded before handing it back to her. Meera watched the bobbing graphics that said the app was contacting nearby drivers.

'Eight minutes away,' she said with saccharine good cheer.

Jeet rubbed the back of his neck, still looking at her. 'Why don't you sit down while you wait?' he said finally, pointing to the chair. He picked up the towel on the armrest and bundled it up.

Was he blushing? It was hard to tell with his colouring, especially in the dim light from the table lamp.

'Thanks,' Meera said and went towards the chair, even though she wanted to stay plastered against the door.

He sat on the mattress, the balled-up towel on his lap. The driver was six minutes away.

'Would you like some water?' Jeet asked.

'Sure.'

He got up and she looked down. His feet were clean and his toenails were neatly clipped, Meera noted. Some dry skin at the heels, but not too much. Meera thought of her own feet. She hadn't had a pedicure in months. In yesterday's meeting, she'd surreptitiously peeled a few strips of thick, dead skin off her left heel.

The driver was four minutes away.

'Here you go.'

Meera took the glass of water from Jeet, emptied it in three gulps, and put it on the table after nudging another glass away.

'I should go down,' she said. 'The cab will be here soon.'

'Right. Of course.'

They walked to the door. Jeet suddenly stopped and said, 'Meera, I'm sorry if I …'

'You have nothing to apologize for,' Meera cut in quickly. 'This is just … complicated.'

Jeet nodded, staring at his feet. Then he looked at her and Meera wanted to press her lips on the twitching nerve at his jaw.

'I don't understand.' The words blurted out of him. 'Stay?' he said.

Meera shook her head, and for no good reason, she pulled his face down and kissed him on his lips. His arms went around her and after two tongue tangles, her phone started ringing. She pulled away, and for a moment, his arms didn't move.

'Hello? Yes, I'm coming down,' Meera said to the cabbie who had called her. 'I'll be there in a minute.'

Jeet stepped away.

'I should go,' Meera said, not for the first time, and turned to open the door. It was a strange lock with too many knobs and levers. Jeet watched her fumble with it for a few seconds, before he unlocked it for her. Meera turned around to say thank you and saw a small woman in pajamas, standing behind him.

So, he did have a flatmate.

'Hey, I heard a noise,' said the other woman, slurring just a little. She was barely awake.

Jeet turned around and took a few steps towards her and away from Meera. Everything about the way he was holding himself changed in an instant. It was as though he'd been standing in a harness all this time. 'Hey, sorry,' he said. 'Ishita, this is my boss, Meera. My ex-boss, actually. This is Ishita, my flatmate. She's a filmmaker.'

Ishita waved. 'Aspiring filmmaker,' she said with a grin. 'Currently just contract labour and sleepy.'

Meera smiled and said, 'Hi, actually I'm not his boss. As in, I wasn't even when we worked together. His boss, Faisal, is a friend of mine. I'm just an ex-colleague. Anyway, it doesn't matter. I was just leaving. I'm sorry to have woken you up. I didn't realize my phone's ringtone was so loud. I should have kept it on silent.' *I should also stop babbling*, Meera told herself sternly. 'Jeet, thanks for tonight and maybe I'll see you around?' Tasing him with her brightest smile, Meera turned around, left the flat and thanked all the gods in the pantheon that the lift was still on the tenth floor. She got in, stabbed at the button for the ground floor, and looked up to see the doors close on Jeet as he stood on the other side, barefoot, brow furrowed and with a noticeable bulge in his pants.

At the same time but in a different time zone, Aalo stared at the mug of cider in front of her and wondered what the hell had happened to her life. She was twenty-four hours away from turning twenty-nine. She was sitting in a pub in London. All of which sounded great until she added the minor details that she couldn't really afford this drink (but her father could) and neither could she afford the holiday (but her father had paid for the tickets and the stay was free, thanks to her old friend Kekoo) and that she didn't really have a career despite having an undergraduate degree in law, a master's in mythology and work experience in three unrelated industries. Also, she was overweight, 5'10" tall, single and practically thirty.

'Sorry I'm late.' Kekoo gave her a quick hug and settled into the chair opposite Aalo.

'It's fine. I was very busy pondering about how much of a mess my life is.'

Kekoo took a large gulp of Aalo's drink and made a face. 'Cider? Hold that thought while I get myself a real drink.'

Aalo watched Kekoo, slim and determined, as he cut a path across the pub, through the crowd at the bar, and caught the attention of the bartender. If that had been Aalo, she would probably have crashed into four tables and spent forty minutes being ignored by the bartender. Meanwhile, in the time that it had taken her to articulate her self-pity, Kekoo had got himself a whisky and her another cider, both of which he was holding with secure grace.

'So. What's this about life being a mess?' he said, putting the glasses down.

'I just realized I'm a really good person,' Aalo said, finishing off the last of her cider and wrapping her hands around the one Kekoo had just deposited on the table.

Kekoo clinked his glass with hers. 'Agreed, but what brought on this epiphany?'

'The fact that I love you despite the fact that you're a walking, talking reminder of what a complete screw-up I am.'

'I'm sorry, what?'

'You're Parsi, you look gay, you can't do simple addition, you studied mythology in university … and despite all this, you live in London, go on exotic holidays every other week …'

'Oh please. Hardly …'

'Where were you last week?'

'Paris, but …'

'And when did you go to Dubrovnik?'

'Three weeks ago, but that was originally for a conference.'

'Which you extended into a holiday that included a random fling with a ridiculously hot human.'

'That was just …'

'Stop interrupting,' Aalo said in her sternest voice. 'You have everything. I meanwhile am jobless, clueless and on holiday because I have a rich dad.' She ran her hand through her hair and groaned. 'Oh, and all my hair is falling out. But despite the obvious contrast in our circumstances, I love you deeply and not just because you're letting me stay in your stupidly cute flat. In London. Ergo, I'm a good person.'

'You're the best. Also, if you ever need a transplant, the organically-grown hair shirt on my back is at your disposal.'

'Your back?'

'I'm not giving you my chest hair. It gets me action.'

'Ew. No. Please. No sex talk.'

'Said the desi internet's favourite sex educator. Ha!'

Aalo groaned again. 'What is my life? I have a proper education, a law degree no less, and my claim to fame is that I answer people's sex questions on Instagram.'

'That,' said Kekoo, 'is not the crazy part. The crazy part is that the last time you had sex, you were practically underage.'

'Stop exaggerating.'

'Ok, how long has it been?'

'Five years.'

'Wow.'

The two friends sipped their drinks in silence.

'It wasn't even good sex,' Aalo said glumly. 'I think I was just turned on by the fact that he wanted me.'

Kekoo made a face. 'I need another drink if we're going to talk about your ex.' He got up and zipped to the bar.

Aalo sighed. Why couldn't she be crushing on Kekoo? Even if he was gay, it would make sense to crush on Kekoo. He was good-looking, single, caring, intelligent and just a *good* person. Instead, continuing her life's theme of being generally useless, Aalo had gone and fallen for a married man who slept around, didn't use a condom and was, in polite terms, a conservative.

Kekoo returned with no glass for her and two glasses of whisky for himself.

'Why didn't you just get one large?' Aalo asked.

'I'm pacing myself,' Kekoo said primly. 'We—by which I mean my sobriety and my bank balance—have to last till midnight. Just so I'm clear, we're bringing in your birthday by talking about your miserable life choices, yes?'

Aalo stared glumly at her cider. 'How the hell did I become a sex educator?'

'Now that you are, can you at least educate yourself to not jump into bed with someone who wears saffron-coloured underwear?'

'Rudra didn't wear saffron-coloured underwear. That's the thing! I didn't know he was one of those!'

'What rubbish. Of course you knew.'

'I swear on my mother.'

Kekoo rolled his eyes. 'Listen, anyone who has seen Rudra's Facebook profile knows he's so saffron, he makes Donald Trump's orange face look pale. How could you not know?'

'I honestly didn't notice his politics. Why would that be such a big deal? I mean, it hasn't been for my parents. My mother's like me and my dad is, well, like Rudra. Oh god! Do I have to deal with daddy issues on top of everything else?'

'Everything else?'

'Kekoo, I know how his political beliefs are more problematic for you than the fact that he was married. But Rudra was and is married. To a woman who is now six months pregnant.'

'How do you know she's six months pregnant?'

'I chanced upon it on Facebook.'

'Ah, so you can "chance" upon his wife's gynaecological updates on Facebook, but you missed the twenty status updates he puts up in a day, adoring Hindu fascists?' Kekoo asked, his smile dripping sweet poison.

Aalo sighed. 'Fine. I admit it. I just ignored that side of him. Not my brightest call, I agree. But I will tell you that despite the fact that we hooked up five whole years ago, my skin still crawls when I think that I let him touch me with the same fingers he uses to type those disgusting updates.'

Kekoo took Aalo's hand in his. 'I know my saying it won't make a difference since I've been saying the same thing for only about ten years, but you really do deserve better than bastards like Rudra.'

'Then why do only idiots with questionable politics and no sense of fidelity fall for me?' Aalo started ticking names off on her fingers. 'Rudra, we've established, is a loser. Roy cheated on me within a week of us starting to date. Ravi thought Clinton was within his rights to screw around with Monica Lewinsky. Ritwik told me that if I'd been thin, he wouldn't have been forced to cheat on me.'

'You really do have a talent for picking amazing men whose names begin with R,' Kekoo said.

'I'm telling you. I just gravitate towards entitled, Hindu idiots. It's like I was Clockwork Oranged.'

'You're like that girl in that podcast we were hearing yesterday, you know, that Asian-American woman who realized that even though she wasn't racist, she had been conditioned into rejecting Black men as potential partners.'

'The one who decided she's just going to date Black guys from now on?'

'Yes.'

'Such a well-made podcast.'

'Superb. NPR is just a class apart.'

A phone on a nearby table started ringing, and instead of a regular ring tone, Divine Comedy plaintively declared the owner of the phone to be a gin-soaked boy. Aalo and Kekoo sat up.

'What are your feelings on kebabs?' Kekoo asked.

Aalo, with her eyes shining, said, 'It's time for a new resolution.' She reached for Kekoo's untouched glass of whisky, ignored his anguished protest, and held it up. 'I, Aloukika Mukherjee, popularly known as Aalo, vow that in this my twenty-ninth year, I will take a hammer to my upper-caste, Hindu socialization and only date or have sex with non-Hindu, non-savarna men.' She knocked back the whisky and choked a little in the process. 'May they be hot and may I have orgasms worthy of a professional sex educator. May they also not have names starting with R.'

Kekoo raised what was left of his whisky and said, 'Oh crap.'

Three days later, when Aalo made her way home from the airport—after her flight from London landed in Mumbai at an ungodly hour of the night—she expected to enter a dark flat. Instead, the lights were on, music was playing at a low, comforting hum, and Meera was sitting on the sofa, in her pajamas, cradling a bowl of Maggi.

'Hello, flatmate,' Aalo said with a big smile.

'Hello, you!' Meera got up and gave Aalo a hug.

At first glance, the two women were a study in contrasts. Aalo was tall; Meera was not. Meera had long hair; the longest Aalo's hair had been was a bob till the base of her neck. Aalo's skin looked like milk with a few drops of coffee in it; Meera's colouring was like strongly-brewed, milky tea. Meera had large, doe-like eyes; Aalo's were narrower and heavy-lidded. Meera had thin lips; Aalo's looked like she was pouting even when she pressed them together to their thinnest. Meera's face was long, making her seem slighter than she was, until you realized that she had the curves that could have easily belonged on a classical Indian sculpture. Aalo's face was round as the moon, making her look fuller than she actually was—until you noticed how toned her arms were and the taut muscles of her calves. Most of the time, their clothes added to the difference. Meera tended to wear saris and long skirts. Aalo paired anything with everything in a bohemian adventure and somehow, it worked. Yet when they stood face to face, like now in their living room, it was obvious that Meera and Aalo fit, like two interlocked jigsaw puzzle pieces that belong next to one another despite all their differences.

'Where's your luggage?' Meera asked, looking behind Aalo.

'The airlines lost it,' Aalo replied cheerfully.

'What!'

'Apparently, it's gone to Hong Kong or Dubai instead of Mumbai.'

'Oh no!'

'I'm keeping my fingers crossed they lose it,' Aalo said as she toed off her shoes and made her way into the living room. 'Is that cheese Maggi?' she asked, peering at the bowl.

'It is. But that's not important. Is there someone we can call? Should I check with the guys on the aviation beat?' Meera sat down and reached for her phone, which was charging on the side table.

'So good!' Aalo said, as she forked some of the unnaturally yellow noodles into her mouth. 'Aviation beat? Woman, keep your journalists away from these airlines people and let them be their inefficient best. If they lose my backpack, I can claim it had diamonds and designer wear in it instead of dirty underwear and old clothes, and then I will be rich.'

Meera shook her head. 'You're impossible. You're also already rich.'

'No, my dad is. This would be wealth I would have earned independently.'

'Give back my Maggi and tell me how London was.'

'London was great. Kekoo is still a doll. He sends his love and says you should visit soon. His flat is like something out of a rom-com. Everything ok here? How did the farewell go? And why are you eating Maggi at 3 a.m.?' Aalo filled her mouth with noodles before returning the bowl to Meera.

'I was hungry,' Meera replied with a shrug.

Aalo raised one eyebrow. Meera raised both in response.

'Meera,' Aalo said in a low voice that radiated gravity. 'Please tell me there is or was a strapping sex god in your room and these are post-coital noodles.'

'Post-coital noodles? Seriously? What is wrong with your generation?' Meera groaned. 'The post-coital cigarette is a thing of elegance, irreverence and defiance. A noodle has none of that and really, Freud could go to town with the whole wilting phallic symbol angle.'

Aalo frowned. 'I feel you're focusing on the wrong detail.'

'There is no detail to focus on. I was just eating noodles.'

'Because you needed carbs after an energetic aerobic workout that involved exchanging bodily fluids?' Aalo asked hopefully.

'No.'

Aalo made a face and sprawled wide on the sofa. 'Dammit, Meera! I rely on you to make my PG-13 life interesting. You can't just be eating noodles for fun. Honestly, one of the main reasons I chose you as a flatmate was because I was hoping you'd use the flat as a place to sow your wild oats, rage against the patriarchal machine, sexually liberate yourself in the process, and all that.'

'Which I've done in the past.'

'Which is why I expect your noodles to be post-coital in the present. You've become very boring and celibate these days.'

'Sorry to disappoint you,' Meera said with a grin.

Aalo raised her head, her face suddenly serious. 'You could never disappoint me. The way you held your ground after the divorce, especially with your family going all Taliban and disowning you? Yas queen!'

'Well, I wouldn't have had much ground to stand on if you hadn't given me this place to stay.'

'The one good thing that came of my terrible stint as an intern with that wretched newspaper of yours—us meeting.'

'It's not my newspaper. I quit, remember? But yes, you were a pretty terrible intern and yes, thank god we met. Don't tell anyone, but I think I got the better end of the deal.'

'Are you kidding me?' Aalo snorted and reached for the bowl of noodles. 'First of all, I have earned enough good karma for a lifetime with the brainwave that we should share this flat. It got my overprotective parents off my back. Plus, if I had a rupee for every time my dad tells me to be sensible and pursue a career like you, I'd be able to afford two flats in Bandra and maybe a 1BHK in Thane.'

'I still think it's hilarious that your parents think I'm a good influence on you,' Meera said, handing the bowl to Aalo.

'It's because they only see the petite, sari-wearing journalist. They have no idea that when night falls, you become a man-eater while I am basically a nun.'

Meera winced, but Aalo didn't notice because she was too focused on spearing a bit of noodle.

'Speaking of man-eating, you should know that I am on a mission,' Aalo told Meera solemnly.

'Is that so?'

Aalo nodded. 'I've decided that the only socially responsible thing to do as a privileged Hindu in present-day India is to date non-Hindu, non-savarna men.' Aalo raised a forkful of noodles in the air. 'Take that, love jihad!'

Meera stared at Aalo in disbelief. 'You're joking.'

'I am 100 per cent serious.'

'So you're going to single out Muslim, Christian, Jain, Sikh, Dalit and Adivasi men?'

'I'm not very keen on Jain,' Aalo said, finishing off the noodles on her fork. 'I don't think I can do the diet.'

'Aalo, are you for real?'

'Like I said, 100 per cent.'

'Have you any idea how completely wrong this whole thing is?' Meera shook her head. 'It's like you're treating these communities like guinea pigs you want to experiment on.'

'You're getting it all wrong. *I'm* the guinea pig I'm experimenting on.' Aalo put the bowl down. 'Look, I'm twenty-nine years old, I've had access to all the freedoms a girl can hope for, and yet I have not ever had a non-Hindu boyfriend. This isn't a coincidence. It's social conditioning and I'd like to re-condition myself. Challenge my upbringing. Which is what I will do with a little help from those damn dating apps that everyone seems to swear by. Did you hear? Raunak married the guy she met on Tinder.'

'You're not on Tinder.'

'I will get on it now.'

'In order to date non-Hindu, non-savarna men.'

Aalo nodded cheerfully while stuffing her face with noodles. Meera buried her face in her hands. 'And I thought I was losing it.' She looked up and frowned. 'Maybe it's something in the water supply that's messing with our heads.'

'I don't understand why you think my idea is so terrible,' Aalo said as she got up to put the empty bowl in the kitchen sink. It was only once she'd put the bowl down that she realized what Meera had said.

'Wait a minute,' Aalo said, returning to the living room. 'What do you mean you're losing it? What have you done?'

Meera released a long breath, but didn't say anything.

'Meera?'

'Hm?'

'Don't hm me. What have you done?'

One second Meera was looking straight at Aalo and the next, she'd dived under a cushion and was mumbling something into the sofa.

'Oy!' Aalo complained. 'Get out of the cushion. I can't understand a word of what you're saying.'

Meera didn't emerge, but she did raise a corner of the cushion. 'I almost slept with one of the kids on the desk,' she said in a small voice. 'Oh god. It sounds even worse when I say it out loud,' she groaned.

'Holy mother.' Aalo stared at Meera's cushion-covered head. 'You banged a deskie! Do you realize how much punning potential that has? Was it thumpingly good?' She perked up. 'Wait. Do I know him?'

There was motion under the cushion that suggested Meera was nodding to answer in the affirmative.

'Let me guess,' Aalo said excitedly.

The corner of the cushion lifted. 'It was Jeet,' Meera said. The cushion came down again.

'Jeet of the scruffy beard?'

Meera raised the corner of the cushion again. 'He shaved,' she said.

'Wow. Jeet is like my age. Meera,' Aalo said, clutching her friend's shoulder, 'is this you having a mid-life crisis?'

Meera said something under the cushion that may have been 'yes' or 'fuck you'.

'Oh, come out from under there,' Aalo said, impatiently pushing at Meera's shoulders. 'I need details!'

After a couple of seconds, Meera sat up and the cushion that had been covering her head was clutched to her chest. Aalo was sitting cross-legged in front of her, leaning forward with shining eyes.

'There's no need to look so excited,' Meera snapped. 'It's not the new Christopher Nolan movie.'

'Are you kidding me? This is like a desi Lolita, in reverse. Way better than anything Nolan could dream up.'

Meera groaned and buried her face in the cushion again.

'Except that Jeet, unlike Lolita, is of legal age, obviously,' Aalo amended. 'Tell me everything.'

Meera looked up and sighed. 'That's the only difference that comes to your mind between Lolita and Jeet?'

Aalo swatted the question away. 'Tell me what happened!'

'There's not much to tell. The office guys threw me a farewell dinner. We were at Ling's. There were more people than expected, so we all squeezed in. He was sitting next to me. And then, I don't know, it just happened.'

'Nonono, don't skip the details,' Aalo wailed. 'What happened?'

Meera threw her hands up in the air. 'I don't know! Maybe I had too much vodka. It was just a game at first because he practically jumped out of his skin when I grabbed his knee by mistake.'

'By mistake?'

'I was trying to keep my napkin from slipping off my lap.' Meera sighed. 'And then it just escalated, I guess. I found myself finding different ways of, well, touching him.' She grimaced as she remembered. 'Discreetly, you know? Fingers while reaching for food, ankle under the table,' Meera squeezed her eyes shut, 'upper thigh under the napkin.'

'You gave him a handjob during an office dinner?' Aalo yelped, scandalized.

'Are you mad!' Meera yelped right back. 'No, I just sort of brushed past … the area. Anyway, soon enough, he was doing pretty much the same. By the time we were done with dinner, both of us were, well …'

'Ready to tear each other's clothes off?'

'Basically, yes. So, everyone was outside and getting ready to go their own way. I obviously hugged each person. When I hugged Jeet, I …' Meera's voice trailed off and she shut her eyes again.

'Go on.'

'I asked him to take me home.'

'I wish my mum and dad were hearing this. So then?'

'Then we walked to Churchgate station, kissed in the shadows along the way, took the train, got off at Kandivali …'

'Why Kandivali?'

'Because that's where he lives.'

Aalo scrunched her face. 'Why wouldn't you bring him here? It's not like you haven't brought men home before.'

'I don't know. At that moment, it just seemed to make sense to go to his place. In hindsight, I'm glad I didn't bring him home because basically, at some point, the hormones settled and common sense finally returned, and I ran out of his house. Literally ran.'

'After you ...' Aalo's voice trailed off and her eyebrows rose like the legs of a water ballet dancer.

'I didn't have sex with him, if that's what you're asking,' Meera said.

'But you did want to.'

'God yes.'

'So, what stopped you?'

'Aalo, he's almost old enough to be my son.'

'Only if you rewind a couple of centuries so that it's normal for you to pop out babies at age ten.'

Meera shook her head. 'It felt like cradle-snatching.'

'Wow.' Aalo sat back. 'I know I only lasted in that horrible office for two weeks, but Jeet did not strike me as someone who'd hit on a colleague.'

'Did he seem like the kind of guy who would be hit on by his boss?'

'Since his boss is a balding man named Faisal, no.' Aalo looked pointedly at Meera. 'You're not his boss. You're his senior. It's not the same thing.'

'I wonder if this is a sign of peri-menopause.'

'On the plus side, at least you never have to see him again now that you've quit. Unless he stalks you on social media and follows you to the next place that you join. Have you figured that out, by the way?'

Meera sighed and plucked at the cushion. 'About that, guess who called me yesterday?'

'*The New York Times*?' Aalo said hopefully.

Meera made a face. 'Navin. He wants to meet.'

'Navin, editor-in-chief of *The Daily*, the newspaper you just quit because they've basically been exploiting you for the last seven years and whose deskie you molested?'

'The very same.'

'Bloody hell.'

'Yup. I didn't know whether to get it over with or stall it, so I compromised: I'm meeting him at the end of the week.'

'Wow. I wonder what he wants to say to you.'

'Yeah, me too.'

'By the way,' Aalo said, stifling a yawn. 'Thanks for setting up that meeting with Rucha Phadke. I'm seeing her tomorrow morning.'

'You mean, today. In a few hours.'

'That only.' Aalo surrendered to the yawn.

'Was that wise?' Meera asked gently. 'Rucha has the reputation of being a dragon. She's not someone I'd want to meet jet-lagged, especially if I want her to hire me.'

Aalo shrugged. 'Let's hope she's in a good mood?'

Judging from the way Rucha Phadke was scowling while yelling into the phone and pacing on the pavement outside the office of the Society for Women's Empowerment through Education, Aalo concluded Rucha Phadke was not in a good mood. Aalo mentally patted herself on the back for having stopped her cab a short distance away. Something about Rucha, with her salt-and-pepper hair tied into a bun, sunburnt face, sturdy chappals and general fury made Aalo certain that the older woman would not have approved of Aalo's air-conditioned cab. Should she wait? Should she call Rucha by name or as Mrs Phadke? After hovering for a few seconds, Aalo took a deep breath and walked towards Rucha.

She was just about five steps away when her phone rang. It was the airlines.

'Hello,' Aalo hissed.

'Good morning, Miss Allaoh, I mean, Miss Aloo, I mean …'

'Aloukika, you mean Aloukika. Yes, that's me.'

'Good morning, ma'am. I am calling from the airport office of Island Airways. Your bag is with us.'

'Are you sure?'

'Yes, ma'am.'

'It's a green and grey backpack.'

'Yes, ma'am.'

'With a black ribbon tied to the front clasp.'

'Yes, ma'am.'

Aalo cursed under her breath. There went her hopes of reimbursement for things she'd never possessed. 'Ok. So send it to my address.'

'I'm sorry, ma'am, our policy is for customers to collect their belongings from the airline counter at the airport. That way the customer can confirm that it is definitely their …'

'Who am I speaking to?'

'Shikha, ma'am.'

'Shikha, is it your employer's policy to lose customers' baggage?'

'No, ma'am.'

'Good to know. Now, since your airlines has already broken its policy by losing my bags, I would urge you to break your policy again and have the luggage delivered to my address.'

'But ma'am …'

'And before you tell me more about your policy, I should tell you I'm recording this call and that I'm a journalist with *The Daily*.'

'Ma'am, let me just check with my supervisor and get back to you.'

'Just take my address down and make sure the backpack is sent to my residence. I'm going to be in a meeting and I may not be able to take your call.'

She hung up on Shikha of Island Airways apologizing profusely, and then stopped short. Rucha Phadke was standing four steps away, a quizzical expression on her face.

'You're a journalist with *The Daily*?' Rucha asked drily.

Aalo felt blood rush to her cheeks. 'Umm, well, no, not exactly.'

'Are you getting your bags back?'

'I think so.'

Rucha grinned. 'Well played. You're Meera's friend? Aloo …'

'Aloukika. Like a lauki plus a kick with an "a".' The older woman looked thoroughly confused. 'You can call me Aalo,' Aalo added. 'Everyone does. Aloukika is a bit of a mouthful.'

'Call me Rucha. Come inside … and Aalo …?' Rucha pinned an unblinking stare on Aalo. 'Try to stick to the truth while we talk.'

When she turned and strode up to the green door that had above it a sign that read 'Society for Women's Empowerment through Education', Aalo released her breath. Feeling a little like the baby elephant in Colonel Hathi's march, Aalo followed Rucha Phadke inside.

'So,' Rucha put a cup of milky tea on the glass-topped table in front of Aalo and then went around to sit on the other side, 'why sweet?'

Aalo looked at her tea. Was it sweet? Had jet lag hit her so hard that she'd blanked out on what had happened between walking in and sitting down at the desk in this office? Had she said she wanted sweet chai, which looked very milky? Should she tell Rucha she was lactose intolerant?

'Sweet?'

'Society for Women's Empowerment through Education. S, W, E, T, E … SWETE.'

'Oh SWETE!' Aalo felt like a lightbulb had lit up above her head.

'Or Sweetie, if you talk to Nadkarni in the education department of the BMC,' Rucha said with a grimace. 'He thinks I named the NGO after my daughter. Even though I don't have a daughter.' She blew on her tea, all the while watching Aalo. 'Meera speaks very highly of you,' she said finally.

Aalo smiled and took a sip of her tea. 'She's a good friend.'

'Very kind woman. Terrible judge of character, of course, especially when emotions enter the equation, but yes, she's lovely.'

Aalo choked a little on her tea. Rucha sipped from her cup serenely. 'So, why SWETE?' Rucha asked again.

Aalo carefully put her teacup down. Meera had told her that Rucha did not take kindly to people who had their heads in the clouds. 'She's straightforward, angry and tremendously passionate about the work she does, and she's been this way for the past twenty years. Don't waffle when you're talking to her,' Meera had warned. Aalo knew what she should say—that she was looking to challenge herself and that she felt strongly about gender justice and social equality.

Maybe it was the jet lag, but Aalo threw caution to the winds and decided to be honest. 'The truth is that I have no idea what I'm doing with my life, and I'm here because Meera told me that she thought your organization would be a good place for me, because she thinks you are a brilliant mentor,' Aalo said to Rucha. When Rucha didn't say anything, Aalo barrelled on. 'My resumé isn't unimpressive. I've studied law and my results are good. I'm great with languages. I have experience in event management and video production, both of which are useful skills in this day and age. I've spent the last six months becoming something of a sex educator online and I don't know if you need any of these skills, but I'm hoping you'll give me a chance.'

'How did you become a sex educator?'

Aalo grimaced. 'I wrote a series of tweets about the kinds of things we are told as girls to keep us from exploring our bodies and sexuality, and wailed about the lack of sex education in schools, especially since so much of visual media nudges people towards being sexually active. The thread went viral, and I started doing small videos on Instagram. Then a school called me and asked if I would basically say in person what I was saying online, so I did. They asked me to come back, and then that led to another school calling me over, and then another.'

'Did you know someone at the first school that hired you?'

'My cousin's child goes to the school, so she'd suggested my name to the school.'

'Which schools have you worked with so far?'

Aalo told her. Rucha stared for a few seconds at the bottom of her now-empty teacup. 'After making presentations at some of the priciest schools in the city, you'd now like to work with me in government and charity-run schools.'

'Yes.'

'You do understand that it's unlikely that anyone from your friend or family circles would be in these schools.'

'I know. I look forward to that.'

'Because you think these kids need your charity?'

The question was spoken softly, but Aalo felt like Rucha had taken her hand and stuck her finger into a live plug point. 'No, not charity. I wouldn't be surprised if I needed them more than they need me. But I do think that few people put in the work that the children in these schools deserve. When it's a rich school with rich kids, everyone falls over themselves to cater to them. When it's a government school with underprivileged kids, it seems like people expect them to be grateful for whatever little they get, which is ridiculous.'

'What do you mean when you say you'd need the kids we work with more than they'd need you?'

Aalo felt a vague tingling in her ears. 'Look, I'm a good public speaker. I can put a spin on my resumé to make each of my career choices seem calculated, but the truth is that I'm still in the process of figuring out what I want to do. I think Meera felt that the kind of work you do would be a challenge that would be good for me.'

'And my girls are supposed to risk becoming collateral damage in your quest for self-discovery?'

'No! I would never …'

'What? Be careless? Disrespect them? You think you're equipped to work with them despite knowing nothing of them and being in the process of figuring out what you want to do? That shows just how little you respect the needs of these girls.'

Aalo balled her fists to stop herself from pointing out that the other woman was twisting her admission out of shape.

'Don't hold back,' Rucha said to Aalo, who couldn't tell if she was hallucinating the twinkle in the older woman's eye or not.

'I think,' Aalo said slowly and carefully, 'you care too much about your girls to let them become collateral damage in my quest for self-discovery, as you put it. I know I don't have much experience in the field you work in, but I have had access to a lot of opportunities and information that can be of help to those who, those who …' Aalo floundered.

'Those who are poor,' Rucha supplied drily.

'Actually, marginalized more than poor, but yes. That's essentially it. I want all girls to be able to walk into a room with the same sense of entitlement that I possess—not because they're faking it, but because they *are* entitled, even though society does its best to convince them otherwise. I want them to look at me and think, "If she can do it, then so can I." I'm not an idiot, I know that I have advantages that a lot of girls and women don't get, but a lot of my confidence and sense of entitlement comes from things that can be shared.'

After a short but awkward silence, Rucha said to Aalo, 'In the spirit of honesty, I should tell you that Meera asked me if I would take you in because, and I quote, "Aalo needs a kick of reality on her privileged ass." I'm not really interested in dilettantes, but I have to admit, I do like you for some reason and I can see the girls liking you too.'

Aalo felt relief crawl into her even while a part of her brain noted that Rucha had used the phrase 'take you in' as though Aalo was a stray in need of shelter. She wondered if she was supposed to say something, but fortunately Rucha didn't let her get a word in.

'We're hopefully going to get a grant to do a series of workshops and a survey in government and charity-run schools in the city,' Rucha said. 'Until it comes, I'll make sure you're paid as much as I can afford and as much as I think your work deserves. Should you choose to work with SWETE, of course.'

'That's a bit vague,' Aalo said.

'It is,' Rucha agreed. 'I'll be more specific after I've seen you work. Right now, I'm taking a chance by hiring you, and if you're interested, then I'll work out what I can pay you and message the number to you by this evening.'

'And from when would you like me to start coming in?'

'Whenever you feel ready to take the plunge. I have a very small team. We keep flexible hours because two of them have families and kids that need them at home.'

'And where would I fit into it?'

'You'll be working with Hema and Farhana,' Rucha said. 'Start off by watching them do workshops, pay attention and learn. You're a decent public speaker, you should be able to start doing them on your own soon enough. Who knows, maybe we can use your sex educator skills with a few of the older girls. What languages do you speak?'

'English, Marathi, Hindi and Bengali, in that order of fluency.'

'Marathi?' Rucha raised an eyebrow.

'Fluently.' Aalo braced herself for an impromptu test.

'Good. So, when do you want to come and meet Hema and Farhana?'

Aalo blinked. 'You're not going to test my Marathi?'

'Do I need to?'

'No.'

'Then why are we having this conversation?'

'Sorry. How about you let me know how much you can pay me, and I come in on Monday to meet everyone, and then start coming in regularly from next week?'

'Welcome to SWETE.'

'Sweet,' Aalo replied with a grin.

When Aalo came out of the office, she sent Meera a message, telling her she'd got a job with SWETE. Meera sent back a string of emojis and said she'd call once she was out of her meeting. The big question, Aalo thought while waiting for the cab that was apparently three minutes away, was whether she should tell her parents, particularly her father. They'd be happy to know she'd got a job, but at the same time, they'd give her a lecture about how she must not act rashly. Her father would tell her that he had spent forty years in one company and that her generation had no staying power. It would all be entirely unbearable, so Aalo decided as she got into the Uber that she wouldn't tell her parents anything for now. She'd tell them after a couple of weeks—provided she survived Rucha for that long.

2

Two days in SWETE and Aalo felt like she'd found a home away from home. So much so that while on her way to the office on day three, Aalo heard herself humming. Yes, Aalo was a glorified intern at present. From researching topics, to getting Farhana a cigarette, making slides for a presentation and setting up the whiteboard before a workshop, she was doing a little bit of everything. But at SWETE, it didn't feel like a bad deal. There was a happy buzz all around. The walls were colourful, with posters and children's artwork. The chaiwala from across the road sent his 'boy' with cups of tea every few hours, and already, he'd started sending one glass of black tea for Aalo because he remembered that the new didi in SWETE didn't drink milk. Rucha's team was small, energetic and welcoming. Farhana and Hema radiated warmth and good cheer as though they were human Care Bears, and watching them develop the workshops that SWETE did with schoolkids was fast becoming Aalo's favourite pastime.

This morning, Aalo realized she must be late because when she walked into the office, Farhana and Hema were already there, and Rucha was sitting on the floor, playing with hand puppets shaped like female reproductive organs.

'Ok, so we start with the body, cover how it will change over the decades, move on to good touch and bad touch, then menstruation and desire?' Rucha noticed Aalo at the door and waved an ovary-covered hand at her. 'Hello, Aalo. Join us. We're brainstorming the sex-ed workshops.'

'Sorry, I got stuck in traffic.'

Rucha waved both ovaries at Aalo to indicate it wasn't a big deal.

'Isn't ten or twelve a bit young for desire?' Hema asked, flipping through her notebook.

'When you say it like it's a Mills & Boon title, probably,' said Farhana.

Rucha threw the uterus at Farhana, who caught it neatly.

'The point is, you may not be there for the girls to ask questions later, so why not lay the ground a little early?' Rucha said. 'These workshops should be about more than where the penis goes in and how to make babies. We want to give these girls life skills. We want them to be kind to themselves and to others, especially those that they're told to treat unkindly, like trans folx and queer people. And all of that will happen if the girls understand their bodies and don't misunderstand desire. Because that's going to happen sooner rather than later, especially with everyone constantly telling girls that the be-all and end-all of their lives is to get married and produce sons. So, first things first: puberty. What's the first thing we need to talk about while discussing puberty?'

'Hormones,' said Hema.

'As good a place to start as any,' Rucha agreed. 'Now, how do we explain what hormones are?'

'It's like a juice?' Farhana suggested.

'Because they're secreted, you mean?' Rucha made a face and shook her head. 'That just suggests hormones are fluids.' Rucha stared at the whiteboard on which they'd written some points to remember. 'We need to think of a parallel that shows what hormones do and relates to their reality.' Rucha's stomach growled. 'Where is that Swiggy guy? I want my idli, dammit.' Her face went from grumpy to delighted in less than a second. 'Delivery partners! Hormones are the couriers of the human body. They take messages from one part of the body to another. Sometimes they get it wrong and need a little help to find their way, sometimes they get confused. Most of the time, they follow two standard routes. How does that sound?'

As Rucha expanded on her idea, the workshop started to come together and Aalo found herself crushing on Rucha just a little.

It would be unfair to call the small explosion of whipped cream, drizzled sauces and sprinkles in front of Navin Kapur, editor-in-chief of *The Daily*, a coffee. He unpeeled a paper straw and as it slid through the frothy drink, a satisfied sigh bubbled out of the large man. Meera lifted up her cup of black coffee for a sip and hid her grin behind it.

'Laugh, laugh. When one day you're forced to go on a draconian diet, you'll remember me fondly,' Navin said, all his attention focused upon his first mouthful of the drink.

'I'm glad your doctor has given you the all-clear, but does your wife know this is what you order when her back is turned?'

'I get one cheat day every three months. Don't spoil it by bringing my wife into it!' Navin paused for a moment as he savoured his drink. 'Now, shall we cut to the chase?'

'Sure.'

'I want you to come back to *The Daily*.'

For a second, the white noise of the coffee shop thickened to a sharp, metallic buzz in Meera's ear. 'Would it be too cocky if I told you that you should have thought of that earlier?' she said, careful to ensure Navin could hear the laughter in her voice.

There was, however, no laughter in his voice when he said, 'Sagar had a heart attack.'

'I heard. His wife told me he's stable now.'

'He's still in hospital, in the ICU. I doubt he'll come back to work any time soon.' Navin looked up at her briefly, before returning his attention to the confectionery before him. 'When he does, he's going to have to take it easy.'

Meera put her mug down carefully. 'I'm not sure what any of this has to do with me.'

'Sagar was one of the best political editors around, but he needs to take a step back. He was your mentor, so I'm saying, this is a great opportunity for you. We're going to need someone excellent to head up the political bureau, especially with elections around the corner.'

'Elections are about two years away.'

'Just come back, Meera.'

The buzzing started in Meera's ear again, and for a moment, the coffee-shop faded away and she was transported to the corner of the office that *The Daily*'s political team occupied in the newsroom; she saw the faces of the people who had been her colleagues till a few days ago, their desks with piles of paper and bric-a-brac. She thought of how desperately she'd wanted Navin to ask her to take back her resignation every day of the two months' notice she had served; how she had dreamt of Sagar sitting at her desk while she sat at his.

'I know you haven't got an offer from anywhere else …'

'That's because I haven't been looking.' It came out sharper than Meera had intended, but Navin didn't seem to mind.

'Well, I'm telling you to not look. It's not like you wanted to leave,' he told her, as if she needed reminding.

'No, I didn't, but I did leave. And you let me.'

'You didn't give me a choice. Political editor or nothing, you said. No conversation. Well, now I'm saying I'll make you the political editor.'

'Really …'

'You did do a great job of handling the bureau while Sagar was out doing the drought series.'

'Thank you. That's why I asked you for the job in the first place—because I know I can do it.'

'So I'm giving you the job you wanted.'

'And Sagar?'

Navin let out a noisy breath. 'Don't make me choose between you and Sagar. The point is: there's enough room in *The Daily* for both of you.'

'Really? Is that why we didn't have this chat before my last day?'

'I wanted to. Believe me, I did. But I needed clearance from the top, and that took a lot longer than I thought it would.' Navin savoured a spoonful of whipped cream. 'Look, Sagar's not in good shape. He's going to be in hospital for a while, and even once he comes back, he's not going to be 100 per cent.'

'Who will he report to once he is?'

'Sorry?'

'When Sagar returns to work, who will he report to?'

'To me, just like you will. You'll both be the same rank.' Meera made a face. 'You know that if I tell him to report to you, he'll have a much bigger heart attack,' Navin said, while searching for an elusive sprinkle in his coffee.

Meera decided to ignore Navin's callousness and focus on practical details. 'So you'll have two political editors? That makes no sense.'

'We'll come up with some fancy designation for him, so that he doesn't throw a tantrum.'

Meera shook her head. 'This whole thing feels like it's more about Sagar and less about me.'

'Can I be blunt with you, Meera?'

'Would it matter if I said no?'

Navin smiled. 'Sagar is a better reporter than you are and you're a better manager than he is. I can't afford to lose him, and I didn't want to let you go, but you refused to give me the time I needed to nudge Sagar out of the managerial role without him throwing a fit. Believe me when I tell you that I would have eventually poached you from wherever you would have gone on to work. Sagar's heart attack just made everything easier.'

'That's a terrible thing to say.'

Navin shrugged. 'It's not like I'm saying I want him dead. Quite the contrary, actually. But you do see that this is the smoothest possible way for you to return to the office?'

Meera didn't say anything for a moment.

Navin finished his coffee. 'Come back for the girls on the team, Meera. Let them know that a woman can be the political editor.'

'Only if the male political editor gets an unexpected heart attack.'

Navin gave her an exasperated look. 'Stop putting yourself down like that.'

'And how much of a raise am I getting?'

'Twenty per cent on your take-home, in addition to those rubbish bonuses they keep promising us, but don't actually give.'

'And I want Sagar's desk.'

'Done. You'll join next Monday?'

'No, in a week. What? I didn't know this was going to happen. I booked a holiday.'

'Where are you going?'

'Turkey.'

'For a week?'

'Navin! Stop eyeing my well-deserved break. I'll join a week later, on Monday, provided HR gets its act together.'

Navin settled into the sofa and said, 'HR hasn't even processed you've left. Now, let me tell you the gossip I heard in Delhi about our dear leader.'

In her defence, it wasn't as though Aalo hadn't noticed the backpack looked grubbier than she remembered it, but she thought that extra layer of dirt was because it had travelled around Asia before returning to her. That's why she'd signed the delivery boy's form without examining the backpack too closely or looking, for instance, for accessories like locks. It was only when she tried moving it—about thirty minutes after the delivery boy had left—that Aalo felt the first prickle of unease. It took another few seconds for her to see that the suddenly-heavier backpack was further proof of her life being a disaster. Because yes, this backpack looked like the backpack she had carted to London and then carted from Kekoo's flat to the airport, but for two tiny details—the black ribbon she had lovingly tied on the front clasp was missing; and tucked under the hood, keeping the two metallic loops of the zips together was a lock. A lock whose combination Aalo didn't know because it wasn't hers.

Groaning, Aalo flung herself on the backpack and then righted herself quickly. God knows where the damn thing had been. She found her mobile phone and called Island Airways.

'Good afternoon, thank you for calling Island Airways. My name is Parth. How may I help you?'

Aalo took a deep breath and explained to Parth that the airlines had first misplaced her backpack and then returned the wrong backpack to her, so could he please help her get the backpack that was hers back?

'Surely, Miss Mukherjee. Please hold the line for a minute while I check the system to find your bag,' Parth said courteously.

'Of course.'

'Miss Mukherjee?'

'Yes, I'm here.'

'Thank you for holding the line, Miss Mukherjee.'

'No problem.'

'Miss Mukherjee, according to our records, your bag was returned to your home address earlier today and you have signed for it.'

'Like I told you, Parth, I received a backpack that I thought was mine, but it isn't mine.'

'But you have signed for it.'

'Yes. Because I thought it was mine. But it isn't. So can you find out where my bag has gone?'

'Ma'am, according to our records, your bag has gone to you.'

'But it hasn't!'

'But you've signed for it.'

'But it's not my bag!'

'But ma'am, why would you sign for someone else's bag? That would be stealing,' Parth sounded perplexed.

'I didn't realize it was not mine.'

'Did you realize it was not yours after opening it?' There was a hint of steel in Parth's voice.

'It's locked. I can't open it.'

'So you mean to say that you claimed the bag was yours, but now want to return it because you can't open it?' The steel was getting steelier.

'Parth, I am not interested in someone else's bag. I want mine.'

'But ma'am, you have yours. As per our records ...'

Aalo hung up on Parth and sat on her bed, staring at the backpack that looked like hers—but wasn't—when she heard laughter from Meera's room. Hoping for distraction, Aalo wandered over and poked her head in through the door.

'Whatcha watching, Ms Political Editor of *The Daily*?' Aalo said to Meera. 'It does feel nice to call you that.'

Meera was sprawled on her bed, giggling at her phone. 'Come and be regaled by your crush, Zeb Shams,' she said.

Aalo joined Meera on the bed enthusiastically. 'That sounds promising,' she said gleefully. Zeb Shams was delicious. She'd found the photographer on Instagram entirely by chance, through the Explore tab. It didn't hurt that the photos he took were nice—Meera insisted she followed him for his photos—but given he was a photographer, nice pictures had to be the bare minimum expectation from his Instagram feed. What made Aalo virtually stalk him was that he was hot, as she'd discovered from his Insta stories, in which he turned the camera on himself. Plus he had a lovely, posh British accent.

'So basically, his bag has got exchanged with someone else's,' said Meera, 'and he's documenting what he finds in it while trying to find out whose bag it is.'

Aalo felt her stomach wiggle uneasily. 'It's a bloody epidemic. What's wrong with these airlines?'

'What do you mean?'

'Island Airways sent me the wrong bag.'

'Oh no!' Meera looked sympathetically at Aalo for a second, before returning her attention to her phone. 'Oh my god! He's found a bra!' she gasped.

Aalo snatched the phone from Meera when she saw her favourite bra on the screen. It was perfectly balanced, so that the two cups fell on either side of a long index finger that presumably belonged to Zeb Shams. Aalo found herself imagining that finger trailing down her cleavage. She shook her head to clear the thought. Another chapter of the story was up. This time, it showed Zeb's gorgeous face—winged black eyebrows, green eyes that glittered, square jaw covered by a trimmed beard, a hawkish nose, full lips that were currently pulled into a half-smile of exasperation. The accompanying text read, 'Pretty. Let's hope the person who owns it thinks my three-year-old boxer shorts are a fair exchange. P.S. If you're seeing this, the shorts need laundering.'

Meera protested when Aalo took the phone and started tapping the screen manically to go back to the start of his story.

'What are you doing?' Meera asked, thoroughly confused.

'That was my bra,' Aalo hissed the words with elemental fury. 'And the bastard is waving it around to his million followers.'

For a moment, Meera looked even more confused, and then her face cleared before arranging itself in an expression of fascinated horror. 'Aalo? Did you walk off with Zeb Shams's backpack?'

'I did nothing of the sort. It came to me,' Aalo replied in a distracted huff.

The first of Zeb Shams's Instagram story was just text: 'Dear Person with my backpack, I have just one word for you: WHY?'

Next: 'Actually, I have many words for you, beginning with this question …'

Aalo found herself staring at a photograph of a backpack that looked very familiar, bathed in soft sunlight, lying on a patterned rug. Behind it was a white wall, which was the perfect backdrop for the message that had been typed on the image: 'Which fool doesn't recognize their own bag?'

Below the backpack, in a smaller font, it said, 'I, for instance, saw this and knew it wasn't mine. Because it's cleaner, lighter and has a black ribbon tied to it.'

Aalo moved to the next photograph. It was a close-up of the front clasp on which she'd tied the black ribbon. 'Unfortunately, @IslandAirways tells me this must be my bag because the only other backpack "of the same description" has been delivered to its owner. Which is actually me. Except I have this bag and the owner of this bag, for some reason, would rather keep mine.'

The Insta story moved on to show the backpack with the top flap opened. 'NO LOCK!' he'd written.

Next: a close-up of the zip, with him saying, 'Dare I pull this open? What will I find? Is it a bomb?' He'd also written '#WitnessMe'.

Then came the post with the bra. He hadn't added any more to the story.

Aalo looked up at Meera. 'What. An. Asshole.'

'You have Zeb Shams's bag.' Meera said the words slowly. 'How? Why?'

'Not because I wanted it, you idiot. It was a mix-up by the airlines. They sent me his bag and sent mine to him.'

'But you've had that bag for a whole day.'

'Calm down. It's been about forty-five minutes since that delivery boy left.'

'But it's his!'

Aalo thrust Meera's phone at her. 'You have to tell him I have his bag.'

'I still don't understand how you didn't know you were taking someone else's bag.'

'Meera. Focus,' Aalo said sternly. 'He's going around waving my bra to the public, and you're wagging your finger at me for a human error. Island had already lost my bag. How was I to know they'd fuck up a second time? You need to write to him.'

'You're the one with his bag,' Meera said. 'Why do I need to write to him?'

'Because he doesn't follow me on Instagram. He follows you, Ms Fancypants Journalist. If I send him a message, it'll be a random request, and god knows how many of those he gets and ignores. You two follow each other. Your message will show up in his inbox.'

'Bloody hell, he's updated his Insta story,' Meera said, peering at the screen. 'Did you find a Wonder Woman-themed Moleskine?'

'Limited edition,' Aalo said. 'I got it for you. Glad you like it.'

'Well,' Meera said firmly, 'Clearly, I have some messaging to do. I want my Moleskine.'

Aalo watched Meera type a message to Zeb Shams, and wondered if there was a word for what was going on here, because 'ironic' didn't cover it. How weird was it that Meera was technically going to introduce Zeb Shams to Aalo, when in fact Aalo had introduced Meera to his Instagram profile? Aalo had spent practically a year gently stalking Zeb Shams online. She knew he had a twin brother named Baz, that his mother was from Kashmir, that he had family in Tehran, that two years ago, he'd started a photo agency with a friend from Iraq and called it Cameraderie. Also, he had beautiful, long fingers, and hair that seemed straight when it was cut short, but broke out in waves when it outgrew the severe haircuts. She'd watched videos of him on YouTube and once in a while, she'd even come up with a witty comment to leave under his latest Instagram photos, which he'd heart. But Aalo wasn't the one he had followed back.

'Ok, here's what I've written,' Meera said to Aalo. 'Hi Zeb, this is Meera. We haven't actually interacted before, but just wanted to say your photos are fantastic.' Meera grimaced. 'Does that sound sappy? It seems a bit weird to go straight to the subject without some small talk, no?'

'Sure.'

'Ok, so yes, photos, fantastic. Then: I just saw your Insta story about the bag, and I think the airlines mixed your bag up with my friend's. Aalo's bag looks like the one you've shown in your story, and it's been missing for the past few days. Is there an email or number that Aalo could reach you at to clear this up? She's also on Instagram as,' Meera looked up, 'I've given your ID.'

'It sounds perfect. Now send it.'

'Should I give him your number?'

'No!'

Meera started. 'Ok, calm down. Do we not want him contacting you?' She looked puzzled.

Aalo had no idea why she'd reacted so violently, but she decided there was no reason to explore that right now. 'I'm not going around giving my number to random men.'

'Random men whom you ogle regularly.'

'He doesn't know that. Also, I don't just follow him because he's hot. His photos really are very good.'

Meera half-rolled her eyes. 'I believe that's my line, but ok, sending,' she said.

Both of them crossed their fingers and waited. In about five seconds, Zeb had sent Meera his number and asked Aalo to write to him. Aalo noted, but didn't mention, that Zeb Shams hadn't followed her back on Instagram.

—Hello, this is Aalo Mukherjee. My friend Meera follows you on Instagram and saw the story you put up earlier today. It seems you have my backpack while I possibly have yours. :)
—Hey Aalo, thanks for writing in. Can you send me a photo of the backpack you have?
—Sure. Here it is. By the way, I don't think it was very nice of you to open my bag up like that.
—Well, I don't think it was particularly smart of you to take my backpack. Also, I was hoping to find your name or address so that I could send it back to you, if you really want to know. Pro tip for the future, in case you walk off with someone else's bag again, write your contact details under the flap.
—It's not like I took your bag deliberately. It was an honest mistake.
—I don't understand how you made this mistake. Your backpack weighs half of what mine does. It's also thirty times cleaner. Anyway, I'll delete the story. How would you like to do the exchange?
—So I'm in Mumbai.
—With my bag?
—Obviously.
—Brilliant. When do you return to London?
—That's the thing. I live in Mumbai. Where are you?
—London.
—I was in London last week, for a holiday. But that's not helpful at the moment.
—Wow.
—I have a friend who lives in London and I'm sure he can pick up my backpack from wherever is convenient for you. But I'm not sure how to get your backpack to you. Do you have any friends or family in Mumbai? Or India?

—This is a disaster. Let me get back to you.
—Sure. :)

Aalo wondered whether Zeb had tried to Google her while they were exchanging messages. It wouldn't help him much since Aalo was her nickname. Her personal favourites of the options that Google's image search threw up, when someone put 'Aalo Mukherjee' in the search bar, were the bespectacled woman hugging a newborn baby and the tentatively smiling middle-aged man with a regrettable haircut. Aalo took a critical look at her Instagram profile. There were a lot of silly selfies in there. If he looked through the 'photos of' tab, he'd find pictures in which Aalo looked like a giant, grinning while she towered over people. There was a lovely black-and-white photo of her that Meera had taken recently. Maybe he'd linger over that one. He still hadn't followed her back.

—Hey Aalo, it's Zeb. Will you check with your friend if they can pick up your backpack from my office? I'll send you the address. It's reasonably central.
—Hi, thanks for getting back. Please send the address. Wherever it is, I'm sure it won't be a problem. My friend's name is Kekoo Shroff.
—You can give him my number and then we'll figure out when and where.
—Great. Thanks!

Five minutes later:

—So any idea how we can get your bag to you? :)
—Plan a trip to London? Not on Island Airways though.
—Haha. Seriously, I'm really sorry about this.

—You should be. Anyway, I've asked around to see if anyone I know is going to Mumbai in the near future. If they are, I'll be in touch.
—Ok. I don't suppose there's much point trying to get Island to send it to you?
—You're welcome to try. I doubt you'll be successful though.
—Fair point.

Five minutes later:

—Zeb, what if I send you your stuff piecemeal?
—I don't understand.
—I mean in parts. Kekoo once made me send him his favourite shorts and T-shirt when he left it behind after a trip home. I don't think it was mad expensive.
—You want to courier me my luggage as individual items? To London?
—Yes. No?
—That is a ridiculous idea. But I just remembered something. If you open the bag, you'll see there's a box wrapped in cellophane. It has sweets in it and you should eat them. I doubt they'll last very long, even though the box was vacuum-sealed. It's from one of the best sweet shops in Istanbul.
—Hand over the combination to your lock immediately.

Two minutes later:

—It's really delicious! I can definitely send this to you, by the way, if you want.
—It won't last. Enjoy it. It's called kunefe, by the way.

—Fantastic. Thank you. Please feel free to eat the chocolate that you pulled out of my bag in the last update of your story.
—I've deleted the story.
—And the chocolates?
—There are unconfirmed reports of a few missing pieces.

3

The moment Rebecca opened the door for Aalo and Meera, she issued a warning. 'I may have gone a little overboard,' Rebecca said, her face red and her curly hair held back by a dinosaur-print bandana.

'Hello to you too, and thank you, I got this dress on sale from OMO,' Aalo said, as she stepped inside and blew a kiss to Rebecca.

Meera grinned. 'Hello you. What's up?' she said as she gave Rebecca a hug.

'It's just that I found this blog with amazing recipes, and then I couldn't decide between two of the dishes, so I ended up making both of them,' Rebecca said, while absently hugging Meera back. 'Then I found another recipe, which sounded like something Jo would love, and well, basically, you're all taking dabbas back with you.' She shut the door behind them.

'Well, for once, I have something for you.' Aalo held out a box, which Rebecca eyed suspiciously. 'Don't look so worried. I didn't make it. It's a Turkish dessert called kunefe. Might be originally

Syrian, according to the internet. Anyway, point is, it's delicious. Cheesy and sweet and syrupy …'

'And nicked from an award-winning photographer whose bag Aalo has stolen,' Meera added.

Rebecca looked puzzled. 'Is this supposed to make sense? Because it doesn't right now.' She sniffed at the box. 'Do I need to refrigerate this?'

'Did you say kunefe?' Fatima said, walking into their living room. 'Where did you get that in Mumbai? Kunefe is like food-of-the-gods delicious. Just keep it outside, Becks.'

Before Aalo could get into the story of her kunefe, the doorbell rang. 'That'll be Jo,' Meera said, as she gave Fatima a hug and went over to the rocking chair.

Not that anyone had planned it that way, but over the years, Rebecca and Fatima's home had become the place where the Not-So-Famous Five group, as Jo had named them, would meet once a month. Rebecca's love for cooking and the other four's love for eating had started this tradition. Once or twice, Jo or Meera would contribute a dish, but usually, everyone just brought alcohol and left the cooking to Rebecca, who reacted to good recipes the way physicists did to the discovery of the Higgs boson.

Mentally, Meera took a snapshot of this moment. Aalo, on the floor as usual, half of herself draped on the beanbag and her long legs stretching out. Rebecca and Fatima on the sofa, with Fatima using Rebecca as her pillow. Jo, on the floor, near the coffee table, with her knees up to her chest. Meera, on the rocking chair in the corner, where she could curl into a little blob. This was her family of choice—Aalo, with her big eyes and laughing lips; Fatima, with the twinkling nose-pin and tattooed arm; Jo, with her permanently sardonic expression; and curly-haired, warm-as-molten-chocolate Rebecca—and Meera silently gave thanks.

'Ok, now that everyone has arrived, I have an announcement,' Fatima said, the excitement shining in her eyes. 'Is everyone ok with champagne?'

'Wow, champagne,' said Jo, the unofficial bartender of the group. 'This is special. Champagne coming up.'

The bottle was popped, the bubbly was poured and everyone raised their glasses. Fatima and Rebecca looked like they desperately needed to pee. 'It's happiness,' Rebecca said, when Aalo asked her if she wanted to use the loo before Fatima started talking.

'The adoption papers are finally, totally and officially through. Rebecca and I will be bringing our daughter home next week!' Fatima squealed.

Gasps and cheers filled the room. Rebecca and Fatima were soundly and tightly hugged. They'd been running from office to office, with copies of papers and certificates in triplicate, for more than a year now. India's rules for adoption were strict, and when the person who wanted to adopt was single on paper (and in a committed relationship with another woman otherwise), it got much harder and infinitely more complicated.

'This is the best news ever!' Jo hollered delightedly, as she refilled the glasses. 'Wait, does that mean that we're going to have to behave when we meet here the next time?' she asked, clutching the champagne bottle to her chest.

'No, because my mum is there to kidnap the kid whenever necessary. Keep pouring,' Fatima replied.

Jo exhaled in relief. 'Everyone, drink up so that we can open the actual good booze.'

Rebecca giggled. 'Isn't it awesome to be able to drink a week before having your baby?' she said.

'What did your mum say when you guys found out?' Meera asked Fatima.

Fatima's mother had been by Fatima's side for every meeting and every appointment, repeatedly assuring government officials and social workers that she would be helping her daughter raise the adopted child, who would be the one spark of joy in her bleak life as a widow. The weeping-widow act was hilarious for Fatima to witness, because her father had been violent and abusive, which meant that, as far as Fatima was concerned, she'd only seen her mother joyful after her father had passed away.

'Ammi's bouncing,' Rebecca said, beaming. 'She's put together a proper dossier—a schedule for when the baby is going to be with her, a list of schools and their feeder schools, how much money to put aside for college, and god knows what else.'

'She needs to calm down,' Fatima said, shaking her head.

'No,' Rebecca said firmly, lacing her fingers through Fatima's. 'She's never to calm down and we're damn lucky to have her on our side. I hope I always see her shiny-eyed and smiling.'

'What about names?' Aalo asked. 'At least now start thinking of names.'

In the past, Fatima and Rebecca had put their foot down and refused to discuss names because, as Rebecca put it, 'I can't deal with the disappointment if it doesn't come through. I can't keep losing pieces of my heart because of fucking bureaucrats.'

So, no one had mentioned names until now.

'My mother is obviously drawing up a list,' Fatima said.

'Just remember,' Jo said, pouring herself a vodka. 'Anything but Jhalkari.'

Everyone burst out laughing. It was hard to imagine Jo—mixer of drinks, solo traveller extraordinaire and the woman who chose pole dancing as her preferred form of exercise—as Jhalkari, but that was what she'd been named by the astrologer her parents had consulted when she was born. At age eighteen, she'd hired a lawyer and filed an affidavit to change her name to Jo, the name she'd picked out for herself at fourteen after reading *Little Women*.

'I don't know,' Fatima said with a grin, sipping her champagne. 'Jhalkaribai Mirza-Menezes sounds pretty badass.'

Rebecca oohed delightedly. 'It has … cadence!'

'That name is like unity and diversity's wet dream and British imperialism's nightmare,' Aalo said, her mouth full of a crunchy appetizer.

'I have to say, it really does sound damn feisty,' Meera agreed.

Jo looked at her friends disbelievingly. 'You're all sadists,' she said finally.

Aalo raised her glass and said, 'To Jhalkaribai Mirza-Menezes, light of Rebecca and Fatima's lives, and destined to be a rockstar. Come home quickly so that your aunts can pamper the crap out of you.'

Everyone cheered and knocked their glasses back, much to Jo's displeasure. 'I get that this is desi champagne, but there's no reason to treat it like tequila,' she grumbled as she laid out five glasses on the table that was doubling up as their bar. 'Is everyone having their usual? Or any special requests?' she asked.

'Usual,' Meera said and then raised her hand, like she was asking for permission to speak in class. 'Guys, I have a little announcement too. So, Navin asked to meet me. He asked me to come back to *The Daily*.'

Angry abuses and contemptuous noises whooshed out of Rebecca, Fatima and Jo. Too many of these dinners had been devoted to Sagar and the way he'd gone from being a wonderful mentor to a complete bastard. It hadn't helped that Navin had either ignored him or sided with him.

'No, no. It's good. He offered me political editor,' Meera said, and gave a quick recap of her meeting with the editor of *The Daily*.

This time, her friends reacted with whoops of joy. 'Political editor! FINALLY!' Rebecca gave Meera a big hug.

'Hashtag: *bade log*,' Fatima said, with a grin.

'You're going to have minions!' Jo said excitedly.

Meera clinked glasses with her friends, telling herself to stop grinning like an idiot. 'I feel like I've climbed Everest or something,' she said.

'At the risk of being a downer, can I ask the obvious question?' Rebecca said, after the second round of celebratory whoops had died down.

Meera sighed. 'No, I haven't spoken to Kapil, but I will.'

'You're ok about meeting him?' Rebecca asked.

'Obviously I'd prefer not to.' Meera could hear the hint of bitterness in her voice as she spoke of her ex-husband. 'I mean, I haven't forgotten the detail that he cheated on me, refused to grant me a divorce for the longest time and said shit about me to anyone who would listen, but it's been two years. I've moved on. I don't think I would have pushed for this job like I did if I hadn't moved on … because, let's face it, there's no way I could be a political editor without at least occasionally bumping into the spokesperson of the ruling party in the state.'

'You know, whenever I see him on TV, I just can't imagine you as Mrs Kapil Patil,' Fatima said.

Meera shrugged. 'I'm just glad that our marriage ended before he became a political bigshot. It was hard enough to get a divorce from Kapil Patil, the aspiring politician. I don't even want to imagine what it would take to get out of a marriage with Kapil Patil, blue-eyed boy of the prime minister, leader of the Maratha people and general champion of all things saffron. My sympathies for that poor secretary he screwed around with while we were married.'

'They're married now, right?' Fatima asked.

Meera nodded. 'Last year, I believe.'

'If he says or does anything dodgy, you just call me,' Jo said. 'I'm sure my dad knows thugs we can set on him.'

'Jo!' Rebecca, Fatima, Aalo and Meera all glared at Jo.

'What? My dad's in construction. My mum's dad owned a textile mill. Of course my family knows thugs. Who knows? Papa might even have a few on the payroll,' Jo said calmly.

'I feel the need to change the subject,' Aalo said, and looked pointedly at Meera. 'You, madam, have more news to report, do you not?'

Meera looked blank. 'I do?'

Aalo waggled her eyebrows. After a couple of beats, Meera realized what Aalo meant.

'Oh god, that!' Meera groaned. 'I can't talk about that without a lot more alcohol in my system.'

'Let that not be an obstacle,' Jo said, handing a drink to Meera. 'Gin, just the way you like it. Now, what's this business that you can't talk about?'

'Meera made out with a boy,' Aalo said, bouncing with excitement as she took her drink from Jo. 'Like almost literally a boy. As in, someone who was barely senior to me when I was interning at *The Daily*.' She suddenly clapped her hand over her mouth. 'Dude! You're going to be working with him again! Holy shit!'

'Thanks, Einstein.' Meera took a long gulp of her drink.

'Which one of you is going to rewind for the rest of our benefit?' Fatima asked.

'Can we start this story over dinner, the way Meera did with her boy?' Aalo asked. 'I'm trying the warrior diet. I shouldn't eat after 7.30.'

Everyone but Rebecca rolled their eyes.

The story about the 'boy' was pushed to the back burner when Rebecca unveiled dinner. Even by Rebecca's standards, a six-course meal with dishes from Kashmir, Italy, Ethiopia, Morocco and Nagaland was impressive. Everyone heaped their plates with food and soon enough, the living room was filled with chewing noises and little huffs of satisfaction. Eventually, their collective attention returned to what Aalo termed as 'Meera's brush with Kandivali'. Meera quickly recapped what had happened with Jeet on the night of her farewell. She ignored how her internal organs fluttered at the memory of that night. After describing how she'd raced out of Jeet's apartment, Meera summed up the incident saying, 'So, in concrete terms, nothing happened, but I think I might be having a mid-life crisis.'

'You had chemistry!' Rebecca crowed, her eyes glazed with romantic hope. 'Did you take a photo of him? How old is he? Is he tall? Hairy chest or non-hairy chest? Tell me everything!'

'For a lesbian, you're way too interested in this guy,' Fatima observed, even while most of her attention was trained upon getting the marrow out of the mutton bone she'd snagged for herself.

'Sexuality is a spectrum, and I love you, but hello, this is someone who got Meera to take a train to Kandivali. This is special,' Rebecca replied. 'Tell me what he looks like!'

Meera didn't even have to close her eyes to conjure up the image of Jeet—the head of curly hair that made him look like he'd just got out of bed no matter what time of day it was; the sharp slash of his nose; the square jaw that his shave had revealed; the thin upper lip and full lower lip; the broad shoulders; the black rings that were tattooed like an armband, just below his elbow; the chest that she'd touched but not seen. She didn't say any of this, and was saved from answering Rebecca when Fatima said, 'It's also a really bad idea, given she's going to be in the same office as him.'

'Office romance!' Aalo exulted.

'No, I will not be making out with him again, obviously,' Meera said blandly. 'Becks, the food is insanely good, as usual.'

'Do not change the subject, but thank you,' said Rebecca.

'Have you had a chat with him since that night?' Jo asked.

'I don't have his number,' Meera said. In a cacophonic chorus, Fatima, Aalo, Rebecca and Jo started listing out the many ways in which Meera could have got hold of Jeet's number.

'Ok fine, I could have contacted him, but I didn't. Happy?' Meera said. 'Look, it's not like he sent me a message or called or anything. So, really, we're on the same page of denial. It's fine.'

'So, when you see this Jeet in the office, you're not going to imagine yourself tearing his pants off?' Jo asked.

'Seriously?' Meera tried for a withering tone, while her brain insisted on remembering how low he wore his pants and the way he'd twitched when she'd run a finger down his thigh during dinner at Ling's. She clenched her hand into a fist.

'If you're going to blush that much just at his name, you definitely need to have a chat with him first. Not just so that he knows where you stand, but so that your hormones process the fact that he's out of bounds,' Jo said. 'Unless you want to …'

'Are you mad? After all this, when I get to head up the political team, I turn around and start boning a junior?' Meera shook her head. 'I'd be crucified, and no amount of chemistry is worth my career. Look, it was two drunk people and it's in the past. I'm not making a big deal of this. Hormones under the bridge and all that.'

'Just talk to him once,' Jo said again. 'I mean, the last thing you want him to think is that you came back to *The Daily* to be with him.'

Meera's jaw dropped. 'I'm returning as political editor and he's going to think it's all about him? That makes no sense.'

'The male ego does not make sense,' Jo reminded her.

To that, the Not-So-Famous Five raised a toast.

Later the same evening, Fatima played for them her newest find. 'You have to hear this guy,' she said, opening up her laptop. 'I loved his sound so much.'

'Please tell me this is not going to be like those punk rock chicks you made us hear the last time,' Aalo begged. Fatima worked with a company that organized music festivals across the country. Sometimes, the music she discovered was a little more experimental than her friends' tastes could handle.

'Those girls were amazing. You should have seen how they got the crowd on their feet in Shillong,' Fatima said, while setting up her laptop. 'But no, this boy is more mellow. Listen.'

It was a song of heartbreak and rage, lamenting how all that was good, warm and beloved had been wrung out, leaving behind only a husk of a dream. He didn't sing as much as croon. Accompanying his soft voice was a violin, and the song's melody settled upon the room like dew.

'This is so, so beautiful, Fatima,' Meera sighed. 'What's his name? I'm going to ask someone at the paper to write about him.'

'Sarfaraz Aziz. He's just twenty-five. Can you believe it?'

'Maybe you should set Aalo up with him for her social experiment,' Meera said drily.

'What's this now?' Fatima asked.

'Aalo here has decided that, for the sake of the nation, she is going to only date … what was it again?' Meera looked at Aalo. 'Non-Hindu, non-savarna men, right? By which we basically mean Muslim, Christian, Sikh, Dalit and Adivasis. Parsis are too posh and too few to count for her project.'

'Stop making it sound like I'm kicking puppies in my spare time,' Aalo protested. 'I basically realized I've only dated Hindu men whose names begin with R. And we all know how well that's gone for me, so I thought I should push the envelope on the dating front by widening my range.' She looked at Meera. 'I genuinely don't see why you think it's a bad idea …'

'Because it is offensive!' Meera practically wailed. 'It's like saying you're friends with Rebecca because you want to be able to say you know a lesbian or a Christian.'

'But if I was a repressed or closet homophobe, who had never thought of being friends with a queer person, then the fact that I have real trust and intimacy with Rebecca would be a good thing, right?'

Meera made an exasperated noise and then looked around at the others. 'Am I overreacting here, guys?'

'If you ask me, ditch men altogether and come over to our side,' Fatima said with a shrug.

'What I want to know is, what's the sample that you're selecting these men from?' Jo asked.

Aalo sighed. 'That's sort of the problem. I don't have a sample.'

'Great, not only are you profiling the men you want to date, now you want a sample.' Meera threw her hands up in the air. 'I give up.'

'Stop reading the worst possible meaning into what I'm saying,' Aalo said to Meera. 'Also, everyone profiles, consciously or unconsciously. Maybe what I need is to give it a name. Like, Operation Liberation.'

'I actually think it's a very interesting idea,' Rebecca said. 'It's like trying to reverse your socialization.'

'Thank you!' Aalo said triumphantly, while Meera groaned.

'It's been a while since I used them, but what about setting filters on the dating apps?' Rebecca suggested.

Aalo wrinkled her nose. 'I was thinking about that, but dating apps just feel weird.'

Jo looked confused. 'What feels weird?'

'I don't know, just this whole thing of deciding on the basis of a photo, then messaging instead of talking …'

Meera burst out laughing. 'Says the girl who has been glued to her phone ever since she got on WhatsApp with …' She stopped short and sat up. 'Wait a minute.' Meera looked at Aalo and a huge grin stretched across her face. 'Zeb Shams! He fits the criteria perfectly!'

'Oh, please,' Aalo huffed.

'Time out,' Jo interrupted. 'For those of us who don't live with you, what is going on?'

'Zeb Shams, he's a photographer and the reason we had kunefe for dessert,' Aalo said.

'You're doing a terrible job of explaining what's going on, FYI,' Jo told her, which led to Meera and Aalo recounting the tale of the backpack, the Instagram story and Aalo's new friendship with Zeb Shams, which included ransacking his backpack for dessert.

'I feel like I've heard of him before,' Fatima said after listening to the whole saga. 'Is he a big deal?'

'He's a photographer who started his own agency with an Iraqi photographer, Akbar Salih,' Meera replied. 'Their agency is called Cameraderie, and they basically train and hire locals to take photos, which these guys place in news publications.'

'Cameraderie is such a lovely name for this,' Fatima said.

Meera nodded. 'Yes, and basically, if you're getting a photo from Cameraderie, then it's from someone who really knows the area and the conflict. Not the standard outsider or white man's gaze.'

Everyone looked suitably impressed.

'So, Aalo is now friends with our man Zeb,' Meera continued.

'Please,' Aalo protested. 'He doesn't even follow me on Instagram. He does, however, follow Meera.'

Meera kept talking as though Aalo hadn't spoken. 'And ever since they exchanged numbers, madameji keeps checking her phone every two seconds. I think the longest she's stayed away from the phone has been while eating dinner.'

Aalo rolled her eyes. 'Zeb and I are just trying to figure out how to exchange these damn bags.'

'We're on first name basis already!' Rebecca said, waggling her eyebrows.

'Yes, Rebecca, we are. Because I'm not *The New York Times* that I'll refer to him as Mr Shams,' Aalo replied primly.

'Odd surname,' Jo said, popping the last of the kunefe in her mouth.

'Is he cute?' Rebecca asked.

'He is gorgeous. Part-Iranian, part-Kashmiri, and 100 per cent hot,' Meera supplied and swiftly pulled out photos of Zeb to prove her point.

'Fuck me, I'd be on the next flight to London if that guy was tapping me,' Jo said, taking Meera's phone to look more closely.

'First of all, he's not "tapping" me and secondly, I can't afford to go back to London,' Aalo said archly. 'So, no. Seriously, guys, most of our chats have been about his stupid bag.'

It was obvious from the other women's faces that she might as well have been talking to herself.

'Have you checked if he has a girlfriend?' Fatima asked. 'Or a wife? I mean, I don't want to be horrible, but given Rudra ...'

Aalo shuddered. 'No need to even utter that name, thank you very much. And no, I don't know if he has a girlfriend or wife, because it does not matter. He is not a candidate for Operation Liberation.'

'But why not? He is non-Hindu,' Fatima said with a grin. 'Also, if Operation Liberation is in the interest of social justice, even part-Kashmiri is a bonus. Though, come to think of it, maybe he should be left available for Kashmiri girls rather than us mainlanders?'

'Listen, the man got all of us dessert before even the first date,' Rebecca pointed out. 'I say he's a keeper.'

Aalo rolled her eyes again.

Partly because of the food coma, and partly because Meera was thinking about how her friends had urged her to tread carefully about working with Jeet—now that the two of them had some history—Meera and Aalo didn't talk on the way home.

'I'm crashing,' Aalo said once they were inside. 'Too much good food. This Rebecca should just quit PR and start a catering service.'

'She really should. You want some green tea? I'm making myself some,' Meera said.

Aalo shook her head. 'I can't keep my eyes open.'

The two of them said goodnight to each other, and Aalo stumbled to her bedroom, while Meera made her way to the kitchen.

It was that rare, precious time in a day when everything was quiet. No noises from the street or neighbours, no alerts from the phone. Meera felt wide awake, and it was all Jo's fault. Why had she mentioned tearing off Jeet's pants? Now all Meera could do was remember how Jeet had felt against her. Only, each time she had that flashback, she also felt a little queasy as she recalled how much younger than her he was. Was he even thirty years old? He didn't look it. If anyone in the office ever found out about that night … Meera frowned. It could destroy her career, because once news got out about this promotion, there would be enough people looking to bring her down. What Meera did on her own time was her business, and she was fairly confident about being able to cut down anyone who tried to moral police her, but with Jeet being in the same newsroom and her junior … it was messy.

Jo was right. She had to send Jeet that message sooner rather than later. She couldn't let this get out.

Waiting for the water to boil, Meera tried to figure out what she would write to Jeet. It couldn't sound like she was writing to him as an excuse to get back in touch. It had to seem casual and friendly. For some reason, an image of Audrey Hepburn from the poster of *Breakfast at Tiffany*'s popped up.

The kettle clicked to let her know the water was ready.

'Hey Jeet,' Meera whispered to herself while dipping a teabag in the mug full of hot water. 'How goes?' She shook her head. That sounded fake. And vaguely needy. She had to get him to understand that their make-out session was never to be brought up in conversation, ever, with anybody. Ever. But she had to do this without sounding urgent, because it wouldn't do to let him have even an inkling that he could affect her life in any way. Or that she was still thinking about him in or out of his pants. There was also the question, thought Meera as she took the teabag out, of whether or not she should get hold of Jeet's phone number. It wouldn't be too hard, but if she WhatsApped him, he'd know she had made an effort. Twitter, Meera decided, was a better option, even if it was now X and a hellsite. She followed him, he followed her; a DM was the most obvious way forward. Settling down in the living room, Meera took a few sips of her tea and then tapped out the message on her phone.

> —Hey, I'm going to be back at *The Daily*. Navin offered me political editor. Just thought I'd let you know. I'm sure you realize that as far was what happened that night is concerned, we need to be discreet and keep it to ourselves. I hope it's not going to be awkward if and when we bump into each other at work eventually.

Meera looked at the time. It had taken her fifteen minutes to come up with that message, and she still had misgivings about it. He replied in about thirty seconds.

—Congratulations on the new gig. :) When do you join?
—Next week.
—I'll be on leave then, but thanks for the heads-up. Congratulations again!

Meera frowned at the exclamation mark in his message. It looked so … happy. As though he'd written it while lounging on a beach, chugging a beer and watching a sunset. Never mind that it was the dead of the night. The message was strangely carefree, and it made Meera furious.

Meanwhile, in the other room, Aalo was not asleep. Instead, she was at her phone, staring at the profile photo that Zeb used on WhatsApp. She zoomed in on his beard-covered jaw. His lips were now a rusty, pinkish smudge. Aalo wondered how the beard felt. Was it wiry? Did it leave a rash on his lover's skin? When her brain started wandering into X-rated territory, imagining the feel of that beard against different parts of her body, Aalo tried to railroad her head back to being polite and PG-13.

—My friends loved the kunefe. Thank you for that.
—You're very welcome. I'm glad it didn't go to waste. By the way, I just thought of something you could send me by courier.
—Tell.

—There's a black pouch in there. About six inches wide, in the middle of the backpack. There's a small jewellery box inside it. Let me know how much it costs to send that and I'll wire the money to you.
—Wait. Let me find it first.
—It's in there, Aalo. No one's robbed my bag. Except you.
—It was an HONEST MISTAKE. BY THE AIRLINE.
—Lies. You just wanted my kunefe.
—No, the universe wanted me to have your kunefe, and who am I to mess with the universe?
—Heaven forbid. If you don't mind me asking, does your name mean potato?
—I'm Aalo, not aloo. Aalo means light in Bengali. Aloo means potato in Hindi and Bengali.
—Ah. Got it.
—It's actually short for Aloukika, which no one but my parents can either spell or pronounce.
—Impressive, but I've still got one letter on you.
—Meaning?
—Zeb's short for Aurangzeb.
—Aurangzeb! Seriously?
—Yep. I think I was about fourteen when I finally learnt how to spell my name. Still not sure if I pronounce it right.
—Wow. Is it still on your passport?
—Haha, yes, it is.
—Don't come to India. It's not a good time for Aurangzeb in India, given he's supposedly the Mughal emperor who hated Hindus and razed temples.
—Really?
—I sucked at history, but I vaguely remember he paid for the upkeep of a lot of temples too. Also won wars in South India and put his daughter in prison.

—Cheerful chap.

—If you compare him to the kings in *Game of Thrones*, Aurangzeb's basically a marshmallow.

—Counting my blessings as I type.

What Aalo wanted to ask him was whether the jewellery in the box was a gift for a girlfriend. Instead, she sent him a gif of Madhubala doing a salaam, from *Mughal-e-Azam*, and tried to ignore the lack of resemblance between herself and the exquisitely beautiful actress. He didn't write anything in reply, but Aalo noticed that on Instagram, he'd posted a photo of a shop in Istanbul that, as per his caption, made the best kunefe in the world. It had been uploaded a couple of hours ago, while they'd been at Rebecca and Fatima's. Aalo felt as though he'd put up the photo for her. Then she frowned. It wasn't as though he was following her, and really, he could have just sent her the photo on WhatsApp if he really wanted her to see it.

Absently, Aalo tried one of the new selfie filters that Instagram had introduced. The filter added flattering shadows that contoured her face, made her eyes look smoky and festooned her hair with sparkling flowers. It should have looked tacky, but weirdly, the filter made her look … ethereal. Aalo clicked a selfie with the filter and wrote, 'I put a spell on you, and now you're mine.' Then she uploaded it as a story. She scrolled through her feed for a few seconds, before checking who had seen the photo. Ten people had seen it already. One of them was Zeb Shams. Something warm and triumphant fluttered through Aalo, even as she imagined him humming the Nina Simone version of the song.

'This needs to stop,' Aalo said out loud to herself. She went to the settings on her phone, turned off notifications for Instagram, and instead downloaded Bumble, the dating app that Jo and Rebecca had praised highly during dinner.

Within seconds, Aalo regretted her move. Jo had made it seem so breezy and simple. 'Just pick a photo of yourself that you like,' she'd said at dinner. 'That's the only bit that takes time.' Actually, the photo had been the easy part. There were hardly any photos of herself that Aalo liked. Most of the time she looked like a giant, especially in group photos, since even the men were usually shorter than her. She wasn't fat, but she wasn't petite either, and that just didn't translate well into photography. The only one who did take nice photos of Aalo occasionally was Meera. Consequently, the list of acceptable photos was short, which made selecting one simple. Far more complicated was the bio that Aalo needed to put in her profile. Aalo stared at the blank field. If only someone would set up a profile for her, the way fictional friends tend to do in stupid rom-coms. But no, her friends were too busy being normal and not invading her privacy. Useless creatures.

Aalo pulled her laptop to her lap and opened up Google. She searched for 'what to put in Tinder bio', even though she wasn't using Tinder. Three articles offered advice to men on how to frame their bios so that they did not sound creepy. 'What about women?' Aalo muttered to herself. One article advised her to speak from the heart and embrace what the universe and algorithms had in store for her. Aalo decided it was time to call the cavalry. She texted Rebecca, whose insomnia kept her up till ridiculous hours. Rebecca responded by calling Aalo.

'You're up late,' Rebecca said instead of hello.

'If you had to describe me, what would you say?' Aalo asked.

'Gorgeous, incandescent and not to be trusted with kitchen appliances,' Rebecca replied.

Aalo figured she could use the kitchen appliance bit. It would ward off anyone looking for a domestic goddess.

'What's going on?' Rebecca said when Aalo didn't say anything in response.

'Sorry, I'm just jotting that down. I'm trying to write up a bio for that dating app that you and Jo recommended. It's damn hard.'

'Ooh! Can I give it a shot?'

'Be my guest.'

'What's the aim here? We're looking for hot sex, right?'

'I'm open to all possibilities that are not right wing and chauvinist.'

'Ok, let me think.'

Aalo patiently waited, idly putting Zeb's name in Google's image search. The man seemed to have different hair in every other photo. There were also new photos of him with a stubble rather than a beard. Aalo decided she liked the bearded look better.

'I've got it,' Rebecca said finally. 'Feminist, fabulous, open to possibilities, closed to chauvinists.'

Aalo raised her eyebrows. That was actually pretty good. 'Not bad,' she said. 'Now add interests.'

'That's easy. Interested in movies, ballroom dancing, travel and trying new things.'

'Since when am I interested in ballroom dancing?'

'There are few things as sexy as the firm grip of your dance partner. Trust me on this. Plus, Prakash and Neena have just set up a dance studio where you can book a single class to try it out. It's an excellent setting for a first date.'

'Who the hell are Prakash and Neena?'

'Friends of mine. They're lovely. More important: they teach modern ballroom dancing. Like the stuff you see on *So You Think You Can Dance*.'

Aalo had a sudden vision of herself standing in a class, facing a dance partner who barely reached her chest. Her toes curled immediately. 'You think I should mention my height?' she said to Rebecca.

'Why is that relevant?'

'I'm 5'10". Most men are shorter than I am.'

'So, is it their height that's the issue or yours? Because from where I'm sitting, neither should be an issue.'

'Rebecca Menezes, you're a good mother. I feel gently schooled.'

'Put the bio up already.'

After she'd hung up, Aalo stared at the profile that was one click away from entering god knows how many millions of phones. What was the worst that could happen? She'd delete the profile and then just sit at home and silently go back to stalking Zeb Shams on Instagram and YouTube.

So, at 1.45 a.m., after eating her weight in dinner, Aalo Mukherjee debuted on Bumble as 'Feminist, open to possibilities, closed to chauvinists, not to be trusted around kitchen appliances. Interested in movies, travel, ballroom dancing and trying new things.'

By 2.15 a.m., she had found two men who looked promising. Feeling vaguely triumphant, Aalo decided it was time to call it a night. She had slides to make for Farhana and Hema's new workshop.

4

The next morning, in the SWETE office, Aalo was in early, searching for images that she could use as slides, when Rucha suddenly popped up and said, 'You're wasting time with this nonsense.'

Aalo almost jumped out of her skin. She mumbled something about following Farhana and Hema's instructions, but Rucha shook her head. 'You want the kids to listen to you, not get distracted by some strange woman in a sari. Also, for most kids, a woman in a sari is a teacher.' Rucha peered at Aalo's laptop screen. 'I know her.'

'It's Sridevi,' Aalo said. 'From *Mr India*.'

'Right. I thought she looked familiar. Anyway,' Rucha turned her back to Sridevi and faced Aalo, 'the point of visuals is that they should be aids. Not distractions. Focus on the research and how you're going to put that information in a way that the girls will want to believe you. Trust your voice. If you don't trust your own voice, then why the hell should these girls?'

When Rucha looked straight at Aalo in that unblinking way of hers, Aalo's stomach turned into concrete. 'My voice is well and good, but Sridevi makes everything better,' Aalo said finally.

Just then, Rucha's phone rang. Mercifully, she walked away to talk to whoever had called. Aalo started breathing normally again. She was growing more and more fond of Rucha with every passing day, but that didn't mean the older woman's growl didn't make Aalo feel the need to sit up straight and cross her legs neatly.

By the time Rucha sauntered back into the office, everyone was in, and the room was full of the low, happy hum of conversation and work. Aalo was telling Farhana what Rucha had said about Sridevi, when she heard Rucha's voice. 'Guys, I need you all for a moment,' Rucha said in a tone that suggested something serious was up.

Aalo looked up to see that Rucha had perched herself on Hema's desk.

Rucha asked another colleague to request those who sat in the next room to come in and join them. 'Group chat,' Rucha said, with a smile. When everyone had gathered, Rucha began, 'I just got a call from Principal Apte, who was very unhappy. She says she expected me to do "A-grade" workshops and not send "B-grade" people.'

While the rest of the room tittered angrily, Aalo felt like she'd been slapped. Principal Apte ran the school that she and Hema had gone to yesterday. Hema had been doing a fantastic job, and she had given Aalo a tiny, five-minute segment to do, of which Aalo had made a mess. In no time, she had lost the kids' attention, and it had taken all of Hema's skills to bring the class' wandering attention back to the workshop. Taking a deep breath, Aalo said loudly, 'It was my fault. I lost the room.'

Rucha looked at Hema. 'Did she lose the room?'

'She had a bad day,' Hema said. 'It happens to all of us. We recovered fine.'

Rucha nodded. 'It's got nothing to do with you, actually,' she said to Aalo. 'Apte's problem is with Hema. She doesn't want a Dalit teacher, when she can get a Brahmin one. Now, I've already given her an earful, because obviously I'm not going to sit quietly while people talk nonsense, especially about Hema!' She reached out and gave Hema's hand a squeeze. 'But my question is, how do we go ahead? How many more workshops do we have in that school?'

'Seven more,' Hema supplied.

'Do you want to go back?' Rucha asked her. 'Because I will completely understand if you don't.'

After a moment's silence, everyone started cursing that principal and saying what they thought Hema should do. Most of the room thought she shouldn't go back.

'If this is how they react, they don't deserve Hema,' said someone angrily.

'We should file a complaint against this Apte,' someone else suggested.

'What do you want to do?' Rucha said again to Hema. 'Take more time to think about it if you want. We have till next week.'

'I'll go back,' Hema said after a moment. 'The kids deserve better than Apte. If she's disrespectful to me, I'm pretty sure I can handle it. But if it gets too much, I'll let you know, and we'll file an official complaint.'

'Great. That's sorted then. I'll have a chat with the lawyer about the legal bit. Meanwhile, I think you should slip in some anti-caste messaging in the workshop. The kids will be better off for it.' Rucha leapt off the desk. 'Can't wait for the end of the workshop when that cow of a woman realizes that her students adore you,' she said, a big smile on her face.

Aalo almost hugged Rucha at that point.

For the second time in forty-eight hours, Meera found herself drafting a message that was essentially her asking a man to not make things awkward for her in her professional life. From a random not-quite-one-night-stand to an ex-husband, she was really covering a spectrum, Meera thought to herself.

When Meera had gone on Tinder right after the divorce, she had claimed to be a housewife, and ignored anyone with even the slightest connection to journalism or politics to make sure her personal and professional lives would never intersect. Now here she was, with the two of them entangled like chow mein. Meera sighed as she started typing the message for Kapil. Somehow, it was easier to draft this one than the DM she'd sent to Jeet.

—Hi, I'm joining *The Daily* as their political editor. Just thought I'd let you know. Of course this changes nothing between us, but I hope it won't make things awkward for either of us. Hope you're well.

It was the first time she was contacting him since the divorce, Meera realized, as she sent the message. Kapil replied immediately.

—Congratulations! This is great news. May I request a meeting? It would be good to talk in person.

Meera grimaced at the sight of Kapil's message. She couldn't say no, but the thought of having to sit in that waiting room, surrounded by hangers-on and sycophants, ignoring the hostile or pity-slick gazes of the staff who remembered her as the pathetic ex-wife—it was distinctly unpleasant. But this was not an ex-wife meeting an ex-husband. This was a political editor meeting a party spokesperson. She couldn't really say no.

—Spokesmen for the ruling party don't need to request meetings with political editors. If it's a meeting about work, I'll come to your office whenever is suitable for you.
—Give me thirty minutes? My secretary will be in touch with details.

As promised, within thirty minutes, a man named Narendra called her and said Patil saheb would meet her at 2 p.m. at his office. He asked her if she needed the address. Meera said yes, even though she knew exactly where his office was located.

The next day, at 1.45 p.m., Meera reached the address and settled down for a long wait. Politicians and movie stars were never on time. She looked around the office. Not much had changed. There were still three doors and no windows in the waiting room. One door led outside. The door to the left led to Kapil's office and the other door opened into what used to be a nap room. She looked for the futon that used to be in that room. It wasn't there. Maybe he'd thrown it out when he'd walked out of their marriage. Or maybe his second wife had thrown it out.

Meera checked her phone. It was only 2.15 p.m. She was surprised that she was the only one in here, barring Narendra and the guards at the door. No politician's office was this empty in the middle of the day, and certainly not when the politician was Kapil Patil. Maybe he had another office that she didn't know about. Meera figured she had at least forty-five minutes ahead of her of staring at the carpet and the walls. Which was why, when two minutes later, Narendra told her that she could go in, it took her by surprise.

Meera couldn't stop herself from saying, 'He's here already?'

Narendra gave her a blank stare of disapproval and did not reply.

She had just stood up when the door to the left opened and Kapil stepped out. Narendra scrambled to standing position. Meera waited to see if he'd salute, but he didn't. Kapil walked up to her, smiling and with his hand outstretched. 'I'm sorry to have kept you waiting,' he said, shaking her hand. 'There was a call I just couldn't get out of.'

'It's not a problem. I was actually expecting to wait much longer.'

'Shall we go inside?'

'After you.'

Kapil cocked his head. 'Ladies first. It's not like I need to show you the way around here.'

As she led the way, she heard Kapil order two black coffees. Of course, he assumed she still drank what he did. 'Actually, I'll have green tea, if you have it,' she said and walked into his chamber. He duly changed the order and followed her, shutting the door behind him.

'Congratulations on the promotion,' Kapil said as he made his way to the sofa rather than the imposing desk that was adorned with photos of the party leaders.

'Thank you.' Meera sat down on the sofa facing him. It should have felt stranger than it did to be sitting here, doing small talk with Kapil, she thought to herself. Not that this felt normal, but it didn't feel awkward.

'How's Sagar taking it?' Kapil asked. 'Has it given him a second heart attack?'

Meera had to applaud his shrewdness. Of course he knew about Sagar's heart attack—after all, Sagar was one of the most respected and well-networked reporters covering Maharashtra politics—but Meera hadn't expected Kapil to have gauged Sagar's dynamic with her so well.

'He's recovering fine,' Meera said diplomatically. 'How have you been? I was expecting a mob out here, but things seem to be quiet.'

'It isn't usually. I had them clear everyone out. I figured we didn't need witnesses.'

They were quiet for a moment. The green tea and coffee came and settled with a ceramic clink in the thick silence.

'I wanted to apologize ...' Kapil began, and Meera immediately shook her head, while reaching for her cup of tea.

'I'm not here to talk about any of that,' she said. 'I thought you wanted to talk about work.'

'I do.'

'Then don't apologize. As far as I know, there's no reason for the ruling party's spokesperson to apologize to *The Daily*'s political editor.'

Kapil sipped on his coffee, all the while looking at her. He carefully put the cup down and said, 'Ok. So, going forward, are you going to be my point of contact for *The Daily*?'

Meera shook her head. 'It'll still be Sagar. I don't intend to interfere with that side of things.'

'Is there anything you would need from me?'

'Will I get the cold shoulder from other party members because of our history?'

Kapil shrugged. 'Everyone knows I've remarried, but I'll have a chat and make sure you don't get any hostility.'

'I've no trouble with pity, if it will get me the news I'm looking for,' Meera said, smiling sweetly.

Kapil laughed. 'We run a tight ship these days, Meera. Leaks are a thing of the past. But I promise you, you'll get the cooperation you need from my office and the city unit of the party. I can't promise how the allies or the Opposition will behave, but let's just say, I would be very surprised if anyone gave you trouble.'

'Thank you.'

'Would you like me to …' Kapil paused, as though searching for the right word, '… encourage Sagar to play nice with you?'

Meera wondered what Kapil had on Sagar, even as she kept her face deadpan and shook her head. 'I can handle Sagar,' she said.

'He can be quite nasty, I've been told,' Kapil warned.

'What's the worst he'll do? Tell people I'm an embarrassment, a barren slut?' Meera casually tossed the phrases that Kapil had once used to describe her to her parents in order to justify his affair and his decision to walk out of their marriage. 'Been there, survived that.'

Kapil's face crumpled. 'I really do regret how I behaved back then. I know an apology isn't enough, but …'

'Would you believe me if I told you I don't really hold it against you anymore? You being horrible forced me to stand up for myself. I'm not going to thank you for it, but you know what they say—every cloud has a silver lining.' Meera found herself smiling, and it wasn't a sad or unpleasant smile. It was a smile of indulgence. 'We can leave all of that behind now, Kapil. I think we've both moved on. Everything's changed, and it's changed for the better.'

Kapil nodded, also smiling. 'You know, I almost didn't recognize you when I saw you outside. You look well.'

'You too. This white kurta look is good on you.'

'I'm becoming fat.'

'Take a tip from our prime minister and do more yoga.'

She stayed for ten more minutes and then left. As she walked out of the building, Meera realized that she hadn't felt tense or nervous for even one moment. She had met her ex-husband after two years and there had been no flutter, no anger, no anxiety. She'd felt nothing.

Closure was a beautiful thing.

One thing that Aalo could say in Bumble's favour was that there was no false advertising. This date was certainly best described as a bumble. Through the app, Aalo had met Parvez of the pretty face, and now here they were, in a coffee shop, getting to know each other. After fifteen minutes of introductory small talk, Aalo was already plotting how to get out of the dinner that they had tentatively planned after watching a film. She wondered whether she was being unfair to Pretty Parvez, because he really was very nice looking. And he was tall, about 6 feet, which was a big point in his favour. If only he wasn't also, well, vain.

Sitting in the coffee shop where they'd arranged to meet before heading to the film, Aalo could tell Parvez had picked a table that let him check himself out in the mirrored wall behind her. He was talking to her and, at the same time, between the long moments he spent admiring himself, scanning the coffee shop. Aalo wondered if she wanted him to scan her, too, or if that thought was meant to feel offensive. If he looked at her like he was looking at himself, Aalo was convinced that she would end up slapping him.

She should have been liking this man and focusing on him, but it was hard. Parvez, bless his poofy hair, was terribly boring. For the last five minutes, he'd been telling her a story that involved an Uber and his friend and his friend's phone. Told by a good storyteller, maybe this would have been fun to hear, but as things stood, it just convinced Aalo to plot her exit strategy well. She'd tell him that she needed to go home because her flatmate was locked out. He had no reason to know that Aalo was the one who usually left her keys inside and that her flatmate wasn't likely to come home before 11 p.m.—one of the joys of working for a newspaper.

'Sorry, I'm droning on,' Parvez said with an embarrassed smile. 'You've had much more interesting travels than my Uber rides. I saw on your Insta that you were in London?'

Aalo felt a wave of frantic guilt wash over her, and she compensated for it by pouring out her heart and soul, telling Parvez about London, and asking him about himself. Sure, he was boring and for some reason reminded her of a pigeon (maybe it was his puffed chest?), but he was trying. She needed to give him a chance.

Her positivity pep talk to herself seemed to have helped and it was all going much better until they reached the cinema hall.

'Should we get popcorn or something?' Aalo asked.

Parvez's expression withered, as though he was feeling sick. 'I don't actually do much junk food. Thing is, I used to be really fat and unhealthy, and I'm just a little paranoid about slipping, and you really need to be disciplined about what you eat. But I have some carrot sticks,' he offered.

'You're carrying carrots?' Aalo asked.

Parvez patted his bag. 'Baby carrots. They're in a pouch that the security always mistakes for a pencil case,' he said with a triumphant grin. 'Actually, could I leave my bag with you? I just need to go to the ...' He tilted his head towards the sign for the toilets.

'Of course,' Aalo replied, taking Parvez's bag from him. The moment he'd turned his back, Aalo pulled out her phone and sent Meera a message.

—Need you to ping in one hour sharp. Will tell you when to call. But definitely ping in one hour.

—Everything ok?

—He brought baby carrots to the movie, so that we don't have to buy or eat popcorn. What kind of satanic behaviour is this?

—Just think of the six pack those carrots are probably making possible.

—I'd rather have popcorn.

—Such a shame. He's such a nice-looking boy.

—Ten per cent conversation, 90 per cent preening.

—He does sound a bit dull. But hey, at least he's not married and his name doesn't start with R. And he's not Hindu. Give him another chance?

—Just remember to ping in an hour.

Meera sent her a salute. Aalo sighed. She was never going to live down falling for Rudra. The worst part was that stupid dates like this ended up reminding Aalo how good Rudra had made her feel when she was with him. Everything Rudra said was a cliché, but he delivered them well and dates with him had been fun. Rudra was living proof that practice made perfect. By virtue of practising his lines on pretty much every willing female who crossed his path, he'd perfected the art of making women feel as though no one else existed in the world.

While waiting for Parvez—since when did boys take this long in the bathroom?—Aalo absently opened up Instagram and looked through Rudra's feed. His last three posts were of himself in the gym, lifting weights. She scrolled through his comments. There were men and women complimenting him. One woman had written, 'What stamina!' and placed a heart-eyed emoji. He'd replied with, 'Thanks. It's always easier when buddies like you are supportive.' If Rudra wasn't already sleeping with this woman, he was definitely laying the ground for it.

Aalo tucked the phone back in her bag, when she looked up to find Parvez walking up to her. She hoped he had washed his hands, and thanked god that Indian cinemas had intermissions.

The film wasn't bad, and when the lights came on at intermission, Parvez and Aalo smiled politely at each other and sat in awkward silence. Aalo could think of nothing to say, and clearly, neither could Parvez. She wondered whether he was also trying to think of excuses that would get him out of this date. Why the hell wasn't Meera texting anyway? Aalo wished Parvez would take out his phone. That would make her feel less guilty about pulling out her own. Finally, Aalo couldn't do it anymore. She took out her phone, and wouldn't you know it, Parvez gave her a look.

'I think I'm addicted to the phone,' Aalo said with an apologetic smile.

Parvez nodded grimly. 'I know what you mean. No, really. I literally was, am, addicted to mine. That's why I've gone on a phone detox. No looking at the phone if I'm outside the house. It's crazy hard, but I'm going to win this.'

Aalo nodded, while trying to think of something to say that wouldn't be taken as being sarcastic or dismissive. 'Be strong,' she managed finally and looked at her phone. Meera had sent a message about a minute into intermission—'Hello. should you need to exit left, I'm locked out and helpless, a damsel in distress who needs her princess charming. SOS'—but Aalo had turned off the vibration feature, so she hadn't felt the message coming in. Annoyed at herself, Aalo turned on all notifications and got ready to tell Parvez that her flatmate needed her. The lights dimmed.

'I think I'm going to have to run,' Aalo whispered to Parvez, but her voice was drowned out by the movie's dramatic background score as it resumed. She tapped Parvez on his shoulder to get his attention and then gestured for him to come closer. He obliged. She sat up to whisper in his ear that she was going to scoot, but he decided that Aalo's approaching face could only mean one thing: a kiss, with tongue. The next thing Aalo knew, Parvez's tongue was writhing in her mouth like an angry sea creature's tentacle while his lips pulled at hers like they were a vacuum cleaner determined to suck up every three-dimensional object in its vicinity. Parvez finally moved away. He was smiling. Leaning in towards her again, Parvez whispered in her ear. 'That was nice.'

Aalo wasn't sure what her face had done in response because the area around her mouth felt vaguely numb. If he was so confident that the kiss was 'nice', she definitely needed to leave, but how was she going to get out now? There was no way he'd believe her if she claimed she'd got a message from a friend. Would he think she was leaving because he was a bad kisser? He was a bad kisser, but she didn't want to hurt his feelings. She also didn't want to be sitting next to him. What if he kissed her again? Just then, a loud beep shrieked out of her bag. It was her phone receiving a message. Another beep pealed out.

'Sorry!' She quickly took the phone out and put it back on silent. 'Sorry, I have to take this,' she whispered to Parvez and made her way out of the theatre. Their seats were bang in the middle of the row, which meant that Aalo had to step on at least ten sets of toes to make her exit. If you're small, you can scuttle out of places. When you're 5'10", there's no such option. All you can do is trample feet and hope that gods and humans will shower only minor curses on you.

Outside the theatre, in the bright light of the cinema's foyer, Aalo released a slow, long breath. She checked her phone to see who had saved her from Parvez's tongue. It was Zeb. He'd sent her a screenshot of a Reddit thread that read, 'Real history has no sea monsters. Just whale penises mistaken for a tentacle. Whales often mate in threes, so while one male is busy with the female, the other will pop his dick out and swim around, waiting his turn.' Below the text were photos of a whale penis, emerging from a submerged whale and waving around mid-air. Aalo burst out laughing. What were the chances that Zeb would send her messages about the reality behind tentacled sea monsters, just when she felt like she was being attacked by one? She quickly tapped out a message to Zeb as she made her way out of the mall.

—Of all the things that I thought I'd see in my inbox today, a whale penis was not one of them.

Aalo looked at the screenshot he'd sent her and giggled. She was booking an Uber when Zeb replied.

—Shit I am so, so sorry. I thought I'd sent that to someone else. This is mortifying. And hugely inappropriate. I'm so sorry.
—Huge seems to be appropriate.
—I really am sorry. I'm an idiot.
—Don't be. It's great trivia and the timing was extraordinary.
—The timing?

Aalo hesitated for a second. Should she tell him that there was another man kissing her (badly)? Would that be too much information or too awkward? Then again, what could be more awkward than kidnapping someone's backpack and sending the wrong person whale penises? With a little shrug, Aalo wrote to Zeb.

—Your message came precisely when I was being attacked by a tongue that seemed to be flopping around in my mouth as aimlessly as the third-wheel penis in those photos. Thanks to your messages, I was able to escape. So, thank you, for facilitating my flight and providing infotainment.

—I'm feeling a little bad for your date, but am glad the science behind sea monsters had some practical use.

—Can I ask why you're looking up whale penises?

—I was actually looking up sea monsters. The penis was extra.

—That's what she said. (Sorry, couldn't resist.)

—Haha. Not according to Freud.

—Listen, if Freud had been given a decent sex ed lecture, we'd all have been spared his penis envy theory and a whole lot more misinformation. I say this as a professional sex educator.

—I'm sitting on my hands to not reply with 'Come again?'

—They did a study with women in America and the UK, and guess what they found? Eighty per cent of heterosexual women reported that they didn't have orgasms during intercourse or penetrative sex. Stats for lesbians—more than 90 per cent did.

—Wow. Really?

—Damn straight. #TakeThatFreud

—So this is what you teach in your sex education workshops?

—I don't teach clitoral stimulation, if that's what you're asking. My talks are more about knowing the body and bodily processes, like menstruation and stuff. I work with kids, mostly girls in government schools.

—Ah. That's fantastic.

—It's fun. Not glamorous like your job, but fun.

—Trust me, there is nothing glamorous about the photography I do.
—It looks pretty amazing on Instagram.
—Amazing, sometimes. Exhausting, all the time. Glamorous, never.
—Says the man who gets featured in fashion magazines.
—Wait, how do you know about that?! And it was ONE fashion magazine. We were a little desperate to get the word out about, regarding the photo agency my friend and I started. How on earth did you see that article in India anyway?
—I'm not sure if the news reached Britain, but India's been in the twenty-first century much like the rest of the planet. With a reasonably open economy and internet.
—Fair enough, but I doubt the UK edition of *Vogue* is passed around like Amar Chitra Katha comics.
—Look at you with your local references.
—Confess, Mukherjee. Have you been Googling me?
—You stole my bag. Of course I Googled you. Are you saying you didn't Google me?
—Stole YOUR bag? Ahem. Pot, meet kettle.
—I notice you're not responding to the question. I'll take that as a yes. Did you think I was a middle-aged man with a com-bover?'
—It might have been easier to get my bag back from the middle-aged man with a comb-over.
—My namesake looks like a nice, respectable family man. I doubt he'd be up for helping you if you sent him whale penises.

They continued bantering for a few more minutes before the conversation tapered off. It was only once Aalo reached home that she realized she hadn't sent a message to Parvez to explain her departure. Quickly, she tapped out an apology and told him she had to rush because her flatmate had a medical emergency. Some women leave men at the altar; Aalo had left Parvez at the cinema—blame it on the giant third penis. Parvez didn't reply. Aalo couldn't blame him. When she opened Instagram a little later, Aalo spotted she had a new follower. His name was Zeb Shams.

5

Meera almost jumped out of her chair when the phone on her desk rang. Ten days into her new job in the old office, this was the one part of the political editor's cabin that was taking some getting used to. When you sat in the open layout of the main newsroom, surrounded by everyone else's chatter and clatter, the landline didn't seem quite as loud. In a cabin—in *her* cabin—the ring sounded like a fire alarm. Meera picked up the phone.

'Meera madam, you have a visitor,' said Manoj from the front desk, his voice as bored as ever.

'A visitor?' Meera asked. 'Who is it?'

Meera heard him asking the mystery person for their name, not getting their name and then asking for it again.

'Meera madam, she says her name is Aalo.'

Why was Aalo in the office?

'Ok. I'll come out. Thanks, Manoj.'

Meera quickly checked her phone, in case she'd missed calls or messages from Aalo, but there was nothing. She shut off her computer monitor and walked past the clusters of reporters' desks to get to the main door. Her old team of reporters had been wonderfully supportive. They'd brought cake and taken her out for a drink on the day she joined the office formally. Meera had no doubt that at least a few of them were reporting her every move to Sagar, but that was fine by her. They were working hard, and they were working well, which was all that she could ask for at this point. Over the last ten days, she hadn't been asked to drop a story and neither had her team missed a story. Both felt like big victories.

Meera walked out to the reception to find Aalo standing there, towering like a golden Amazon warrior over the puny men around her. She had two large cups of coffee in her hands and one huge smile on her face. As usual, Meera let herself imagine for a moment that she was Aalo's height and had Aalo's legs.

'Hello political editor saheba,' Aalo said.

Meera did her version of the royal wave. 'Hello ex-intern, what brings you here?'

'You just finished ten days on the new job. I brought you celebratory coffee.' Aalo came forward to give Meera both the coffee and a hug. 'Happy tenversary.'

'You just made up a word and it's a terrible-sounding word,' Meera said, taking both coffee and hug.

'Also,' Aalo said in lowered tones, 'since you didn't mention you-know-who, I figured I'd go to the source as it were. He's back at work today, right?'

Meera sighed. 'Doesn't SWETE give you enough to do?'

'I still can't get over that name. I feel like I should be coming out with a cupcake instead of a presentation on good touch and bad touch. Also, don't think I'm not noticing how you're changing the subject.'

'There's not much in the subject to talk about … but come inside and see the new newsroom. Manoj, you got her to sign the register?'

'All done,' Manoj replied, not even looking up from whatever it was that he was watching on his phone.

When Aalo had interned with *The Daily* almost three years ago, they'd been housed in a crumbling building in South Mumbai that was beautiful to look at and had the potential of collapsing like a house of cards at any moment. Now *The Daily* lived in one of the glassy towers of central Mumbai and had fingerprint scanners at the entrance that let only the right ones in.

Aalo said, 'This new office is swanky. I might have lasted a couple more weeks if I'd had to do my internship here.'

Meera made a face. 'I hate it. It's got no character.'

'Well, it has a lift and that, as far as I'm concerned, is way more relevant. Climbing up those awful stairs every day was a nightmare.'

'It was only the third floor, and you were walking up a historic eighty-year-old staircase. Also, at least there was a staircase. I'm pretty sure if there's a fire here, I'll have to throw myself off the balcony.'

Meera opened the door to the newsroom and the two women walked in. Aalo stopped to scan the place that Meera had nicknamed 'The Daily Dungeon'. It was a strange combination of overwhelmingly grey and brightly lit. Neon tube lights dangled from the ceiling—on paper, they were probably blue, but in reality, they coloured everything a miserable shade of pale. Rows and rows of desks filled the room. The windows looked out on a grey, smoggy sky.

'I see what you mean about it not being an improvement,' Aalo murmured.

'It's less bad when you get past how bloody grey the whole thing is,' Meera told her. 'My cabin's in that corner.'

'Corner cabin,' Aalo said with a proud smile. 'Me likey. Let me go and say hi to the desk first, and then I'll come to you.'

'You're going to say hi to the desk?'

'They're my friends. I worked with them for almost three months.'

'Almost three years ago.'

'Time is irrelevant when it comes to friendship.'

'So, if I tell you Jeet isn't there, you'll still be consumed with this need to say hello to the desk?'

'But you said he's coming back from his holiday today.' Aalo looked at her phone. 'It's 6 o'clock. What do you mean he isn't here yet?'

Meera sighed. 'He's here, but …'

'I just need to see the piece of man flesh that convinced you to take a train to Kandivali, because genuinely, I do not remember Jeethamitra V as a male siren.'

'That's because he isn't. Anyway,' Meera pointed in the direction of the desk, 'they're over there. Try to be something close to discreet? And don't forget to say hello to Faisal. He actually was your boss, even if you never treated him like one.'

'Will do.'

While Aalo bounded towards the desk's side of the office, Meera stopped on her way to the cabin to check on a couple of reporters who were filing their copy for the day. Even though her back was turned, she heard the desk greet Aalo, their cheers spiking through the low hum of newsroom conversations. Back in her cabin, Meera wondered whether Jeet would find it odd that Aalo had shown up out of the blue. It was weird to think the last time she'd actually spoken to Jeet was in his flat. She'd studiously avoided him after he'd come back from leave. It hadn't been difficult to do. She was too senior for their paths to cross unless she, or he, deliberately set out to meet.

Aalo returned to Meera's cabin a few minutes later. 'I have to say, I don't entirely get it. He's,' Aalo wrinkled her nose, 'scruffy.'

'He is, now that the beard is back,' Meera agreed. 'And I'm incredibly thankful for it. Because if he was still making me hormonal, work would have been a nightmare.'

'I mean, Jeet's a lovely guy.' Aalo slurped some of her coffee. 'And he has such a nice voice. Deep, gravelly. But just at a purely superficial level, that is not a face that would launch a thousand ships.'

Meera tried not to think of how close she'd got to becoming topless—a la the towers of Marlowe's Ilium—with Jeet. 'Helen of Troy might be raising the bar a little too high, but I will say, in my defence, you haven't really seen his face. You've seen his beard, which, like I said, I was very happy to see return. Because we both know what happened when it was absent.'

'Seriously? It made that much of a difference?'

'Huge.' Meera stopped herself from launching into how without the mess of facial hair, you could see the thin slash of his upper lip and the fullness of the lower one that just seemed to beg to be nipped. Even his nose seemed more aquiline without the beard.

'I wish you'd taken a photograph,' Aalo grumbled. 'Then I wouldn't have to do this mental photoshop. If he shaves again, make sure you smuggle a photo.'

'Can we please pray that never happens?'

Aalo smiled slyly. 'Why not? Are you afraid you'll do a repeat performance if he loses the beard?'

'Yes, Aalo, if he shaves and flashes that jawline at me again, I'll have no choice but to swoon and beg him to ravish me. In Kandivali.'

And on cue, who should appear at the doorway, but Jeet.

'Hi, sorry to bother, but Faisal was wondering if we'll have something on Sharad Pawar's meeting with the press?' he asked, after nodding at Aalo.

'Sahil is there. He'll file a small copy. There wasn't anything particularly newsworthy.' Meera hoped her face was not as red as Aalo's.

'Great. Thanks, Meera.' Jeet smiled and turned to Aalo, 'Tell me when you're leaving? I'll come down with you for chai and cigarette?'

'Sure,' Aalo squeaked. 'Definitely.'

Neither Meera nor Aalo said anything for a few moments after Jeet left.

'If he's clean-shaven tomorrow …' Meera whispered.

Aalo cut her off. 'I will find out if he heard us when I meet him downstairs and totally fix this situation if he has.'

Meera shook her head and drank the coffee, wishing it were something stronger.

About twenty minutes later, after Aalo had left, Meera got a message from her: 'Pretty certain he didn't hear. He didn't even mention you, so I'm guessing we weren't loud enough.'

When Meera came into work the next day, Jeet was at his seat with his beard very much intact. She spent the rest of the day telling herself that there was no hint of disappointment tainting her relief.

Over the course of the week, Meera also told herself that her repeated trips to Faisal's cabin were only for a change of scenery and because Faisal was one of the few people who wasn't lapping up the bitchy gossip that Sagar was circulating about her. It definitely had nothing to do with the path to Faisal requiring her to walk past Jeet's desk, or the pleasant distraction that Jeet's voice provided when the air felt like it was full of sly whispers.

One afternoon, she found Faisal standing outside his cabin, evidently in the middle of a heated argument with Sheila, his deputy. Everyone else was watching the two of them like it was a blockbuster movie.

'Should I come back later?' Meera asked Faisal, who shook his head and asked her to join in the conversation.

'You know that order to make Hindi mandatory in all schools in Maharashtra? We were talking about that,' Faisal said. 'Sheila's convinced this means the end of civil liberties as we know it and is saying we should do a full package.'

'Faisal doesn't want to do it because he's afraid Navin will fire all of us if we prod the beast without provocation,' said Sheila. Her chin jutted out mutinously. 'Those are his words, not mine,' she added.

Meera shook her head. 'Your jobs are safe,' she promised. 'The current education minister's a nobody. However, I do think this is a bit of a non-issue. Hindi imposition is one of those topics that gets trotted out whenever someone needs to distract the public's attention from boring but relevant matters, like how far behind the BMC is on its monsoon prep or a spike in the number of farmer suicides.'

'Oh please, Hindi imposition is not a non-issue. It has been on this party's agenda pretty much since the day they were born,' Sheila replied. 'Now that they're in power, they've done it.'

'So you have a problem with a directive that requires Hindi as a mandatory third language in English and Marathi medium schools?' Meera tilted her head and looked questioningly at Sheila. 'Leaving aside how much pride the average Marathi manoos takes in his mother tongue, would Hindi in schools really be that bad?'

Sheila looked at Meera like the latter had turned into an alien. 'They're imposing Hindi as part of a project to Hindufy the country. Yes, I do think it would be that bad.'

'The proposal is to make Hindi a mandatory third language,' Meera countered. 'I don't see how that's a bad thing, or how that would demolish Maharashtrian culture, or any other regional culture for that matter. It's ridiculous that the only language we have in common as a country is English.'

'I cannot believe you're saying this,' Sheila said, shaking her head.

Meera shrugged. 'Look, if you tell me English is an Indian language today, I'll agree with you, but grudgingly. It's a foreign language that comes with a lot of baggage.'

A deep voice entered the debate. 'Sure, but we're very much in the process of claiming it as our own,' Jeet said, as he got up from his desk to stand next to Sheila.

Meera tilted her head to show she accepted what he'd said. 'Even so, the privileged and "correct" version of English is the foreign one, not Indian English,' she pointed out. 'Indian English is still mocked, and more importantly, it's not as widely prevalent as Hindi. The only Indian language that's anywhere close to being pan-Indian, across socio-economic demographics, is Hindi. I don't see why learning it is such a big deal.' Meera shrugged.

'Because it attacks our diversity,' Sheila wailed.

'The Swiss learn German and French. In some regions, they learn Italian too. Plus English. They seem to be doing ok. Why can't we learn a third language, in addition to English and whatever mother tongue you inherit? The only thing going for English is that it isn't steeped in caste politics like all other Indian languages. And that's only because it's essentially a foreign language.'

Sheila turned to Faisal. 'Help me out here!'

Faisal scratched his head. 'I'm just wondering that if the whole Hindi-in-schools thing is about keeping a language alive, why not Urdu? It's definitely more dead than Hindi, but I don't hear of any campaigns to revive it.'

'Thank you!' Sheila said triumphantly.

'But Faisal, the idea of Hindi as a third language is not about keeping the language alive, but about making it pan-Indian. No one's saying Hindi is dead or dying, or that the only way to revive it is to make it the third language in schools across India.' Meera considered Faisal for a moment. 'But let's go with your point, about reviving a language that's losing ground. Your father's family is originally from Lucknow, right?'

Faisal nodded.

'And your mother's?'

'Hyderabad,' Faisal replied.

'Do you speak the posh Urdu of Lucknow or the Deccani Urdu of Hyderabad?' Meera asked.

'I speak both very badly,' Faisal said sheepishly.

'And that's because you studied Hindi in school?' Meera asked.

'No Hindi. I had Marathi as my second language in school. Byculla boy, remember?'

'What did you speak at home?'

'English, mostly,' Faisal replied.

'So, which do you think is more responsible for you not knowing Urdu—studying Marathi in school or speaking English at home?' Meera didn't wait for him to reply. She turned to Jeet. 'What about you? Would you say English is your mother tongue?'

'No. Mother tongue is definitely Tamil,' he replied.

'Are you fluent?'

'Absolutely.'

'Because you studied it at school?'

'To some extent, definitely.'

'Really? Not because your parents spoke it at home?' Meera asked.

Jeet was about to say something, but Sheila spoke first. 'I don't see the point,' she said impatiently.

'I'm saying that there's only so much that you can blame or attribute to a school curriculum,' Meera said. 'What language you ultimately speak and preserve has a lot more to do with what goes on outside school. If we don't learn and use regional languages, they will disappear. Not because the state is telling us to learn Hindi, but because we're spending all our time learning and speaking in English,' Meera said.

'So you're saying it's ok to impose Hindi on all Indians now because English was imposed on us in the past?' Jeet asked.

'No, I'm saying Hindi as a third language is not an imposition,' Meera said. 'It's a third language. You're still free to study in a Marathi- or English-medium school, and speak whatever language you want outside school. Just because it's in the curriculum doesn't give the language power or influence. I mean, if you tell me German is as alive as Hindi in India because they're both offered as a third language in certain school boards, I would beg to differ. Instead, I'd ask why it is that Hindi, an Indian language, feels more foreign to you than English or German, which are actually foreign languages?'

There were a few moments of angry silence.

'Right,' Faisal said to Meera, 'since we have ten minutes before the edit meeting, can I interest you in something other than the English we got thanks to colonization—chai?'

'That's actually why I came here in the first place, to ask if you wanted chai,' Meera said, smiling at Faisal.

As she and Faisal walked away, Meera was sure she heard someone whisper, 'Who knew Meera's a bhakt?'

She knew Faisal heard it too, because he turned to her and said, with amusement bright in his eyes, 'You picked one helluva day to wear an orange sari.'

'I know it's a slow news day, but letting Sheila work herself up like that? You've got to have other ways to entertain yourself. When are you going to tell her the education minister has announced they're rolling back the decision to make Hindi a mandatory third language?' Meera asked.

Faisal laughed. 'Sheila as a righteous liberal tornado is great fun to watch.'

'It's too easy to rile these kids up,' Meera said with a grin. 'They're also not very good at constructing arguments. The problem isn't with Hindi as a language, but with the right wing's agenda to use the language. Should I tell Sheila that a little research into the educational work that the RSS does will go a long way towards helping her make a better case?'

'You could, but it's so much more fun to see their brains melt at the thought of you being a sanghi,' Faisal said with a grin, holding the door open for Meera.

Aalo looked at the box and felt extremely pleased at how neatly she'd packed everything. Instead of only sending the jewellery box Zeb had asked for, Aalo had decided that she'd send him a larger box—a shoebox, to be precise—with some of his belongings from the backpack and some Indian mithai to make up for the lost kunefe. She had also sneaked a peek at what was in the jewellery box. It was a ring, and Aalo recognized the designer from the logo—T for Talisman, which was one of those madly expensive and exclusive jewellery brands—printed discreetly on one corner of the lid. Zeb Shams was a generous man, Aalo decided. Then, to keep herself from doing something terrible like trying the ring on, Aalo added a handwritten note to the box.

Dear Zeb,

Yes, I have gone through your bag, but only with the noble intention of figuring out what I could send to you in this package. I know you said that sending you the luggage in parts was 'ridiculous', but under the circumstances, I really think it's the most sensible idea. So, here's your first instalment. Let me know if there's anything in particular I should pack in the next box. Oh, and in return for the kunefe, I've sent you some Indian sweets. In case you're not familiar with our array of sweet snacks—in India, sweets are way more versatile than just dessert—it's an assortment from all over the country. The box has been vacuum-packed, so what's inside should last, but the guy at the shop said that once you open it up, try to finish it within a week. Let me know which one you like, and if you want, I'll give you a TED talk on it. Hope you're well!

Friendly, warm and not betraying any indication that the writer of the note spent her nights dreaming about Zeb's beard and fingers. Aalo sighed and taped the box shut. She'd probably have to send about ten more boxes like this to clear his backpack, but at least this was a bulletproof reason to go through his things. Aalo had hoped that taking out the first few items from his luggage would somehow gross her out or puncture the hot air balloon of fantasy that she was floating on, but precisely the opposite had happened.

Now, she knew that he used handmade soaps, and she could smell him on the T-shirts that were obviously well-worn. From the bag that had cleanser, toner, face scrub, hair serum and two kinds of moisturizer, she could tell he took skincare seriously. There were pressed flowers in the books that he'd packed (all non-fiction).

'I'm invading his privacy, aren't I?' Aalo had said, while piling two bowls with gelato for Meera and herself.

It was one of those nights when Meera had come home late, and both women had felt that the future of the world as they knew it depended on scoring the perfect midnight snack—raspberry gelato, sprinkled with pistachios and dark chocolate. Meera had taken charge of chopping up the chocolate and nuts.

'I can imagine it's Sagar's head under the knife,' she'd said grimly. 'And no, I do not want to talk about him. I would like to talk about anything, literally anything, other than Sagar, *The Daily* and journalism. Anything.'

Fortunately, what Aalo had on her mind had nothing to do with any one of those topics. Meera sprinkled the nuts and chocolate on the gelato contemplatively. 'Anyway, to answer your question about invading privacy, it's not like you're doing anything evil,' she said.

'It's actually a bit pathetic, isn't it?'

'A little bit. But in a sweet way. He sends you whale penises, you cuddle his dirty laundry.'

'It's not dirty,' Aalo protested.

'The point at which you can smell an absent man on his T-shirt is not a point at which said T-shirt can be termed clean,' said Meera.

'Well, it doesn't look or smell dirty. It smells nice.'

'Of cinnamon and manhood?' Meera asked, a smile dancing on her lips.

'What?'

'That, according to Ryan Reynolds, is what David Beckham smells of.'

The two women meditatively ate gelato for a few moments.

Aalo was the one who finally broke the silence. 'So, yesterday, he sent me a link to a YouTube video that shows you how to make origami vaginas.'

Meera's eyes widened. 'Origami vaginas?'

'Vulvas really.'

'Was there a context to this?'

'I'd told him how we're constantly trying to find fun aids for SWETE's sex education workshops.'

'So, he found a video about making origami vulvas for you.'

'Basically.'

Meera raised her eyebrows. 'Honestly, I can't tell if this is innocent or not. Normally, I'd say a man who sends you whale genitalia …'

'By mistake,' Aalo pointed out.

'Whatever, he still sent it. So, yeah, conversations that involve whale genitalia and origami vulvas wouldn't traditionally qualify as innocent, but with you and Zeb, I don't know.'

'Sometimes, I think I'm imagining the whole chemistry. Or maybe I'm just projecting my crushing on him into what he sends me.' Aalo sighed. 'I don't know. I just wish this whole stupid backpack thing had never happened.'

'He is ridiculously good-looking though,' Meera said after a minute.

'He really is,' Aalo agreed. 'And I swear, in the past week, he's put up more pouty selfies on his Insta stories than he has in months. It's like he knows that I see him going down on me in my dreams.'

'Considering how much time you two spend on the phone with each other, I wouldn't be surprised if he guessed.'

Aalo stuck her tongue out at Meera. The fact was that her conversations with Zeb were confusing. The backpack that stood in the corner of her room rarely surfaced in their chats anymore. Instead, they talked about things that were happening around them, shared little curiosities, made each other laugh and, in Aalo's case, spent an unhealthy amount of time stalking the other on Instagram.

Frequently, Aalo would look at her own feed and wonder if someone could fall in love with what was here in her photographs and captions. Was this a reflection of her or was it a reflection of someone she thought could catch Zeb Shams's eye?

Because you could fall in love with what Zeb Shams put up of himself on Instagram. Aalo should know. While most of the photographs in his feed were from different conflict zones—streets with skeletal buildings, people with shuttered faces, landscapes flattened by fear; the images almost always stark, melancholy and sometimes even sinister—the stories that he put up were wry, funny and filled with sunshine.

She mentioned that to him, which was how they started talking about Cameraderie. He'd told her about Akbar, whom he had met when he had first been sent to Iraq for an assignment.

Akbar was his local contact, and quickly, the two men became friends. 'He's one of the funniest and sunniest people you'll ever meet. Seriously, it's exhausting how optimistic he is,' Zeb told Aalo. 'To hold on to that temperament while growing up in Iraq is a kind of courage that is truly in rare supply.' Letting Akbar take him around different parts of Iraq, taking his friend on assignments to other countries in the region, was an eye-opener for Zeb. 'Most foreign correspondent sorts go and chase the same big stories—car bomb here, shelling there—but there are smaller stories that aren't considered important enough. Except, a lot of the time, those smaller ones tell you a lot more about the situation.' Akbar knew how to find the small stories. They started working together more and more. Eventually, it was Akbar's idea to set up Cameraderie. He imagined it as a network of local photographers from different parts of the Middle East, whose photos could be distributed to news agencies around the world. 'We're not Magnum, but we do alright,' Zeb said, when she asked him whether he'd describe Cameraderie as social work.

Aalo lapped up Zeb's stories, and in return, he asked her a million questions about Mumbai, her work, her friends. She sent him photos of markets, vivid sunsets, traffic jams and potholes. He delighted in the videos she sent him of the kids at SWETE workshops and street food being made at crowded roadside stalls.

He started sending voice notes, which made Aalo feel like he was in the room with her. All this sounded (and was) innocuous on one hand, but there was an undercurrent that was difficult to pinpoint. She heard it in the way he spoke to her in the voice notes, how his voice would dip, the hesitation that would slow his sentences down—this was a friendship that was a little more than friendship, but what exactly was going on below the surface was anyone's guess. All Aalo knew was that she'd got into the habit of listening to his voice notes before going to sleep at night.

A week after she'd sent the box to Zeb, Aalo's phone lit up while she was at work. It was a message from him.

—Today in Wonders from the Western World, a photograph from my friend Marike. Her six-year-old attempted to make a mini replica of the Taj Mahal. Your package reached me safe and sound, by the way. You're insane for having sent so many things, but thank you for the notebooks and the sweets. Much appreciated.

—Dude, that is not the Taj Mahal from any angle.

—Use your imagination, Mukherjee.

—If I used my imagination, that would at best be five small dildos. Not the Taj Mahal.

—That's just your Land-of-the-Kama-Sutra imagination acting up. What I sent you was an innocent and admittedly inept attempt at replicating an architectural wonder.

—Come to think of it, the Taj Mahal was made for a woman who died in childbirth and spent the better part of her life pregnant thanks to her 'loving' husband. Dildos are probably the most poignant stand-ins for the Taj Mahal. Your jewellery box reached safe and sound, right?

—Very much so. Along with everything else. You really shouldn't have, and what you really should do is tell me how much it cost so that I can transfer the money.

—It's not a big deal—unlike that piece of jewellery. Which I'm guessing is a very big deal. Girlfriend or mother?

—Girlfriend.

—She's a lucky lady to get a Talisman piece. You're a good man.

—You know Talisman? I thought only minor royalty and billionaires with dirty money knew Talisman. Confess, Mukherjee. What's all this social work a front for?

—I should be asking you that. You're the one who can afford a Talisman.

—Honestly, I doubt I could. Talisman is a friend's brand. It's a gift.

—Tahira Ceylan is a friend of yours?

—We were in uni together. How do you know Tahira?

—Wow. I can't believe there's just one degree of separation between Tahira Ceylan and me! You have seriously fancy friends.

—Make a trip to Istanbul and I'll make sure she takes you for a walk. I have a feeling she'll do cartwheels when I tell her she's a known name in India.

—Don't get her hopes up. I only know about Talisman because I worked for a few months with a diamond merchant who was one of her suppliers.

—A diamond merchant hired a sex educator? I've got to say, Mukherjee, the India you live in just redefines exotic.

—That would have been brilliant, but sadly, it was a lot more prosaic. I wrote the text for his sales brochure. Come to think of it, the English in that brochure was pretty exotic. Let me dig it up.

Aalo sent him a few excerpts from the glorious, ridiculous purple prose about gemstones she'd written for the brochure, and their conversation cheerfully wandered into other tangents. It was only hours later, when she was going to bed, that Aalo acknowledged that she'd done her best to stretch out the conversation with Zeb and ignore the detail that he had a girlfriend. In the darkness, Aalo felt disappointment sit with a heavy, dull thud on her chest. 'From tomorrow,' she whispered to herself, 'we focus on work and forget about Zeb Shams.'

Fortunately, there was enough work at SWETE to distract Aalo. It had only been a couple of weeks, but Aalo felt like she'd found her groove in this little organization, even though most of her 'work' was following Hema and Farhana. Still, when Hema asked her how she was liking SWETE, Aalo had no hesitation in saying that this was the first time that she was actually enjoying work. 'I don't think I've had this much fun ever. You and Farhana are amazing,' she said to Hema. 'Everyone's so nice, and everyone does all this amazing work. I don't mean to sound soppy, but you guys have made a really inspiring place in SWETE.'

Hema and Aalo were sitting at Pappu's chai stall, which was across the road from the SWETE office. It seemed counter-productive to leave the air-conditioned office to sit under a tree in the sultry, pre-monsoon heat—especially when Pappu was more than willing to send his 'boy' to SWETE with regular cups of tea—but there was something about Pappu's little shop that drew everyone to it.

'Pappu, you need to start selling ice tea,' Hema wailed.

Pappu ignored her and focused on boiling tea.

'Meera was saying the IMD forecast says the monsoon is going to be at least two weeks late,' Aalo said.

Hema groaned. 'I miss the days when IMD got everything totally wrong. Back then, if IMD said it wouldn't rain tomorrow, you knew for sure that it would pour cats and dogs on that day.'

Aalo laughed. While they waited for the tea, Aalo found herself humming what Farhana had titled 'The Alphabet Song'. Along with the health and sex education workshops, SWETE also had basic literacy workshops. 'The Alphabet Song' was its closing item and it was very popular with kids in primary school.

'Are you singing "The Alphabet Song"?' Hema asked, grinning.

Aalo nodded. 'That song is an earworm.'

'It really is.' Hema sighed wistfully. 'I wish Farhana would come up with something like that for our sexual abuse workshops.'

Aalo almost choked on her tea as she imagined a peppy musical take on distinguishing molestation from appropriate touch. 'Did the literacy workshops come first or the gender ones?' she asked.

'Gender. Rucha's focus was always sex education and health,' Hema replied. 'I don't think anyone else had thought of doing sex education as a proper course, which is effectively what SWETE does. We don't go in and do just one workshop. It's always a set of six to eight workshops.'

Aalo nodded. 'It makes a lot of sense. You can't cover everything in one workshop.'

'That's one point. The other is that if you want to find out if anyone in a class may be in an unhealthy environment, you need time to build a sense of trust with the kid. When a kid has seen you for a month, they have more of a chance of trusting you. The kid also knows that you're not going away.'

'Has that happened? Someone comes up to you and says they've been abused?'

'Too many times.' Hema finished her tea and asked for another. 'That's actually the good part, when someone tells you. The crap part is not being able to do anything to help them when the system makes a mess of things and basically puts the kid right back in their abuser's clutches.'

'Fuck.'

'Yup.' Hema took a sip of her second glass of tea. 'I have very seriously told Farhana we should be vigilantes on the side and beat the crap out of these bastards who abuse kids in their homes. Because, most of the time, the whole process of bringing the fathers and uncles to book is so damn traumatic on the kid that they just drop the cases.'

'Shit.'

'And don't even get me started on the number of times the bloody court will send the kid back to live in the house with their abuser.' Hema shook her head in disgust. 'We actually started doing the literacy workshops as a feel-good distraction—it was for us rather than the kids. Farhana said she needed to do something that was just pure fun and came up with reading workshops. You know how mad Farhana is about reading and books.'

'I know. Half of that bag's weight is made up of the books she's going to distribute at the school,' Aalo said, pointing at the bag she'd packed in preparation for the workshop she was going to do with Farhana later in the day.

Hema laughed. 'If you stick around, you'll go back to the school with us in a few months or in a year, and see how much the kids love those books, and how carefully they keep them. It's really sweet.'

'Does Rucha still do workshops?' Aalo asked.

Hema shook her head. 'She used to till last year, but the whole fundraising thing is a full-time job. She keeps saying she wants to hire someone to handle the fundraising side of things, but no one's fit so far … so, it keeps falling on Rucha. It's a shame, because she's such an amazing educator. Kids watch Rucha like she's Cartoon Network.'

'Are you calling me a cartoon?' Rucha said, as she walked up to them. 'Pappu, a big glass for me.'

Pappu did a salaam to Rucha, and Aalo felt herself sit up straighter when she realized Rucha was going to have chai with them. It was the first time Aalo would be hanging out outside the office with this woman. It felt a little weird.

'I was telling her about your workshops,' Hema said.

'The good old days when I could actually spend time with the kids instead of with stupid BMC officials or someone in a corporate office with an unpronounceable designation that basically means "handles charity",' Rucha said grumpily. 'By the way, have you any ideas for the menstruation workshop we'd talked about?'

Hema nodded. 'I have some, but I've got to admit, they're not very good. Farhana was thinking about using the felt body. You know, the one that has all the major organs Velcroed to it.'

Rucha shook her head. 'It's fine to use that when we're talking about body parts, but I'm not sure if it's as good an idea for an introduction to the menstrual system. Not because of the kids, but the adults. Everyone who's past puberty associates menstruation with sex. It takes one idiot teacher or parent to complain that the body with the Velcro vagina is pornographic or obscene, and we're screwed.'

'But that's stupid,' Aalo blurted out. 'I mean, when you get your period as a kid, the last thing you think about is sex. Even if you're told that now you can have babies, most Indian kids don't know what penetrative sex is at that point.'

'Okay, Miss Social Media Sex Ed Expert,' Rucha said, 'imagine you're conducting this workshop. How will you start?'

'What age group?' Aalo asked, forcing her voice to work, even though all her internal organs were feeling like they were shrinking and freezing simultaneously.

'Let's say fifteen,' said Rucha.

Aalo gulped her tea down. 'Give me one second,' she said and went to give her empty glass to Pappu. 'Can I borrow a pen?' He gave her the pen he had tucked behind his ear. Aalo scribbled something on her palm, returned the pen to Pappu and came back to Rucha and Hema.

'Are you my class?' Aalo asked them.

'Obviously,' Rucha replied.

'Ok, so how many of you get cramps during that time of the month?' Aalo asked.

Hema raised her hand.

'When you get the cramps, is it a little pain, like when you stub your toe?' Aalo showed the size of the pain using her hands. 'Or is it a big pain that feels like it's all over your stomach and back?'

'Big, big pain,' Hema replied.

'Do you know what part of your body is responsible for that pain?' Aalo said to Hema, who shook her head in imitation of the students they met in schools.

'The big pain that wraps itself all around you, that makes it hard to sleep—it's all because of the uterus.' Aalo held up her palm. It had a drawing of what looked vaguely like two unspooled balls of wool and a funnel, but it was clearly meant to be the uterus. 'And that's how big the uterus is. It's so small that it could fit in my palm, but this little organ plays perhaps the biggest role in your life as a girl and a woman.' Aalo put her hand down and shrugged. 'I'd go on to explain the different parts of the uterus, how the lining works, the shedding, and so on. The main idea though, is to start off with getting the girls to understand that this is what the uterus looks like and that it's a small, natural part of you; rather than something horrible, huge and alien.' Aalo shrugged again. 'But I think we need to start with much younger girls, so that they don't freak out when they get their period.'

'A lot of girls you know got their period early, right?' Rucha said knowingly. 'Age at menarche reflects the health of that demographic. The less prosperous, the worse the general health of the demographic, the later the age of menarche.'

'You mean it's only rich people whose girls get their period early?' The thought made Aalo's head spin.

'More than rich, we're talking about societies that take care of their women, keep them in good health. By and large, studies show that girls from poorer and more marginalized communities get their period later.'

'Bloody hell,' Aalo said incredulously.

Hema reached for Aalo's hand and looked at the drawing. 'You know, it never struck me that the uterus can fit in the palm of our hands,' Hema said.

'The worse the cramps are, the bigger we think the uterus is. But if you think about everything that's packed in that part of the body, there really isn't space in there for a huge thing,' Aalo said.

Hema was smiling. She looked impressed. Rucha was more inscrutable. 'You should work on this,' Rucha said finally to Aalo. 'It has potential.'

Aalo almost whooped with delight. Two weeks later, she did her first solo workshop, which Farhana filmed and Hema photographed like proud parents. One of the photos showed Aalo holding up origami vaginas in different flesh tones. Aalo didn't send any of this to her actual parents, but she did dump all the videos and photos on Meera, Rebecca, Jo and Fatima. The four women sent out celebratory messages, as though Aalo had won the Nobel Prize. Aalo put up the photograph with the origami vaginas on Instagram, and Zeb liked it. Soon after, he sent her a message.

—Glad the origami link came in handy.
—It did. Thank you. Did you try making one?
—I did. Failed miserably.
—I sympathize. I botched it up completely. Fittingly, the person who got it right at one go is a lesbian friend.
—Fittingly?
—To quote her: 'First-hand knowledge helps.'
—If that were true, then I wouldn't have ended up with a crane at my first attempt.
—How many tries did it take to go from bird in hand to bush in hand?
He sent her a 'haha' in response, and for the next couple of nights, Aalo saw—and felt—his fingers in her dreams.

By 10.30 p.m., Meera had admitted defeat.

It had been a little more than a month since she'd come back to *The Daily*, and with every passing day, work was getting harder to do and the office was becoming more and more unpleasant. Everything had changed because Sagar was back, of course. He'd returned ten days ago, after his doctors had said he could work part-time. This meant he now came into the office twice a week, and Meera still wasn't sure whether she preferred him in the office—being obnoxious to her face—or at home, rumour-mongering behind her back. It made Meera laugh when she remembered how she had thought her biggest challenge as political editor of *The Daily* would be political backlash. So far, that had been the least of her problems.

Meera hadn't expected Sagar to be polite about losing his position (and cabin) to a reporter he'd mentored. So, the snide comments Sagar made in her earshot didn't surprise her. ('Look, they can't keep the political editor's post empty, and you know Meera. She comes cheap. In terms of salary, I mean, of course.') The way he called her 'chief' and salaamed when he passed her desk radiated sarcasm, but she took comfort in knowing that when she smiled sweetly in response, it probably gave him indigestion. He told anyone who cared to listen that her ex-husband was Kapil Patil, who had left her for another woman. If Faisal was to be believed, Sagar had also told some people that Meera had been given Sagar's job because the newspaper wanted to keep Kapil happy.

'That makes no sense,' Meera had said to Faisal when he told her about this particular bit of gossip.

'It's gossip. It doesn't have to make sense, it just has to sound scandalous,' Faisal told her.

Meera shook her head. 'It's been five years since our marriage fell apart, two years since the divorce, and guess who made it possible for me to basically survive that divorce?'

'Sagar?'

'Sagar. He could have steered clear of me and stayed on Kapil's good side, but he actually helped me get this job. He didn't let me quit when things got bad and everyone at home demanded I leave the job to "prove" I was a good wife to Kapil. Now the same Sagar is saying I've got my job because of Kapil. It's just insane.'

'He's a bastard.'

'He isn't though. That's the problem. He's just,' Meera shrugged, 'jealous, I guess.'

'I repeat: he's a bastard,' Faisal said.

What Meera really couldn't wrap her head around was how Sagar was ignoring the way his ploys against Meera were damaging *The Daily*'s reputation. He had got into the habit of calling up reporters—even when he was at home—and sending them on assignments without bothering to inform Meera. This meant that often Meera ended up sending someone too, and two reporters from *The Daily* would end up at the same press conference or chase the same official for quotes on the same topic. It made Meera look bad, but it also made *The Daily* look disorganized. On top of that, Sagar pitched his own stories directly to Navin, who would approve them without bothering to involve Meera or let her know. Which meant Meera found out at the last minute, usually at the evening edit meeting. It was embarrassing as hell to learn at the nth hour that there was a 'special story' from the political team that she officially headed.

Then there was what had happened minutes ago. The prime minister was in the city and meeting the chief minister for dinner. Of course, all of *The Daily*'s other bureaus from across the country were waiting for the Mumbai team to file a story, in which party representatives would say something about this meeting. Navin had told Meera to get comments at once. By 10 p.m., other centres had called multiple times, asking when they could expect inputs from Mumbai.

Meanwhile, the person who had promised to get the comment—who else but Sagar?— was flatly refusing to cooperate. The two other reporters who covered politics said they couldn't get through to party representatives, but something about their tone made Meera certain they were deliberately steering clear of getting a byte. Both of them pointedly told her that Sagar was most likely to get the necessary inputs. The calls she had made to the chief minister's personal secretary were being politely deflected, which was to be expected since the personal secretary was a childhood friend of Sagar's. Sagar, of course, was not taking her calls.

She finally got him on her fourth try. 'They're not saying anything,' Sagar said and hung up on Meera. Gritting her teeth, Meera called him back. Sagar apologized profusely for the bad phone network and repeated that no one was taking his calls. This was difficult to believe but impossible to refute. When she pressed him a little more, reminding him he was one of the best networked political journalists in the city, Sagar suggested Meera make the calls. 'Maybe it'll make a difference if they know Kapil Patil's ex-wife is calling,' he said. Meera slammed the phone down. It started ringing immediately. It was Navin, asking about the inputs.

'I'll need twenty more minutes,' she told him.

'It's 10.45 p.m. What's taking so bloody long?'

'I'm sorry, Navin. Just give me twenty minutes.'

'Are you going to put the blame on Sagar?' Navin asked.

'No.'

'You should. Because, at least that way, you could try to pass off as being victimized, instead of coming across as just incompetent.'

Meera tried not to yell. 'Twenty minutes. I promise.'

He hung up on her.

Taking a deep breath, Meera did what she should have done hours ago. She sent a message to Kapil, asking for a quote on the meeting. He sent her a reply within five minutes. It had everything she needed and, of course, it was to be attributed to 'a source close to the CM who had requested anonymity'.

Fifteen minutes later, having filed the copy, Meera sent Jo a message asking if she was home and in the mood for company. Now that Jhalkari Mirza-Menezes had arrived, Meera made sure she gave Fatima and Rebecca enough of a warning before showing up. Childless and 'man-free' Jo replied saying she'd be home in thirty minutes and she was up for being bad company, which sounded perfect. Suddenly, Meera felt a sharp craving for a cigarette. She hadn't smoked in years, but it felt like one of those days when regressing felt acceptable. She poked her head out of her cabin. Vivek, who liked to think of himself as the Shiv Sena expert at age twenty-five, was still in the office. From him, she got two cigarettes, one lighter and directions to the part of the terrace adjoining the office that had been designated 'the smoking corner'. It was apparently before 'the make-out corner' and after the coffee machine.

'We have a make-out corner?' Meera asked.

'It's basically this little closet-like space on the terrace, next to the room that the auditors use when they're here.'

'That room has glass walls!'

'I don't use it,' Vivek added quickly. 'But you know, the hours are long …' his voice trailed off.

'That they are,' Meera agreed.

'Anshul from marketing swears he saw Faisal there once,' Vivek said conspiratorially. While everyone knew that Faisal and Aishwarya from marketing were having an affair, a junior reporter had no business gossiping about them to Meera.

'Vivek, what kind of a reporter trusts anything marketing says?' Meera said sternly. 'Now go and check with Vaishnavi or whoever is looking at page two, to see if they need anything.'

The smoking 'corner' was less terrace and more a narrow strip of balcony that wound its way around three-fourths of the office. Meera got there just as two people were leaving, so it was all hers and never before had the term 'refuge area' felt so apt. The night sky was made darker and more opaque by the lights of the city under it. Meera stared at the view unseeingly, as she lit her first cigarette in five years and took a deep drag. The city and the cigarette—both foul, toxic and perfect, all at the same time. Meera blew out the smoke and felt a little bit of tension leave her body. Somewhere nearby, an insomniac pigeon cooed gutturally.

'What the hell was I thinking when I took this job?' she whispered out loud, watching a skein of smoke rise from the cigarette. Something flickered in Meera's peripheral vision. She turned to see the light in the auditors' room had been turned on. It lit up a part of the shadowy niche next to it, the unofficial make-out corner. Wedged between the stored cleaning equipment and the glass wall of the auditors' room were two people. It took Meera a moment to recognize Jeet because half of his face was in shadow and the rest of it was under that damned beard. Facing him was Vaishnavi. She was one of the better kids on Faisal's team—a good sub-editor for political stories in particular, Meera thought absently, even as she stared at them. They were so engrossed in their conversation that they didn't seem to register that the room next to them was no longer dark and they could be seen from across the terrace. Vaishnavi said something to which Jeet nodded. Both of them laughed, and he wrapped his arms around her.

'Yup,' Meera whispered to herself as she put the cigarette to her lips. 'A proper, fuck-all day.'

Three bottles of wine and two bad pizzas later, the day felt less hopeless. Not quite hopeful and definitely not better, but manageable. It was 2 a.m. when Meera decided it was time to call it a night.

'You sure?' Jo asked, smothering a yawn. 'I could make a bed for you on the sofa.'

'It's Mumbai and it's 2 a.m.,' Meera said, getting up. 'I'll be fine. Plus, the cab's already here. Thank you for tonight.'

'Anytime, every time,' Jo said. 'Give me a hug first.'

The two women stood near the door, holding each other close and tight.

'Did I make a huge mistake by pitching for this job?' Meera asked softly, her arms still around Jo.

'No. Stop being so hard on yourself. Just think of all the crap Sagar pulled. You're barely a month into the job. You're allowed to stumble. And that's all you've done. You stumbled. And it was fine at the end of the day.'

Meera pulled away with a sigh. 'Only because Kapil is my ex-husband and he's now feeling guilty about having been a bastard in the past. I can't rely on exes to save the day every time I fuck up.'

Jo put her hands on her hips and looked sternly at Meera. 'Listen to me,' she said, enunciating every word slowly and clearly, 'you did not fuck up. Sagar fucked up. You managed things.'

Meera released a long breath and said, 'I hear you. I just don't entirely believe you.' Her phone buzzed. 'That's the Uber.'

The two women hugged goodbye once again. Jo asked Meera to message when she reached home, and Meera told Jo to stop behaving like she was her mother.

'I'm older than you,' said Meera, getting into the lift.

'By seven days,' Jo retorted, as the doors of the lift closed. 'Message!' she yelled to Meera.

Back inside her flat, Jo sent a message to Fatima.

—Meera's not doing so good. Think she needs to relax a little. Take her out somewhere?

—Not good in the sense?

—Whoa. I was expecting a reply at 6 a.m. tomorrow. How come you're up?

—I have a kid now, remember? Sleep cycles have gone to hell. Tell me about Meera.

—She's having a rough time at work and she's beating herself up about it.

—Kapil?
—No. He's been fine, it seems. Sagar.
—Bastard.
—Hundred per cent.
—You think she wants to talk about it?
—I think she needs to talk about it less. She was at mine this evening. Talked about it non-stop and I don't think it really helped. She needs a distraction.
—Ok. There's a gig next week by a band I think she'll like. I'll take her for that.
—If it's not on her day off, she'll put up massive resistance. This work thing is really getting to her.
—I will drag her kicking and screaming if I have to.
—Sounds like a very good idea. Let me know how it goes.

Meanwhile, on her way home, Meera noticed there was a WhatsApp message from a number she didn't have in her address book. It just said 'Hi'. She was wondering if she should ask who this was, when Aalo messaged, checking in on Meera. Once she was assured that Meera was fine and would be home in about ten minutes, Aalo shared her epiphany of the day.

—It's all my dad's fault.
—What is your dad's fault?
—This whole Operation Liberation. The reason I need it is him. I just remembered something he'd told me on my eighteenth birthday. It was the first time we had a drink together. He gave me a full lecture about how I was an adult now, and that I was free to do whatever I wanted, etc., and that I was free to date or marry anyone I wanted, BUT the person had to be a he and couldn't be a Muslim!

I'm genetically predisposed to crushing on bhakts because of my dad!

—Is that why you've been crushing so hard on a man named AURANGZEB?

—That's not real. That's just internet stalking. It's not like there's any realistic chance of me having sex with him or anything.

—You never know. You do seem to spend a lot of time chatting with him about penises and vulvas, no less.

—A relationship with Zeb is out of the question.

—Why?

—He has a girlfriend. Also, very, very high probability that he uses toilet paper.

—I'm sorry, what?

—Bathroom! Personal hygiene! I bet he doesn't have a bum shower.

—You can't have sex with Zeb because he doesn't have a health faucet in his bathroom?

—Exactly.

—Not because you're in Mumbai and he's in London?

—I'm saying, if we get to that point, I can't because hello, toilet paper is just not enough to clean things up.

—You're crazy.

—I just take cleanliness seriously. Where have you reached?

—At our building.

—See you upstairs.

6

Three days later, when Fatima called Meera, begging her to come to a house concert, Meera couldn't put a finger on exactly what was weird about the request, but there was something that didn't feel quite right.

'Please!' Fatima wailed into the phone. 'My mum can't babysit because she has to go to some ancient aunty's birthday party, which means Rebecca has to stay home, and I don't have a plus-one. You *have* to come! I can't go to this thing alone.'

'Fatima, you're always going for gigs alone. I have vivid memories of you actually abandoning us when we went to see Roger Waters, so that you could have your "alone time" with the music.'

'That's at big concerts. This is a house concert. I need a wingman. Wingwoman. You know what I mean.'

'I actually have zero idea what you mean.'

'Why are you being so difficult?'

'I have work, Fatima.'

'Oh, come on, you can bunk work one evening. It's not like the government is going to fall if you're not at your desk. Anyway, you've been saying how crappy work has been. So, ditch it one evening. It's a nice, mellow band. Ashu and Kavita, the guys who are hosting the concert, they're really nice.'

'I genuinely don't see why you need a wingwoman under the circumstances.'

'Stop being such a brat and just come with me already.'

Meera looked at her computer screen at work. The emails were either banal or irritating. Sagar was in the office today, which meant the evening meeting would be even more painful than normal. At the same time, technically, Meera could leave him to handle things. It would mean he'd have to do some work, which would mean he'd have less time to gossip.

'Meera, I swear I'll come and start a dharna at *The Daily* office if you don't say yes,' said Fatima.

An email popped up in Meera's inbox. They were instructions from the Delhi office to carry an incoming interview with the finance minister on page one. The minister had spoken about how the centre was committed to helping farmers in Maharashtra. This was news to Meera since she also had statistics from the office of the minister for relief and rehabilitation that said 700 farmers had died by suicide between January and June this year, and on an average, eight farmers killed themselves each day because of spiralling debts. Meera suddenly felt exhausted and disgusted.

'I guess I'm feeling a migraine coming on,' she said slowly into the phone. 'What time?'

Fatima whooped in response and said she'd text Meera the details.

The house concert was happening in a building in Santacruz, which was a bit of a trek from the office. Meera told Fatima she'd probably be a little late.

'Don't worry about it. I'll meet you at the paanwala near the building. You can't miss his shop. It's next to graffiti of a purple alien,' Fatima said.

True to her word, that's exactly where Fatima was, when Meera reached the address. She was taking photos of the paanwala—who wore a jaunty little cap and had a collection of funky pins that he wore on his shirt the way army officers wear medals.

'I'm sorry I'm late,' Meera apologized as she walked up to Fatima.

'I got here just two minutes ago.' Fatima gave Meera a hug and then stepped back to look at Meera. 'Damn girl, do you dress like this for work every day?'

Meera looked down at her cotton sari. 'Pretty much. Why? Is the sari and jhola look going to earn me bad karma from hipsters?'

'Bad karma? They're going to need drool buckets, if you ask me. Jesus, that waist.' Fatima shook her head. 'You do good things for saris, Miss Meera. Now let's go inside.'

As they walked to the address, Fatima told Meera about the couple that had started hosting these concerts in their house.

'I know Ashu and Kavita because we all worked for the same ad agency in the early days. Ashu was in the copy department and Kavita was a stylist,' Fatima said as they walked into the lift. 'They've always loved music, but Kavita's a bit like Jo—she hates crowded places. So, she'd have a horrible time every time she went to a gig. That's when they decided to start this Moonlighting thing.'

'Moonlighting?' Meera asked.

'That's what they call their house concerts. They invite a new-ish band to perform and send out invites to a bunch of people who are asked to bring one person and whatever booze they like. It used to be really small, like ten or fifteen of us. But, over the years, they've made quite a name for themselves for picking great bands, so now it's more crowded. About fifty-odd people in the audience, usually,' said Fatima.

'How do they find these bands?'

'I guess they hear stuff online? I'm sure bands send them demos too. To get a spot for a Moonlighting concert is pretty prestigious now. It also means exposure to, well, people like me.' Fatima grinned. 'Like Yacht, the band that's playing today, they've done a few smaller concerts and there's a bit of a buzz about them. Nice, mellow music.'

'Wait a minute. You've heard them before?'

Fatima's paused for a second. 'Only on Soundcloud.'

'You're lying.'

'Why would I lie?'

'That's what I'm trying to figure out.'

'The problem with you journalists is that you're all paranoid.' Fatima rang the doorbell. 'If you don't believe me, ask Ashu. He's been after my life to hear this band. Why would he do that if I already knew them?'

Fatima had barely finished her sentence when the door was opened by a giant-sized man with a bald head and eyebrows that looked like outsized caterpillars. 'You came!' he roared delightedly.

'I came,' Fatima replied, giving him a hug. 'Ashu, my friend Meera. How late are we?'

Ashu beamed. 'They're setting up. You're just in time. Come in, come in.'

The flat was enormous, beautiful and filled with people who looked impossibly young and vaguely in need of a bath. One part of the living room was in shadow, and it was obviously the stage, because it had microphones set up and there were a few people fussing over instruments.

'The bar's over on the terrace,' said Ashu, pointing at a door at the far side of the room. 'But you two should go and join Kavita at the kitchen island because I've "reserved" the best seats in the house for you guys. I'll bring you the special cocktail.' He winked at Meera and said in a mock whisper. 'It's only for friends.'

'Ashu's cocktails are amazing,' Fatima said with a grin. 'I'm pretty certain that's why all the Moonlighting concerts seem to be so good. He gets me drunk, so that I have only happy thoughts.'

Ashu laughed loudly and told them to go grab their 'seats'. Fatima and Meera walked over to the island from where Kavita, a small woman with a cloud of grey hair, was waving at them. Fatima did the introductions, and Kavita said to Meera, 'I'm sorry if this sounds forward, but I'm so glad you're wearing a sari!'

Meera laughed. 'It's a bit out of place here, but I'm coming straight from work.'

'No, no, you look stunning, and oh my god, now I don't feel like a freak.' Kavita hopped off the high stool. 'See!' She was wearing a mundu under a strappy top.

'Thanks ladies,' Fatima said drily. 'I'm feeling totally part of the gang in my jeans.'

Ashu showed up with three glasses. 'Coconut water with vodka and a hint of green chilli and Gondhoraj lebu,' he said proudly.

'Fantastic, but will you please go and get these kids to start playing, so this awful dhinchak that's currently on, stops?' Kavita begged her husband.

'It's progressive house!' Ashu protested.

'No, it's my house and that music is nonsense,' Kavita replied.

'I married a philistine,' Ashu grumbled. 'Ok, I'm going to go introduce them.'

As Ashu walked up to the stage, Kavita fiddled with something that looked like a remote, and the stage area lit up, while the rest of the room got darker. The band members were all visible now. Meera settled on the stool and turned to face the stage, only to break out in a coughing fit.

'Are you ok?' Fatima whispered, while Ashu made the introduction.

'The guy on the left with the beard?' Meera took her hair out of its bun and let it fall around her face.

'With the curly hair?'

'That's Jeet.'

'Who's Jeet now?'

'Kandivali.'

'Holy bloody shit!' Fatima squeaked, as Yacht began their concert.

Maybe he hadn't noticed her, Meera thought as she tried to breathe normally. It wasn't just Jeet. The woman on the drums was the flatmate Meera had seen at Jeet's place. She wondered whether Jeet and his flatmate had talked about her that night. It wouldn't be surprising if they had. As the band set up, Meera figured the one silver lining was that, unlike in office, there was no reason to not have her fill of staring at Jeet neck down, since neck up there was that ghastly beard. After all, everyone was looking at the band, right? Meera found her eyes drawn to the way his fingers moved on the guitar, the ripple on his forearm as he plucked strings. His tattoo moved as he played, and Meera wondered whether the black lines encircling his arm meant something. She remembered how soft his messy cloud of hair had felt, and noticed the contrast between the paler tones of the wooden body of the guitar and his darker arm. Now and then, the short sleeve of his T-shirt rode up, and she could see a tan line. Her eyes lingered over how closely he held the instrument. It was like a lover's fit. His jeans were torn at the knees—one of those bizarre fashion trends that Meera couldn't understand, but now appreciated, because it showed another bit of Jeet's milk-chocolate skin. She itched to draw a lazy circle on that exposed knee. How would he react if she did that?

'They're good,' Fatima whispered into Meera's ear after the first couple of songs.

Meera nodded. Not that she knew much about music, but when a room full of people bobbed to the rhythm of the songs being played, there was obviously something in the music that was working.

Kavita leaned over to Fatima and asked, 'How do you like them?'

'I was just telling Meera they're good,' Fatima replied.

'Wait till you hear Jeet and Jo jam,' Ashu said, grinning.

'Jo?' Meera asked.

'He's the bassist,' Ashu replied. 'Jawahar, but goes by Jo. He's a good singer and a fantastic bassist. Him and Jeet together?' Ashu closed his eyes and beamed blissfully. 'It's magic.'

'I hope Jeet does some of his own songs too,' Kavita said, crossing her fingers. 'He's got a lovely voice, that boy.'

Meera tried not to wince at 'boy' and focused on staring at him. She was imagining tracing the dark wing of his eyebrow with her finger, when he looked up and his gaze came at Meera like a physical force. He'd definitely seen her.

About twenty minutes into their performance, the band put its instruments down and the frontman and singer spoke into the mic. 'I just want to thank Ashu and Kavita for inviting us to do a Moonlighting concert. It's very cool to be here, because we've all been in the audience and heard so many awesome bands, so this turning of tables is kinda fantastic. Moonlighting is also on the money since all of us have other things that we do to make rent. So, let me quickly introduce Yacht. On the drums, we have Ishita. Filmmaker by day, drummer queen by night.'

Clapping with the rest of the room, Meera wondered whether Ishita had also seen and recognized her.

'On the bass, we have Jo, who is a pretty awesome sound engineer, and if you've heard our tracks online, he's the genius producer behind them. On the lead guitar, my man Jeet. And I'm Nakul. And we are Yacht, because that's the dive in Bandra where most of these songs were written. Thanks for coming to listen to us. Now,' he turned to Jeet and said, 'I think it's time for my song.'

Jeet looked blank for a second and then shook his head to say no. It wasn't a coy gesture. Meera wondered if she'd imagined him darting a glance in her direction. Nakul turned to the audience and said, 'I know you don't know which song I'm talking about, but trust me on this. You want to hear it.' Jeet muttered something in a language that Meera didn't recognize. Nakul ignored him entirely. Ashu and Kavita catcalled from behind Meera.

Now, Jawahar lowered his head to speak into the mic for his guitar. 'So, what you should know,' he said, while Jeet audibly groaned in the background, 'is that my man Jeet here is an amazing singer-songwriter. Are you going to sing the song or not?'

Jeet lowered his head to catch the mic that was positioned for his guitar. 'Not,' he said.

Everyone laughed. Ashu and Kavita booed. Ishita played a low drum roll, while making a sad face.

'Don't make me embarrass you into doing it, man,' Jawahar said to Jeet. 'I've known you since we were seven. I'm pretty sure I could come up with something, especially today in front of this lovely audience,' he said.

Fatima, who had an amused smile dancing on her lips, looked at Meera and raised her eyebrows.

'Fine, fine,' Jeet said, repositioning the mic so that it would catch his voice and his guitar. 'Fucking blackmailer,' he grumbled.

There were loud cheers, the loudest from Ashu and Jawahar.

Jeet sang a simple love song with just the guitar and Jawahar harmonizing with him. It was about falling in love with someone, and making your way through a careless world that couldn't be bothered about you feeling alone because the love was one-sided. Meera felt Jeet's voice, with its hint of roughness, on her skin, like the slow lick of a tongue.

Within seconds, the song settled softly upon the room, wrapping everyone in its gentle, bittersweet melancholy. Between the verses, Jeet played a little guitar solo, with Jawahar on the bass and Nakul on the keyboard. They started improvising, and the rich but tender tones of the guitar, keyboard and bass were everywhere. Fatima rested her head on Meera's shoulder. It was the kind of song that made you want to reach out and hold hands with the nearest person.

'Your boy's good,' Fatima whispered.

When the song ended, the room was in silence for a beat.

Jeet looked around and shrugged awkwardly.

Everyone sighed audibly before erupting in applause.

Yacht played for another twenty minutes. At the end of their last song, there were loud cheers, and as Meera joined in the enthusiastic applause, she realized she was feeling proud of Jeet. This was ridiculous. What she should have been figuring out was a way to leave quickly. How rude would it be to leave without congratulating Jeet on a good performance? She could always tell him at work tomorrow, Meera reasoned.

'Should we make a move?' Meera said to Fatima.

Fatima looked a little taken aback. 'Sure, if you want to,' she said. 'Just give me two minutes to talk to the band?'

'What do you mean "make a move"?' Kavita demanded. 'You're staying for dinner.'

Fatima looked at Meera and said awkwardly, 'We've got to go, unfortunately ...'

'But you promised you'd chat with the band!' Ashu said.

'I made the mutton you like so much!' Kavita said hopefully.

Fatima was about to say something, when Meera responded, 'You should stay. I'm the one who has an early thing tomorrow. I'll just be on my way.'

'Nonsense,' Kavita said, grabbing hold of Meera's hand, as though she were going to physically restrain Meera from moving away. 'Neither of you is leaving. I refuse to let you go without having dinner.'

'But I really need to …' Meera protested.

'Whatever you have to do tomorrow, you need to have dinner tonight. It'll be quicker to eat here than eat anywhere else. So, you will have dinner here,' Kavita said decisively. 'You two sit here, while Ashu and I herd all these people out.' She winked. 'We have a system,' she said.

Then off went Kavita and Ashu.

'So, this is the boy,' said Fatima, her voice rich with amusement. Meera didn't say anything. 'You can leave if you think it'll be too weird.'

'How?' Meera wailed. 'I can't imagine anyone getting past Ashu and Kavita. Were they bouncers before they got into advertising?'

Fatima giggled. 'I can see it though.'

'What? Ashu and Kavita as bouncers?'

'No. Why you've fallen for this boy.'

'I haven't fallen for him. I've just … pawed him.'

Fatima made a disbelieving face. 'Those fingers are going to be doing a lot of things in a lot of people's dreams tonight,' she said, smiling. 'If I didn't bat for the other team, I might have fantasized a little about him, too. Great jawline. If only he'd lose that beard.'

'I know.'

The two of them watched Jeet and the rest of the band pack up their instruments and deal with all the people—mostly young women—who were hovering around them. Even from a distance, the adoration shining in the women's eyes as they looked at Jeet and Nakul was obvious. Ashu and Kavita were considerate enough to give each person a few moments with the band, before shepherding the audience towards the exit.

'It must be so weird for him to go from this to being a mediocre deskie,' Meera murmured almost to herself.

'Unrelated to your lust, but I kind of love that they have a woman drummer,' Fatima said.

'Who happens to be Jeet's flatmate,' said Meera. 'Should I say hello to her? I mean, does being introduced to her that night count as an introduction?'

'We'll find out in about thirty seconds,' Fatima said, while tilting her head in the direction of the band members who were walking towards the kitchen island, accompanied by a beaming Ashu and Kavita.

'I thought we'd never get rid of them,' Ashu said as they approached Meera and Fatima. 'Ladies, meet the humans of Yacht. Guys, this is Fatima, whom I told you about. She's one of the people who puts together the Electric Fields and Daytripper festivals.' There were murmurs of appreciation and shaking of hands. Under the counter, Meera wiped her hand, which suddenly felt clammy, on her sari.

'And this,' Ashu said, coming round to put his arm around Meera, 'is ...'

'Meera,' Ishita said cheerfully, extending her hand to shake Meera's. 'We've met.'

Meera shook her hand. 'This is true,' she managed. 'You were great tonight. You all were.'

'How do you two know each other?' Ashu asked and Meera felt like her heart had stopped beating. She couldn't stop herself from casting a panicked look at Jeet, who was studiously looking away from her.

'She's Jeet's boss,' Ishita said, grinning.

Ashu and Kavita did a double-take. 'You didn't say you know Jeet!' said Kavita.

'I'm not his boss,' Meera said, having somehow found her voice. 'But yes, we do work together. At *The Daily*.'

'How did I not know you're a journalist?' Ashu asked Jeet.

'Because I'm not,' Jeet said.

Meera's brow furrowed. 'Really? So, I'm just imagining you in the office six days a week?'

Jeet shrugged. 'I just cut and paste paragraphs from a Word document to the page. That's not journalism.'

'What is it then?' Kavita asked.

'It's making rent by doing time in a newspaper office,' Jeet replied. 'Now, we've literally sung for our supper. Are you going to feed us or what?'

Dinner ended up being surprisingly fun. Ashu and Kavita were wonderful hosts. The food was delicious. Fatima and the band talked about music with an infectious enthusiasm that made their conversation entertaining for Meera, even though she didn't know most of the people or songs they spoke about. And then there was the awareness that Meera felt burning under her skin every time Jeet looked at her. He wasn't obvious, as far as Meera could tell, but she could feel his eyes on her, and it made her want to do things; like preen a little in the hope of tempting him. She spent the duration of the meal watching his fingers, drinking in the sight of him talking and arguing, and hearing the song he'd sung replay in her mind, as though he were crooning it in her ear. A mid-life crisis was torture, Meera thought to herself. It was also incredibly erotic.

For coffee and ice cream, Kavita suggested they migrate from the dining table to the sofas. 'And maybe we should try talking about something other than indie music,' she said. 'Meera must be bored out of her skull listening to us go on and on.'

'Not in the slightest,' Meera said, as everyone arranged themselves on two curved sofas. 'Listening to people talk about stuff they're passionate about is great fun.'

'So, what are you passionate about, Meera?' The question came from Jawahar. There was something about the way he asked the question that made the hair on the back of Meera's neck rise. Had Jeet told him about that night, she wondered.

'Lots of things,' Meera said, her tone deliberately light. 'Eradication of caste, gender equality, world peace, the list is long.'

'You forgot to add Hindi imposition,' Jeet said blandly, while spooning some ice cream into his mouth. He was sitting on the sofa opposite the one Meera was on, which meant they were practically face-to-face, and despite the beard, Meera got a hint of how his cheeks indented when he sucked the spoon clean.

'Hindi—what now?' Fatima asked confused.

Meera rolled her eyes and said to Fatima, 'Jeet and another colleague lost an argument with me at work.' She turned to Jeet. 'You do know that I wasn't serious, right?'

'You sounded pretty convinced that we should all be speaking Hindi,' Jeet replied.

'Rubbish,' Meera said. 'I'm Maharashtrian, for god's sake. Looking down on Hindi is coded into our DNA.'

'Also coded into our DNA is massacring English,' Fatima said. 'There's something about Ghati pronunciation that just ...'

'Please, Miss South Bombay, not all of us can sound like we're first cousins of Queen Elizabeth,' Meera interrupted, grinning, but with a steely glint in her eye.

'English comes with so much baggage, no?' Kavita sighed. 'We used to make merciless fun of our college secretary, just because he pronounced English words all wrong. Poor guy was from some obscure village from Andhra, and instead of appreciating the effort he'd made to learn English, we humiliated him all the time. As though the British had left us here to be the pronunciation police.'

'If the British hadn't left and India hadn't been partitioned, Fawad Khan would be ours,' Ishita said wistfully, and all the women in the room sighed.

'I do not understand what it is about that guy,' Nakul said grumpily. 'Ok, so he's good-looking …'

'He's not good-looking.' Ishita looked sternly at her bandmate. 'He's gorgeous. Like jaw-droppingly, heart-stoppingly, ovary-explodingly gorgeous.'

'Like I said, I don't get it,' Nakul repeated.

Fatima waved her spoon at him. 'I'm with you,' she said.

Meera shook her head. 'You don't count.'

'Just because I'm queer? I protest,' Fatima said with mock outrage.

'I'm with Meera,' Ishita said. 'I don't think you can really appreciate the beauty of Fawad Khan unless you're a gay man or a straight woman.'

Ashu, who was sitting next to Jeet, raised his spoon. 'I'm a straight man, and I would like to submit that I have serious feelings for Fawad Khan's beard. I have had dreams of being able to grow a beard like his. So neat, so thick!'

'Ashu can't grow a beard,' Kavita explained to Meera. 'I keep telling him that someone in his family must have had a secret Chinese lover, because nothing else explains his fair and lovely hairlessness.'

'Beards are overrated, Ashu. I'll take a clean-shaven jaw to nibble on over a beard any day,' Meera said, studiously ignoring Jeet, who stroked his beard pensively.

Ultimately, everyone decided to leave after finishing dinner and helping Ashu and Kavita clear up the house a little. Kavita gave Meera a big hug at the door and made her promise that they would meet soon. While waiting for the lift to arrive, Fatima gave her number to Jawahar and Jeet. 'I can't call you Jo,' Fatima said apologetically to Jawahar. 'We,' she said pointing at Meera, 'already have a Jo, and it's hoes before bros for me, I'm afraid.' When the lift came, Ashu was in the middle of a story about the time he'd met Leonard Cohen in a seedy bar near Metro Cinema. 'I'll come down with you guys and tell you the rest in the lift,' he said and stepped inside. The lift wasn't very big and everyone shuffled a couple of steps back. Meera stumbled against someone.

'I'm so sorry!' She turned to find Jeet behind her.

'It's cool,' he said.

Meera turned around and tried not to think about how easy it would be to take half a step back and press herself against him. Suddenly, the lift lurched to a standstill. The lights flickered and went out, as did all thoughts of Leonard Cohen. Everyone gasped and floundered for balance. Meera's hand groped around in the darkness and found a hand. From the muttered 'fuck' that he breathed at precisely that moment, she realized she'd found Jeet, and of their own volition, her fingers intertwined with his. She brought their hands up, pulling him closer to her, holding his hand against her waist, his knuckles brushing against her skin.

Meera felt him stiffen behind her. The lights flashed on for a fraction of a second and went out again. The lift juddered. While the others panicked and tried to figure out what was going on, Meera felt Jeet loosen his fingers from her grip. Instead, he held her firmly and pulled, so that she was pressed against him, and his lips sank into the curve of her neck. The hand on her waist was warm against the soft swell of her stomach. She felt his teeth against her neck and his tongue. Ashu was saying something about the emergency button, and someone else had found their phone and called Kavita. There was something being said about just thirty more seconds, but Meera didn't register anything other than her pulse practically leaping out of her skin, as though it needed to be inside Jeet's mouth. The lights flickered again. Jeet's kiss gentled, and Meera felt him drape the aanchal of her sari around her neck like a scarf, as he moved to make some distance between them. A few seconds later, the lights came back on in the lift, the lift made its descent, and everyone tumbled out gratefully. Jeet practically ran past Meera and joined Jawahar and Ishita as they strolled towards the gate.

Meera readjusted her sari. Fatima came up to her and asked, 'Am I dropping you or are you off to Kandivali?'

'What do you mean?'

'Unless you developed an alien skin condition in the time that it took us to reach the ground floor, that there is a hickey.'

Meera's eyes widened and she reached for the spot that Jeet had kissed.

'Glad I didn't have to tell you exactly where it is,' Fatima said drily. 'Now, what's the plan?'

'I'm going home.'

'With him or with me?'

'You, dammit. Definitely. One hundred per cent.' Meera touched her neck again. 'I work with him!' she whispered furiously. 'I can't do this!'

'Well, he's coming up to us, so you've got about ten seconds to figure out what exactly you mean by "this",' Fatima said, pinning a wide smile to her face. 'Jeet,' she said loudly, holding out her hand, 'I'm so glad we met. You're very talented, and I'm not just saying that. I hope I'll hear more of your music.'

'Thanks.' Jeet looked a little embarrassed as he shook Fatima's hand.

'I really do mean what I said,' Fatima said. She turned to Meera. 'I'm going to get the car. It's a bit of a walk away. I'll see you at the gate?'

Meera nodded. Fatima gave her an encouraging look before walking off.

'That,' Jeet pointed at Meera's neck. 'I'm sorry about that.'

'You are?'

'It's not exactly subtle.'

Meera suddenly remembered Jeet and Vaishnavi in the make-out corner. 'Don't worry. I won't tell Vaishnavi you did this.'

Jeet looked confused. 'Ok,' he said slowly.

'Good night, Jeet. I'll see you at work tomorrow.' Meera walked past him and hoped that Fatima would be at the gate by the time she reached it. She could see Jawahar, Ishita and Nakul standing by the gate, looking in her direction with undisguised curiosity.

'Meera!' Jeet trotted up to walk next to her. 'I sent you a message the other day.' He waved his hand vaguely. 'So that you have my phone number.'

Meera shook her head. 'I don't remember getting a message from you.' They were almost at the gate. Where the hell was Fatima?

'It just said "Hi". I figured WhatsApp would show my name.'

'Oh.' The mysterious 'hi' that she'd got the day she saw Jeet with Vaishnavi had been from him. Meera almost collapsed in relief when she saw Fatima's car coming to the gate just as she reached it. 'Well, guys, thank you for a wonderful night. All of you were really amazing,' Meera said to Jawahar, Ishita and Nakul. She flashed them her brightest smile as Jeet came to stand with them. He looked like he wanted to murder her, which was ridiculous. Meera waved inanely, and then got into the front seat of the car, next to Fatima.

'So … not taking him home,' Fatima observed blandly.

'Drive. Now,' Meera ordered.

Sometime later, while they were navigating the Saturday-night traffic in Bandra, Meera's phone lit up.

—Hi, it's Jeet. Are we cool?'

Meera imagined punching Jeet the way heroes punch bad guys in cartoons, his jaw sliding out of the socket, his face warping, his eyes first wide with shock and then shutting down to become thin slits.

—Cool as dry ice.

—You're sure you don't want to talk about it?

—There's nothing to talk about.

—Noted.

The next day, Meera caught sight of her face in the rearview mirror.

The earrings looked fabulous, her face was glowing, and her turtleneck top covered her neck comprehensively. It was the first time in years that she was wearing something other than a sari to work. Everyone would do a double-take. Aishwarya, head of marketing, would definitely say something outrageous. The key, Meera reminded herself, was to avoid eye contact with Jeet—a bit of advice she completely forgot when he showed up at her cabin and asked if she wanted to get a cup of tea.

'Faisal's taking some of us from the desk to get chai, so I thought I'd check if you wanted to join us,' he said.

She should probably have said no, but Meera found herself saying a jaunty 'sure'.

'The others are already on their way down,' he told her when she didn't make any move to get up. Which was how Meera found herself standing next to Jeet, in another lift that was making its way to the ground floor, and trying her best to not touch the hickey under her turtleneck. The silence in the lift felt like a million invisible blankets piling up on them.

'You were really good at Moonlighting,' Meera told Jeet. 'I mean, the band. How long have you guys been playing together?'

'Thanks. Jo and I grew up together in Chennai. We met Ishita and Nakul at gigs after moving to Mumbai, and it just came together from there.'

'You guys are good,' Meera said again.

The lift doors opened on to the ground floor.

'Not that I know much about music, but Fatima does, and she was full of praise. She said the song you sang reminded her a little of The Velvet Underground.'

'Really?' Jeet laughed. 'That must have been some cocktail Ashu mixed.'

'No, seriously. Have you thought about focusing on music? Because it must be crazy trying to find the time for it while working here.'

Jeet shrugged. 'I've thought about it on and off.' He shrugged again.

'You should do it. Talk to Fatima,' Meera urged. 'She can give you a realistic point of view because she knows the industry.'

He nodded vaguely. They walked in comfortable silence for a bit. As they came out of the building, Meera could see Faisal, who waved at her. She waved back.

'Can I ask who that song was for? The one that Nakul and Jawahar forced you to sing,' she asked Jeet. 'It was beautiful.'

He finally looked at her properly. 'You liked it?'

'So much that I stayed up way past my bedtime looking for it online. I found your SoundCloud page, but that song's not on it.'

He laughed out loud. 'No, it isn't. That SoundCloud page is old. I should take it down. But that's good.'

'What's good?'

'Knowing that I'm keeping you up at night,' he said, as they reached Faisal and the deskie crew.

Going down to have chai with the desk became the new pattern at work.

Sometimes, it was just Jeet and her. On those occasions, they'd often end up talking about the news of the day. One day, he told her how relieved he was to find she wasn't the right-winger a lot of the desk feared she was after the argument about Hindi with Sheila. Meera burst out laughing at this momentary lapse into earnestness.

Sometimes, she'd ask him to tell her about his music, what he liked and disliked about performing, and she'd pester him to call Fatima.

'She genuinely thinks you're good,' Meera told Jeet for what felt like the nth time.

'Yeah, well, maybe she's just being polite to you because she knows you're looking for my SoundCloud page in the dead of night.'

'Fatima does not do polite, and definitely not with me. Just call her. See what she says.'

He didn't say anything, but nodded.

'Wouldn't you like *not* to have to do this?' Meera asked him. 'I mean, I obviously don't get the charm of the desk, but you're …' She shook her head. 'You're better than just sitting there and cleaning up other people's words.'

He looked up from his tea and their eyes locked. 'What would you like me to do?'

The first thought that flashed through Meera's mind was telling him to get down on his knees. Meera shifted her stance to bring her legs closer together. 'More than what you're doing at the desk,' she said.

He held her gaze for a moment and then said, 'I see why you and Faisal are friends. He also gave me a shitty appraisal.' He tipped back his head to finish the tea. He gave the cup to the chaiwala and saluted him. 'I should go back up,' Jeet said. 'You know, so that I can do more at the desk.'

'Has anyone told you you're an incredibly annoying, frustrating boy?' Meera sputtered as she rushed to match his quick, long strides.

'I am not a boy,' he said, not even breaking his stride.

'Agreed,' Meera said loudly to his back as she fell behind. 'You're a deskie. You could be a singer-songwriter, but you're choosing, for god knows what reason, to be a deskie.'

They didn't talk much for the rest of the day.

Barring conversations like that one, the shared chai-break turned out to be a welcome addition to the office routine. Most of the time, Meera wasn't alone with Jeet since a big group of reporters and editors started to go down to the chaiwala together.

'We should have done this ages ago,' Faisal told her one day, as they made their way up to the office. 'Just look at them.'

Ahead of them, the deskies and reporters were laughing about a story that had driven all of them up the wall the night before. They were ribbing each other and groaning. Meera tried not to focus on Jeet, who was throwing his head back in laughter.

'They're getting along a lot better than they usually do, aren't they?' she said to Faisal.

'They're becoming a team,' Faisal said with a note of satisfaction in his voice. 'And all it needed was a shared chai and smoke break.'

7

Meera returned to wearing her usual saris to work after the hickey faded, but she couldn't shake off the feeling that she was still getting looks from people in the office.

'I thought it was because I'd worn pants and skirts for a couple of days in between, but that's not it,' she said to the head of marketing in the smoking corner. Marketing was not a department you usually considered when building a circle of friends as a journalist, but Aishwarya had, over the last few years, become a fixture in Faisal's life. That, in turn, made her a regular in Meera's life in the office, and the two women realized they had a lot in common despite their very different professions.

'Thing is, you're looking great, but that's not why they're staring,' said Aishwarya. 'They're staring because they're gossips, and Sagar has probably come up with another round of crap about you. But at least they're not staring at you because they think you're a combination of Naagin and Mata Hari, which is what I have to go through.'

Meera laughed while watching Vaishnavi and Jeet sitting two tables away. Meera knew she was behaving like a teenager, which was ironic because when she had been a teenager, she had desperately been trying to behave like a grown-up, so that her family would agree to her marrying Kapil. Now, here she was, at age almost-forty-one, trying to spy on a crush.

'You ok?' Aishwarya asked. 'You look a little flushed.'

'I think it's time to return to the air conditioning,' Meera told Aishwarya.

As they got up, Aishwarya complained, 'The humidity this year is a killer.' Meera nodded while cursing her hormones.

That night, at an ungodly hour, Jeet sent her a sound file on WhatsApp.

—Since you liked the song.

—Thank you!

—Ashu had done a recording of our performance that night.

—It's great. Thanks again.

—Nakul calls it his song because I wrote it for him after he came out to me.

—Ah. That must have been difficult, for him particularly.

—For some time, probably. But he found someone else quite quickly. I think he basically just wanted me to write a song for him.

—If that's what he was going for, I can see his point. It's a beautiful song. Thanks again for sending it. I have a feeling I'll be playing it on loop.

WhatsApp told her that he kept typing for a good three minutes.

—You're very welcome. Good night.

Meera spent entirely too long wondering what he'd written but not sent her. After listening to the song on repeat for almost an hour, Meera made it her ringtone and admitted to herself that she wished someone would write a song like this for her.

The next day, the first of the monsoon clouds appeared in the sky, and Meera was sitting with Faisal, chatting about the state of the nation, when the blood in her veins turned to glitter. Because Jeet walked into the office, clean-shaven. Meera nodded absently, barely registering what Faisal was saying. Her phone buzzed, breaking her reverie. It was a message from Jeet and he'd written it in Devanagari script.

—Don't swoon.

Aalo knew something was wrong the moment she walked into the SWETE office. There was none of the usual noise and bustle. Hema, Farhana and Rucha were huddled around Rucha's desk. In stark contrast to the colourful walls, the three women in the room were radiating gloom.

'Hello,' Aalo said tentatively. 'Is everything ok?'

'No, it isn't,' Rucha barked, without looking up. 'Nothing is ok. We're surrounded by assholes in a fascist country and a racist planet.'

'Pull up a chair,' Hema said softly.

'Look, Rucha, maybe it's for the best.' Farhana sounded exhausted and defeated. 'If this is how much trouble they're giving you now, imagine what we'd have to go through to get the money. We'll just make do without it.'

'How?' Rucha got up and practically flung the chair aside. She was glowing with rage. 'How will we make do without it?' Rucha started pacing the room as she talked. 'I'm still waiting for the state funds to come through, and I'm reasonably certain that this is the last time I'm getting it, unless something in the local or central administration changes. You know what pittance we get from CSR funds. How will we make do without the foundation's funding?'

'We'll have to cut back,' Farhana replied.

'I can barely pay you two. That girl,' Rucha said, indicating Aalo, 'is being paid peanuts. What would you have me cut back on?'

Farhana released a long breath. Aalo wondered if this was a good time to ask what was going on.

'The income tax department froze my personal bank account. They're also saying we've violated some FCRA nonsense, so SWETE's bank account was frozen this morning. I'm to be present in the city to answer their queries, which could come any time,' Rucha said abruptly, as though she'd read Aalo's mind.

'Any time or never,' Farhana muttered.

'This would be bad enough, except I was supposed to go to the UK next week for a conference and fundraising event, which clearly won't happen now, which basically means SWETE has gone very badly sour,' Rucha said. She picked up the paperweight on her table with such violence that Aalo almost ducked as a reflex.

'Can't Hema or Farhana go in your place?' she asked.

'My visa was rejected only recently,' Farhana said. 'Apparently my husband and someone on their no-fly list share names.'

'That's ridiculous,' Aalo sputtered.

'Which part of this whole thing is sounding fair and logical to you?' Rucha snarled.

'What about you?' Aalo asked Hema, who shook her head.

'I don't have a UK visa and the last minute one is too expensive.' She laughed sadly.

'Fuck.' Aalo collapsed in her chair. 'Why do you think they froze your accounts?'

Rucha didn't answer or stop pacing. Farhana sighed: 'There are a few options. It could be the piece that Rucha wrote for *The Daily* last week, attacking the state for giving the contract for mid-day meals to that caterer who refused to add eggs in meals for schoolkids. Also, a lot of kids who ate those meals have been hospitalized.'

Aalo nodded. 'Meera was telling me about that,' she said.

'Not just hospitalized,' Rucha added. 'A lot of them died. What a strange coincidence that most of those kids are Dalits and Adivasis. That's not a catering firm. That's a bloody front for those Hindutva bastards. And that damned Kapil Patil said the kids died because the parents didn't get them to the hospital in time. Most of those parents were turned away from at least two hospitals. They carried their dying children in their arms, looking for a doctor that might save them, because the fucking caterers Patil's government has hired gives Dalits and Adivasis rotten food!'

'So that, as you can imagine, hasn't won us too many fans in the health department,' Farhana continued blandly.

'Rucha's also part of the Forum for Democratic Dissent,' Hema said.

'Which is apparently not what we do anymore in India,' Rucha butted in again. 'Bloody largest democracy in the world, my ass.'

'They've been vocal, sending out press statements and stuff about all these arrests and lynchings, and Rucha's name is always there,' Hema said.

'A few of the other signatories have also been getting some heat,' said Farhana, 'like Sudhir Singh, who started that lawyers' collective, which takes up hate crime cases pro bono. Their accounts were frozen last week.'

'The slightly more important part here is that we need the Nightingale Foundation's money,' Hema pointed out.

'And Rucha needs to be in the UK for that?' Aalo asked.

'I can probably push for an interview over Skype or something, but it's always better to be there in person.' Rucha sat on her desk, her shoulders slumped. 'Plus, in person I can tell them about the kind of delays and crap that I expect the ministry will pull to keep us from getting the funding. I can't put that stuff on record, but I can talk about it informally. They manage to get funds to much more complicated places. Maybe they'll have some ideas. Except we'll never know because I'll be here cooling my heels, waiting for the bloody ED to call.'

'It would have been so great if you pulled a Marlon Brando at the foundation's event,' Hema said wistfully. 'You know when Brando had that Native American woman read his refusal speech at the Oscars?'

'Sacheen Littlefeather,' said Aalo. 'Not for Brando a wrinkled elder. Of course, his spokesperson was a gorgeous young Apache woman.'

Rucha jumped off her table. 'Aalo, do you have a valid UK visa?'

Aalo nodded. 'Felt like I'd have to part with my liver when I saw the fees, so made my dad pay for it, which means I'm going to owe him till the end of this decade. But yeah, I have a five-year visa. Why?' Her eyes widened in alarm as a wide grin started spreading over Rucha's face. 'Hold on. You're not, I mean, I can't, that would be ridiculous. No way.'

'Yes way,' said Rucha. 'You're going to be my Sacheen Littlefeather.'

As her delighted father went on and on about how much he loved London and all the things she must do and see, Aalo wondered whether Bengalis would have been as infatuated with Lagos if by some tweak of history, Nigeria had colonized India instead of Britain. Every time Aalo told her parents that she was going to London, she got the same reaction. Her father launched into this lecture-cum-itinerary, which was basically just him being nostalgic about the years he'd spent as a postgraduate student in the city. After about five minutes, her mother would take the phone, berate Aalo's father for talking nonsense, and then tell Aalo about the latest eligible London-based Bengali bachelor she wanted Aalo to meet. Over the years, there had been many candidates, but all of them had three things in common—they were highly educated, their parents had memberships in all the colonial clubs of Kolkata that Aalo's parents had memberships in, and they all wore their hair flat with a neat side parting.

'Aalo? Are you there?'

It was her mother. 'Yes, Ma, I'm still here.'

'Don't listen to your father.'

'Goes without saying.'

In the distance, her father yelled something that may or may not have included the words 'gobbet' and 'whisky'.

'Ignore him,' Aalo's mother said. 'Now listen, Patralekha's friend's son is studying at the London School of Economics. She's asked if you can carry something for him. I said yes.'

'Please call her back and say no. I have no space to carry anything, and I have no time to meet anyone. I'm going for work, Ma!'

'Don't be so difficult. You can't meet one boy? What nonsense. Snehashish is a lovely boy. Patralekha sent me his picture. I'll forward it to you. He's very good-looking.'

'Really? Very good-looking?' Aalo suddenly felt furious. 'Like Zeb?' She'd sent her mother one of Zeb's selfies while telling her about the tentative friendship that had developed between them since their bags got exchanged. Her mother, like most sensible straight women, was suitably impressed.

'No, no. How will a poor Bengali boy have those Pathan-type features?' her mother said wistfully.

'Pathan features? I don't think he's Pathan.'

Her mother wasn't listening. 'But Snehashish is very fair. Patralekha said he's 5'10", so your heights will match!'

Aalo rolled her eyes. 'Ma, even if I wanted to meet this Snehawhatever, I seriously won't have time. I have Rucha's speech to deliver, which I'm totally freaking out about.'

'But why? She's already written it, you said. You're just reading it out. You read out so well, shona. Just remember all the elocution prizes you've won.'

'It's a little different, Ma. Plus, I have to meet the funding people she was going to meet. And on top of that, I barely have space to carry my own clothes because I'm taking that backpack, remember? I have to return it to Zeb. And before you start imagining a love story, he's got a girlfriend.'

'Nonsense!' Her mother laughed. 'As if I would set you up with a Muslim. My god, can you imagine how your father's head would explode if that happened?'

Aalo heard her father asking in the background why her mother was talking about his head exploding.

'Aalo was teasing about setting something up with that Aurangzeb photographer in London,' her mother said, laughing.

'No Muslims!' Aalo heard her father roar. 'Christian is fine. Dalit, I'll consider. But no Muslim!'

'Stop overreacting,' Aalo's mother said to him. 'No one's marrying anyone right now. Aalo? Are you there?'

'I'm here.'

'Your father is a complete lunatic. Anyway, so listen, you're sure you can't fit a little thing for Snehashish?'

'Was Baba always like this, Ma?'

'Like what?'

'Islamophobic,' Aalo said bluntly.

'Your father's not Islamophobic, shona,' her mother said gently.

'He definitely sounds like it.'

Aalo's mother sighed. 'Ever since this government came to power, I feel like your father has lost his mind. On one hand, this man wants to eat biryani from Shiraz and mutton chaap from Arsalan and get drunk on whisky and wine. On the other, he'll go and vote for the party that wants everyone to be vegetarian teetotalers. It's very confusing. But anyway, unless you're planning to give that Aurangzeb yourself along with the backpack, this is not something I need to worry about.'

'Ma, like I said, he has a girlfriend.'

'He is very good-looking though.' Her mother's voice sounded dreamy. 'Such sharp features.'

'Yup. But yeah, Muslim and girlfriend.'

'So Snehashish?'

Sighing, Aalo once again launched into an explanation about why she couldn't carry anything for Snehashish and wouldn't have the time to meet him.

—Have you been praying that you get your backpack back?

—No.

—Because you don't want it back?

—I want it back. Just not that desperately as to contemplate prayer.

—My script was counting on you saying yes, tbh. Because then I could say, your prayers have been answered!
—You found someone to bring the backpack to London?
—In a manner of speaking, yes.
—?
—I think I'm going to be in London. For work.
—That's brilliant! When?
—Next week. I fly out of here on Saturday, fight jet lag on Sunday, get down to work on Monday. Leaving on Thursday, so we'll have to coordinate the handover in that time.
—Coordinate the handover. Look at you sounding like a spy novel. Where's work putting you up?
—I'll stay with Kekoo. Remember him?
—Tattooed on my brain as the man who took away the bag that I wished were mine. Ok, so how about I take you out for lunch or dinner on Sunday? Depending on what your jet lag allows.
—Sounds good.

Aalo couldn't decide if she felt excited at the thought of seeing Zeb in less than a week or if that little kick of vague unhappiness in her tummy came from anxiety that her tiny friendship with Zeb would disappear once he had his bag. To be fair, it was probably gas rather than anything else. That last fish fry had been entirely unnecessary and pure greed, and extra wrong since she had no time to try and lose a little weight before meeting Zeb.

'He's got a girlfriend,' Aalo said to herself, as though speaking the words out loud would stop the wide-eyed romantic in her head from imagining Zeb falling head over heels in love with her on Sunday.

Sighing, Aalo went to the kitchen to check if there was another piece of fish fry in the fridge.

One good thing about a nine-hour flight was that it meant nine hours without the internet, which in turn meant nine hours without opening up Instagram every other minute to obsess over how Zeb had reacted (if at all) to her latest upload. Aalo sighed and shuffled uncomfortably in the cramped seat. Being tall was not fun, especially if you flew economy.

Involuntarily, she found herself going through her phone to open up Instagram and look at old notifications. Zeb had seen the selfie she'd taken while the plane was waiting to take off. He'd seen it within four minutes of her uploading it as a story.

Aalo could close her eyes and see the tiny little circle of his Insta profile photo, she'd stared at it so much. A blurred city street in the background and his face in the foreground; his eyebrows, one a little more arched than the other; his neatly-trimmed beard that was worthy of his imperial Mughal name; his hair, a little long and ruffled by the wind; the collar of a black shirt that must have had the first couple of buttons open because you could just glimpse the dip between his collarbones. She knew that image by heart, and in nine hours and one day, Aalo would have his face before her, life-size.

'What am I doing?' she whispered to herself. Outside, the night sky was punctured by starlight.

Aalo told herself she wouldn't look at her phone again until the plane landed. Closing her eyes, she remembered the last dinner she'd had with the Not-So-Famous Five.

'So, what's going to happen on this London trip between you and Zeb?' Rebecca, the eternal romantic, had asked eagerly.

'While I'd love for him to fall madly in love with me at first sight and sweep me into his arms as the sun sets on Hyde Park,' Aalo had replied, 'I think what's more likely is that I will meet him on Sunday for lunch, give him his backpack and never hear from him again.'

'Really, after all the hours you two have spent messaging and exchanging photos of whale penises and origami vulvas?' Meera had said, shaking her head.

Jo had raised a glass to Aalo. 'I've got to give you serious points for unconventional flirting. No wonder Operation Liberation is such a huge success.'

Aalo threw a cushion at Jo. 'Operation Liberation was a non-starter. I canned it after that disastrous date with Pretty Parvez.'

'In any case, Aalo's been lusting after Zeb long before she came up with that awful idea,' Meera had pointed out. 'So, my bet is on some good old-fashioned staring deeply into each other's eyes and not going any further than, at best, one intense making out …'

'You guys! Zeb has a girlfriend!' Aalo had yelped. 'And seriously, if any of you mention Rudra, I will stab you in the eye with my chopsticks.'

Meera had held up her hands in a pose of surrender. 'It's precisely because he has a girlfriend that I'm saying only one make-out session at best. Then you'll come back, and he'll realize he's in love with you.'

'At which point he will book the next flight to Mumbai, and Aalo and he will get married, and Aalo will divide her time between London and Mumbai, and we'll all live happily ever after,' Jo had finished.

'Until my father finds out I've married a Muslim,' Aalo had interrupted. 'When he cuts me off, that will be the end of this fictional relationship, given my SWETE salary will get me about a week's groceries in Mumbai and a couple of bottles of water in London.'

'Damn, I forgot about your dad,' Jo had sighed.

'Maybe Zeb can pretend to be your dad's driver, like Dharmendra in *Chupke Chupke*,' Fatima had suggested, and everyone had collapsed with laughter at the idea of Zeb's face peeking out of a monkey cap.

'Maybe he won't mind too much if you tell him Zeb isn't religious,' Jo had said when the hysterics had died down.

'There is nothing to tell my dad,' Aalo had reminded everyone. 'Literally nothing.'

'Is he though? Religious, I mean,' Fatima had asked.

'Since he drinks and has mentioned loving bacon, I'm guessing not,' Aalo had said.

'It must be so schizo for him to spend half his time in this cosmopolitan world in London and the rest of the time in places where agencies like ISIS are practically breathing down his neck,' Meera had said with a little shudder.

'Forget him, I don't know how his girlfriend and family deal with the stress of knowing he could be kidnapped or killed at any point,' Aalo had said. 'I don't think I could handle it.'

'So, you've thought about it,' Rebecca had said with a sly smile on her face.

'About what?'

Rebecca's smile got slyer. 'About what it would be like to be his girlfriend.'

At the dinner, Aalo had rolled her eyes and said of course not, but Rebecca was right. Of course Aalo had imagined it and she'd imagined it in meticulous detail. If Zeb ever found out the graphic details that Aalo had dreamed up while imagining them reuniting after one of his trips, Aalo would have to go into hiding.

She looked at her phone to check the time. She had only about eight hours and fifteen minutes to go before she reached London.

Twenty hours after she'd landed in London, it was Sunday and Aalo obsessed over every possible detail of her impending meeting with Zeb.

It didn't help that when she told Kekoo about her crush on Zeb (in brief), he collapsed in laughter and immediately FaceTimed Meera. 'Dude, the two of them have to hook up. Only so that we can sell rights to their story to make a film titled *The A to Z of Long-distance Relationships*,' Kekoo said. Meera and he spent the next twenty minutes discussing what Aalo should wear, which was at least more helpful than the two of them laughing at her.

'I think I should just tell him I'm feeling sick and cancel,' Aalo said about a hundred times over the next two hours. More than once, she begged Kekoo to come with her. He flatly refused. 'It's your date with loverboy,' he said, 'and you don't need a kebab-mein-haddi.'

At eleven in the morning on Sunday, Zeb called Aalo, and just the sight of his name on her illuminated screen made Aalo's heart skip a beat. She was actually going to speak to Zeb rather than hear a voice note.

'Hello?'

'Hey, it's Zeb.'

If salted caramel were a sound, it would be Zeb's voice. Aalo looked for a chair. There wasn't one. She sat down on the floor.

'Hey, it's Aalo.'

He laughed. 'I figured. How are you? How's the jet lag?'

'I'm good. I'm very good. I wasn't expecting it to be so hot in London. It's crazy!' She was sounding like a hyperactive chipmunk. Aalo took a deep breath.

'Yeah, it looks like you brought a heat wave with you.'

'That's me. Heating things up wherever I go.' What was she saying? Why was she saying this? What was wrong with her? Aalo wondered how weird it would be if she just hung up right now, except Zeb was laughing and that sound was like a caress in her ear. 'Joke,' Aalo said weakly. 'So, are we still doing lunch?'

'Depends on you. Do you feel up to it?'

'Zeb, I took a flight, I'm not an invalid.'

He offered to pick her up, but that made Aalo's stomach feel like a snake doing yoga. She said she'd meet him at the restaurant instead, and so he gave her detailed directions, which didn't register, and the name of the restaurant, which did.

'Great. So, at what time do we meet?'

'Are you staying at Kekoo's?'

'Yes.'

'It shouldn't take you more than twenty minutes. How about half past noon?'

'Purrfection.'

Zeb laughed again while Aalo winced. It was like just her mouth was on drugs.

'Aalo?'

'Hmm?'

'I can't wait to see you.'

He said it softly, and Aalo's heart slammed against her chest again. 'Me too,' she squeaked.

When Kekoo came into the room, Aalo was sitting on the floor with a blank expression on her face.

'Oy, you alright? Why are you on the floor?' he asked, bending down on his haunches to get to Aalo's eye level.

As she turned to Kekoo, her gaze focused. 'He sounds like he should be on the radio, or have a sex chat channel,' she told him.

Kekoo made a face. 'This is why you shouldn't go through a sex drought. If you'd just got on Tinder after that bastard Rudra dumped you, then you wouldn't be swooning like this just at the sound of a man's voice. Where's lunch?'

Aalo told him.

'You'll need at least forty minutes to get there because I know you, you'll definitely make some sort of idiotic mistake on the tube. Get up!' Kekoo yanked at Aalo's arms ineffectively a couple of times. She started moving. Kekoo shook his head. 'I'm not sure if this is the right time to discuss this, but will you check with your boss if they can pay for a hotel?'

The haze of lust in Aalo's head cleared. 'What happened?' It finally registered that Kekoo looked worried. 'Is everything ok?'

'Dad had some heart thing.' Kekoo ran his hand through his hair.

'Oh shit, Kekoo. Is he ok?'

'He sounds fine. They're keeping him in hospital overnight. Mum keeps saying it's minor, but I think I'm going to fly down anyway.'

Aalo wrapped him in a hug. 'Of course you are. What can I do? Shall I ask Meera to check in on them? Which hospital are they at?'

Kekoo pressed a kiss on Aalo's forehead. 'No, no. Don't worry about all that. The five Parsis still alive in Mumbai are there, helping Mum with stuff. It's not serious. He's flirting with the nurses and he's not even in the ICU.'

'Ok, but give her Meera's number. You never know what she might need help with and Meera's damn resourceful.'

Kekoo nodded. 'Yeah, she's lightning in a shot glass.'

Aalo laughed. 'Shot glass instead of bottle because she's so tiny?'

'Nope, because lightning in a shot glass is more of a miracle than lightning in a bottle. You're the same. The two of you make the most everyday thing feel exciting. Just look at how much drama you've managed to pack into coming to attend a dull as duds conference on social work.'

Aalo frowned. 'Can we just focus on your dad right now?'

'We don't need to because Mum says he's fine and, in any case, he's in hospital. Which is the best place for him right now. And yes, I've given Meera Mum's number and given Mum Meera's number. Dad is not the one I'm worried about right now. The thing is, I'm not sure my landlord will be ok with you staying here if I'm not around.'

Aalo shook her head. 'Don't worry about me. I'll get a hotel sorted after I come home from lunch. What's the point of being a spoilt little rich girl if I can't get my dad to pay for a hotel in London?'

Kekoo made a sad face. 'I'm sorry about this. I've texted my landlord, asking him if he'll be ok, but the fact that he hasn't replied yet doesn't look good.'

'Kekoo,' Aalo said sternly. 'You will stop worrying about me and get your ticket to Mumbai. Right away. When I come out of that bathroom showered and dressed for heartbreak, you should have your flight details. Is that clear?'

'Yes, ma'am.'

Unsurprisingly, thanks to all that drama, plus the extra five minutes that Aalo wasted trying to again convince Kekoo to come with her and then getting lost as Kekoo had predicted, Aalo arrived at the restaurant a good twenty minutes late. On her way, Aalo sent Zeb profusely apologetic messages—effectively a running commentary of what was happening practically every minute of her journey. Zeb replied to the first few texts. He asked if Kekoo was okay and then asked after his father. After that, he made gentle fun of how bad Aalo was with directions, even while assuring her that the wait wasn't a big deal. The last message she got was a laughing emoji, which struck Aalo as odd because Zeb rarely used emojis. He was more of a 'haha' man than an emoji user.

It was when Aalo reached the restaurant, with that wretched backpack, that she realized why Zeb's messages had got progressively shorter. He was waiting for her at a table that had two women—one blonde, one dark-haired—and another man. Aalo cursed Kekoo for not coming with her and suddenly felt like she was going to cry. (Except she wasn't, dammit. She was definitely not going to cry.)

When he saw her walk into the restaurant, Zeb got up and walked up to her, smiling. The neurons started flaring in Aalo's brain; it was like someone had set off thousands of fireworks at the same time. She'd imagined he'd be taller than her, but he wasn't. He was her height, and he was wearing a shirt with sleeves rolled up, so she could see his forearms. As the distance between them shrank, Aalo registered details—the neat, glossy darkness of his beard; his lips that were pink and his teeth that were even; the stray white hair that glinted brightly now and then; the green eyes that were shining. The camera didn't do his eyes justice, Aalo thought to herself, and realized where she'd seen that colour before—his eyes were the colour of the water of the Sindh river in Kashmir, catching autumn sunlight. She could stare into his eyes all day. Except that was what girlfriends did. Not people like Aalo, who existed to traffic misplaced backpacks.

'Hey,' Zeb said. There was a hint of crow's feet at the corner of his eyes. 'You made it.' His face creased with concern. 'Are you ok?'

'Your stupid backpack weighs like you've got a dead body in it,' Aalo said abruptly. She swung it off her back to hand it to him, narrowly missing a waiter and a table.

Zeb laughed as he took it from her and put it down. 'Yeah, I'm not a light traveller, am I?' He stepped forward. 'Thank you for bringing it all the way here.'

Aalo didn't say anything. She was feeling furious, but at the same time, her eyes and brain drank in the sight of Zeb like this was the first time she'd been given the gift of sight.

'Can I give you a hug?' Zeb asked, forcing Aalo out of her reverie.

'Yes, of course.' Aalo shook her head to clear it and stepped forward to accept what she figured would be a quick, perfunctory gesture. Except Zeb put his arms around her in a way that folded her body into his. Even though they couldn't have been like that for more than a second or two, Aalo felt like he had imprinted himself upon her.

'Let me introduce you to the others,' Zeb said, as they parted. 'They're all dying to meet you.'

Aalo bit the inside of her cheek and reminded herself to keep her smile intact, as they walked up to the table at which he'd been sitting. The two women and man got up, smiling to welcome Aalo. Thanks to her extensive googling and photographic recall of everything Zeb had told her about himself, she guessed the other man was his twin brother, Baz.

'This is Baz,' Zeb said, confirming Aalo's deduction when making introductions. 'I've told you about him.'

The twins looked nothing like each other, beyond the fact that both men had the same eyes and colouring. Baz had a lovely, crinkly smile and he didn't make Aalo feel like she couldn't breathe. His hair was outgrown and looked like he'd been pulling it at, which made Aalo immediately feel a certain kinship with Baz.

'That's Lara, Baz's wife and a fantastic illustrator,' Zeb continued, pointing out a lovely blonde woman with dark eyes and a musical voice. 'And Meher, this is Aalo,' he said to the petite beauty who held out her hand. Aalo saw a ring on Meher's third finger that looked familiar. It was the Talisman ring she'd couriered to Zeb. Clearly, he believed in saving the best for last, Aalo thought to herself.

'The backpack thief,' Meher said, smiling warmly. 'I've heard so much about you.'

'That's me,' Aalo replied. 'Sex educator by day, backpack thief by night.'

Everyone laughed.

He'd brought his girlfriend to the lunch that Aalo had thought was going to be just her and Zeb. Aalo bit the inside of her cheek harder so that she didn't shriek hysterically, while trying to not dwell on the detail that her thumb was probably wider than Meher's entire wrist. Meher wasn't just thin, she was gorgeous, like a miniature painting brought to life and dressed in elegant, modern fashion. She and Zeb were a perfect pair, matched in beauty and grace and height. Aalo felt like a runaway character from *Shrek*. Did she really need to be here? She'd given him the bag. If she made a run for it, would anyone come after her?

'Ok, we have officially stood around the table long enough to look totally dysfunctional,' Lara said finally. She grinned. 'Should we sit?'

Murmurs of 'yes of course' made the rounds as they tried to figure out who would sit where. Zeb hoisted the backpack on his shoulder and said, 'I'll just ask these guys to keep this thing somewhere so that it doesn't trip people up. We should order food.' He looked at Baz. 'Definitely the lobster crumpet toast. I'll be right back.'

'And we're still standing,' Lara pointed out again.

Aalo pulled out the chair that was closest to her—the one that Zeb had been sitting on—and sat down. Baz sat next to her, while Meher and Lara took the sofa, leaving for Zeb the seat at the head of the table, where Baz had been earlier. Aalo steeled her nerves for the reality that she would spend all of brunch watching Zeb and Meher as a couple. They would probably kiss. Maybe Meher would feed Zeb a bite or two. This was going to be a horrible, indigestion-inducing meal, Aalo thought to herself.

'Zeb mentioned that you were in London for work,' Meher said to Aalo. Try as she might, Aalo couldn't find anything but warmth in Meher's voice as they talked about Aalo's trip. Aalo pretended she'd known that Meher was a human rights lawyer, since Meher seemed to know everything about Aalo. 'You're meeting the Nightingale Foundation? I know Philippa, one of their founders, quite well. She mostly goes by her nickname, Pippa. She's lovely. I'm sure you'll get along famously,' Meher said. Aalo couldn't figure out if Meher was name-dropping or if she really did know the founder of the Nightingale Foundation.

Zeb returned to the table just as Aalo was asking Baz about the design firm he ran.

'Oy, shift,' Zeb said to Baz.

Baz looked at Aalo with an apologetic expression. 'Do you have any siblings, Aalo?'

'Only child, I'm afraid,' Aalo replied.

'You're lucky. The thing with siblings is that one of them is invariably a spoilt brat who exists to annoy the other,' Baz said conversationally, before turning to mock scowl at Zeb. 'There's a place for you at the head of the table, with the girls,' he said, indicating the spot next to Meher.

'I want to sit next to Aalo, you go sit next to the girls,' said Zeb.

Aalo froze. She couldn't resist darting a look at Meher.

'Also, I've been tasked with taking a photo with Aalo by our common friend, as proof of life,' Zeb continued, as though there was nothing weird about a man refusing to sit next to his beautiful girlfriend and choosing to sit next to a random stranger instead. 'To do that, I need to sit next to her. So, shift.'

Baz got up slowly and muttered something to Zeb that Aalo didn't catch and Zeb didn't acknowledge. Once they were all seated, Zeb brought his head close to Aalo's while holding his phone up. 'Smile,' he ordered softly. The click of the phone sounded louder than a gunshot to Aalo. Zeb moved away and examined the photograph. 'It's nice,' he said and showed it to her. 'You think this will convince Meera you're safe and sound?'

Aalo barely glanced at the photo. Since when were Meera and Zeb messaging each other? 'If it does, it'll be fake news, because I'm pretty much starving to death here,' she said.

'That is me being a bad host,' Baz said, and hustled to get the waiter's attention. While he and Meher rattled off what sounded like entirely too much food—'Rovi's all about sharing plates,' Baz said. 'I promise you've never had Middle Eastern food like this'—Aalo tried to ignore how close she was sitting to Zeb, and learnt that Lara was the illustrator who had done the cover of one of Farhana's favourite kiddie books.

'My friend will be so jealous I've met you,' Aalo told Lara. 'We've got to take a picture.'

'We definitely must,' Lara said. 'Zeb, should you and I exchange places ...?' Lara's low voice trailed off, and she batted her eyelashes at Zeb who pointedly held her gaze for a second before immersing himself in the menu. Aalo shot a glance at Meher, who didn't appear to have heard Lara, since she and Baz were busy ordering the food.

The rest of the meal went smoothly, thanks to truly delicious food and the easy warmth that Baz, Zeb, Lara and Meher shared.

The conversation eventually returned to Aalo and her plans in London.

'I'm only here till the end of the week, and I think all the days will basically be tied up at the conference,' she told Baz when he asked if she would like to come to his and Lara's for dinner one of these days. 'But I might need to move to a hotel or Airbnb type thing, so if you have any reccos, hand them over.'

'I thought you were staying with Kekoo,' Zeb said.

'I am tonight, but he'll be flying out tomorrow or day after, for his dad,' Aalo replied.

'You could stay with me.' Zeb dropped that bombshell calmly and reached for more food to put on his plate.

Aalo diligently avoided looking at Meher or responding to Zeb. She reached for her spoon and took a little from the dish in front of her. It was sweet, rich, chocolatey and slick with indulgence. 'What is this?' Aalo asked, changing the subject.

'Beetroot and chocolate fondant,' Meher replied. For the first time since Aalo had met the other woman, her voice sounded brittle.

'It's obscenely delicious,' Aalo said. As she took another spoonful, Aalo added, 'So yes, hotel or homestay, if you have any reccos.' She looked at Lara and Baz.

'I just gave you one,' Zeb pointed out mildly. 'You'd get a room in a flat that's clean and centrally located. There might even be breakfast on some days.'

Aalo couldn't help looking at Meher now. Their gazes locked for a second, but Meher didn't say anything. How was Zeb ignoring this, Aalo wondered to herself, as she valiantly tried to keep things light while refusing Zeb's offer. If there were a god, Aalo hoped he was taking note of the maturity and selflessness that Aalo was displaying right now.

'Dude, considering how much grief you've given me for this backpack—which, I'd just like to state for the record, was an honest mistake—I am not going anywhere near your property,' Aalo said, waving her fork threateningly at Zeb. 'You wouldn't believe the number of times he's accused me of stealing his stupid bag in these past few weeks.'

'And my kunefe,' Zeb added.

'And the kunefe.' Aalo rolled her eyes. 'Considering my thieving tendencies, you should be finding me a hotel in the other end of the city just to make sure you're safe. Hell, what if I put my greedy paws on your family jewels?'

Zeb's eyes widened and Baz had a small coughing fit. There was a clattering sound, as the cutlery dropped from Lara's fingers. Only Meher didn't have any reaction. It took a second for Aalo to realize what she'd said. 'I mean, silver. Your family silver,' she quickly corrected. 'Joke,' Aalo said, while laughing weakly and wanting to disappear.

Meher called for the bill soon after, and despite Aalo's best efforts, the others didn't let her pay. While she was walking to the tube station, Aalo felt her phone vibrate in her pocket. She pulled it out to see Zeb had sent her a message:

—You're welcome to my family jewels.

8

—Meera? You up?

—Hello. Zeb just sent me the selfie. You two look so cute together.

—He asked me to stay with him.

—What?!

—It was crazy. First, he introduces me to his girlfriend, and then, in front of her, he's like, 'Stay with me,' in that deep, sexy voice of his, and then he's sending me messages about his family jewels. I'm so confused.

—He's sending you messages about his family jewels?

—Ignore that. It's part of a longer, stupider story involving my motormouth. What should I do???

—What do you want to do?

—Have him tie me up and make sweet love. Obviously. But that's not an option, is it, when he has a girlfriend? Also, there is no version of reality in which a man who has someone as gorgeous as Meher by his side is going to think about me in *that* way. Did I mention she's gorgeous?

Like, she could be a model gorgeous. I felt like one of those Japanese mascots sitting opposite her at lunch. By the way, I tasted beetroot and chocolate fondant today and it is the bomb.

—Beetroot fondant? Why is that even a thing?

—Beetroot and *chocolate* fondant. It's delicious. But can we please focus on the important part, which is not the dessert that I had this afternoon, but the fact that I need a place to stay in London.

—Actually, the important part is that you need to stop putting yourself down. Aloukika Mukherjee, I would kill to have your body. If I had a penny for every time I've ogled your legs with envy, I'd be able to retire. Or pay for a hitman to get rid of Sagar. But never mind me. When is Kekoo flying out? His landlord has definitely said no to you staying?

—Kekoo's leaving tomorrow and yeah, his flat is not an option. I could ask my dad to help.

—Or you could stay with Zeb.

—Who has a girlfriend and with whom I've had an imaginary romance just because he's looked at my Insta stories and liked a few photos.

—Maybe staying with him will make you realize you're crushing on a fantasy and that the real, flesh-and-blood version of the man is a creep like Rudra.

—I feel a little bit pukey at the idea of Zeb being Rudra 2.0.

—The point is also that you're not the same person that you were when you met Rudra.

—I know Zeb isn't hiding his girlfriend like Rudra did—in fact, might have been better if he hadn't included her at today's brunch—and maybe I'm just imagining he's flirting with me. And I feel like an idiot even thinking that he might be flirting with me because, Meera, there's Meher. And did I tell you—she's a human rights lawyer.

—What are the chances that he was just being nice when he offered you a place to stay?

—That's what would make sense, right? I'm just not sure. I know his offer took Meher by surprise. She didn't even try to hide it, and I just got this weird feeling that I was in the middle of something that is none of my business.

—Speaking as someone with a lifetime's experience in messed-up relationships, it's only when the relationship between two people is already broken that anyone else can bend it out of shape.

—They look so beautiful together. I was watching them the whole time, and it's like they're perfect clockwork.

—Then maybe Zeb's offer is innocent.

—It just didn't feel innocent. But maybe that's because I was more preoccupied wondering whether that beard leaves a rash.

—You're only there for four-and-a-half days. Just stay with him. Don't harbour what-ifs.

—This is your mature advice? Walk into a potential minefield of adultery and god knows what other kind of mindfuckery, just so that I don't have what-if regrets?

—Pretty much. It's what I'd do. Anyway, you keep saying yours is a one-sided crush.

—This is true. In any case, like I said, there is no chance of competing with Meher.

—Aalo, this is not a competition, and you are gorgeous, so if you keep doing this comparison with her or say Zeb's out of your league, I'm going to have a stroke.

—You know what I mean.

—I don't actually. But if you tell me that he's in love with a gorgeous woman, and so probably isn't interested in throwing himself at another gorgeous woman—i.e., you—I get that.

—You're right. As long as I don't throw myself at him, we're fine. And even if I do throw myself at him, he'll probably just politely set me aside, which will be embarrassing as hell, but then I've already made regrettable comments about his family jewels, so how much worse can it get?

—At some point, you need to tell me this family jewels story.

—Later. Right now, I'm going to check prices on Airbnb for a place in London, which of course I can't afford, but still.

—Aalo, don't give your dad another chance to think you need him as your saviour and that you can't be independent.

—Yeah, well, he's right. I'm not independent, am I?

—You can be. And there is more to independence than money. Money helps, paying bills helps, but really, independence is about making decisions for yourself (and dealing with their consequences).

—I don't know why I feel so nervous about staying with Zeb. Realistically, I know that there's zero chance of anything happening. But …

—I might have a solution to your problem.

—Tell me, O wise one.

—Remember what you said about the bum shower? Every time you feel the hormones, just remember he uses toilet paper.

—Oh god. I'd forgotten about that. Thank you for reminding me. Meera? It isn't wrong for me to stay with him when he's asked me in front of her, right?

—Just make sure she knows you're staying with him. If they're into threesomes, who are you to resist?

And so, at around 9 p.m., Aalo wrote a message to Zeb, telling him that if his offer was genuinely meant, Aalo would be very grateful to stay till the end of the week with him, but she was not interested in his family jewels, literally or metaphorically. Further, Aalo would take him up on his offer only if it was okay with Meher.

When Aalo woke up stupidly early, she found a message from Zeb. It had detailed directions to reach his address, which Aalo read twice to make sure she wasn't dreaming herself into a Richard Curtis film.

But she wasn't.

Zeb really did live in Notting Hill.

Sitting at the kitchen island, Aalo tried not to pinch herself. She knew she wasn't hallucinating because this was all just too ridiculous for any self-respecting person to imagine, no matter how much of a romantic they may be. Zeb didn't just live in Notting Hill. His house was on a road in which one bit of *Love Actually* had been shot. As if that weren't enough, the house had ivy on its façade, and because he lived on the top floor, Zeb had a little terrace. Aalo tried to think of a cliché from a Hollywood romance that wasn't here in Zeb's unreal home, and came up with nothing.

'This cannot be your real life,' she finally blurted out.

Zeb raised an amused eyebrow and Aalo felt his Sindh-river-coloured eyes on her like a physical sensation. 'I'm sorry?'

Aalo flapped her hands like a duck trying to fly. 'In St. Luke's Mews, in a house with ivy on the front and a terrace, and just all of this,' she said. 'Who lives like this?'

'Someone whose father had the good sense to buy property in the 1970s,' Zeb replied. His smile was a little smudged by embarrassment.

'Even that sounds like something out of a Richard Curtis film,' Aalo said, shaking her head. She looked around the sunlit kitchen and living room, trying to find something that would distract her attention from the fact that Zeb, with his beard and twinkling eyes, was doing a whole lot more for her hormones than Hugh Grant. 'So, did Meher do up this place?' Aalo asked as brightly as she could.

'No.'

'Oh.'

'Do you remember what time you got off the train?' Zeb asked conversationally.

'9.27,' Aalo replied promptly.

Zeb looked up at the clock on a nearby shelf. 'In the past fifty minutes, you've mentioned Meher four times.'

'You're keeping count,' Aalo said, laughing nervously. 'That's good. Good boyfriend behaviour.'

'Considering how you keep bringing her up, I think you're doing a better job of good boyfriend behaviour than I am.'

Aalo laughed again.

'Meher and I, we're not together anymore,' Zeb said. He didn't take his eyes off Aalo.

'Oh. I'm sorry.' Aalo gulped. The barstool-like chair she was sitting on suddenly seemed impossibly high and precarious. Had Meher and Zeb broken up right after she had lunch with them? Had Aalo been the reason? Even as she felt guilt curl her toes, her pulse quickened; a part of her brain noted that if Zeb was single, then Aalo was entirely within her rights to … to do what? Walk up, push his knees apart and fit herself against his body, pelvis to pelvis, and start unbuttoning his shirt? Aalo felt her cheeks go warm. She reminded herself of all the vows she'd taken to behave with sense and caution after discovering Rudra had used her to cheat on his wife. Only, even at his most charming, Rudra had never made Aalo feel like this. When Zeb looked at her, like he did right now, Aalo forgot all the reasons why he wouldn't really fall for her and why they couldn't be together. He seemed to be at the point of saying something, but Aalo jumped off her seat at the kitchen island. She needed to get away from him and settle her brain, so that she didn't do something stupid. 'Would you look at the time! I've got to get ready,' Aalo said too brightly. 'Listen, can I ask you for another favour?' She pulled up the itinerary that had been sent to her. 'Can you tell me how to get to this address?' She handed her phone to Zeb, who nodded and returned the phone to her.

'Why don't you go ahead and get ready? I'll tell you the route afterwards.'

'No! Don't tell me anything,' Aalo yelped. 'I'll never remember it. I'm terrible with directions.'

Zeb looked at her for a moment before nodding. 'Got it. I'll write out the route for you on a piece of paper.'

'Or just message it to me. Better that way. Less chance of me losing it.' With every word, she took a step back. He was looking at her in a way that made Aalo feel tingly. Zeb got up, and for a second, Aalo's heart hammered against her ribs because she thought he was following her to the guest room. 'You've got the spare key I gave you?' he asked.

'I have the key. No locks stand a chance. By the power of the spare key, I will stick it to them and twist. It's all good. Thank you.' Aalo had to physically put her hand on her mouth to stop herself from rattling on.

Zeb looked like he was going to burst out laughing, which made Aalo want to smack his beautiful face with a wet, rotting fish.

'Ok, so I'll head in there,' she said, smiling and pointing at the room he'd shown her.

'Best of luck with your presentation!'

'Thanks. And thanks again for letting me stay here. I don't know how I can repay you ...'

'I'll think of something,' he said.

'Right. Of course you will. You just let me know,' Aalo said, refusing to entertain the idea that there could be any innuendo in Zeb's tone. After saying bye to him again, she practically ran into the room and shut the door behind her.

'Remember. He doesn't use a bum shower,' Aalo whispered to herself. 'There is no future without a bum shower. It doesn't matter how hot he may look, and the way his voice dips, or how those jeans hug his bum—forget all that. Remember the bum shower that isn't there.'

Aalo breathed in and out deeply. She felt a little better after the pep talk. She checked her phone. She had loads of time. Google Maps had told her that she needed just fifteen minutes to reach the venue. She heard the muffled sound of the front door shutting, which meant Zeb must have left the house—without sending her the directions. Still, Aalo felt relief flood through her.

Taking her towel and toiletries, Aalo stepped out of the room and padded her way to the door that Zeb had earlier pointed out, identifying it as her bathroom. Aalo felt herself blush as she remembered their conversation.

'I'm sorry, the guest room doesn't have an ensuite bathroom, so you'll have to use that one in the hallway,' he'd said.

'No problem. I wasn't planning on prancing around your house stark naked anyway,' she'd replied.

'Shame,' Zeb had replied, and smoothly followed this up with, 'Tea?'

Shaking her head in embarrassment now, Aalo opened the bathroom door and fumbled for the light switch, while appreciating the lemony scent of disinfectant that was in the bathroom. It was only when she came out of the shower that Aalo's heart leapt out of her chest. Because there, next to the toilet, was a bum shower.

She stared at it for a moment and then gingerly lifted it from its holder and pressed to see if it worked. It squirted water on the toilet seat and made a little mess. Aalo's hand quivered as she replaced it and then took some tissue paper to wipe the toilet seat dry. Then she ran out of the bathroom like she was being chased by the hounds of hell or immigration officials or both.

Back in the guest room, she threw herself face down on the bed. The mattress was nice and firm. Aalo felt herself bob on it for a moment. A bum shower! In London! Since when did the British do personal hygiene? 'Damn you universe, y u do dis?' Aalo wailed.

She reached for her phone to break the news to Meera that Zeb had a bum shower in his guest bathroom, when she realized Zeb actually had sent her detailed instructions on how to reach the venue. He hadn't bothered to explain how she should get back, but Aalo reasoned she just needed to do the route in reverse.

The phone vibrated in her hand again. It was Meera, wishing her luck for the presentation.

'Focus, dammit,' Aalo hissed at herself. 'You have more important things to do right now.'

Putting all thoughts of Zeb and personal hygiene aside, Aalo started to go over Rucha's speech again.

The nerves didn't kick in until Aalo was at the venue, and a pasty-faced young man was efficiently attaching a mic to Aalo's person.

'You should be able to hear my boss in your ear right about now,' he said cheerfully. 'Her name's Alison.'

Right on cue, a woman's voice hummed in Aalo's head. 'Hiya, this is Alison. We have about five minutes to your segment. Please make sure your phone is switched off or on airplane mode when you go on stage, so that it doesn't interfere with the speakers. I'll give you a heads-up when we're about a minute away. Please stay backstage, and if you need anything, Aidan will get it for you.'

Aalo figured the pasty-faced one was Aidan. 'I'm fine actually, thanks,' she said to whoever was listening.

Aidan gave her a grin and a thumbs-up.

'Aidan?' she asked. 'I'd emailed the text of what I'm going to say to someone, to put on the teleprompter.'

'Yeah, don't worry about it. It's there,' Aidan assured her. 'When you get to your mark on stage, you'll be able to see the teleprompter right in front of you. But, just in case, I've got a printout too, in case you want to hold on to it as a backup.' He handed her a few pages, which Aalo grabbed gratefully.

'Thank you,' she said.

The next few minutes took forever to pass. By the time Aalo finally heard Alison's voice in her ear, there was a bit of her brain telling her to just bolt and run. Except Philippa 'Pippa' Markham, one of the hosts of the evening and a member of the Nightingale Foundation's board of trustees, was on stage, introducing the next speaker, who happened to be Aalo Mukherjee, colleague and collaborator of Rucha Phadke, founder of the Society for Women's Empowerment through Education, from Mumbai, India. As Aalo came up to the microphone, she could see the teleprompter and the circle of light that was to be her domain.

The first few words of Rucha's speech were already on the screen. Aalo took a deep breath and was just about to start when the teleprompter flickered and then went dark.

Aalo's smile froze on her face. She'd left the printout Aidan had given her backstage. The room was silent. She could feel the expectation of the audience. It was heavy as a handkerchief doused in chloroform. Someone apologized to her through the earpiece and said they'd have the teleprompter up in five minutes.

Aalo took another deep breath, pulled out her earpiece, and reminded herself that she knew Rucha's speech and she knew what SWETE did. The earpiece felt heavy on her collarbone. With a little nod to herself, Aalo started talking.

'Every couple of weeks, my boss Rucha Phadke makes a trip to the headquarters of Mumbai's municipal corporation's headquarters, BMC. There's a man she meets there. His name is Hemant Nadkarni. He knows Rucha and the Society for Women's Empowerment through Education very well because he's the one who signs the papers that release the payment that Rucha gets from the BMC for conducting workshops in government-run schools. Mumbai has the richest municipal corporation in the country, but what Rucha gets for her workshops is so minuscule, it didn't even get mentioned in the annual budget they presented this year, which amounted to about Rs 744 million. I can't do the math, I just teach sex ed, but I do know that's a lot of zeroes and a lot of money. Nadkarni isn't a very important man in the larger scheme of things, but since he does sign the cheques that Rucha has been getting, Rucha and he meet every quarter. She asks him how he is, and they chit-chat for a bit, before Nadkarni gives Rucha the cheque she's come to collect. For the past fifteen years, despite knowing the organization and many of the people involved, Nadkarni hasn't bothered to learn the name Society for Women's Empowerment through Education. He's just shortened the name of the organization. S, W, E, T, E, or *Sweetie*. Rucha lets him because, as she puts it, if Sweetie is what it takes to get the money she needs to run the workshops, so be it.'

There was laughter.

Aalo nodded. 'It is funny. But it also hints at what Rucha is up against. After all these years, Nadkarni doesn't care to refer to the organization by its real name. That comes from a lack of respect, a readiness to dismiss. And he's not an opponent. If anything, he's supportive and still, SWETE—that's what we call it affectionately, because what it does, it's sweet—SWETE doesn't occupy enough space in Nadkarni's mind to deserve the respect of being called by its correct name.

'Now imagine what Rucha is up against when she encounters someone committed to standing in her way. Because, right now, there are many people who fit that description. Why, you ask. What would anyone have against a non-profit organization that holds workshops about women's health, sex education and literacy? Why would it scare groups that have social and financial capital, political backing and often, even the support of community elders?' Aalo paused for a second. 'Because, with the workshops, Rucha gives the girls something that our societies systematically leech out of their lives—confidence and imagination. She teaches boys that they must see the girls as equal and that the dysfunctional gender relations they see in their everyday lives—the wife who gets beaten, the sister who is taken out of school, the girl that the older boys catcall—isn't normal. Rucha, Hema, Farhana and the other warriors in SWETE, who go out and work with the community, they become heroes and confidantes for the girls and boys they meet. The children tell them when things go wrong, they trust SWETE to help them, they participate in the workshops with shining eyes and bubbling comments and loud laughter. Because SWETE helps them imagine a better, fairer, more empowered future. That's why Rucha is special. That's also why, to some people, she and SWETE are scary.'

The teleprompter lit up. There were no words on it, but at least there was a sign of life.

'It's an honour for me to be able to read out Rucha's words before all of you. But if you're feeling a little ripped off that you don't get Rucha in person, you're absolutely right. I'm not a fair exchange by a long shot. Rucha couldn't be here because she's fighting battles back home, battles that I can't fight or win for her. All I can do is be her voice for today. Many of you, who are in the audience, you can do a lot more than I can. And I hope, by the time I'm done reading Rucha's speech, she'll have your support. That would be, well, sweet.'

Aalo flashed a grin at the darkness facing her. A little laughter rippled through the audience. After sending out wordless thanks to the tech gods and humans, Aalo began reading out the words on the teleprompter.

When she finished, the room erupted in applause and half of the audience was on its feet. Aalo breathed easy for the first time since she'd walked on stage and she did a namaste before walking off. In the wings, she took off the mic and gave it to Aidan, who told her she'd been brilliant and apologized profusely for the technical glitch with the teleprompter. Alison also showed up to apologize and congratulate Aalo.

Wading past the regrets and praise, Aalo made her way to one of the green rooms at the back and turned on her phone to update her girls. The moment her phone latched on to the venue's Wi-Fi, Aalo's phone was full of congratulatory messages from Meera, Fatima, Jo and Rebecca. There were even screenshots that showed her on stage. Rebecca added that she loved the outfit. Jo had sent a photo of herself making a kissy face while holding up a glass of what looked like whisky. Meera said that she loved the intro Aalo had given. Fatima, with the eagle eye of an experienced producer of live shows, asked if the intro was to cover up a technical glitch. A perplexed Aalo quickly tapped out a message to the gang.

—How the hell did you guys know about the speech?

Meera wrote back first.

—Zeb livestreamed it on Instagram. Looked like he was pretty close to the stage.

What on earth was Zeb doing here? And was Meher with him? Aalo looked at herself in the mirror. Her cheeks looked pink, as though she'd been running. Apple-cheeked, as her mum would describe it.

She tapped out a message to her parents, letting them know the presentation had gone well, and then made her way to the fourth floor of the building, to the restaurant where the dinner was supposed to be held. Rucha's speech had been the second-last item of the day, so Aalo figured those in the audience who were attending the dinner would probably take some time to reach the place. This was a good thing. Aalo felt like she needed to knock back a couple of glasses of wine before meeting Very Important People. She was debating between red and white as she walked in. A few people were already there. One of them was coming up to her. It was Zeb, in a tailored jacket that was clearly designed to make Aalo's jaw drop and mouth dry up.

'Red or white? They've only got wine here, so that's all the choice you get,' he said, as though reading her mind.

'Red. I wasn't expecting you here. Is Meher here?'

He ignored her question and manifested two glasses of red wine, seemingly out of nowhere. 'That was a brilliant speech and you were fantastic,' Zeb said, raising a glass to her.

'All credit to Rucha,' Aalo said, clinking her glass with his. 'The brilliance was her words. You livestreamed it on Insta, Meera said. Thanks for that.'

He shrugged. 'Not sure if that will be of any help in real terms, but I figured your friends would want to see you being a rockstar on stage.'

'Rockstar almost peed her pants,' Aalo said wryly. 'The teleprompter blipped for a few minutes. That's why I was faffing in the beginning.'

'No one could tell.'

'My friend Fatima did,' Aalo said, grinning. 'She said she almost had a panic attack on my behalf because she was imagining the worst-case scenario of the technical glitch remaining glitched. Is Meher here?'

'No.'

'Oh.'

'I wangled an invitation for myself at the last minute.'

Aalo looked confused. 'Why?'

Zeb looked at her for a moment and then gulped down some wine. 'I presume you want to meet potential donors,' he said, taking her by the elbow.

Aalo nodded, still unclear about how and why Zeb had become her wingman. 'I have been sternly told to mingle by Rucha,' she told him.

'Right, then, let me introduce you to the fat cats that I know in this room, courtesy Cameraderie,' he said, steering her towards a man who looked about one hundred years old. 'He should work almost as well as a cold shower. I had to be interviewed by him three times to get a measly grant, and it was only at the end of that interminable process that his secretary fessed up that there were so many interviews because he kept forgetting to wear his hearing aid when he met me.'

Aalo stumbled on the flooring that was completely smooth and ended up clutching at Zeb wildly. 'I'm sorry did you say cold shower?'

'Keep up, Mukherjee,' he said mildly, as he put his arm around her waist to steady her. 'I'm this close to throwing caution to the winds and kissing you senseless in front of all these old farts after that amazing presentation. You keep up that wide-eyed, lips parted look, and I swear I will kiss those lips shut.'

Aalo clapped her lips together immediately.

'Spoilsport,' he murmured, before extending his hand to an ancient-looking man and introducing Aalo to him. Aalo made what were hopefully polite noises and told the gentleman about SWETE. She stumbled at a couple of points, but Zeb smoothly stepped in and covered up for her. When they'd moved away, Aalo said, 'I need more wine. And some explanation of what's going on here.'

'Well, this, Mukherjee, is what we in London call a gala dinner. By which I mean, it's full of obscenely rich people, who are looking for opportunities to spend a little bit of money that will make them feel like modern-day miracle workers.'

'I meant here,' Aalo said, waving her hand between herself and Zeb. She put her empty glass down on a tray that appeared with a smiling human attached to it. After a moment's hesitation, she picked up another glass of wine.

'That's white,' Zeb pointed out.

'Details. Why are we talking about cold showers and kisses?'

'It's not mandatory,' Zeb said, plucking a glass of wine for himself, before the tray floated away. 'I mean, we can keep sending sexually-charged messages to one another, and not actually do anything if that's what you want.' He looked around the room. 'Do you see anyone you want to meet? Or food? I'm feeling a bit peckish.'

'There's some appetizer-type thing floating around in that corner,' Aalo pointed out.

'Good girl. Pippa Markham's there too. Two birds, one stone.'

'Markham? As in the Nightingale Foundation woman?' Aalo remembered Meher had said during that godawful brunch that she knew Philippa Markham.

'The very same. Let's go.'

'You have a girlfriend. A beautiful, amazing girlfriend. I couriered jewellery for your girlfriend,' Aalo pointed out as they walked across the room.

'You're a bit obsessed with Meher, Mukherjee. I did mention we're not together anymore.'

'No, I'm obsessed with not being the other woman.' Aalo stopped walking abruptly and yanked Zeb to a stop. 'I can't be the person who broke you two up or the person you use while waiting for her to come back.'

She saw him look at her closely and wondered what he saw. Could he tell she was feeling like she could burst into tears at any moment and that she wanted desperately for everyone to disappear so that he could kiss her, with tongue? What if he was Rudra 2.0? What if she was subliminally looking to upend other people's long-term relationships?

'What Meher and I have done with our relationship has nothing to do with you. I'm sorry if it sounds harsh, but it really isn't even your business,' Zeb said finally.

'It is if you're going to cheat on her by having sex with me.'

He raised his eyebrows. 'Slow down, Mukherjee. Can we just take baby steps and introduce you to Pippa Markham first?'

'I think I've had too much wine on an empty-ish stomach.'

'Feeling dizzy?' He sounded concerned.

'Feeling blurty.'

Zeb looked confused. 'Blurty?'

'I want to kiss you too. See? Blurty. To be honest, I want to do a whole lot more than kiss you. I've had some very, very graphic dreams involving you and me and no clothes. See? More blurty. I don't know what happens when I'm around you. I've been blurty since the first time you called me on the phone. So, maybe it's not the wine. But despite what I sound like, it's not like I have no impulse control. Meher and you …'

'Are not together.'

'You're sure?'

'I'm sure.'

'If this Markham woman tells Meher that she saw us kissing, it won't mean that she'll show up with a chainsaw and cut me into little pieces.'

'I don't think chainsaws are really Meher's thing.'

'The device is not the point. The intent is.'

'I think she'll feel sad, which I don't want, so please don't kiss me in front of Pippa Markham. Or, really, anyone in this room. Most of them know Meher, even if they don't know me. The philanthropy set is very much her crowd.'

'Did you break up with her because of me?'

Zeb clicked his tongue disparagingly. 'So judgemental, Mukherjee. And so convinced that you're the reason the world goes round.'

'I'd love to not be.'

'Well, in this case, you're not. As for the tent pole that I'm in danger of sporting, you're very much the reason that's happening. No, Aalo, for the love of god, do not look down.'

Aalo's eyes and head snapped back up. 'We need to talk about this.'

'If you insist. Personally, I'd prefer to "do" about this.' His face took on a puzzled expression. 'Wait, you want to talk now, here?'

'No. Now, we do Markham. Then, we go home and do each other. Then we talk.'

Zeb inhaled sharply. 'Well, don't just stand there, Mukherjee. We're on the clock here.'

He grabbed her by the hand and practically marched towards Philippa Markham.

9

Aalo had thought that everything—the buzzing in her ears, the tingly feeling under her skin—would hit a fever pitch after that exchange with Zeb, but the opposite happened. Everything slowed down, as though time had decided to take an extra beat between seconds. Aalo felt almost like she was watching herself from a distance. She approached Philippa Markham and heard herself speak confidently about the issues that Rucha had told her to raise, and added a few points of her own after gauging the British philanthropist's interest areas. Markham was impressed enough by Aalo to introduce her to two more board members. They spoke about SWETE and the difficulties that a lot of non-governmental organizations in India faced with foreign funding. Aalo suggested setting up a meeting on Skype with Rucha, even while taking them through SWETE's aims. All these months of shadowing Hema and Farhana held her in excellent stead. She wasn't pitching blindly. She knew what SWETE did in detail, and as she spoke about the work, she remembered why Rucha wasn't here to do the talking. Far away from her office and her colleagues, Aalo felt in every fibre of her being just how difficult it was for Rucha to ensure this organization existed and how hard she fought to make sure it didn't surrender to the obstacles she faced.

While she did her bit, Aalo also registered Zeb was being pulled into different conversations. People came up to him, and from their body language and his, she could tell that they were complimenting him. He worked the room skilfully to bring himself closer to her and she heard someone congratulate him on the work Cameraderie was doing. She noticed how nice he was to the server, who nervously came up to him to say she was a photography student and wanted to be a photojournalist. Even when they made excuses to get out of the formal dinner, everything stayed quiet in Aalo's head.

Once outside, she saw Zeb hail a cab, she felt him hold her hand in a light grip the whole way. Every thought in her head felt like it was sunken in honey. At one point, it started to drizzle, and for some reason, the sight of the raindrops on the window reminded Aalo of her father. She absently wondered how he'd react if he knew she was in a cab with Zeb, minutes away from (hopefully) making love to him. A tendril of cold anxiety uncurled somewhere inside her. Aalo looked at the neat fit of her hand in Zeb's. He squeezed gently and the warmth from his fingertips sank into her skin.

They didn't say anything when the cab reached home. Not even when Aalo tried to pull out her wallet to pay at least some of the cab fare and Zeb didn't let her. They didn't say anything as they walked up the stairs and Zeb unlocked the door to the flat. The quiet wasn't uncomfortable. It felt right against the night sky that you could see from the large windows in Zeb's living room. She heard Zeb toe off his shoes once they were inside and she did the same. He came in her line of sight when he went to switch on the table lamp next to the sofa.

'The blurty feeling has passed, I gather,' he said, as the light pushed the shadows to the corners of the room. He sounded only mildly curious.

Aalo shrugged. She took a couple of steps towards him when he held up his hand.

'Just stay right there for one second,' Zeb said. 'Don't move.' He walked quickly to his room and returned with a camera which he put to his eye.

'This is a bit weird,' she told him finally, while he took photos of her.

He didn't say anything for a few moments as he kept a distance from her and kept clicking. Finally, he put the camera down. 'It's like you're made of amber and shadow,' he said, touching a finger to her cheek. He put the camera to his eye again.

'Hold up your hand,' Aalo said.

Zeb took another photo and then lowered the camera. 'My hand?'

Aalo nodded and held up her right hand, its fingers splayed as though to show the number five. Zeb held his left hand against hers. Their palms touched lightly. Aalo's fingers were pudgier and her nails were longer, but in terms of size, their hands were the same. The tips of their middle fingers were even, the joints of their thumbs met at the same point; there was a little hollow created by the dips of their palms. His hand didn't engulf hers or make her feel small or delicate. It was her equal.

A soft click brought Aalo out of her reverie. She looked at Zeb. The lamp was behind him, and he had the camera to his eye, which transformed him into a lens-eyed creature. A benevolent, sexy cyborg, with slender fingers and a smile on his lips.

'Are you going to put that thing down and kiss me at some point? Because if something has to be glued to your face, I'd rather it be my face than your camera.'

Zeb's face appeared from behind the camera looking a little stunned.

Aalo shrugged. 'I guess blurty is back,' she said.

Zeb capped the camera's lens and put it down on the table, and before Aalo had taken another breath, he was standing so close to her, the tips of their noses were almost touching.

'Blurty's the best,' he murmured and touched his lips to hers. He kissed her softly, learning the shape and feel of her slowly, gently. With each little kiss that he pressed on her lips, Aalo felt herself relax and unravel. She slipped her fingers into his hair and took a step closer to him, so that their bodies touched. His hands came around to her hips, steadying them both and holding her close. He deepened the kiss, as his hands followed the shape of her butt and pulled her closer.

Aalo pulled her head away, while carefully maintaining pelvic contact and keeping her arms wrapped around him. 'That's an erection, right?'

'You sound unsure.' There was a twinkle in Zeb's eye.

'So you should know I haven't had much sex. In fact, I haven't had any sex in five years. I would say that I've forgotten how to do it, but I don't think I knew how to do it very well in the first place. Which means …'

Zeb kissed her a little harder and then harder still when she tried to keep talking. She gave up and kissed him back the way she wanted to—with a lot of lip, some tongue and a little teeth. He finally pulled away.

'You're the one who said Blurty's best,' she said, through lips that felt vaguely swollen.

'My feelings about Blurty remain unchanged,' Zeb said, turning his attention to her ear. 'I'm just not particularly interested in your previous partners.'

'I was just trying to prepare you …'

He frowned and kissed her mouth again.

'Is this going to be a pattern?' Aalo asked. 'Are you going to use your tongue to shut me up?'

'Only if I get the feeling that you're about to say something unnecessary,' he said, and the kiss that followed went on for much longer than Aalo had expected. Long enough for her to untuck his shirt and slide her hands underneath to feel his skin, the firm points of his nipples and the graze of body hair in certain patches. He looked down to where the contour of her hands, placed on each of his pectorals, slightly tented the fabric of his shirt. 'How did you get ahead of me?' he said.

'I'm very target-oriented,' Aalo informed him. She ran her nails down his chest, before flattening her palms against his stomach. She could feel him clench under her touch. 'I'll have you know, that's censorship,' she said.

'What's censorship?'

'Kissing me to prevent me from expressing myself.'

'In that case, I should up my game from PG-13,' Zeb replied and got down to work. This time, when he kissed her, it was urgent and ready. His hands were holding her face one moment, backing her against a wall the next, fitting her against his body; all the while lingering and learning the shape of her. His lips and fingertips were turning parts of her into erogenous zones that she hadn't ever associated with desire, like her shoulder. Who knew teeth grazing against the ball of the shoulder could be erotic? Or that the back of his fingers caressing the inside of her arm could make her feel shivery? He hadn't even got to the X-rated bits of her yet, she thought. Just then he cupped one of her breasts firmly. Aalo suddenly stood very still and realized her eyes were shut. She opened them to find his eyes—those green, green eyes—looking straight at her. His hand was no longer at her breast.

'Ok?' he asked.

Aalo nodded. 'How did we get to your bedroom?'

'We used our legs, Mukherjee, because they're still working, miraculously enough,' Zeb replied while pressing kisses along her jaw and the curve of her neck.

'I want to see.' Aalo twisted to look around once they stumbled through the door. It was neat. There was a big bookshelf, Aalo noted approvingly. One of the doors of his closet had a full-length mirror with an ornate frame that should have looked out of place in the otherwise modern room, but didn't. The only light came from behind the headboard of his bed, which looked like it was glowing, like it was part of an alien spaceship. Then she felt something firm behind her knees and reflexively clutched at Zeb to keep herself upright.

'That's the foot of the bed,' Zeb told her.

'You don't sleep on a waterbed or something kinky like that, do you?' She looked up at the ceiling.

'No, Mukherjee, I don't have either a waterbed or a mirror on the ceiling.' Zeb gave a light little whack on Aalo's bum. 'This is my bedroom, not some love motel.'

Aalo let go of him and sat down on the bed abruptly. The mattress was firm and didn't sink under her. She took a deep breath and pulled off the blouse she'd worn for the presentation. The bra wasn't lacy, but it was nice, Aalo figured. Less nice: now her love handles were on display and her panties—currently not on display since they were under her pants—didn't match her bra. She realized she hadn't shaved her legs and winced.

'What happened?' Zeb asked.

'I have hairy legs.'

Zeb shrugged. 'So do I.'

Aalo gave him a withering stare. 'Ha. Ha.'

'It's true.'

'You're sure it won't gross you out?'

Zeb folded his arms across his chest. 'I'm a thirty-five-year-old man whose past exploits as a boy include eating booger and bringing roadkill home. And you think your hairy legs are going to gross me out?'

'I was just checking,' said Aalo, while her heart did a small, happy, feminist dance. 'Take off your clothes,' she told him.

'Are you demanding a striptease?'

'Basically.'

He burst out laughing. 'Who knew there was a pervy businessman lurking inside you, Mukherjee?' He shrugged off the jacket he'd been wearing and let it fall to the floor, before slowly unbuttoning the remaining buttons of his shirt. 'Maybe I will invest in a mirror for the ceiling, after all,' he said. She watched him peel off his shirt. He wasn't bulky, but his muscles were visibly delineated, from a solid chest to a flat stomach. His arms rippled with each movement they made and Aalo realized she had, in the space of the time that it had taken Zeb to lose his shirt, developed a thing for triceps. Also, he wore his pants very low.

'Do you ever worry your pants will just fall off?' she asked him.

'That's why we wear belts,' he informed her, while taking his off.

Aalo tilted her head. 'Your belt is off but your pants are still on.'

'They're being held up by my erection at present.'

'Oh.'

Something close to nervousness started bubbling in Aalo as she watched Zeb peel off his pants. And then he was naked, and she was sitting on his bed, which meant her head was basically at the level of his penis.

'You didn't have any underwear on!' Blurty really was something, Aalo thought to herself.

Zeb shrugged. 'I go wild sometimes.'

She pressed her lips together to make sure she didn't end up telling him that she was sure she'd forgotten how to do sex and that she was halfway in love with him right now. For good measure, she shut her eyes as well. After a moment, she felt Zeb's hands travel up her pant-covered legs, from her ankles to her knees and then her thighs. She felt him rest his hands on her thighs as though she were a table he was sitting at. Seemingly of their own accord, her hands went to his triceps, and then rested on his shoulders. He felt as beautiful as he looked, and Aalo really wanted to see him, but somehow, she couldn't open her eyes.

'Hey,' Zeb said softly. 'What's going on?'

Aalo shook her head. She felt a little weight on her thighs as he levered himself up to kiss her. He tugged at her lower lip with his teeth. 'Bring Blurty back,' he said.

'You don't want to hear this.'

Her eyes flew open when she felt his beard against the swell of her breast. He pressed a kiss on her breastbone and Aalo's breathing went haywire. She closed her eyes again, this time to savour the feel of him on her skin. Then, she felt his hands go around her waist. He gripped firmly and scooped Aalo up, which meant she was suddenly airborne and clinging to him like an orangutan on a vine.

'Zeb!' She was officially squeaking. 'This is way beyond my sexual syllabus. Like way, way beyond.'

'Calm down.' Zeb walked with her around to the other side of the bed, closer to the heap of pillows, and sat down so that now she was on his lap. 'Ok?'

'Ok. What are we doing?'

'For future reference, say ok after figuring out what you're doing.'

'Ok, but what are we doing?'

'We're sitting on a bed and if you want, I'll get my clothes on.'

'Are we doing standing-up sex?'

'No.'

'Are you offering to put your clothes on because I just freaked out at the thought of standing-up sex?'

'No, I offered to put clothes on because you seemed like you freaked out.'

'I'm fine.'

'I know the visual cues might suggest otherwise, but we don't have to do any kind of sex.'

'What!' Aalo yelped.

'If you don't want to, I mean. Don't get pressured by a naked man with an erection. It will take only thirty seconds to put my clothes back on.'

'I'm sitting on you practically topless and you want to stop this here?'

He kissed her cheek. 'I don't want to stop in the slightest, but this works better when one of us isn't freaking out.'

Aalo touched his chest and felt his heart under her palm. It was racing. 'I do mixed martial arts and my belly dancing teacher says I'm very flexible. But I eat more than I work out,' Aalo told him. 'Hence the love handles.'

Zeb's eyes glittered. 'You belly dance?' he asked, a big grin on his face. 'Damn Mukherjee, you're an Oriental dream.'

A half-smile on her face, Aalo pushed at Zeb's shoulders, and he obediently fell back, so that he was lying on his back, on the bed. Aalo got off the bed and took off her pants and panties in one go. Then she resumed position, with one knee on either side of Zeb's hips. Back straight, arms firm but gracefully bent on either side, her waist moved like rippling silk in slow motion, as Aalo did one undulation and then another and then one more. Zeb's eyes were fixed on her belly.

'You know, I've never really understood the whole thing about women's navels being sexy, but it's starting to make a whole lot more sense now,' he said conversationally.

Aalo sat back down on her haunches, careful to make sure she didn't sit on his erection. Hesitantly, she wrapped her hand around his penis and looked up at him.

'I sense a question coming,' Zeb said, in a voice that seemed slightly choked.

'Should I be sitting, so that this is behind me?' She held him a little more firmly. 'You feel nice, by the way.'

'Thanks. You should move up so that this, as you put it, is behind you.'

Aalo nodded. 'I thought as much, but figured I should check. I mean, I wouldn't want to lean over and break it or something.'

'Can we take a moment to appreciate just what a superior quality erection I'm sporting that not even the casual mention of you breaking my dick is making it wilt?'

Aalo blushed and settled herself, so that the erection in question made its presence felt against a butt cheek.

'I seem to recall a passing mention of graphic dreams,' Zeb said, drawing lazy patterns on her skin with his fingers.

'Now that I think about it, they involved you doing all the work,' Aalo said, a little embarrassed.

Zeb reached around to unsnap her bra. 'Work like this?' he asked.

Aalo nodded. He peeled off her bra and threw it aside. Then his lips closed around one nipple while his fingers played with the other. Aalo felt everything in her snap to attention.

'How am I doing?' he whispered, lips still on her breast. She pressed her pelvis down on him, and he groaned against her.

The next thing Aalo knew, she was on her back and Zeb was looking down at her. She brought his face down to kiss him and she felt his hand on her stomach. He broke off from the kiss and asked, 'Can I, you know, keep going?'

'Yes, please.'

'Fair warning—we're going to need to do a repeat performance of this very soon, so that I can redeem myself, because I'm fairly certain that I'm going to make a mess of this round.'

'We seem to be ok so far. Better than ok.'

He pressed a quick, hard kiss on her lips. 'Music to my ears, but in all honesty, I think I'll be exploding in about ninety seconds, so yeah, this is going to be a bit of an embarrassment. In fact, I'm sort of impressed I've kept it together for this long. Also,' he reached down to flick his tongue against first her left nipple and then her right, 'I might be a little obsessed with your breasts.'

'I thought it was my belly-dancing navel.'

'I'm drawing up a list,' he said, kissing her shoulder, while his fingers walked down below her navel. Aalo wondered how long it would take him to find her clit. In about fifteen seconds, she almost jack-knifed off the bed.

'You found it,' she gasped.

He didn't waste time replying to her and focused on the task at hand.

'Zeb?'

'Hm.' His lips had found her ear.

'Condom. Now. And find a way of doing this without lifting your hand from what it's doing right there.'

'Doing this or this?'

'Oh god.'

'No?'

'Yes! Fuck me, yes.'

'I'm trying to. Give a man points for effort at least.'

'Zeb! Condom!'

'Did you know, someone told me most women don't orgasm from penetrative sex, so fingers or tongue are much better suited for that task?'

'How and why are you having this conversation while doing—oh god—that to my nipples?'

'I'm a multitasker.'

'If you don't put on a condom now—oh!'

'Aalo?'

'Yes?'

'Come for me. Now.'

As it turned out, he wasn't enough of a multitasker to be able to put on the condom while doing everything else, but Aalo didn't hold that against him.

When Aalo woke up hours later, she realized she was thirsty, and there were parts of her that felt achy. At one point, Zeb had groaned, 'Fuck, Aalo, at this rate neither you nor I are going to be able to walk tomorrow.' As Aalo padded her way to the kitchen, she felt her thighs quiver, and she remembered what he'd gone on to do despite that warning. A stupid grin and a blush spread across her face. In the living room, the table lamp was still on. She pulled out her phone from her bag before switching the lamp off and going to the kitchen island. She filled a glass of water, sat on one of the high stools and went through her messages. Rucha and the SWETE gang sounded like they were happy with her presentation. Aalo made a note that she needed to let Rucha know whom she'd met and what meetings she'd set up for the next few days. The city was silent outside in a way Mumbai never was. The clock on the counter told Aalo it was 4 a.m. Around this time, four days from now, she'd be on a flight back to Mumbai.

—Aalo: Guys, is anyone around?

—Meera: Hey you. Everything ok?
—Rebecca: Hey rockstar, whatcha doing up at 4 a.m.?
—Fatima: Yeah, it's not like you have a tantrummy toddler.
—Jo: ?
—Aalo: So much for me thinking I'd be intruding into your day.
—Jo: More like the day is intruding into my life. What's up with you?
—Meera: What she said.
—Aalo: I'm thinking of extending my stay in London.
—Fatima: For work?
—Aalo: For play. Like sexy play.
—Rebecca: Wait, is that innuendo or is there actually a sexy play?
—Jo: Seriously, Becks?
—Rebecca: What? She's in London. Maybe there's a really good play at the West End. It can happen. She's Bengali.
—Meera: Fair point.
—Fatima: Aalo, are you thinking of staying on for the theatrical excellence of the West End?
—Aalo: So Zeb and I, we did the deed last night.
—Jo: Whoa! The drought is over!
—Rebecca: What?
—Fatima: REWIND. RIGHT. NOW.
—Aalo: I don't really know what to tell you.
—Rebecca: Please tell me he is dumping his girlfriend.
—Aalo: It seems Meher and he haven't been together for a bit.
—Meera: But he told you they were together, right?
—Aalo: Yeah, I'm not sure why. I was going to ask him, but then he did a striptease and I got distracted. But they're definitely not together. He made that quite clear. Also, at

the party, he introduced me to people who know Meher, work with her, and he was holding my hand quite obviously. So yeah.

—Rebecca: WHY ARE THERE NO PHOTOS BEING UPLOADED? I DEMAND PHOTOS. SEXY PHOTOS OF ZEB. SHIRTLESS. CLOSE-UPS.

—Fatima: Babe, you sure you're lesbian, right?

—Jo: How's the sex?

—Aalo: Why do you think I'm saying I want to extend my trip?

—Meera: Bloody hell. And all because the man has a bum shower.

'Are you just sitting in the dark, giggling to yourself?'

Aalo turned around to see a sleepy Zeb standing there, hair mussed up and not a stitch of clothing on his person.

'Hey, I was just talking to Meera and the gang.'

Zeb rubbed his eyes and then peered at the clock on the counter. 'It's only been about two hours since. Are you sure that's enough of a gap to get an objective perspective on the sex?' He walked up and put his arms around her, resting his face on her upper back. 'Just warn me if for some reason they want to kill me or something,' he said, his voice still heavy with sleep.

'I don't think anyone's looking to kill you. But Rebecca does want a photo of you.'

'Who's Rebecca now?'

'The one who just adopted a baby with her girlfriend.'

'Ah yes. Becks.'

'That's her.'

'Can we take a photo when I have some clothes on?'

Aalo laughed. 'Come on, sleepyhead. Back to bed.'

'In what sense?' He sounded significantly more awake.

Aalo turned the stool around, so that she was facing Zeb. He had a half-smile on his lips, and once again, Aalo felt herself swoon a little at the sight of him. 'Meera was a bit confused about why you said you and Meher were together when you weren't,' she said. 'I told her I was going to ask you, but you distracted me with a striptease.'

Zeb laughed and came to stand between her legs, his hands at her waist. 'Honestly? I just figured I'd seem less creepy if I didn't admit to being single. I mean, I was sending you origami vulvas. That's borderline pervy, surely.'

'The jewellery?'

'Tahira made it for Meher, so I thought she should have it, and I didn't want to delay things, because then it might seem like I'm using the jewellery to get back in touch or something messed up like that. So, I asked you to send it to me. We had no way of getting my backpack to me at the time, remember? And before you ask, the brunch was just a huge mess. Among the many downsides of having a twin is that apparently you both end up planning brunches at the same restaurant. Baz, Lara and Meher were already at Rovi when I got there, and obviously they hadn't told me they were meeting up. But when I walked in, there they were, and I figured it would be more awkward if we were sitting at separate tables.'

'Makes sense.' Aalo ran a finger down a meandering path from Zeb's clavicle to his navel and lower.

'Are you even listening to what I'm saying?'

'Not really.' She looked up at him and tilted her head. 'Would you describe yourself as experienced? Sexually, I mean.'

Zeb drank the few sips of water remaining in Aalo's glass and cleared his throat. 'I'm not sure I'd go with experienced per se.'

'But you know how sex and the human body work.'

'More or less, yes, I think I do.'

'So given I'm feeling a little sore, do you think it'll actually hurt if we have sex again now?'

Zeb breathed in sharply. 'I think we should do some practical research into figuring out a way to do this without you feeling any kind of discomfort. For science and the greater good of women.'

'And men, judging from what's coming up at your end.'

'Eyes on my face, Mukherjee.'

'Why?'

'Because I'm more than an erection. Also, I'm about to go down on you.'

Hours later, it felt like Aalo's life had taken a sharp left into fantasy, and usually, that would make Aalo brace herself for a reality check and a rude shock. Here, with Zeb and in his picture-perfect apartment, Aalo relaxed. It was easy to pretend that this life in London was normal. Zeb had woken up at an ungodly hour to go to the gym, which explained that beautiful body of his, along with signifying a certain level of insanity, because not even the combination of an earthquake and a tsunami would have persuaded Aalo to do anything more strenuous than snoring after the mostly sleepless night they'd had. By the time he got back though, Aalo had dragged herself out of bed, showered, become human and made breakfast. They drank tea, and she stared at him while he read the newspaper on his tablet. He took more photographs of her, and they took a selfie that Aalo sent to Rebecca. Then Zeb retreated to the 'the cave', which was what he called his home office, while Aalo skipped out of the house—literally—for her meeting with the Nightingale Foundation.

The meeting was long, but it went well, with everyone promising to extend their support to SWETE. Rucha joined through Zoom, and Aalo squirmed with happy embarrassment when Philippa Markham and a few more directors of the

Nightingale Foundation told Rucha that Aalo's presentation had been one of the best at the conference. Later, Philippa Markham sat Aalo down and gave her some advice about pitching projects to some of the other potential donors whom Aalo planned to meet over the next two days. Aalo took down the details of what kind of projects were likely to receive funding, made notes on what to avoid, and generally felt very grown-up. 'I'm probably jinxing myself by saying it out loud, but I think I'm kinda-sorta good at this business of making pitches and fundraising,' she told Farhana and Hema on a group video call, after bringing them up to speed with all the meetings she'd had.

'I did notice right from the start that Excel spreadsheets and PowerPoint presentations don't scare you,' Farhana said, grinning. 'It was very suspicious. But listen, don't jump into the fundraising side of things. All the people who work on that side of social work are absolute idiots, in my experience.'

'Stop it!' Hema said to Farhana. 'Aalo, don't listen to her. We've just had very bad experiences. Most of them didn't know what we did, and they'd make us do all the work for their decks ...'

'Which was really annoying because they were being paid humongous salaries to do all that rubbish,' Farhana cut in.

'True. Also, most of these guys had networks that proved to be useless for SWETE,' Hema said. 'So, that's why Farhana's calling them idiots. If you're liking the job of fundraising, it would be pretty incredible, because you actually do know the work we do.'

'And you're not an idiot,' Farhana added.

Aalo laughed. 'Thanks for the vote of confidence. I've got to talk to Rucha about this when I get back, but this side of networking, pitching, budgets—it takes me into a world where it's easier for me to impress people. I have all the markers of privilege they're used to and respect, which is obviously frustrating at one level because, hello, how are we ever going to take a hammer to elitism if people are *still* so easily impressed by posh accents? But, in the short term, I can use these shiny, superficial bits for good.'

'Which is great,' said Hema.

Aalo grimaced. 'I have a feeling Rucha will tell me I'm being lazy and she might be right. What you guys do is really, really hard for me to crack …'

'Trust me when I tell you that working in fundraising would be really, really, *really* hard for me, and I doubt I'd ever be able to crack it,' Farhana told Aalo. 'So no, it's not lazy.'

'I think the word you're looking for is aptitude,' Hema said with a smile.

After finishing the call with Hema and Farhana, Aalo found her way to the Tate Modern and spent a few hours there, ate a cheap and cheerful lunch, and then made her way back to Notting Hill, where she sat at a cafe and made calls to confirm her meetings for the next day. Then, giving thanks to free internet, Aalo checked how much it would cost her to change the date of her return ticket to Mumbai.

Zeb joined her a little while later, and they roamed aimlessly from one neighbourhood to the next, telling each other stories. They took trains and buses, wasting time and taking detours. At one point, they ended up in a little Japanese restaurant in SoHo. She told him stories of the Not-So-Famous Five and her parents. She asked him about having a twin brother, growing up in London and travelling to the dangerous places that he did for work. He wanted to know everything about Mumbai and he asked to see photographs, which he'd zoom into and stare at like they were precious artefacts. He told her about his parents, who had met as students in England; how Farsi made everything sound a little more dramatic and poetic; and how he couldn't come up with a list of favourite places, even though he loved lists. He told her about his father, who loved breaking out into song, and his mother, who had grown up in Srinagar. She asked what his mother remembered of Kashmir, and Zeb said he hadn't actually thought of asking her. 'My parents are throwing a little party next week. You could ask her yourself, if you want,' he told her.

'A party? Next week?' Aalo took a big gulp from the little tumbler of sake she'd been nursing.

'Monday, actually. Who else but a bunch of retired people would think Monday night is good for a party?' Zeb said drily. 'Not that it's an elaborate party. Just a get-together because my dad's cousin is in town, from Tehran.'

'There's this technical hiccup of my return ticket, which would have me leave at the end of this week,' Aalo said, not looking at Zeb.

He was quiet for a couple of moments. 'It would be high-handed, pompous and arrogant to expect you to put your life back home on hold and stay here just because the sex is great and I'm around,' he said finally.

Aalo shrugged. 'On the other hand, if I went ahead and changed my tickets without you asking me to stay back, it would be pretty high-handed, pompous and arrogant on my part. You know, to assume I'm not overstaying my welcome.'

Zeb narrowed his beautiful green eyes. 'Are you trying to tell me something, Mukherjee?'

'I'm just saying that one of us has to take the risk of seeming like a bit of a prick. Otherwise, this is all going to be over too soon.'

'So, cancel your ticket. Stay back for me.' He winced. 'That sounded worse when I said it out loud.'

'It's actually music to my ears.'

Zeb raised his eyebrows. 'Because there's a submissive lurking in there somewhere?'

Aalo studiously stared at the surface of the table. 'Because I sort of went ahead and changed my return ticket this afternoon. And while roaming around in the city, I ended up at a sex shop, where this woman told me that my life is basically not worth living, because I haven't experienced Rough Rider Studded condoms.'

Zeb almost choked on his sake. 'Rough what?'

'It's supposed to be very good.' Aalo pulled out a square, blue packet from her bag and put it on the table. On the box was a garish cartoon of a woman with what looked like inflated balloons for breasts.

Zeb picked it up and examined the product description. 'That artwork certainly is something. Is your friend sure these are latex? Because I've seen corrugated sheets that have fewer ridges than what's on the "representative photo". How many packets did you buy?'

'Two.'

'And how long are you staying?'

'Not important. I'll leave whenever works for you. I mean, I'll leave day after if that's better for you.'

'It obviously isn't, Rough Rider.'

Aalo blushed. 'Ok, so we can figure out …'

'When's your ticket for, Mukherjee?'

'Thirteen days from tomorrow.'

Zeb held up his fingers to do some mental maths and then grinned. 'Perfect. You can come with me for that party. What are you flying?'

'Turkish Air.'

'It has a stopover at Istanbul, I imagine?'

'Yes, eight hours if …'

'Right.' He sat up straighter and waved for the bill. 'Come on, we need to get back home and sit at the computer.'

'We do?'

'We're going to convince Turkish Air to change your tickets again. London over the weekend, party on Monday, then I'm showing you Istanbul for a few days, after which you can go east and I can go west.' He leaned over and gave her a quick kiss. 'Well done, Rough Rider,' he said, tossing the packet of condoms back to Aalo.

10

The meteorological department had predicted heavy rainfall in Mumbai for 29 August, but no one had anticipated 944 mm of the stuff. Later, when they'd tell their stories of surviving the flood, people would talk about buses and cars that sputtered to a standstill, trains that stopped moving, and wading through waist-deep water. Some watched their walls wilt, turning from solid to sponge, as steel-grey sheets of rain battered the concrete jungle of the city. Everyone got wet that day, and those who made it to safety and shelter watched the city crumple against the force of the monsoon. When the rain started that Wednesday, no one thought it would be quite so cataclysmic. In fact, Meera, sitting in the office of the chief engineer of BMC's roads department, had actually interrupted the official, as he vented to her about how the BMC had to take the heat for the inefficiencies of the PWD and other agencies.

'Nadgoudar saheb, any reports about the rain?' Meera asked. She pointed to the dark sky outside his window. 'It's been pouring for more than two hours now.'

He brushed Meera's concerns away and assured her that everything was fine and that there was no need to panic. 'This is not 2005,' he told her with a big smile.

When she came out of the meeting, Meera checked her work WhatsApp groups. Two of her reporters had written that streets in both the suburbs and south Mumbai were getting waterlogged. Of all people, Srikanth, who headed up *The Daily*'s crime bureau, was the one with information. He'd met a spokesperson from the IMD, who was 'shitting bricks' because the forecast was looking terrible for the next twenty-four hours. Meera sent messages to her reporters, asking them to let her know where they were, and then asked Srikanth to call her when he could. He seemed to be the only one who actually had any real information. While waiting for Srikanth to call, Meera wrote to friends telling them to get home as quickly as possible because the city was flooding. Fatima sent a reply immediately, asking Meera if she wanted to come over, but before Meera could reply, Srikanth called.

'See, this guy from the IMD had come to the police station because a guy stole his bag from the signal,' he told her. 'But he got a call and he just looked like he was going to pass out. So, I talked to him. He said that the forecast was crazy.'

'Some of my guys are already reporting waterlogging.'

'This guy said that it was going to get much worse in a few hours.'

'Where are you now?'

'Near Cuffe Parade. I just left the police headquarters.'

'Go back. I'll try and pick you up. I have a car.'

Over the next hour, the sky got gloomier, the rain fell harder and the city sank a little deeper in misery and dirty water. Local trains on the Central line started reporting delays. Meera sent messages telling her team to go home if they could or to come to the office. Whatever else a newspaper office may or may not be able to do, it could give shelter.

Meera found herself praying as she plotted a route through South Mumbai. She needed to pick up two of her stranded reporters—Mithil from Colaba and Dhanya from Walkeshwar—as well as Srikanth from the police headquarters. The rain beat down on the roof of the car, elemental in its fury. When she neared Colaba, Meera called Mithil.

'Is there a suitcase shop near you?' Meera said.

'Did you say suitcase?' Mithil asked. 'I'm not sure. I can check?'

'Find one and buy four. Not too large—they should fit in my car. I'll reach you in about fifteen minutes. Hopefully.'

The car picked up the beleaguered journalists and valiantly stayed above water as it went through the sinking city, but gave up about 500 metres from the tower in which *The Daily* had its office. The water had risen high enough to create a small whirlpool outside the main gate. Meera, Srikanth, Mithil and Dhanya were not looking forward to making their way through it.

'Isn't this where that doctor guy fell into an open manhole the last time there was a flood?' Srikanth asked gruffly.

No one answered. All of them knew the answer was yes. Near them was the bridge that Meera used on the days she was compelled to take the car to go to South Mumbai for meetings. From it, a mini waterfall cascaded down, adding to the watery chaos. Fortunately, among those taking shelter under the bridge were a couple of taxi drivers who recognized Dhanya's face, peering through Meera's car window, because Dhanya regularly took cabs when leaving the office at night. Six complete strangers yelled out and told Dhanya and her companions to stay in the car. They waded into water that was almost up to their waist and pushed the car, so that it stood at the gates of the office complex, which was on slightly higher ground. Here, they could get out without fear of being sucked into open manholes. The four journalists thanked their saviours.

'I don't know if the owners of the buildings will let us bring you inside, but I'll check and Dhanya will call you. She has your number, she said. Meanwhile, can we give you some food and water?' Meera asked. She had charted a route that took her past a string of restaurants and had picked up all the food she could. The taxi drivers laughed and said they were fine under the bridge. Meera and Dhanya insisted that they take some food and quickly packed some bottles of water and food packets in a spare plastic bag that Dhanya had in her tote. Then, the four journalists abandoned the car, picked up a suitcase each and trudged up to the office. They walked into the newsroom looking like garbage and feeling like superheroes.

'Turn on some music and get plates,' Meera announced, as she, Dhanya, Mithil and Srikanth walked in, 'because we come bearing pizzas, dal khichdi and chilli chicken.'

'And vada pao,' added Srikanth.

Everyone in the newsroom stood up. Most of the deskies were there, along with Faisal, Navin and Unni, who headed the sports section. A few reporters were in the crowd, looking as bedraggled and wet as Meera and her little gang. The office boys and guards were watching them like they were ghosts. Meera noticed Jeet looked like all the blood had drained from his face. He was staring at her, and Meera decided she'd better say something before he did.

'Jeet, help me with this? Actually, first, let's get some newspaper to put on this row of desks.' It took him a moment to react to her, but soon enough, Jeet and a couple of others were turning newspaper pages into tablemats.

Jeet came up to Meera and pointed at the suitcase she was still holding. 'Can I help you with that?' he asked.

'Just put it on the table and we'll unpack it.'

Meera noticed a little tremor in his hand as Jeet reached for the suitcase.

'You think we have enough?' Dhanya asked.

'We can only hope,' Meera said, as Jeet hoisted the suitcase onto the nearest desk. She unzipped it. Inside were boxes and boxes of food, which she started unpacking. The other three followed suit.

'Some of the pizza boxes are a little damp around the edges,' Srikanth said unhappily. He opened one. 'It looks ok inside though.'

The row of desks started to turn into a bizarre buffet spread.

'You guys bought food,' Faisal said slowly. 'You were out there, in that rain, in which people are probably dying, and you bought food.'

'It was Meera's idea,' Mithil said, trying to dislodge some water from his ear. 'She said we'd need food since none of us are going to get home till tomorrow, probably.'

'The four of us will probably die of leptospirosis, but at least we won't go hungry tonight,' Meera said with a grin.

'I have the best edit team in the world,' Navin roared, and charged towards Meera to give her a hug that would probably have given HR palpitations, but to everyone who was witness at *The Daily* office, it felt like the most appropriate way to give thanks.

It turned out that more challenging than finding food in a submerged city was getting hold of dry clothes for Srikanth and Mithil. Dhanya and Meera kept a change of clothes in the office, but the men didn't have that backup.

'Why the hell would you keep clothes in the office?' Srikanth said as he stared at Dhanya pull out her neatly folded set from the bottom drawer of her desk.

The two women spoke in unison. 'Periods,' Meera said; while Dhanya went with, 'Last-minute booty call.'

Ultimately, marketing ended up being the saviour. 'Aishwarya says there are T-shirts and track pants in the marketing closet.

Some promotional nonsense,' Faisal said. 'She's also said to give you a hug, which I'm not going to, because I think Navin's filled the hug quota for today,' he said to Meera with a smile.

When they returned to the newsroom, clean and relatively dry, Navin held a quick edit meeting.

'Two buildings may have collapsed because of the rains,' Meera said, perching herself on an empty desk. 'One in Malad and the other in Bhendi Bazaar.'

'The collapses are confirmed?' Navin asked.

'I just got a message from Vivek. He has an aunt who lives near the one in Malad, she saw it collapse from her window. The Bhendi Bazaar one is hearsay at the moment.'

'I'll ask a friend. He has family in the area,' Faisal said, pulling out his phone. 'Oh shit, I completely forgot. Aalo has been trying to reach you. I didn't know she was in London, but anyway, she's called Jeet and me about a hundred times.'

'Jeet?' She turned to him. 'Why did she call you?'

Before he could answer, his phone rang. Jeet signalled to Meera that it was Aalo calling. Meera took the phone from him. 'I'm just going to take this outside, ok?' she said to Jeet, who nodded.

'Hey,' Meera said, making her way out of the newsroom to a corner of the terrace that wasn't exposed. 'I'm alive and on dry land.'

'What the fuck, Meera! I've been going nuts trying to get through to you!' Aalo wailed at the other end. 'What happened? Zeb's asking if you're ok. Which you obviously are, I can tell from your voice, but fuck! I was so worried. We were so worried! Are you ok?'

Outside, the rain was so loud and angry that Meera could barely hear Aalo. 'My phone died pretty much the moment it got wet, and it's been a bit of an adventure getting to work, but everything's fine now,' Meera said.

'How bad is it?'

'It's like something out of a disaster movie. I've never seen anything like this. Do you know if Jo, Rebecca and Fatima are fine?'

'Jo's at Fatima and Becks's place. Fatima's mum is with them.'

'That's good. I just heard a building may have collapsed in Bhendi Bazaar.'

'Damn. Are people going to die?'

'It's been raining like mad since 7 a.m. I have no idea how the fire brigade will reach anyone who needs help. Maybe use their rubber dinghies. I don't know.'

'Shit. I'm so glad you're ok.'

'Very ok.'

'How will you get home? Zeb's saying you should just stay where you are, but that's just him being all First World.'

Meera laughed. 'I hate to say this, but I think he's right. The few of us who are at work now will be sleeping on desks in the office.'

'Wow. You're going to spend the night with Jeet.' Aalo giggled.

'Ok, I'm going now. I'll email or message, depending on the state of my phone if it recovers. Say hi to Zeb, and you take care, ok?'

'Yup. You stay dry. Oh, Meera?'

'Yes?'

'I'm sorry about calling Jeet, but honestly, I was just frantic, and I couldn't get through to Faisal, so I messaged Jeet on Facebook, asking about you. He's been really sweet and has been updating me. I think he was mad worried too.'

'It's fine. Do me a favour? Let Jo, Fatima and Becks know?'

'Of course. Ok, I'm going to go now.'

'Bye.'

By 9 p.m., it was obvious that no one was going home. Meera and Faisal had to practically bully Navin into talking to the company that owned the business complex, but he finally did pick up his phone and make the calls, so that at least some of the people who were stranded outside could take shelter in the lobby and parking areas. By 11 p.m., the owner of the printing press called Navin and said his machinery was underwater, which meant that there would be no newspaper the next morning. Faisal didn't let that stop them from making pages. 'We'll put the PDFs online,' he said. 'It's the digital age, after all.' Everyone in the office grumbled and cursed Faisal's work ethic, but it was also strangely comforting to get into the familiar rhythm of filing reports and making pages. It made everyone feel like they had a handle on the chaos that was swirling around them. Of course, they had nothing of the sort, but the illusion was calming. Besides, as Faisal kept reminding them, they were in a building that wasn't leaking, they had electricity and the distraction of work. 'Make the most of it,' he ordered.

By 1.30 a.m., the rain finally started to slow down, and Faisal, Jeet, Vaishnavi, Sheila and the intern Rahul uploaded the next day's paper online. Most of the office was asleep. Some had bent over their desks. A few were using books and dictionaries as makeshift pillows. The ones who were awake made their way to the other end of the office. It was Sheila's idea to play a version of Truth or Dare that involved a spinning pencil and only telling the truth. That was how Meera learnt that Faisal's grandfather had wanted to call him Prince and his mother had wanted to name him Rocky, after the Stallone film. Rahul's nickname was Lulu. Dhanya had run away from home at age nineteen and married the guy who was her maths tuition teacher. He still gave maths tuitions and was a stay-at-home dad and husband. Srikanth had fed his strictly vegetarian grandfather keema, telling the older man it was a special kind of soya. 'He loved it,' Srikanth said. 'Took three helpings.' The first time Sheila had sex, one of her partner's chest hairs had got caught in her teeth. 'I haven't been able to have sex with hairy men since then,' she said, shuddering. 'Just thinking about it makes me want to brush my teeth.'

'So, then what? You tell the guys you date to shave themselves before the big night?' Srikanth asked, while everyone else collapsed in laughter.

'I have a couple of times. Fortunately, I met Temjen. Naturally hairless chest,' Sheila replied.

When the pencil chose Meera, Sheila came up with the idea of making Meera play a game of Kiss, Marry, Kill.

'Give me candidates, guys!' Sheila urged the others. 'I need hot men.'

Meera studiously kept her gaze on a random spot on the wall that was not Jeet.

'George Clooney,' Faisal supplied.

'Akshay Kumar,' Dhanya said.

'How is he hot?' Rahul complained. 'He's all teeth.'

'You have no taste,' Dhanya pronounced.

'I need one more. Don't we have any hot politicians?' Sheila asked.

'Rahul Gandhi?' Srikanth suggested.

'That'll do,' Sheila said happily. 'So, Meera, these are your choices: George Clooney, Akshay Kumar and Rahul Gandhi. Who would you kiss, marry or kill. You can only do one thing with one man. No repeats.'

'This set doesn't work,' Meera said. 'First of all, there's only one officially single man—Rahul Gandhi—and he isn't even that hot.' When Sheila sputtered, Meera held her ground. 'I'm not saying he's ugly. He's nice-looking, but we're mostly swooning at him taking after his white mama.'

Srikanth raised his hand. 'As someone who is constantly mistaken for being Nigerian when I'm in Colaba, I'd like to state for the record that we Indians are racist bastards.'

'Correct,' Meera agreed. 'But coming back to your game, I don't care who you're dropping on my lap, marriage is out of the question. Been there, done that, and not doing it again, not even as a joke.'

'Tinder zindabad!' Dhanya roared.

'You're married,' Faisal pointed out. 'But thanks for supporting us single types.'

Meera could feel Jeet staring at her and she resolutely did not look in his direction. 'So that leaves me with the option of kissing or killing. Rahul Gandhi, kiss. As for George Clooney and Akshay Kumar, can I kill both of them?' she asked.

'There should be a film called *Clooney and Kumar*,' Dhanya said dreamily.

'You can't kill Clooney!' Sheila said incredulously.

'He's in a relationship,' Meera said with a shrug. 'I can't kiss him.'

'Maybe he's unhappy with Amal and waiting for you to help him break free,' said Rahul.

Meera shook her head. 'Still no-go, Lulu. If he isn't single, I don't mingle. But since he's hotter than Akshay and supposed to be faithful to his wife, I'll let him go with a kiss on his cheek and kill Akshay.'

'Who's left?' Vaishnavi said, looking around their little circle. 'Jeet! Bugger, how did you manage to get away from the pencil?'

Jeet, who had stretched out on the floor and was using a pile of newspapers as a makeshift pillow, shrugged. 'Out of sight, out of mind,' he said.

'Kiss, marry, kill—who would you pick from the office?' Sheila asked.

'From the office?' Jeet started. 'Go screw yourself. I'm not touching that with a bargepole.'

'Ok, among the men in the office.'

All the men in the group groaned. 'Stop being homophobes, you guys. It's a game! And hello, Jeet is obviously straight,' said Vaishnavi.

'Fine,' Jeet said, peeling himself partially off the floor to sit cross-legged. 'Kill is easy. Shashank from HR.'

Everyone cheered. 'Kiss, I'd say Faisal,' he said. Faisal did a curtsy.

'Why Faisal?' Rahul asked.

'Because he always has mouth freshener on his desk.'

'And marry?' Vaishnavi asked.

'Definitely Navin,' Jeet replied.

'Navin? Really?' Faisal spoke for all of them.

'He gets paid the most. I could totally be his house husband if he'll be my sugar daddy,' Jeet replied.

Everyone applauded Jeet's fine set of choices.

'Right, guys, I'm calling it a night,' Faisal said. It was about 2.30 a.m. The others murmured in agreement.

'You're not sleeping on the floor?' Meera asked Jeet when he settled back into his newspaper pillow.

'It's not like the desks are particularly comfortable,' he said with a grin.

'But the floor's filthy.'

'Life, ma'am, is filthy.'

'Ladies, you should take the conference room table,' Faisal suggested. 'I'm sure at least three of you will fit comfortably on it. Well, as comfortable as you can be on a table.'

'That's a great idea,' Vaishnavi agreed. She turned to Meera. 'I think you, me, Sheila and Dhanya can fit on that table, no?'

Dhanya grinned. 'Great. I'm going to sleep with my boss. Move over *Disclosure*.'

When the women were gone, the lights were switched off, and the men were enveloped in the sound of the rain that was still loud but a little less furious. Or maybe they'd just got used to it.

'Am I the only one who's going to think of the four of them lying on that table the next time we're in the conference room?' Srikanth said in the darkness.

'Srikanth,' Faisal said in a tired voice. 'Some things don't need to be shared.'

'I'm just saying what we're all thinking,' Srikanth protested.

'Macha, go to sleep,' Jeet said.

Srikanth made a grumbling noise, and then there was only rain.

Meera woke up a few hours later. It took her a moment to remember where she was. Her shoulders and neck felt stiff when she tried to turn—signs of old age, she told herself as she slowly levered herself up to sitting position.

Meera slipped out of the room, leaving behind the soft snores and sleep-rich sounds of the other three women. In her cabin, she turned on her computer. It was 5 a.m. She had emails from people she'd forgotten she knew, asking if she was ok. Jo, Fatima and Becks had sent multiple emails, the last one filled with relief after Aalo had informed them that Meera was staying put in the office. Aalo and Zeb had sent emails. Zeb had clearly reached out to his network, because she had photographers she barely remembered writing to ask if she was ok. There were no emails from her parents or anyone else in her family. It took a moment for Meera to realize that rejection didn't hurt quite as much as it used to and it didn't make her angry. If anything, she found herself smiling cynically.

Still, she checked the rainfall in her parents' neighbourhood and mentally dismissed all thoughts of them when she saw it was puny compared to the rest of the city.

If the updates she'd been sent were accurate, then the city was still standing, but only barely. The eastern and northern suburbs were badly hit, as was central Mumbai. Fortunately, the meteorological department was confident there would be less rainfall today. Meera made note of the fact that it didn't say the rain would totally stop. Switching off her monitor, she went out of the newsroom, walking as quietly as she could to the terrace. The sky was still dark and cloudy, but the rain had softened to a dull hum. A cigarette now would be perfect, she thought to herself.

'Are you an early riser?'

Meera spun around to find Jeet standing behind her. His hair was messier than normal and the first couple of buttons of his shirt were undone. Meera told herself to focus instead on the pronounced stubble.

'Not this early usually. Did you get any sleep?' she asked him.

He came up to stand beside her. 'A little, but newspapers do not make for good pillows.' He rolled his shoulders and stretched his neck. They stood and looked out at the city, watching light tentatively dab the cloudy sky.

'So, Vaishnavi and I are not seeing each other,' Jeet said suddenly. Meera didn't say anything. 'I'm not sure how you got that idea,' he added.

'It's a shame,' Meera said, steadfastly looking ahead of her.

'It is?'

'You two looked good together.'

'We do?'

'You did when I saw you in the make-out corner.'

'Where we weren't making out.'

Meera found herself wishing once again that she had a cigarette. 'It doesn't matter anyway,' she said, before turning to look at Jeet. 'Can I ask you something?'

'Sure.'

'How old are you?'

'Twenty-eight.'

Meera turned away from him and looked out at the city sprawled below them. 'I'm practically forty-one,' she said.

'Ok.'

The sky turned from the colour of shadows to a pale pink smudged with grey.

11

Aishwarya had been venting to Meera about how working with sales meant being stuck with the most foolish people in the world, when Faisal charged into Meera's cabin with a big grin and said, 'Check your email.'

'You're very chirpy today,' Meera said suspiciously to him. 'What's in this email?'

'Srikanth being a genius.' Faisal sat down in the chair next to Aishwarya's.

'This email better be worth interrupting my venting session about idiotic men,' Aishwarya told him.

Meera clicked on the email. It was a brief about a story, written in the florid English that everyone knew was Srikanth's style: 'In an ideal case of completely no control over criminal elements, the police are unable to apprehend or even hinder the Dhak Dhak gang as it runs unleashed, driving fear into the hearts of Mumbaikars.' Before Meera could take a moment to moan about Srikanth's literary flourishes, she realized the email had an attachment. Faisal had taken the trouble of crudely

Photoshopping a street scene in Mumbai, so that Madhuri Dixit, in that famous orange outfit from *Beta*, popped up randomly next to cars and lamp posts.

'This is genius,' Meera said, turning her monitor around, so that Aishwarya could see Faisal's work of art.

'Isn't it the best?' Faisal said, gleefully. 'The gang is actually known as the Thak Thak gang, because their first move is to knock on car windows. But our star crime beat reporter has renamed them the Dhak Dhak gang. How's that for genius?'

'Almost as incredible as your Photoshop skills,' Aishwarya said, giggling.

'Thank you. You should know I took an hour to make that image, while twitching involuntarily in my chair, because my headphones were filling my head with "*Dil dhak dhak karne laga*".'

'A great image if there ever was one. How does he do this? Doesn't he read what he sends out?' Aishwarya asked.

'Sure, Srikanth reads. It's just that he reads while he's slightly drunk,' said Meera.

'My personal favourite so far,' said Faisal, 'was the article he "edited" and sent out, so that it said "crime beach" instead of "crime branch". Not once, not twice, but for the whole thing. I almost felt like I should be on vacation on crime beach, with a cocktail called Jai Shri Rum.'

'Don't let Navin hear you saying stuff like that,' Meera warned.

Faisal's smile faded a little. 'He has been getting his knickers in a twist quite a bit of late, hasn't he?'

Meera nodded. 'Apparently, some foreign journo in Delhi is trying to do a story on press freedom in India, so everyone's gone from zero to sixty in paranoia. Navin has stopped sending emails for anything that he thinks might be "misinterpreted", which is damn annoying, because the last thing I want is to have to rely on his crappy memory.'

'But we haven't done anything that Navin needs to worry about in terms of killing stories, have we?' Aishwarya asked.

Meera looked at her like she was speaking in tongues. 'Do you and I work for the same paper?'

'I just mean that we've always killed stories. This foreign bugger is only sniffing around to get news on how we've sided with the current party and its people … but the fact is *The Daily* was a slave to the previous regime too,' Aishwarya said.

'We weren't slaves to the earlier regime, we were friends with it,' Faisal corrected her. 'It's not the same.'

'Seriously?' Aishwarya asked. 'You don't think you're overreacting just a little?'

'Ash, if anything, we're all underreacting to this stupid government,' said Faisal.

'Meera? What do you think?'

Meera leaned back in her chair. 'Earlier, when I did stories that weren't pro-government, Sagar would pitch them for page one and they'd go through without Faisal or anyone else getting a call with the order to change the story on the page. Did you work with Karthik? He was editor-in-chief before Navin.'

'Briefly,' Aishwarya said.

'So, whenever there was a sensitive story, Karthik would roll his eyes and be like, "Bloody fools, because of you I'm going to have to take X or Y out to dinner or lunch,"' Meera said, mimicking the previous editor's erudite Tamil accent.

'Or: "I just had to spend three minutes being verbally abused because of your damn story,"' Faisal said.

Meera smiled. 'But he'd still let us do the stories and he'd carry them prominently,' she said.

'That was true of Navin, too,' Faisal pointed out. 'Until recently.'

'Absolutely. Until the last couple of months, that was definitely true of Navin. What's changed is this—the people he's trying to pacify. Lunches and dinners don't seem to cut it anymore. If they get upset, these guys don't let it go,' Meera said. 'Just look at how they're going after small fry like Rucha Phadke.'

'I'm not sure how that's better than burying news about politicians who are friends with the family that pays our salaries,' Aishwarya said.

'Pissing off people in power didn't feel as dangerous before as it does now,' Meera said. 'I can tell you that, as a reporter, there are a lot of times we can sense there's a story, but it amounts to nothing because everyone is fucking terrified. Sources won't talk on or even off record. Journalists back away because they know these stories won't get published. Hell, it might be worse if they do get published because what if there's a court case or the journalist gets arrested? Not one of us feels confident that the newspaper will have our back.' Meera clawed at the air in mock frustration. 'It's like being put in a straitjacket while the house is on fire. And you're right, we've always had to make our overlords happy, but in the past, we could do stories that exposed them too.'

'That last part is what I'm not so convinced about,' Aishwarya maintained.

'I'll give you concrete examples,' Meera said. 'The Bofors story came out because of the press. The government was given enormous amounts of grief by the media about the Babri Masjid demolition. Protests against the Defamation Bill saw editors take to the streets. The Commonwealth scam was reported. We know of these things because the media covered it, and in a lot of cases, there were consequences. Ministers took responsibility and resigned. Can you remember the last time a minister did that?'

'At least you and I can remember that past,' Faisal said. 'Just think of the kids who are in their twenties now. A compromised mainstream media is all they know. It's always been true that a fraction of the news reported makes it into the newspaper, but in the past that was mostly because of space constraints. Now it's a survival tactic.'

'And as angry as I am at all of us for sleepwalking into self-censorship, I get why everyone's afraid,' Meera added. 'Two reporters and one editor I know spent a day in a police station last week. Their "crime"? They'd carried an article on their website about a government hospital in a Muslim neighbourhood of a small town not getting the funds it was supposed to from the state. Their article had a quote from the guy who ran that hospital. He didn't say it was a case of Muslims being systematically targeted. He just said his hospital desperately needed money. That was all it took. The journalists got arrested first, and the police came up with charges later.'

'This is pretty much standard now, but it wasn't when I joined journalism,' Faisal said grimly.

Aishwarya sighed. 'It's much too scary to believe that things have gone so far and so quickly into the belly of hell,' she said.

They were all quiet for a few moments.

'You know what scares me most?' Faisal said finally.

'What?' Meera asked.

'That they're fucking with the data,' said Faisal. 'I know it's a really deskie thing to say, but what do you do when you can't rely on figures released by a government?'

Meera sighed. 'Now you're making me worry about the numbers we'll get for the drought stories we're doing.'

'You're getting ground reports?' Faisal asked.

'Yeah, I've sent a reporter down to Marathwada.' Meera released a long breath. 'It's crazy right? Here we are, halfway to building Noah's Ark, because the bloody BMC won't desilt drains, and over there, in Marathwada, everything is turning to dust.'

'It is crazy,' Faisal agreed. 'But the flooding isn't just a case of the BMC being twits. The amount of rain we've been getting in the city is abnormal. I swear to you, the environment is going berserk, and these extremes are the real problem. This is the first time since 2005 that my walls are dripping. The ceiling in Jeet's flat collapsed, and it's not an old building. It's just …'

Meera sat up. 'Jeet's ceiling collapsed? When?'

'The day after we spent the night in the office. He's been house-hunting and is not getting anything.' Faisal sighed. 'I felt quite bad for him, honestly. He's a good kid and very big on being independent. He wants to make it on his own, but this city can be a bitch. He told me that he's thinking of quitting because he isn't finding a flat in his budget. He might go home to Chennai, he said. Poor guy sounded so defeated it broke my heart.'

'Ask him to come and see me?' Meera said to Faisal. 'He can stay with Aalo and me while he's house-hunting. There's loads of space in our flat.'

'That's very generous of you, Meera,' Faisal said.

'I know how tough it can be to do things on your own. I'll never forget house-hunting when I first wanted to move out,' Meera said. 'Sagar had just got me the job with *The Daily*, but I didn't have enough money for the kind of rents people were asking for, let alone the deposit. I've never felt so worthless.'

Aishwarya nodded in agreement. 'Seriously. It doesn't matter what you're earning. Nothing makes you feel more like an outsider than house-hunting in Mumbai. You can't afford anything, everything is crap, the brokers are sharks, it's just awful.'

'So yeah, if I can make it a little easier for someone going through that circle of hell, I will,' Meera said.

'I'm sure he'll take you up on that offer,' said Faisal. 'From what I know, it hasn't been going well.'

Just then, Aishwarya's phone lit up, as did Faisal's. 'Shit!' Aishwarya jumped out of her chair. 'I forgot I have a 2 o'clock! I'll see you later.' She scampered out of the room, while Faisal looked at his phone balefully.

'I have to take this,' he said. 'Chai at 4.30?'

'Sounds good,' Meera said with a smile. 'Will you tell Jeet?'

'You tell him,' Faisal said with a grin. 'It's your good deed of the day.' Faisal gave her a mock salute and walked out of the cabin.

Meera waited for a minute and then opened WhatsApp on her phone. She drafted a message asking Jeet about his flat and then wondered if she wasn't supposed to know. Faisal knowing something was no indication of the news being private or public. He managed to dig things up about everyone, and he was open with Meera because he trusted her to be discreet. Meera put her phone away and decided she'd ask Jeet in person. Hopefully he'd come down for the chai break.

When Meera came out with Faisal to go down for chai, there was a massive group of reporters and deskies attending the chai break. Jeet and Vijay, one of the reporters on the crime beat, were having an animated conversation in Tamil. Intruding to talk about Jeet's housing situation would be awkward, so Meera joined the other conversation about Shah Rukh Khan's best film instead. At one point, another reporter asked Jeet how the house-hunt was going, which led to Jeet sharing the story of the ceiling collapse with everyone.

'Bro, that's dramatic,' said Vivek from Meera's team. 'Listen, my uncle said his friend wants a PG-type tenant from next month. His friend has a place in Dadar Parsi Colony. You want me to check if the place is still available?'

'Yeah, that would be great. But just check if he's ok with late nights and music?' said Jeet.

The conversation moved on to other topics and the group lingered for a while longer before trudging back upstairs. Meera lagged behind intentionally and felt a little spurt of triumph when Jeet let the others go on ahead and waited for her to reach him.

'Your ceiling collapsed?' Meera asked.

'Yeah,' Jeet replied.

'Why didn't you tell me?'

There was a bit of a pause before he replied, 'It didn't come up.'

'Clearly it came down.'

Jeet made a face at her.

'It wasn't that bad a pun,' Meera defended herself. 'Where are you staying now?'

'In the same place.'

'With the collapsed ceiling?'

Jeet shrugged. 'It can't collapse again.'

'Don't be ridiculous. What if another chunk of it comes crashing down?'

'My room's fine. A bit of the ceiling in Ishita's room looked dodgy, so she's staying with Nakul.'

'While you live in rubble?'

'The rubble is only in the living room and it won't be for very long. I'll move out in a couple of weeks max.'

'Do you want to stay at my place until you find something?'

That stopped him in his tracks. 'I'm sorry, what?'

'Our flat has only two bedrooms, but it's very spacious and the living room is huge. You can sleep on the sofa. The ceiling is firmly intact,' Meera said.

Jeet looked at her like she'd grown nine heads and a moustache. 'You're asking me to move in with you?'

Meera decided to ignore the phrasing, because he looked stunned and incredulous. 'Look, I've been where you are now. If Aalo hadn't saved me from house-hunting, I don't know what I would have done. So I'm just …'

'Scoring good karma points?'

'Something like that.'

Jeet stared at her, a strange expression on his face.

'You don't have to decide now,' Meera said, feeling strangely thankful that they'd reached the lift. The way he was looking at her felt odd. 'Think about it. See how it goes with the flat in Dadar.'

'Thanks,' Jeet said finally. 'You go on ahead,' he said, gesturing towards the lift. 'I'm going to take the stairs.'

'To the thirteenth floor?'

'It's good exercise. I'll see you later?'

'Sure.'

Meera watched him lope towards the fire escape and tried not to think of the way he'd kissed her in the malfunctioning lift at Ashu and Kavita's.

—The ceiling collapsed in Jeet's flat. I offered him the sofa at our place until he finds a place of his own. Hope that's ok?

—Of course. Ceiling collapse is scary! He and his flatmate are ok?

—Seems so.

—He's welcome to use my room till I get back. Can't remember where the spare key is, but it's somewhere in my room. Probably the bedside cabinet. See if you can find it?

—Thanks. Are you ever coming back?

—I am, but let's just say it's damn tempting to keep postponing the date.
—Mumbai's going to feel like one massive letdown after this London trip, isn't it?
—Actually, I'm in Istanbul right now.
—Istanbul?! How come?
—Zeb wanted to show me the city.
—So he flew you to Istanbul?
—Pretty much. Turns out Indians can get visa on arrival if you have valid UK and US visas. #PrivilegeRox
—Unreal.
—I'll send you photos. I haven't put them up on Instagram because I haven't told my parents I'm here. Rucha doesn't know either. Just told her that I needed a few more days. I meant to tell you, but got distracted.
—Distracted, huh? Try and get out of the bedroom. It's a gorgeous city to walk around in.
—We're doing a lot of walking!
—Is that what you kids call it these days?
—Zeb says to tell you that you're only five years older than him. But speaking of 'kids', you're sure about having Jeet in the house, right? I'm cool with it, but I'm not the one who's gone to Kandivali with him.
—That was ages ago. I think we've put that stuff behind us now.
—Really?
—Really. By the way, you're going to tell the rest of the gang you're in Istanbul?
—Yeah, sending a message to the group in a bit.

Aalo looked out of the window and stared at the Bosphorus as she thought about the wording of the message for the Not-So-

Famous Five. 'Hey guys, I'm in Istanbul for a week!' with a smiley face? A photo of this gorgeous view with the caption, 'Mine for a week'?

It really was unreal. This whole trip was unreal, Aalo thought, as she remembered the party at Zeb's parents' home last week.

The Shams family home was outside London and the cutest cottage Aalo had ever seen. Her first thought when Zeb introduced her to his parents was that it was unfair how good-looking the whole family was. Reza and Firoza, Zeb's parents, looked like they could be in a Pixar film—petite, perfect features, twinkly eyes, loud laughter—and all of Aalo's niggling anxiety about gatecrashing evaporated within minutes of meeting them.

'Aalo wanted to ask you what you remembered of Srinagar,' Zeb said to Firoza, soon after making introductions.

'Have you been?' Firoza's face lit up, and Aalo realized Zeb had got his eyes from his mother.

Aalo nodded. 'I went last year with a few friends. We spent a few days in Srinagar, before going to Sonamarg and Gulmarg. I don't think I'll ever see anything more beautiful than that landscape.' She plunged her hand into her bag to find her phone. 'I can show you photos. I'm a terrible photographer, but Kashmir is so beautiful, you just can't make it look ugly.' She opened up the folder with the pictures taken in Kashmir. 'Unless you find a tank or an armed soldier in the frame, I suppose, which happens way too often,' she laughed awkwardly. 'But anyway,' Aalo started selecting photos from her Kashmir album, 'this is Srinagar now.'

Firoza put a hand to her heart as though to steady herself. 'I left when I was seventeen,' she said. For the next few minutes, Firoza took Aalo through the Srinagar she remembered and asked

Aalo about the city as she'd seen it. They were both speaking of the same place, and yet it also felt like two different worlds. The Srinagar that Firoza had left was not the one Aalo had seen, and the Srinagar that Firoza had in her heart was a place that Aalo could only imagine. Despite the warmth in Firoza's voice and the smile that didn't falter, there was so much loss that glinted along the edges of her words. Seeing one particular photo from Aalo's gallery, Firoza called her husband over. It was a street lined with abandoned, dilapidated houses that once belonged to Kashmiri Pandit families. Aalo had taken the photo because the guide had pointed out the wood and brick façades, saying these were traditional Kashmiri façades and were fast disappearing.

'I think this was the street,' Firoza told Reza, zooming in. 'I think this is where Aarti's family lived. We'd meet at this corner, and then go from here to the bridge, and cross it to go to the market.'

Aalo moved away to give the couple their privacy, but Baz and Zeb both peered over their parents' shoulders to see the photo. Baz was the first to move away.

'Aarti Aunty and Mamma came to England together as students,' Baz said softly, as he came to stand beside Aalo. He handed her a glass with a bright pink drink. 'It's lemonade. I wasn't sure if you wanted alcohol.'

'Thanks, this is good,' Aalo said, watching Firoza describe the street and market visits animatedly to Reza, who was listening with rapt attention as though he were hearing the story for the first time.

'He's heard that story about a million times,' Baz said, affection evident in his voice. 'I say a million because I've heard it at least a hundred thousand times, and we were born five years after they got married.'

'So she came here to study and met him?'

Baz nodded. 'She was allowed to go abroad to study on the condition that she'd come back after her degree and marry the guy her father had chosen for her. Instead, my mum brings all of her family's nightmares to life by informing them she's hooked up with this Persian rake instead.'

'Wow. Dramatic.'

'Very.'

When Firoza looked up enquiringly, Baz said, 'I was just telling Aalo about how you came to England.'

'It was like a Bollywood film,' Firoza said, grinning, 'complete with my father disowning me for marrying Reza.'

Just then, there was a gleeful shout, and they looked up to find a large man walking in through the gate, carrying a crate of wine.

'That's the uncle for whom this party was thrown. Brace yourself,' Zeb said.

The lawn filled up with people quickly. Everyone seemed to know everyone else and Aalo felt like she was crowd-surfing, as one Shams family member or another got her to meet one person and then another, and then one more. Glasses of wine and lemonade kept coming to her like magic, and soon enough she was scampering into the house to take a pee. Fortunately, the bathroom was right next to the kitchen and not hard to find. When she came out, she couldn't resist taking a little wander through the drawing room. It was a large but cosy room, full of bookshelves, tables with neat piles of papers and magazines, and the sofa had doilies on it. There was a fireplace too and on it were family photographs. One of the photographs was of Zeb and Meher. They were holding each other close, and Meher was laughing, while Zeb had a rose stem between his teeth.

Aalo put the photograph down carefully and tiptoed her way out of the room. She was near the kitchen when she heard Zeb's voice. Aalo inched closer, knowing this was eavesdropping and that she shouldn't be doing it. Except, of course, she was going to listen in on this conversation. She heard another voice. It was Baz.

'All I'm saying is don't throw yourself into the deep end without telling her the lay of the land.'

'That's a horribly mixed metaphor,' Zeb replied.

'Don't deflect, you twat,' Baz said. 'Have you talked to her properly?'

'It's only been a few days.'

'Long enough for you to get her to meet your parents.'

Zeb didn't say anything. There was a small clatter of plates or bowls clinking against each other.

'Look, I'm not trying to interfere. I'm just looking out for you,' Baz said with a sigh. 'You've fallen hard for Aalo. It's obvious. And that's fine. She's great, but so is Meher. Meher and you seemed solid, until everything went downhill. With Aalo, there's a lot more to think about. It's not one elephant in the room, it's a whole bloody herd. She lives in another country, for fuck's sake. Our family is as confused as a bowl of punch and we're good with that, but what about hers? Do they expect her to marry a nice Indian boy? Add to that the whole stress of dating you while you go off chasing stories in crazy parts of the world. If this is just a fling, then neither of you need to think about all this, but in that case, why the hell are you bringing Aalo to meet the parents?'

'Because the parents threw a garden party while she was here?'

There was the sound of a door opening, and someone yelled for Baz to bring out his guitar because it was time for music. Aalo made her way out, sliding by quickly so that she avoided coming face to face with either of the brothers. She didn't hear Baz saying, 'Bollocks,' and Zeb replying, 'You're right. That's bullshit. I need to talk to her.'

Sitting in the apartment they'd rented for the week in Istanbul, Aalo tried to prepare herself for this thing between her and Zeb coming to an end. Absently, she found herself imagining Zeb pulling her into his arms and the two of them striking a pose fit for the cover of a romance novel. 'Marry me,' he'd whisper against her lips and pull out a ring. And then, she'd call her father and tell him she wanted to marry a man named Aurangzeb, after which he'd disown her, and that would be the last Aalo would see of her mother. She'd live in London, in Zeb's picture-perfect world, dependent on him for every little thing, from the money for the Oyster card to the phone bill. A couple of months later, she'd be tiptoeing in the dark, going through Zeb's phone like the suspicious wife that she was, and find messages exchanged with beautiful, perfect Meher, because, of course, he'd come to his senses and realize that Meher was the one for him.

'Everything good with Meera?' Zeb said, coming out of the shower.

He had only a towel wrapped around his hips and he was drying his hair with another towel. There were errant drops of water on his shoulders. He came over and kissed her on the corner of her lips and smiled. His eyes looked greener in the Istanbul sunshine and everything that Aalo had been imagining of their future disappeared from her mind. Instead, she decided that a week of being able to say *this* was her life—this paperback romance perfection that included an impossibly handsome man and jet-setting to exotically beautiful world cities—was worth all the heartbreak that could follow.

'She said hi,' Aalo told Zeb. 'A colleague of hers, his ceiling collapsed, so he may stay at my place for a few days.'

'Shit, that's scary. Is he ok?'

'I don't think he was there when it happened. Meera didn't mention any injuries.' She reached for Zeb's towel and pulled him closer. 'I'm sorry, wearing a towel is basically an invitation to pull it off.'

He clapped his hand over hers. 'Not in front of a window this size,' he said, laughing. 'Cihangir's modern, but they're not that modern yet.'

'Did you say Jahangir? I thought they wrote it with c.'

'They do. In Turkish, the "c" is pronounced like the English "j".'

Aalo burst out laughing. 'I'm with Aurangzeb, in a neighbourhood named Jahangir. All that's missing is Shah Jahan.' Seeing Zeb's confused expression, Aalo explained, while plotting a path from the middle of his chest to his belly button. 'Basics of Mughal history. Shah Jahan, best known for building the Taj Mahal, was the son of Jahangir, best known for being played by Bollywood actor Dilip Kumar in *Mughal-e-Azam*.'

'I know that one. Vaguely. Thanks to my mother,' Zeb said.

'Aurangzeb, who gave himself the title Alamgir, was the son of Shah Jahan,' said Aalo.

'I see. And what does Alamgir mean?'

'Ruler of the world or something banal like that.'

Zeb started walking Aalo away from the window and towards the bed. 'Did he have belly dancers in his harem?' he asked.

'Not a chance. Aurangzeb Alamgir was a very severe and strict Muslim. Banned music, drinking, premarital sex.' Aalo felt Zeb's fingers at the fastening of her pants.

'That seems a bit harsh.'

Aalo slipped her hand between their bodies and loosened the towel so that it fell. 'He did have many wives though,' she said, stroking the length of him.

'That's good.'

'It is?'

'Not the many wives. That just seems like a waste of resources. You can go a little tighter and a bit more … north.'

'Sure, Google Maps.' Aalo adjusted her grip. 'Better?'

'Fuck. Yes, brilliant.'

'You were saying about the women. Waste of resources?'

'Why bother with so many, when all you need is a belly-dancing sex educator?'

Aalo pressed a kiss on his lips before kneeling before him. He reached out to hold her hair and tip her face up to look her in the eye.

'You sure? You don't have to,' Zeb said.

'It would be my pleasure, Alamgir. In any case,' she said after flicking an experimental lick, 'it seems only fair to return the favour.'

Zeb's hand in her hair involuntarily clenched and then relaxed. 'Just to be clear, me going down on you isn't ever meant to be a dick for twat.'

Aalo stopped what she was doing because she had to laugh. 'What for what?' she asked.

'Dick for twat.' Zeb shrugged, grinning. 'A technically more accurate version of tit for tat,' he replied.

'It's a good thing you're not a writer, Alamgir,' Aalo said. 'Now, lie back and think of England, and tell me if I'm doing it right.'

A few hours later, still a tangle of limbs and crumpled sheets, after Zeb had returned the favour with interest, and they'd given up on their plan of going for walk, Zeb said, 'Aalo?'

'Hm.'

'Do you have to go back at the end of the week?'

Aalo clambered on top of him and, resting her chin on his chest, asked, 'What exactly are you suggesting?'

'Stay another week? It's not a solution to …'

Aalo lowered her eyes and sighed deeply. 'I suppose I could tell Rucha I've fallen ill and can't travel. Or that I've been kidnapped by a marauding Mughal named Aurangzeb and become his concubine,' she said slowly.

Zeb smiled and flipped her over so that he was the one on top. 'In which case, I should be treating you as such,' he said, pressing a kiss on one breast, and then another, before travelling further south. 'Part those legs for me right now, Mukherjee.'

Meera was staring at a ghastly and ludicrously expensive proposal to build yet another giant statue, this time in the middle of the bay at Marine Drive, when there was a knock on her cubicle wall. She looked up to see Jeet.

'Do you have a minute?' he asked.

'Sure, take a seat.'

He sat down and leaned forward to rest both his arms on her desk. 'I'll be taking that flat in Dadar,' he said. 'The one that Vivek was talking about.'

'That's great news. Congratulations!'

'Thanks. So, my new landlord can't give me keys until the middle of September.' Jeet drew a deep breath in and said, 'I was wondering if I could take you up on the sofa offer for this stretch. It's two weeks.'

'Sure,' Meera said, smiling widely to cover up the way her pulse had started racing nervously. Jeet living in her flat had just gone from being a vague concept to a concrete fact. She needed to change her ringtone immediately. He couldn't find out that she'd put the song he'd sent her as her ringtone. She kept her phone silent at work, but home was a different matter.

There was quiet for a few moments. Meera noticed Jeet hadn't shaved today and there was a dusting of stubble. It didn't look bad.

'When do you want to bring your stuff in?' she asked, dragging her thoughts to practical matters.

Jeet did a little shake of his head. 'I wanted to get some basics straight first.'

Meera raised an eyebrow. 'Ok.'

'I'm not comfortable with taking favours. Staying with you for free doesn't ...'

'I'm not taking money from you, Jeet.'

He tilted his head in acknowledgement. 'Which is why I'd like to propose that I do the cooking for the time that I'm staying with you, and I'll pay for the groceries.'

'You cook?' Meera asked.

'I'm not a candidate for *MasterChef*, but yeah, I cook.'

Meera couldn't stop the smile that was tugging at her lips. 'If we're doing payment in kind, can I also ask you to sing for your supper? Sorry, sing for the sofa?'

'I'm serious.'

'So am I,' Meera replied, still smiling. Jeet looked at her, an exasperated expression making the square line of his jaw more pronounced. 'Look, you don't have to do all this, but if it makes you feel better, then yes, you're welcome to cook and do the groceries,' she told him. 'We do have domestic help, so you'll have to fight Sujata, who takes her cooking duties very seriously. But that's on you.'

Jeet breathed in deeply. 'One more thing,' he said. 'Outside of this office, I'm not your junior or your colleague or anything to do with office and its hierarchy.'

'Of course.'

He narrowed his eyes a little. 'I'm serious. Inside your house, I'm just a guy on your sofa, with a guitar and two suitcases. I'm not the deskie, and I'm not going to tiptoe around you like you're my senior.'

Meera leaned back in her chair, folded her arms, and looked at him for a moment. 'I wouldn't expect you to,' she said. 'Outside of this office, you're a twenty-eight-year-old who needs a place to sleep and I'm the nearly-forty-one-year-old with a free sofa.' That, Meera figured, would bring everyone's hormones down to common sense levels.

Jeet nodded slowly. 'As long as we're clear that the office stays in the office,' he said again.

When she tipped her head in agreement, Meera noticed that his shoulders relaxed visibly.

'When should I come with my stuff?' he asked.

12

Jeet came with two suitcases and a guitar case at 8 a.m. His ringing the doorbell should have woken Meera up, but thanks to Sagar and Navin, Meera had been up since 6.45 a.m. The morning call at 7.30 a.m, with the team that handled *The Daily*'s website, was supposed to be Sagar's responsibility since he mostly worked from home now. Last night, he'd asked Meera to sit on the call. No, he'd ordered her to do it. At 11 p.m., Sagar had forwarded her the email that had the login details for the morning call, with just two lines: 'Make sure you have the list of important stories. Don't be late.' Of course, he'd cc'd all the other editors who would be on the morning call. They were the audience for Sagar reminding Meera that he was the boss. He knew the email would make her colleagues start whispering behind her back. Some would pity her, a few would sneer; most would want to speculate on what Meera must have done to turn Sagar against her.

'Just ignore him,' Faisal messaged. He was among those cc'd on the email Sagar had sent to Meera.

There were only a handful of people who had known the old Meera who cared about what people thought, and Sagar was one of them. Maybe he thought he could make her regress to being the people pleaser she used to be when she was married or the anxious stranger she'd briefly become after Kapil left her. If that was Sagar's plan, then there was a lot of frustration coming his way. Unfortunately, it also meant Meera would have to get used to being annoyed by Sagar, which was saddening and rattling at once. Sagar had been her staunchest ally. To have him politick against her made Meera question herself even when she knew she shouldn't.

After staring at Sagar's email for ten minutes, Meera had decided that silence was the most dignified option. In the morning, Meera got up early, changed out of her threadbare nightshirt, made herself presentable for Zoom, and joined the call at 7.31 a.m. Sagar was already on the call. He didn't even acknowledge her and started listing the major stories of the day. 'If there's anything that breaks, I'll let you know,' Sagar told the website in-charge once he was done. 'Or I'll have Meera inform you,' he said, as though Meera were his secretary.

'Thanks, Sagar, but that's unnecessary. Shivam is part of the WhatsApp group for senior editors, so he'll probably know if anything breaks before you do,' Meera said. 'I'd add you to the group, but Navin has told all of us to make sure you don't get stuck in all these day-to-day work things.'

Sagar laughed. 'That's sweet. I wish you'd mentioned that and replied to the email I sent you last night, so that I wouldn't have to handle day-to-day responsibilities like the morning call, but I guess Navin still wants me to keep an eye on things,' he said.

'We all want you to keep an eye on things, Sagar,' Meera said, smiling as sweetly as she could manage. Then, feeling just a little reckless, she added, 'None of us want you to feel like you're irrelevant.'

Faisal stepped in at this point and defused the situation by asking if editors from other city editions had any stories they wanted the website to feature. The rest of the meeting passed without incident, but by the time Jeet rang the doorbell, Meera was feeling heady with the rush of having stood up to Sagar. She was also still in her shorts, she realized, when she opened the door, because she'd only changed her top for the Zoom call. It was too late to do anything about that; besides, the shorts weren't disreputable. They just seemed absurdly casual next to Jeet's neatly ironed T-shirt and jeans. He looked like he was appearing for his first day at a new job.

Meera showed him around the house and told him Aalo had said he could use her room since she was travelling. He said he would use the bathroom in Aalo's room, but that he'd be more comfortable on the sofa. Jeet had been in the house for only about thirty minutes when Meera admitted to herself that it had been a terrible idea to offer the sofa to him. For fourteen days, he was going to be in the living room. He'd be here, outside her bedroom, within touching distance, all the time. She watched him bend down to rummage through his suitcase for something and found herself staring at the strip of chocolate-coloured skin that became visible as his shirt rode up. Fourteen days. Did he wear pajamas to sleep, Meera wondered, and then shook her head to change the direction of her thoughts. She forced herself to go into the kitchen and drink some water, even though that was not the kind of thirst that she was grappling with.

'Right, so I'm going to get ready. I need to head to work,' Meera said brightly, coming out of the kitchen.

Jeet turned around to look at her. 'This early?' he asked.

He was right. It was barely 9 a.m. Newspaper offices didn't really wake up till noon.

'Conference call with all the bureau chiefs,' Meera said, hoping her lie sounded credible.

Jeet stood up. 'Shall I bring you a dabba for lunch?'

'No, no. That's fine. But I should give you the spare key.' His fingers touched her palm when he took the key from her, and just at that moment, her phone started ringing. Meera realized that thanks to Sagar, she'd forgotten all about changing the ringtone. Now her phone was literally on song. With Jeet's song. Red-faced and inwardly cursing herself for not changing her ringtone, Meera looked around for the phone. It took one verse and a chorus for her to find it—she'd left it in the kitchen—just as the call from an unknown number ended. Meera came back into the living room to find Jeet leaning against the dining table, a smug expression on his clean-shaven face.

'You made it your ringtone,' he said.

Meera nodded. 'It's a really lovely song,' she said.

He narrowed his eyes for a moment and then stepped closer to her. His hands came to rest at her waist. Despite the thick cotton of her blouse, she could feel his warmth seep into her. Of their own volition, her fingers danced along his forearm, lingering on the rings of his tattoo, and then feeling their way up to his shoulder, before coming down to settle on his chest. His heartbeat was steady and fast under her palm. He bent a little and then lifted her in his arms, holding her against him for a moment before placing her on the dining table. Their heads were almost level now. Meera pressed her knees primly together, which placed the length of her thighs between her and Jeet. He rested his hands on her knees, but didn't move to part them.

'Jeet.'

'Hm?'

'What are we doing?'

He shrugged. 'Nothing. Yet.'

For a few moments, they remained like that—Meera seated on the table, Jeet's fingers drawing lazy patterns on her knees, their breathing suddenly ragged. The noise in Meera's head quietened as she looked at Jeet, his curly hair, his downcast eyes, his long-fingered hands with their rough tips. She exhaled unsteadily, parted her legs and pulled on Jeet's belt buckle to bring him closer. Her fingers travelled up his body and learned his face, lingering over his square jaw, his chin, his lips. 'To think you hid all this under that horrible beard,' she murmured.

He laughed.

'Why did you grow it?'

'I thought it made me look older.'

'Why did you shave it?'

An eyebrow was raised high enough to disappear under his cloud of hair. 'Why d'you think?'

'You did hear me that day, didn't you, when Aalo came to the office?'

He grinned. 'Yup. It almost made up for you leaving me with blue balls that night.'

'I panicked,' Meera admitted.

'That was obvious. What I'm still not sure is why.'

'Because wanting to have sex with you smacks of a mid-life crisis.'

He tugged gently at her top. 'May I?'

Meera lifted her arms so that he could pull it off. She heard him say something under his breath that she didn't understand. Before she could ask him what he'd said, he kissed her hard while his hands palmed her breasts. There was an edge of desperation to his kisses, and it felt as though his hands wanted to be everywhere. Meera drew back gently, taking hold of his wrists, and pulled his hands away from her body.

'Slow down,' she said, leaning into his ear and pressing a soft kiss on the spot behind his earlobe. 'Can I ask you something?'

'Anything.'

'Are you a virgin?'

Jeet frowned. 'Meera, I'm twenty-eight, not eighteen.'

'That doesn't answer my question.'

'No, I'm not a virgin.'

'Any hard no's I should know?'

Jeet looked confused. 'Hardnose? Like a detective?'

Meera laughed as she leaned back on the dining table so that she was resting on her elbows. She could feel his eyes on her and she returned the favour, drinking in the sight of him with his shining eyes, swollen lips, broad shoulders ... and the open belt buckle. 'You're gorgeous,' she said, 'and so very young.' Meera smiled wryly.

Jeet raised an eyebrow again.

Still smiling, Meera sat up. As she spoke, she slowly rolled Jeet's shirt up and off his body, pressing light kisses on the skin that was being revealed along the way. 'One of the few benefits of being an older woman is that you've figured out what works for you and what doesn't. So, by hard no's, I mean no as in negative, not nose like the facial feature. Your nose is just magnificent, by the way,' she clarified, reaching up to boop the tip of Jeet's aquiline nose before returning to his torso. 'Coming back to my hard no's: no anal, under any circumstances. No choking. No coming on my face. This whole semen squirting thing is just not sexy. No hitting of any kind—no slaps, no paddles, no whips, no crops, no rulers, no belts. I don't want them used on me and I don't want to use them either.'

'Jesus, Meera.' He looked like she'd punched him in the gut. 'If the point is that I die of embarrassment, this is going really well.'

'You're twenty-eight. You'll recover.'

'Not if we keep going with this conversation.'

'Have you ever tried a paddle or a nipple clamp?' Meera asked.

'No!'

'Well, for all you know, you may like it, but as far as the hitting stuff goes, you won't be finding out with me. Basically, I'm not big on pain as foreplay. Semi-hard no would be nipple clamps because I do have one pair that I like. But I'm not open to clothespins or binder clips or stuff like that.' She circled one nipple of his with her finger. Her voice was huskier when she spoke again. 'Maybe we should try my nipple clamps on you. I can kind of imagine them peeking out of your chest hair and your nipples seem sensitive.' Obediently, they puckered under her touch. She licked one nipple and then the other.

Jeet swallowed. 'Thanks for the warning, but I think I'll be ok with regular, non-kinky sexual intercourse,' he said.

'Oh, I didn't mean I'm anti-kink,' Meera said. She shuffled forward to the edge of the table and gently rocked her pelvis against his. 'I like tying up as much as I like being tied up,' she said, before pressing an open-mouthed kiss on his Adam's apple. 'Cuffs and silk ties can be a lot of fun,' she whispered, and ran the tip of her tongue along the line of his jaw. She leaned in closer and ran her fingers through his chest hair. 'I've been wanting to do this since that first night in your flat,' she confessed, her voice unsteady. His chest heaved. Meera reached behind to unsnap her bra. She saw his throat convulse. 'You might have guessed from that night at Ling's, during dinner, a little exhibitionism really turns me on,' Meera said, peeling off her bra. She leaned forward to graze his collarbone lightly with her teeth, and then pressed herself against him. Jeet's hands gripped her waist hard. 'I love how your chest hair feels against my breasts,' she whispered and heard him curse under his breath. Meera drew back. 'You look like you're going to have a heart attack,' she observed. Jeet shook his head. Meera slid one finger down to tug at the waistband of his jeans. 'May I?' she asked. Jeet nodded. She pressed a kiss on the corner of his mouth as she undid his pants. 'Also nice, though messy, is using food. I've dreamt of you drizzling honey on my clit and then sucking it off of me.' Jeet made an incoherent noise.

Meera stilled and then slowly pulled back. 'Why'd you stop?' Jeet's voice was hoarse.

'There's no rush.' Meera held his face in her hands, smoothed some of the hair away from his forehead, and kissed him softly. She took his hands and put them on her breasts. 'Gently,' she said. 'Use your fingertips.' He rubbed the pad of his thumbs on her nipples, and this time, it was Meera's breath that caught. She smiled and kissed him again. Her hands slowly travelled down his body to push his pants down a few inches. 'Breathe,' Meera whispered, and then wrapped her hand around his erection. Jeet dropped his head on her shoulder and said something in what Meera figured was Tamil.

'Is that good?' she asked him softly.

'Is there such a thing as a hard yes?' he asked.

'Hey,' Meera pressed a kiss on the bit of his head that was within her reach. 'Look at me?'

He raised his head. His eyes looked glazed and his breath was hot, like he'd been running. 'My head feels like it's going to explode,' he told her. 'Both my heads.'

Meera laughed and pressed a quick kiss on his parted lips. 'Told you you'd recover.' She kissed him again, for longer this time. 'Sex works so much better when you tell me what feels good, what you'd like to try, what you don't want to do, and vice ...' her tongue slipped into his mouth to savour the taste of him, '... versa.'

'How the hell did you do that?' Jeet asked when she lifted her lips.

'What?'

'Turn "vice versa" sexy.' He kissed her, and she matched him, taste for taste, both of them sucking hard on lip and tongue.

Jeet pulled away abruptly and took a deep breath. Gritting his jaw, he took a step back. Breaking out of the circle of Meera's interlocked ankles, he yanked his pants up.

Meera suddenly felt very conscious of the fact that she was sitting, topless, her legs splayed apart on the dining table. 'Are we ok?' she asked.

'You need to get off that table and take me to bed right now, because I swear if we keep this up for five more minutes, my legs are going to give up on me and I don't think my male ego can take that.'

Meera had vaulted off the table before Jeet had finished his sentence.

By the time they reached her bed, they'd clumsily managed to get most of their clothes off each other. They'd bumped and scraped every joint against every surface possible, and each time they pushed the embarrassment aside and kept kissing. At one point, he got down on his knees and pulled her shorts down slowly. Meera heard Jeet say, 'Thank fucking god,' as the shorts gathered at her knees.

'What happened?' she said, stepping out of them.

Jeet got back on his feet and shook his head. 'It's nothing.'

Meera pushed him, so that he stumbled backwards and ended up sitting on the bed. 'Something made you happy. I want to know what.'

'All that kink talk had me a little petrified you'd be the sort that gets Brazilians or shaves down there. But you're not, so that's great.'

'Jeet, you're adorable.'

Pulling her closer to him by her hips, he practically growled against the hair he'd been so relieved to see, 'I'll show you fucking adorable.'

A little while later, they were lying on the bed, their bodies flush against each other. Every bit of skin felt like an electrically-charged erogenous zone. There was a strange expression on his face.

'Now what happened?' she asked.

He touched a spot on her neck. 'This is where I gave you that hickey in the lift,' he said softly and pressed a kiss there. 'I remember thinking that your skin tasted like a wish coming true.' With his index finger he drew a line from the base of her throat down to the tips of her breasts, where he lingered for a while before going down to her navel. Then he slipped his hand lower to cup Meera between her legs. 'You're really wet,' he said, sounding a little stunned. Meera couldn't stop herself from arching against his hand. 'And you're blushing.' Jeet sounded delighted. He tentatively moved his fingers in the slick wetness while kissing her. 'Tell me what you want me to do,' he said against her lips. Meera kissed him hard and then moved away to get off the bed.

Jeet sat up and his eyes followed Meera's naked form as she opened her closet. 'Babe?' he asked tentatively.

Meera laughed. 'Not exactly age-appropriate, is it?' she said, turning around and walking back to the bed.

'Do you mind me calling you that?'

She shrugged. When she climbed on to the bed and made her way to him on all fours, she saw his Adam's apple bob. 'Show me your hands?' she said, as she straddled him.

His brow furrowed, Jeet held out his hands. She brought them together and then tied them at the wrist with a long strip of silk that she'd taken out of the closet. 'Too tight?' she asked.

Jeet swallowed and his Adam's apple bobbed again. 'I don't think so,' he managed finally.

Smiling, Meera sat up taller to guide his arms into a stretch. When they reached the headboard behind him, she said, 'Hold on to that and don't let go.' He obediently curled his long fingers around the top of the wooden headboard.

'You realize your breasts are directly …' Jeet abruptly stopped what he was saying and shook his head. 'Why am I even talking?' he said, before pressing a kiss on her breastbone. Meera held up his face and her tongue lingered over the lines of his lips. Her hands ran all over his arms, his chest, his stomach, delighting in the feel of him. 'I can't stop touching you,' she murmured. She wet two fingers in her mouth and circled one nipple, while lowering her lips to the other.

Jeet fell back against the headboard and closed his eyes.

'Jeet?' Meera's hands wandered around his body. 'Are you listening to me?'

'Mm-hm.' He didn't open his eyes.

Meera's hands cupped his balls lightly while her teeth gently grazed his nipple.

'Fuck!' Jeet's eyes flew open.

'Pay attention,' Meera said. 'I have only two condoms. So, make this count, ok?'

Jeet released a long, slow breath. 'Thanks. I really needed that extra pressure.'

She let one finger travel a slow, meandering, teasing path down to his erection. 'You seem to be holding up ok,' she observed. When she circled the tip slowly with her finger, Jeet's hips bucked. All the while, their gazes were locked on each other.

'I think I'm going to die now, like right now,' Jeet whispered.

Meera wrapped her hand around his erection. 'You're literally throbbing,' she said. After squeezing it a little, she lifted her hand to her mouth and gave her palm a little lick. 'And leaking,' she added.

'For fuck's sake, Meera, would you please do it already?' Jeet groaned. His hands left the headboard, but Meera shook her head and pushed them back while positioning herself.

'You kids are so impatient,' Meera said mildly, holding his erection in the palm she'd licked and pumping him once, twice. Her other hand, she placed firmly on the centre of his chest, forcing him to keep the rest of himself an arm's length away from her. 'No patience whatsoever.' She curled her fingers into his chest hair and tugged gently, while the hand around his erection squeezed a little harder. 'How's this?' she asked huskily.

'I hate you so much right now,' Jeet groaned, his eyes squeezed shut.

A smile on her lips, Meera eased a condom on him and then lowered herself, slowly, onto him. Jeet's eyes flew open to see her eyes widen with pleasure. She took him in deeper and a little whimper of pleasure slipped out as she started moving her hips. Cursing hoarsely, Jeet straightened his back to sit up ramrod straight, and the next thing Meera knew, his arms, though still tied, were around her and he was kissing her hard. His tongue matched the rhythm set by her hips. They were both breathing erratically, each breath loud and unsteady and desperate.

Meera pulled her head back. 'I thought I told you, headboard,' she said, riding him harder and impressed that she'd managed to form something close to a sentence while her orgasm surged towards her.

'Punish me later,' Jeet said and lowered his mouth to her neck.

Her hips still on song, Meera reached behind her and untied his wrists quickly.

Afterwards, when Jeet got up to throw the condom in the trash, Meera said, 'I thought it would take us at least a week to build up to this.' She heard him laugh and mentally gave him another brownie point when she heard him turn on the tap to wash his hands. He came out to stand at the foot of the bed.

'Your nipples are still, well, erect,' he said mildly.

'Air conditioning.'

'Damn.'

Meera raised an eyebrow when he settled down to sit cross-legged at the other end of the bed. 'You're already thinking of round two?' she asked.

He walked two fingers up her leg slowly. 'Did you know how mad it made me to see you coming round to our side of the office only to talk to Faisal?'

'So it wasn't embarrassingly obvious that I was hanging out at Faisal's room so that I could ogle you?'

Jeet took her foot in his hand. 'You have tiny feet.' He kissed the arch and grazed his teeth against the flesh. 'Your ogling was very discreet. I have no grounds to complain to the company's Vishaka Committee,' he said lightly.

The boneless languor that Meera had been feeling evaporated in less than a second. Jeet felt it too. 'Babe?' His tone was still light, but his eyes looked guarded. 'It was a joke.'

Meera tried to stand up, but Jeet didn't let go of her foot. She gave up and lay flat on the bed. 'I know,' she said, 'but you know we can't do this.'

'We've already done this.'

'You know what I mean.'

'Not really.'

'Stop being stubborn. You're my junior at work.'

'I'm also a consenting adult.'

'Still. I'm your senior. You may not report to me, but that doesn't make it ok for me to be naked with you.'

Jeet sighed and let go of her foot. 'You promised office would stay in office so long as I stayed here.'

'Yeah, well, you're the one who brought it up.' Meera sat up and clutched a pillow to her body, covering it up. 'Why can't you just go out there and be the singer you're obviously born to be, so that sleeping with you isn't an ethical violation?' A muscle twitched in Jeet's jaw and Meera reached over to press a kiss just there. 'Seriously, Jeet. Why are you in the newsroom instead of making a career in music?'

Jeet was quiet for a moment and then he pulled her close, so that they were spooning. 'The same reason you take the crap that Sagar keeps dishing out,' he said. 'Because it's nice to have a pay cheque in Mumbai.'

'I keep telling you to call Fatima, and you just keep nodding your head and not making the call. Talk to her. She knows the music business, she'll help you.'

'Why would she do that?' Jeet laughed. 'Because her bestie has my song as her ringtone?'

Meera smiled and pressed a kiss on Jeet's arm. 'Maybe,' she said.

'That's not how I want to do this,' he said softly into Meera's hair. 'There's nothing I'd like better than to quit *The Daily*, but I don't think I'm ready to go full-time with music. I wish I were ... because desk work is so dull, I feel like I could go into a coma and that would be more exciting. Also, *The Daily* is like sleaze central. I honestly don't know how you've managed to work there all these years without going totally insane.'

'Sleaze central is a bit extreme.'

'Meera, do you seriously not see how the men in the office look at you? The way Navin hugged you the day of the flood?'

'That wasn't sleazy. I know what sleazy feels like. That was just Navin being hyper.'

'If you say so. From what I can see, Faisal is pretty much the only decent guy in the newsroom. Sagar is a complete asshole.'

Meera sighed. 'I don't know what's got into him. He wasn't like this before,' she said.

Jeet made a disbelieving noise. 'Yeah, well, we all know he's a complete menace now. He's constantly eyeballing the girls, asking them to have chai with him, standing too close. It's disgusting.'

Alarm prickled Meera's skin. 'Has he done anything that needs to be reported?'

'No. At least I haven't heard of anything, but he makes everyone uncomfortable, and we can all see he's been an asshole to you ever since you became political editor.' Jeet pressed a kiss on Meera's shoulder. 'Why are we talking about the office? I thought we'd decided that's not allowed to come between us when we're home.'

Meera turned around to face Jeet. 'You know this can just be a one-time thing, right?'

'Why?'

'You just called Sagar an asshole for standing too close to the girls. Considering what I've just done to you, what does that make me?'

'A phenomenal lover,' Jeet said and then put a finger on her lips. 'You cannot seriously be equating yourself with Sagar right now. You know as well as I do that this is completely different. You and I have been waiting to do this since that night at Ling's.'

'When I pawed you at an office event.'

'And I pawed you right back.' Jeet kissed the sigh out of Meera's mouth. 'Meera, please don't try to make what we have into something sleazy and ugly, because it's not, and I'm going to start getting offended if you keep trying to convince me you're a female Sagar, because frankly, I have better taste than that.' Meera burst out laughing, and Jeet smiled as he watched her. 'If you say it's complicated, I'll accept that,' he said softly.

'That's putting it mildly,' Meera said. She kissed him, savouring the taste and feel of him against her. 'As political editor, the first woman in that position at *The Daily*, I just cannot be doing this with a junior in my newsroom. It's professional suicide if it gets out.'

Jeet held Meera's wrists and pulled her hands away from his body. 'Do you have any idea how fucking confusing it is for you to be doing what you are with your hands while those words come out of your mouth? A mouth that's swollen because that's how much I've kissed you, and it's still not enough, and I am definitely going to kiss the lights out of you again. And again,' he said hoarsely.

'That's terrible sentence construction, deskie,' she said, bending her leg so that her toe could trail up the taut length of him, ankle to hip. 'I'm sorry for the mixed messaging, but it's just too much fun behaving badly with you.' She arched against Jeet and a soft hush of breath rushed out of him. 'I do mean it though. We can't make a habit of this,' she said.

'So you're saying this is a one-afternoon stand?' Jeet asked. Meera nodded. He narrowed his eyes for a moment and then untangled himself from her to get up and walk out of the bedroom.

'Jeet? What are you doing?'

He came back with a bowl in his hand and sat down beside her. 'If all I'm getting is one afternoon with you,' Jeet said, dipping his fingers in the bowl, 'then I'm making the most of it.' He gently moved Meera's hair aside and smeared a line of honey where her neck met her collarbone and then lowered his mouth to lick her skin clean.

'I think you were a vampire in your last life,' Meera told him in an unsteady voice. 'You have an unhealthy fixation for the jugular.'

'Only yours.' Smoothly, he arranged Meera so that she lay across his lap. He took the bowl of honey and drizzled it over her. 'If you ask me, the whole work angle is stupid,' Jeet said, lowering his lips to the honey dripping off her nipple. 'Jesus, salted caramel has nothing on this,' he breathed before going on. 'So, yeah, you're being ridiculous, but you're not asking me or listening to me, and thankfully, we're not anywhere close to the office right now.' He dipped two fingers in the bowl of honey again. 'So, I'm just going to focus on your clitoris, if that's alright by you.'

Meera said a prayer, and in a distant corner of her mind that wasn't exploding with sensation, she realized that the next two weeks with her new flatmate were going to be a true test of her convictions.

Three days after Jeet became Meera's flatmate, a photograph popped up in the Not-So-Famous Five WhatsApp group. It was of Aalo, shoulders bare, the rest of her wrapped in a white bedsheet, with a big smile on her face and a window that showed a sliver of the Bosphorus behind her.

—Aalo: Hello from Istanbul!
—Rebecca: Hold up. ISTANBUL?
—Jo: Sexy photo. Did Zeb take it?
—Aalo: Yes, to both of you.
—Fatima: When did you end up in Istanbul? Why does no one tell me anything?
—Aalo: OMG. Fatima, HOW CUTE IS YOUR NEW PROFILE PIC WITH LITTLE JHALKARI BAI!
—Jo: Please don't call her that.
—Fatima: It's not new. It's new to you because you're too busy having sex by the Bosphorus to check WhatsApp.
—Rebecca: Tell us everything. Now.
—Aalo: I was flying Turkish Air, and Zeb had the excellent idea of changing my ticket, so that instead of a stopover,

we'd do a little holiday in Istanbul before I come back to Mumbai. So here I am, saying hello from Istanbul.

—Jo: Un-fucking-real. Is this house on Airbnb or does your boy own gorgeous real estate everywhere in the world?

—Aalo: Airbnb.

—Jo: Send me the details? Definitely need to keep this in my travel file.

—Aalo: It's a great location and lovely flat. With bum shower. Highly recommend.

—Meera: Thanks to you going on about bloody bum showers, I keep getting ads for portable bidets on Instagram.

—Aalo: OMG. A portable bum shower! What a GREAT idea!

—Rebecca: Can the two of you get your heads out of your asses—see what I did there with the bum pun? Thank you very much, I'll be here all week—and tell us what is going on with you and Zeb?

—Aalo: Nothing's going on. We're just having a little fling.

—Fatima: Little? Ten days in London and how long are you guys in Istanbul?

—Aalo: Not sure.

—Rebecca: What do you mean not sure?

—Aalo: We're thinking of extending by a couple of days. It's a gorgeous city.

—Fatima: Yeah, I'm sure you're thinking of extending because of its monuments.

—Meera: Did you mean its legendary, sorry, historic erections?

—Fatima: Nicely done.

—Rebecca: Aalo?

—Aalo: Still here.

—Rebecca: Are you sure it's just a fling?

—Aalo: Very sure.

—Jo: From where I'm sitting, it's looking more like you're trying to stall end of said fling. Which isn't very flingy. That's more the sort of thing that people do when they want a proper relationship with the other person.

—Rebecca: It's also not like you to jump into bed with someone randomly.

—Aalo: Oh please. He's hardly random.

—Rebecca: You know him through Instagram! It hasn't even been ten days since you first laid eyes on him in person.

—Aalo: Nonsense. It's been almost two weeks.

—Rebecca: The point is, he's a stranger and you're in bed with him.

—Meera: Is that better or worse than having a stranger on your sofa at home? I kind of ended up offering our sofa to Jeet, and he's taken me up on it, and now for the past three days, when I get up in the morning and come out of my room, there he is. On the sofa. Frequently shirtless. And it's only struck me now that he might be an axe murderer in addition to being a deskie and an aspiring singer-songwriter. Because, really, what do I actually know about him? The answer is: nothing. Fatima, did he call you?

—Fatima: WHAT IS WRONG WITH YOU WOMEN? AND WHY DOES NO ONE TELL ME ANYTHING? And no, he hasn't called me.

—Aalo: Deskie, singer-songwriter AND axe murderer? I'm not sure there are enough hours in the day to do all that. Especially with Mumbai traffic.

—Rebecca: I don't even know what to say. You let a man into the house? Just like that?

—Jo: Am I the only one who clocked the frequently shirtless bit?

—Meera: I've also given him a spare key. That wasn't clever, was it? I mean, he could bring anybody into the house when I'm not there.
—Fatima: YES HE COULD.
—Jo: Stop overreacting. He's a homeless journalist, not a drug dealer. Coming back to that shirtless detail, what's he wearing to sleep? Don't tell me you haven't looked, because I will not believe it.
—Meera: T-shirt and presumably shorts. I don't know what he wears below because that's been under a comforter. But this morning, he was shirtless.
—Rebecca: HELLO. And?
—Meera: I don't understand how he has a body like that, given the schedule I've witnessed for the last three days.
—Fatima: HE'S BEEN THERE FOR THREE DAYS AND YOU'RE ONLY TELLING ME NOW?!
—Jo: Fats, just get off the caps lock already. Meera, explain.
—Meera: He's asleep when I leave for work. He stays at work till 1 a.m. approximately. He's not home when I go to sleep at 1.30 a.m., so he's out partying somewhere, I'm guessing. Comes back whenever he does, cooks and packs lunch for me in the dead of the night, then goes to sleep. Where is he getting that chiselled torso from?
—Jo: Chiselled?
—Aalo: Exactly what do we mean when we say 'chiselled'?
—Fatima: YOU DON'T KNOW WHEN HE COMES BACK AT NIGHT?
—Rebecca: He's making you lunch?
—Meera: Yeah, that's the deal. I'm giving him a sofa for two weeks because the ceiling of his old flat caved in and his new flat isn't ready yet. In exchange, he makes me lunch.
—Rebecca: Any good?

—Meera: Not your level of skill, but way better than mine. Thai curry and rice on the first day, pasta yesterday. Today I have tamarind rice and raita.

—Jo: Marry him. Now.

—Meera: Not. A. Chance. This lunch and occasional fondle is nice and all, but having him in the house has been a great reminder of how much I like being on my own.

—Jo: Wait, did you say 'fondle'?

—Meera: I meant 'ogle'. Freudian slip.

—Rebecca: Really? Not even slightly tempted?

—Meera: To?

—Rebecca: Be with him.

—Meera: Sexually, yes. CONSTANTLY. Which is why this was not my best idea. But definitely don't need a twenty-something hanging around me all the time. Especially if twenty-something's presence requires me to be decently dressed and polite when I get out of my room.

—Aalo: Ahem. He's my age and we're practically thirty.

—Meera: He's twenty-eight. I checked. And you're twenty-nine, which is practically twenty-nine. Not thirty.

—Jo: So basically you'd just like to have him show up, get a little physical on request, and then disappear. Like my dad does with the thugs he uses to clear out places he'd like to buy for cheap.

—Meera: Bingo.

—Rebecca: Does anyone else find it insanely fantastic that Jo ended up being a restoration architect despite her father being a builder?

—Jo: I think I got into restoration precisely because my dad is a builder. Quite apart from the fact that I couldn't have afforded the phoren degree without his earnings from dubious sources.

—Meera: By the way, Jo, I wanted to ask you if you could help me get some information on the plot in the buffer zone of SGNP that the Mulchandani family owns. Someone told me they're looking to sell it to a builder.
—Fatima: And then everyone will be like, 'OH noo! Look, leopard in the complex! Kill the leopard!' Why are you building your house in the forest, idiots? That's the leopard's home.

The conversation turned to development, and Jo and Meera made plans to discuss the sneaky ways of Mumbai builders. In a separate window, Aalo sent a message to Meera.

—Thank you for distracting the girls.
—I got your back. They mean well.
—I know.
—You know what you're doing?
—Not really, but it's just perfect right now, and I don't want to think about anything beyond that.
—Fair enough. If you need to talk or anything, you know I'm here.
—I love you. Oh, and by the way, is Jeet really 'chiselled'?
—Unfortunately, yes.
—I want a photo. Also, Meera, do you know what you're doing?
—Stop using my lines on me.
—Shit. You did it with Jeet!
—Go and do touristy things in Istanbul.
—Yes, ma'am. You take care, ok? And have mercy on the boy.
—Go away, Aalo. And come home soon.
—How long is Jeet staying?

—Eleven more days.
—Wow. You're counting the days.
—I'm practically counting the hours.
—Was it good?
—Let's put it this way. It was good enough for me to think it was worth risking the scandal of everyone finding out I'm bonking a kid who works at the desk.
—Bleddy. Now I really want a photo.

13

Jo figured something was up when a few days after their bombshell group chat, Meera didn't just suggest catching up for 'early brunch', but also messaged to say that instead of ringing the doorbell, Jo should ping Meera once she was downstairs. Instead of pointing out the obvious weirdness of the request, Jo pinged as instructed, but when she was standing outside the apartment, Meera opened the door immediately.

'What's with the no-doorbell thing?' Jo asked, walking in.

'I thought Jeet might be sleeping in since he works late,' Meera said, hovering by the door as though she wanted to pull a Road Runner act. 'We should go. I booked us a table at La Loca. We need to get there on time.'

'We'll take the car. It'll take two minutes. I'll drive,' Jo said, and then looked at the sofa that betrayed no trace of human presence. 'Pity. I was hoping to see this hunk of man flesh that both you and Fats are salivating over. For different reasons, obviously.'

'We should go,' Meera said again, keeping her voice low.

'Where is your MLC, by the way, since he's not sleeping in or on the sofa?' Jo asked, sitting down. She noted Meera's eyes widening. 'Sorry, is no one else allowed on this anymore?'

At just that moment, a freshly-showered Jeet walked into the living room with only a towel around his shoulders, and a pair of worn-out, low-slung track pants barely preserving his modesty. There was an awkward silence for a beat, before Jeet came up to Jo. 'Hi,' he said. 'Sorry, my shirt's over there.' He pointed at the suitcase on the other side of the sofa. He crossed the room and shrugged a T-shirt on, before looking pointedly at Meera.

'Jo, this is Jeet,' Meera said finally. 'He's a colleague from work who's staying over for a few days.'

Jo stood up to shake hands with Jeet. Both of them darted a quick glance at Meera and raised one eyebrow each. Jo turned back to Jeet. 'The collapsed ceiling, yes?' she asked, making it plain that Jeet had been a topic of conversation between Meera and her.

'Ah, you're the Jo Meera talks about so fondly,' Jeet replied with a smile. 'My best friend's nickname is Jo, and Meera won't use it because she said there's only space for one Jo in her life.'

'That would be me. Meera said you're looking for a new place?'

'Actually, I've found one. I'm just homeless while the landlord gets it ready.'

'That's great.' Jo rocked on the balls of her feet.

There was another awkward silence before Meera said brightly, 'Jo, shall we head out?'

'Would you like to join us? For brunch,' Jo asked Jeet.

'No!' Meera said quickly. 'He's got things to do.' She took Jo by the elbow and herded her towards the door. 'And we have a reservation that we shouldn't be late for. Jeet, if you need anything, send me a message.'

Jeet didn't say anything. He just waved.

Seconds after Meera had got out of the flat, she got a message from Jeet.

—MLC?

Meera groaned. 'Did you have to say MLC in his earshot?' she said to Jo, who didn't say anything because she was focused on backing Meera's car out on to the road. Sighing, Meera replied to Jeet.

—It's an in-joke between Jo and me. MLC = mid-life crisis.
—Just trying to figure out whether that's better or worse than 'hunk of man flesh'.

Meera groaned again and hid her face in her hands. 'I need alcohol. Lots of alcohol. You, by the way, did not help. At all.'

'So, the whole message-when-you're-here thing was supposed to ensure you scuttled out of your own home before he got out of the shower,' Jo asked evenly. 'By which I can only conclude that you've had sex with him. More than once?'

Meera looked up at Jo. 'There is no logical connection between the two things.'

'But you have.'

'It cannot be that obvious.'

'Was it good?'

Meera threw her head back to stare unseeingly at the roof of the car.

'He does have a nice chest,' Jo observed, as she illegally overtook a BMW.

'He does,' Meera agreed.

They didn't say anything for the next couple of minutes. While parking the car, Jo asked casually, 'Work must be interesting under these changed circumstances.'

'Are you sure you want to start me off? Because I feel like a pressure cooker that's about to go boom and splatter everything everywhere.'

'Bring it on,' Jo said.

Except when it came to actually venting about the past week, Meera found herself struggling to find the right words. Where should she even begin? With the morning Jeet moved in, when both of them took the day off from work and spent it entangled? Or with the way she felt when she heard Jeet crooning one of those melodies he seemed to conjure effortlessly? Or the fact that she could close her eyes at any moment and shut out the world by just drawing up the memory of Jeet lazily murmuring lyrics against her skin, of songs she didn't know? If any part of Meera had thought that their one-afternoon stand would tie a knot on her desire for him, there were a million nerve endings tingling to prove her wrong. She woke up in the morning, humming like a tuning fork, with the awareness of Jeet being just a few metres away, on the other side of a wall that felt flimsy next to the concreteness of her longing.

If only it had been a matter of simple desire. If only all that drew her to him were the lean, strong and burnished lines of his body and that beautiful face. How had it turned out that they'd ended up talking so much? How had they developed habits and rituals over the course of just one week?

The first time that Jeet asked Meera if she wanted to come out for a coffee, she'd been certain that the invitation was to ensure they didn't end up in bed again. She'd said yes, thinking conversation between them would probably be stilted without the buffer offered by the rest of the chai gang. Nothing like an awkward conversation to get hormones in check. As Jo had once put it, 'Chemistry was not built to survive everyday life.'

However, sitting at the cafe, waiting for their order to arrive, it seemed that the chemistry between Meera and Jeet was thriving in real-life conditions. Meera could feel it in the way he looked at her. Jeet could probably see it in the way she watched the shadows of the nearby mango tree flutter on his skin. And it wasn't as though they only sat there, X-raying each other with smouldering glances. There was also dialogue, and it didn't move awkwardly at all. She told him she preferred to take the train to go to South Mumbai, partly because it was quicker but also because for the longest time, the construction sites for the coastal road had blocked the view of Haji Ali. To not see the dargah and only see concrete blocks and bulldozers felt, to her, horribly depressing. Now Haji Ali was visible again and Meera found herself taking the car when she had a meeting anywhere south of Worli. He told her about dislocating his shoulder while skateboarding, and wanting to see the Northern Lights, but being too chicken to deal with freezing Arctic temperatures. She asked about his family, and listened to him talk fondly about both his parents, who were serious-minded doctors; they found it funny that their only son was 'arty'. They were waiting for him to admit music was best pursued as a hobby. She thought he'd ask about her marriage to Kapil, but he wanted to know if she had any hiding places in Mumbai and how she had become friends with Aalo, Fatima, Jo and Rebecca.

Meera had lied to her girlfriends when she'd said she didn't see much of Jeet and that he spent the mornings asleep on the sofa. If anything, both she and Jeet were sleep-deprived because they were trying to spend as much time with each other as they could without actually admitting that this was exactly what they were doing. When he rushed home after closing the issue, Jeet found

Meera sitting on the sofa, reading a book or watching something on her laptop. In the morning, Jeet was the one who opened the door for Sujata, and he hung around the kitchen while Meera made toast and eggs. After breakfast, it had become a ritual to step out for coffee before going into work together. Meera had taken the car every day since Jeet had come over because going by train would mean being separated during their work commute.

Two days ago, while they waited for the signal near the office to turn green, Jeet asked, 'What do you think has played a bigger part in the person you are today, journalism or Mumbai?'

'Where did that come from?' Meera asked.

'I was just thinking that with most people in this city, if you ask them to say one thing about themselves, they'll tell you their profession,' he replied. 'Their experience of this city is anchored by the way they earn their livelihood. That's not how you are though. For you, the city is something else. When you talk about places and neighbourhoods, it's like you're talking about a bestie.'

'I never really thought about it, but I definitely think I'd be a very different person if I'd spent the last twenty years in, say, Nagpur,' Meera said, grinning.

Jeet laughed and then sighed as she turned her car into the parking area of the office. 'And so it begins,' he murmured, patting his pockets to find his access card. There was a tired blankness that filtered into his voice the moment they entered the premises of *The Daily*. Meera felt it in herself, too, and it was a feeling that she hated. She missed reporting and the fact of being a manager, rather than a journalist, felt like an uncomfortable, persistent itch. As proud as she was of becoming the political editor, journalism now felt like something she squeezed into her day after she'd tackled the male egos in the office.

On one hand, there was Navin who seemed to have decided that an alternative definition of 'editor' was to either reject or mock Meera's ideas in open meetings. Fortunately, with Faisal as her ally, Meera had found a way around that problem. She discussed the stories with Faisal first, and Faisal would go up to Navin and ask for those particular stories to get prominence on page one. If Faisal said it was a good story, Navin would agree to giving it a good spot. If Meera pitched the same story, Navin would tear it apart. His behaviour made no sense, but Meera did her best to ignore it, reminding herself that she had found a way to make sure good stories weren't buried. That was what mattered, rather than Navin's vitriol or Sagar's smug expression when Navin put her down.

Then there was Sagar. One of the new hires on Aishwarya's team had complained that Sagar had got drunk and flirted with her at an event *The Daily* had organized recently. 'She's just a girl, barely twenty-one. I feel so damn responsible,' Aishwarya said to Meera, her voice cold with fury. 'I told her she should file a formal complaint but she's scared. She keeps saying "Sagar sir is senior and knows people."' It was true, Meera had to concede. Sagar did know 'people' and he wouldn't take kindly to being called out. Meera promised Aishwarya she'd figure something out and remembered what Jeet had told her about Sagar making women in the edit team feel uncomfortable. The other conversation that came to mind was Kapil offering to 'help' if Sagar's hostility got out of hand. What did Kapil have on Sagar that he was so confident about making the senior journalist behave? As far as Meera was concerned, if Kapil could convince Sagar to fix his behaviour with Meera, he could probably make Sagar write whatever Kapil wanted him to and use *The Daily* as his party's platform. That was a chilling thought.

In the middle of all this, since yesterday, Jeet had started hanging around Meera's cabin, which had led to Faisal cracking a joke about how Jeet had suddenly become wildly interested in the politics beat.

'I laughed it off because what else could I do?' Meera said to Jo, clutching her third glass of sangria. 'When I told Jeet later that he needs to keep a lid on it, he just stormed out and I didn't see him again until this morning. He began the day sulking. Sulking! I mean, who does that?'

'A twenty-something,' Jo said drily. 'Kids, I tell you.'

Both women held up their hands to get a waiter to refill their glasses. 'Then, after two pouty minutes, he started hitting on me so obviously that Sujata, of all people, told him to calm down.'

'Sujata!' Jo cackled with laughter.

'She literally wedged herself between Jeet and me, slammed a glass of cold water into Jeet's hands and told him to drink up because the heat's becoming too much. I promise you she wasn't talking about the weather,' Meera said. 'I think Jeet had this scenario in his head where he'd flirt a little, stare at me with sexy eyes, and I'd basically collapse in a puddle at his feet and worship his dick,' she said, slurring a little.

Jo wrinkled her nose in distaste. 'Worship sounds like a bit much.'

Meera sighed. 'You haven't seen it. Jeet's dick is worth a matha-teko.' She took another large gulp of her sangria. 'But that doesn't mean I'm going to jeopardize my career for it.'

'It's the fault of these bloody rom-coms,' said Jo. 'All the boys grow up thinking that women are going to choose them over everything else. Bastard writers.'

When Meera got home from brunch, the house was empty. She'd been debating if she should go into the office even though it was her day off, but the silence of the house felt incredibly comforting. Meera pottered around the flat for a bit, before slipping into sleep long before the sunset. At exactly 3 a.m., Meera's phone rang. She thought it was ringing in her dream, but after a couple of peals, she realized the sound was coming from outside her head rather than inside it. Forcing her eyelids open, she looked at the phone. It took a few seconds to see the name on the screen was Jeet.

'Jeet?'

'Hey Meera, sorry to wake you up.'

'Are you ok?'

'Yeah, I'm fine. I just, well, you speak Marathi right?'

Meera was already out of bed. 'What's happened?' she asked while pouring herself a glass of water.

'It's nothing serious.'

'Jeet, just tell me what's going on.'

'This cop, he's stopped us, it's a one-way street and we turned, we didn't think, and the thing is, he only speaks Marathi.'

Meera realized his words were slurring. 'Are you drunk?' she asked.

'No. As in, I drank but I'm not drunk.'

'Where are you?'

'At the corner.'

Meera gritted her teeth and prayed for patience. 'Which corner?'

'The corner of the street where you live.' He hummed a bit of a tune that sounded familiar, and then he stopped abruptly. 'Can you talk to the cop in Marathi so that he lets us go?'

He didn't wait to hear her answer. The next voice Meera heard belonged to an irritated and tired traffic cop, who wanted to have nothing to do with the two obviously-drunk men he'd caught on a bike, not wearing helmets and going the wrong way. Meera let him rant for a good five minutes, agreeing with him emphatically every step of the way.

Finally, she asked him what he'd like to do about the boys. 'I can't just let them go. These idiots will just go crash into something,' he told Meera.

'One of them lives with me, just down the road you're standing on,' Meera told him. 'He's my brother,' she said, feeling blood rush to her face as she trotted out the lie.

'What about the other one?'

'Can you pass the phone to my, umm, brother?'

Meera heard the constable say, 'Sister, sister talk,' to Jeet.

'Did you just tell him you're my sister?' Jeet said.

Meera could tell he was smiling. 'Who are you with?'

'What?'

'The bike. Whose is it? Who are you with right now?'

'Jo. My Jo. Jawahar.'

'Where does Jawahar live?'

'Bandra.'

'How far is he from my flat?'

'About three minutes, maybe five. Isn't it Aalo's flat?'

'Is he sober enough to do the five-minute ride in an auto?'

'We're not drunk, Meera.'

'Give the constable the phone.'

'I'm serious. We're not drunk.'

Meera curled her fingers into a fist to keep herself from yelling at him. Why on earth was she feeling this angry anyway? 'Do you want me to hang up and leave you two to convince the cop in Tamil and whatever other language Jawahar speaks?' she asked with as much calm as she could manage.

When the constable came back on the phone, Meera explained to him that the bike and Jeet could be parked at her building, which was round the corner, and Jawahar could be put in an auto. 'That way, they're out of your hair and you can go back to work, without any worry,' she said.

'And you'll talk to your brother? It's very dangerous to go around like this, without a helmet.'

'I will talk to my brother. He's actually my aunt's son, from out of town. From Delhi. You know how they are over there.'

The constable made a sympathetic noise, and then, after feeling suitably important because of all the gratitude Meera had lavished on him, he said that he would come and deposit Jeet at her doorstep.

When the doorbell rang, a sheepish Jeet and a grumpy constable were faced with a furious Meera. She was wrapped in a dressing gown—with electric pink flamingos printed on it (it was Aalo's)—that was clearly too big for her, but the last thing Meera needed was a constable staring at her nightwear. Especially since she was wearing a strappy top that had 'Beers before bros' written on it. Before he left, the constable complained one more time to Meera about how her 'brother' had no sense, and Meera agreed heartily with him.

After sending the cop off and locking the door, Meera turned to find Jeet standing awkwardly in the middle of the living room. At least he looked steady on his feet.

'I'm so sorry about this, and thank you. He didn't know Hindi,' Jeet said. He was speaking slowly, pronouncing each word with the care and precision people exercise when they know they've had too much to drink.

'You are incredible! You think it's cool to go and ride a bike when you're drunk? And without a helmet! Because just the alcohol wasn't enough of a death wish!' A small part of Meera's brain noted that she had not just raised her voice, but was also charging at him, wearing a flamingo-printed dressing gown. Jeet's head snapped back as though he'd suddenly been woken up. 'You think it's funny that you got pulled over? You think the problem here is that the cop only speaks Marathi? Do you have any idea how dangerous what you did today was? How stupid you two are?' she said, practically yelling.

'Don't talk to me like I'm a child,' Jeet growled at her, and Meera smelt cheap alcohol on his breath.

'Then try behaving like an adult. Step one: learn how to drink without getting drunk.'

'I'm not drunk.' He swayed for a moment, and Meera involuntarily took a step closer to steady him. Meera hoped he wouldn't actually stumble. He was too tall for her to hold up. She was standing very, very close to him, she realized.

'Are you wearing anything under that?' he asked in a whisper.

Meera yanked her eyes away from him and stepped back, putting some distance between them. 'You stink of rum,' she said quietly, after taking a breath. 'If you're going to throw up, do it in the bathroom … or get the bucket from there and keep it next to the sofa.' She pointed at the coffee table. 'I've kept a bottle of water on the table should you feel dehydrated.' Then she went into her room and locked the door behind her.

Meera didn't want to be alert to the noises that Jeet made, but it was that time of the night when the city was closest to being silent and Meera heard a quiet in the house that suggested Jeet hadn't moved, that he was just standing there, in the middle of the living room (swaying?). Then she heard him pour a glass of water. She heard a door shut (probably Aalo's bathroom door). He was an idiot, she told herself, and so was she, because she should be sleeping instead of listening for the sounds made by a millennial who couldn't hold his drink.

When Meera got up in the morning, Jeet was sleeping, face buried in a pillow, while the rest of him was swaddled in the comforter. On the dining table was a lunchbox. She picked up the Post-it note stuck on the box. It read, 'Sorry. Thank you for saving my ass.' He didn't look like he'd wake up for hours, so when

Meera was about to leave for work, she wrote on the same Post-it, 'You're welcome. Thank you for lunch. There's some watermelon in the fridge. Might help with the hangover.' She stuck the Post-it on the kitchen door.

She was coming out of a meeting in which Navin had dropped three stories that Meera had pushed hard to get done, when Jeet sent her a message.

—The watermelon saved my life. Thank you.

In spite of everything, Meera felt the gloom that she was feeling lift a little.

That evening, Jeet didn't come home until 1 a.m., which was when Meera decided to go to sleep. She debated sending him a message to not get drunk again, but stopped herself. Jeet and his alcohol intake were none of her business.

A few hours later, her sleep was interrupted like cracks running across thin ice. Not fully awake, Meera peered at her phone. There were no messages, and through half-open eyes, Meera saw it was 4 a.m.

She heard a soft clatter coming from somewhere in the house. Was it in the kitchen? There was a smell in the air, too. Something oniony. Meera's sleep-fogged brain tried to process the idea of a break-in by a … hungry burglar who … wanted to make himself a snack? She heard a little thud from the kitchen, and someone cursed softly. Meera forced herself to get up. Her eyes still mostly shut, she opened her bedroom door and felt like she'd been slapped by a blast of yellow light.

'What the hell are you doing?' Meera snarled. Her eyes hadn't adjusted to the light, but one glimpse of the tall figure standing at the stove was enough for her to realize there was no burglar in the kitchen. It was Jeet.

As sleep peeled off her brain, Meera registered the sight before her. He was standing over the stove, tossing something in a frying pan, wearing those sweatpants that hung improbably low on his hips. A dishcloth was draped on one shoulder. She noticed that being wet didn't flatten his curly hair much. A drop of water—or was it sweat?—ran down his spine. Jeet saw her and cursed as he switched off the gas. 'I really was trying to be quiet, I'm so sorry,' he said. 'Please go back to sleep. I'm done.'

Meera padded into the kitchen and came close to the stove. 'You're cooking,' she said slowly, trying to make sense of what she was seeing and smelling. The saucepan had something in it that looked like it was made of sunshine. 'What is this?' she asked, reaching to pick a little out for a taste.

Jeet pulled her away from the pan. 'It's hot.'

'What is it?' Meera's attention remained trained on the food. It smelt nice. Maybe she should have a midnight snack. Rather, a pre-dawn snack.

'Kind of like lemon rice, but with amaranth.' He was still holding her arm.

Meera turned to face him. She could smell soap, shampoo and toothpaste on him. 'Tell me you're not making lunch for me at 4 a.m.?' she asked.

Jeet shrugged. 'I have a readymade masala. It didn't take very long.'

Meera groaned. 'It's practically dawn, Jeet! Get some sleep, you idiot! You have work tomorrow.'

'It's my day off actually. So, I'll catch up on sleep. Don't worry. You're the one who needs to get some sleep. I'm really sorry I woke you up.'

Meera didn't properly register what he was saying because right there, just a few measly centimetres away, was all of him, without a shirt. She looked down and saw his fingers around her arm. With her other hand, she traced his tattoo. 'Do these rings mean something?' she asked.

'Not really. I just thought they looked cool.'

It would be so easy to move her finger in a straight, horizontal line, from the tattoo to his stomach bisected by a line of dark hair. Meera stepped aside slowly and deliberately, and backed out of the kitchen.

'You should get some sleep,' Meera said. 'I should do the same.'

'Meera? I'm really sorry about the other night,' Jeet said quickly, taking a small step towards her. He took the dishcloth off his shoulder and wiped his hands on it. 'You were right, it was stupid, but it honestly wasn't as bad as it looked. We were at a friend's, it's two minutes away, and at the risk of sounding like an alcoholic in denial, I really wasn't drunk. And neither was Jo.' He rubbed the back of his neck. It was an embarrassed, awkward gesture. 'But I definitely did drink more than I should have, and we should have left the bike at our friend's and come back by auto.' After releasing a long breath, he stood up straighter. 'So, yeah, I'm really sorry and, again, thank you for saving my ass.'

Meera couldn't stop herself from darting a glance towards said ass, which was out of her line of sight, and then dragging her gaze to the front where the tie of his track pants dangled, tempting her to tug at it. There was an awkward silence that stretched between them, and instead of sensibly retreating to the safety of her room, Meera ended up breaking the silence with the most stupid question ever.

'What do you do?' she said.

Jeet blinked. 'I'm sorry?'

Meera waved her hand up and down as well as side to side a couple of times. She was trying to indicate his torso and had ended up drawing a giant, invisible cross in the air. 'Your body,' she said finally.

Jeet started folding the dishcloth carefully. 'What about it?' he asked casually.

'How do you have it?' Meera asked, while wondering why she was having this conversation.

He raised his eyebrows as he put the folded dishcloth on the nearby counter. 'Everyone has a body, Meera,' he said, coming to stand right in front of her.

'Not one like that, and not while working at the desk.'

'I swim.'

'Have you been swimming for a while?'

'Since I was a kid.'

'Good habit.'

'You think?'

'Definitely.'

'I'm glad. I wondered if you liked gym bunnies.'

'Too much bulk turns me off. Lean is better.'

'I'm relieved to hear that.'

'When do you find the time?'

'I usually go before work. There's a pool near the office.'

'That's good.'

The image of him, bare-bodied, slicing through blue waters, was much more than good. Meera drew in a shaky breath and reminded herself that she was the older one in the room.

'Right, I should go to bed,' Meera said, backing her way to her door. 'By the way, Fatima said you still haven't called her.'

Jeet made a face and the shift in his mood was unmistakable. He folded his arms and leaned against the kitchen's doorjamb. 'I don't understand why it matters so much to you that I haven't called her,' he said.

Meera furrowed her brow. 'I just thought you'd want to follow up with her since you're serious about your music and she's in the business of earning money from music.'

'Maybe it's because I'm serious about my music that I want to get ahead on my own merit. Maybe I don't want to shove my music down the throat of someone who's being pestered by her friend to give a loser kid she knows a break.'

Meera rolled her eyes and said, 'If you actually called Fatima, then you'd know how wrong you are and maybe even get a few tips on how to make a career out of your music.'

Jeet's jaw jutted out. 'Maybe I'm good with it being a hobby.'

'Seriously?' Meera found herself laughing. 'You want me to believe that you like being in a dead-end job at *The Daily*, where you have to take leave if you want to perform on any night other than a Friday?'

'You know what I think?' Jeet straightened and walked up to her. 'I think you want me to be a musical genius because then you can make peace with the fact that you were attracted to me, albeit briefly. But I have to break it to you, I'm at best above average …'

'I have no idea what you're getting at, and I don't like your tone, so I'm going to end this here,' Meera said, turning around.

'You obviously don't think I'm good enough to have a relationship with, but I'm just curious. Have you decided I'm not up to your standards for a random fuck too? Is that why you've just been teasing me since our one-afternoon stand?' Jeet said to her back.

Meera froze.

'Would it be lowering your standards too much to sleep regularly with the random deskie?'

Meera turned to face him again. 'Where the hell is this coming from?' she asked.

'This is coming from you. From you treating me like I'm some dirty secret. If I'm this genius musician, a diamond in the rough, destined for great things, will that afternoon's lapse of judgement be ok? Is it acceptable then to be slumming it out with me because at least you can tell your friends I have potential?' Jeet made 'potential' sound like an abuse. He took a step back from her. 'But what if this is it, Meera?' he asked, holding his arms wide open. 'What if this is all I am? Can you deal with the fact that, at least for an afternoon, you were attracted to a guy with a crappy salary, no savings, no potential?'

There was silence in the room for a moment.

'Is this the part where you say you're just a guy, standing in front of a girl, asking her to love him?' she said drily.

The laughter that snaked out of Jeet sounded unpleasant and bitter. 'Except you'd never settle for someone ordinary like that bookshop owner in *Notting Hill*, would you?' When Meera didn't say anything, Jeet shook his head and moved away. He put the food he'd made into a tiffin box, and then switched off the kitchen light. The apartment was plunged into semi-darkness, with only the light from the streets leaking in.

'Good night,' Jeet said quietly and walked towards the sofa.

'I don't know where this idea that you're not good enough has come from,' Meera finally said in the darkness. 'But I do know that it's got nothing to do with me and everything to do with how you see yourself. You feeling inadequate has nothing to do with whatever has happened between you and me.'

'Nothing happened between you and me, remember.'

'Don't interrupt. Just listen,' Meera said sharply. Her tone was gentler when she spoke again. 'I haven't done or said anything to make you think I don't find you good enough. In fact, I've done the opposite. I'm the one who came on to you, I've invited you to live in the house I live in, I've treated you as my equal. I chose you.' His laughter was bitter and the sound of it made Meera's throat catch for a moment. After taking a beat to collect herself, Meera carried on, 'You don't see that and you're fixating instead on something else. That's probably because you know you can be more than a mediocre journalist at *The Daily*. Which is true. You can be more and you are.

You don't want to call Fatima? Fine. But give your music and your talent the respect they deserve. Grow up and be better.'

Jeet angled himself on the sofa so that he was in darkness, but Meera could tell he was looking at her. 'You're telling me to grow up?' he said in a voice edged with a sneer. 'The woman who lives with a roommate like she's on her first job, fresh out of college?'

'I live with Aalo because I like living with her.'

'You live with Aalo because you're scared of doing things on your own. Or maybe she's your security blanket and you're hers. I don't know what it is, but it sure as hell isn't grown up.'

Meera retreated into her room and locked the door behind her. That night, she didn't sleep.

In the morning, she came out of her room to find the living room empty. Once again, the empty house felt like a comfort. At work, she was surprised to find herself functioning better than normal, despite being sleep-deprived. From Sagar's temper tantrum to Navin curtly informing her that the drought series needed stories from farmers who had benefitted from the state government's schemes, she received it all with equanimity. She ignored Sagar and told Navin she'd look for the stories he wanted, even though it was unlikely they'd find someone who fit the bill. Two reporters said they wanted to quit, and she calmly talked them off that ledge. By the time it was 8 p.m., Meera felt like she'd lived lifetimes, but exhausted as she was, she didn't want to go home. The idea of either seeing Jeet or locking herself up in her bedroom felt intensely claustrophobic. She picked up her phone and scrolled through her contact list idly. She could crash with Jo or at Fatima and Rebecca's. Neither of them would ask questions if she told them she needed some space. But they'd know something was wrong and they'd worry.

Faisal poked his head through her doorway and said, 'I'm ordering some ice cream. You in?'

Meera smiled and shook her head. 'Listen, I do have a favour to ask. Can you recommend a nice hotel? A place I can stay one or two nights.'

Faisal looked at her for a moment and then stepped inside her cabin. 'Alone?' he asked bluntly.

'I'm not sure right now,' she said frankly. 'Maybe not.'

After a moment, Faisal said, 'A family friend has a boutique hotel in Colaba. I've never used it because, obviously, he's a family friend. But it's very nice, and that kitchen makes the best caramel custard in the whole world, I hear. I can set it up for you.'

'It sounds perfect. Thank you.'

'Two nights?'

'Maximum. Maybe even one.'

Faisal nodded. 'I'll talk to him and get you the details in a few minutes.' He made to leave.

'Faisal? Thank you.'

'Anytime. You're ok, right?'

'Yeah. I just need some space and I can't really turf Jeet out.' Meera shrugged.

Faisal nodded. 'I understand. Too much to explain to a random kid you're being nice to. Don't worry about it. You sure about the ice cream?'

'You're the best, and yes, I'm sure about the ice cream.'

Meera ended up spending two nights at the hotel, which was really more of a homestay than a boutique hotel, but still charming. Her room had a balcony where she sat and read books on her phone. She told the girls that she'd found a lovely place for a staycation, and sent photos of the view and the quaintly-decorated room with its old prints and vintage furniture. In a separate chat, Jo sent Meera a hug, a red wine emoji, and a reminder that she was around if Meera needed anything. There was nothing from Aalo, which was unusual, but Meera was too exhausted to ask after her. Instead, she slept.

The first night, she woke up when it was still dark only to feel disoriented by the realization that her hand was not buried in the cloud of curly hair that had felt so real and present in her dreams. She closed her eyes, and her mind wandered to a memory of crashing waves on Worli Sea Face, from back when the Sea Link hadn't been built. That promenade, now cluttered with barricades and construction equipment, used to be one of Meera's favourite places to retreat to when the first cracks appeared in her marriage. She would go and sit by the sea, feeling it salt and mist her skin as she listened to Paul Simon singing 'Bernadette' on her phone. The song had been part of a mixtape she'd made for herself when she was in college. When music turned into MP3s that you could store in phones, Meera had painstakingly pirated each track. '*Come with me*,' Paul Simon sang. '*There's a place I want you to see. / When the leaves are dark, / I've got a hiding place in Central Park*.'

In her hotel room, Meera found 'Bernadette' on Spotify and played it on loop. She fell asleep to Paul Simon's voice, and this time, her sleep was dreamless and restful. In the middle of her second night at the hotel, she got a message from Jeet, in which he said he was sorry. Meera didn't feel like replying to him, so she didn't. He wrote to her again after a few minutes.

—Please let me know that you're ok.

—I'm fine.

He was already in the office when she reached work the next day, but she almost didn't recognize him when she went to give Faisal a dabba full of caramel custard. Jeet's curls were gone. He'd cut his hair so short that it was little more than a layer of fuzz on his head. After a little chat with Faisal, Meera went to her cabin. She had just about switched on her computer when Jeet showed up.

'You're at work early,' she said.

Jeet shrugged. 'Everything ok with you?'

Meera nodded. 'You?'

'I'm fine.'

'Great.' Meera sat down in her chair. After a moment of him standing at the doorway, Meera asked, 'Was there something else?'

His jaw twitched as though he were grinding his teeth. 'I've taken my stuff and left the spare key on the dining table,' he said.

'Your flat's ready?'

Jeet nodded and turned to leave. Then he turned around again and said, 'I'm sorry if I hurt you the other night.'

Meera noted the 'if' and decided to not comment on it. 'Is that drastic haircut part of your penance?' she asked.

His jaw twitched again, probably at the sight of the sarcastic smile that was dancing on her lips. 'It actually looks really good on you. Very *Prison Break*,' she told him.

He thanked her and left the cabin, while Meera turned her attention to her inbox. There was no smile on her face. Now, it was her jaw that was twitching, because she was the one gritting her teeth. 'Well done, Meera,' she whispered to herself, 'on managing to break up with a guy even before you've had a proper relationship with him.'

When the screen turned into a blur for the third time in thirty minutes, Meera accepted defeat and told Navin she needed a sick day.

'But we're doing the package on political alliances today,' Navin said to her. 'It's only 7 p.m. You need to be here.'

'It's one of Sagar's special stories with only a few boxes, which I've already cleared. Sagar discussed the story with you, not me. I'm sure he can handle putting it on the page,' said Meera.

'If Sagar does everything, then what exactly are you handling?' Navin's voice was soft, but there was acid lacing every word, and Meera felt the sting. Usually, she would have left the room with a non-committal reply, but that evening, Navin's unshakeable faith in Sagar made something snap in her.

'What I'm handling is the fact that the principal political correspondent of one of the leading English dailies in the country is under the ruling party's thumb because they have compromising information on him. How do I know this? Because Kapil Patil has told me with great confidence that he can get Sagar to do whatever he wants. This means every article and every special story that Sagar files runs the risk of being biased because he's probably afraid of the dirt they have on him being made public. So, before a story reaches you, I make sure it is as balanced as an article by a compromised journalist can be. It also means that as the political editor, I can't rely on Sagar to bring or pass on any story that isn't in favour of the ruling political party.'

She paused and waited for Navin to say something. He didn't.

'You look surprised,' she continued. 'I'm disappointed. I realize that we don't really have the freedom to carry anti-government stories anymore, but I would have thought you'd be better informed about your senior staff, especially since my personal life appears to be everyone's business in this office.' Meera got up and made a show of straightening the sari that was perfectly in place.

'Now, if you think I'm not handling things well enough and you want me to resign, all you have to do is say the word. I have my old resignation letter saved and it will take me less than five seconds to change the date on it. For now, though, I'm taking a sick day. If you need anything, please contact Sagar. Also, I would strongly recommend you have a chat with him about his behaviour with the new marketing hire who may file a Vishakha complaint after Sagar misbehaved with her at the last *Daily* event.'

With that, she walked out of Navin's cabin. On her way home, she put up a message in the work WhatsApp groups that she had a migraine, but would be available on the phone if anyone needed anything.

14

Meera was sitting on the sofa that had been Jeet's bed till recently and was staring at images fluttering across the TV screen unseeingly. There was a click at the main door that made Meera turn, and she saw Aalo standing inside the house.

'Hey,' Meera got up. 'I didn't realize you were coming back tonight.' She took a step closer and registered Aalo's pallor and her red eyes. It had been a few days since she'd got a message from Aalo, Meera remembered, and a soft, cold dread crept over her. 'Is everything ok?' she asked gently.

Aalo shook her head and tears started running down her face. 'Everything is wrong,' she said. Her voice broke with a sob. 'Zeb's gone.'

A little more than twenty-four hours ago, Aalo had been living what had felt like the perfect life in Istanbul with Zeb. They walked around the city during the day. He fed her profiteroles and licked the chocolate off the corner of her lips. She took photos of him and he took photos of her. She made him do touristy things, like watch a performance of whirling dervishes, and he took her to an island off Istanbul where the water was so blue it was almost blinding. Almost every evening, there was a friend they met either in a beautiful restaurant or in an equally beautiful home. They had changed the date of Aalo's flight to Mumbai again, and the airline had threatened to cancel her ticket if she made any more changes. So now there was a definite date of departure, but it was a week away, and it was easy not to think about that little detail when there was just so much to enjoy.

The night before everything had gone to hell, Aalo and Zeb were walking back to their flat after dinner. She laced her fingers through his and told him that she understood why he kept coming back to Istanbul. 'It's so beautiful,' she sighed.

Zeb turned to kiss her forehead. 'It is,' he said. After a moment's pause he added, 'That's not why though. I keep coming to Istanbul for work. Because the Middle East is just riddled with conflict zones and Turkey's location is very convenient.' He shrugged, but it wasn't a casual gesture. The lightness felt forced.

Aalo nodded. 'I know. I've seen your photos, remember. I just didn't realize that's why you know this city as well as you do.'

'I usually leave my bag with Tahira and then go to one of the borders with a backpack. Travelling light makes sense and Tahira's a useful local guardian.' Zeb offered a small, tight smile. 'When your job includes the risk of being buried under rubble, getting caught in gunfire or being kidnapped, it's a good idea to have a local guardian who has the French president's personal mobile number.'

They walked in silence after that, and they'd almost reached the flat when Zeb spoke again. 'That's what broke Meher and me,' he said. 'Not just that I was always travelling, but that I was travelling to places that felt dangerous and out of reach. She said she couldn't handle the distance and the stress, and I suddenly realized that we'd been apart more than we'd been together. Worse yet, I didn't mind the distance. I hadn't even noticed when I'd fallen out of love with her because all my attention had been on work.'

'Why are you telling me this?'

'Because this,' Zeb turned Aalo to face him and pulled her close, 'is amazing and I want this to go on forever, but it's …'

'It's a fantasy,' Aalo finished his sentence for him. Zeb's brow furrowed.

'Fantasy?' he asked.

Aalo pulled away. 'I know this isn't real, Zeb. You don't have to break it to me gently.'

'Let's go inside. I'm getting the feeling you might have to break things to me gently,' he said.

Once they were upstairs, Aalo didn't feel like going to the bedroom. That was still a happy place, and she had a bad feeling about the conversation that Zeb had started on the street. Instead, she pretended to be immersed in her phone and sat down on the living room sofa. Zeb poured her a glass of the peach wine that Aalo had discovered and fallen in love with on this trip. 'Tell me about this real versus fantasy thing that we started downstairs,' he said.

Aalo felt her stomach knot uncomfortably and she took a sip of her wine to buy a little time. 'I'm not sure what you want to hear,' she said. She forced herself to relax and sank her feet into the shaggy rug at the foot of the sofa.

Zeb stared at her for a moment and then joined her on the sofa. 'Aalo, I think I'm falling in love with you,' he said. 'As stupid as it sounds, it probably started on Instagram. I didn't hit the "follow" button for ages because I had this irrational anxiety that you'd know that I was going through your Insta feeds compulsively, looking at those ridiculous selfies of your beautiful face again and again and again. I haven't ever felt as happy and alive as I do when I'm with you or sending you whale penises and origami vulvas.' He shrugged, a little smile on his perfect lips, and his green eyes blazing brightly. 'And these last few weeks have been brilliant. It's been real, not a fantasy.'

Aalo couldn't take her eyes off him. He was so utterly and completely beautiful. 'You're saying things,' she said.

'I am,' Zeb agreed. 'Feel free to say things too.'

Aalo shook her head. 'You'll snap out of this. You're just drunk on the fantasy Kool-Aid.'

Zeb's eyes narrowed. 'Maybe you should explain this fantasy theory of yours.'

'Look, I'm not saying this hasn't been good,' she said, the words coming out of her jerkily. 'You're like the perfect man, the sex is incredible, every single person in your family is gorgeous and sweet. Your life is like something out of a fairy tale or a movie.' Aalo shook her head. 'I'm not like that. I wish I were, and in the time we've spent together, I've loved pretending that I belong in your world, but I don't. In every way, we're worlds apart.'

'What does that even mean?'

'It means I live in Mumbai and you live in London. In bloody Notting Hill.'

'You live in Bandra.'

Aalo frowned. 'Yeah, where the streets explode with fire. Literally,' she said. 'BMC was digging something today, and boom, they hit a natural gas pipe. Pillar of flame, at everyone's service. It was all over my Instagram. But that's not the point. You and I, we can't work in real life. You're friends with Tahira Ceylan and hugely respected for being brilliant at your job, while I'm just a nobody, with nothing. I don't know what I'm doing, I think I've just about glimpsed what might be my career, but who knows?

Maybe that's just part of the rose-tinted fantasy that this trip has been, thanks to you. Zeb, I've just floated through life. It's why Meera wanted me to interview with Rucha for SWETE. I kept telling her I was coasting, and she kept telling me that I needed to ground myself in the real world instead of making the most of having a father who's damn annoying but can pay for the life that I want.' Aalo took a deep breath. 'What I'm trying to say is that people like you don't fall in love with people like me.'

'You're not a nobody and we probably need to have a longer chat for me to understand what you mean about your dad, but let's put a pin on that for now,' Zeb said in a soft but firm voice. 'Aalo, you're figuring out your place in the world. That doesn't just take time, it's actually an ongoing process. We're all doing that in our own ways. You care about the world around you and you're trying to make it better, which is exactly what I'm doing, or at least trying to do. The rest of it, we can work it out.'

'No, we can't,' Aalo said bluntly.

Zeb's face hardened. 'You mean you don't want to.'

'I'm being realistic, Zeb.'

That was when, bang in the middle of their conversation, Zeb got the call that Akbar had been kidnapped.

And just like that, the dream ended. It was as though someone had taken a dull, jagged knife and dragged it slowly and brutally across Aalo's world, tearing it apart in a way that was messy and irrevocable.

A day later, in Mumbai, the memory of that last day in Turkey made Aalo's breathing ragged. She tried to tell Meera the little she knew of what had happened to Akbar, but her breath started coming in short, sharp spurts. Dimly, a corner of Aalo's mind registered she was having a panic attack. She vaguely felt Meera rubbing her back and saying something about breathing. She closed her eyes and saw that horrific image of the journalist being beheaded on camera by masked men claiming to be part of ISIS.

Aalo forced herself to push that image away and it felt like she was literally throwing her whole body against something that was physically present but invisible; a thick, unmoving fear that was so much more real than her attempts to move past it. Blindly reaching for her phone, Aalo held on to it like it was a lifeline. Her grip woke it up, and on the screen was a photo she'd taken of Zeb in a mosque in Istanbul. He was looking at her with those green eyes of his.

'Aalo, I need you to breathe, baby. Breathe.' Meera's voice finally felt closer.

Aalo drew in a long, fractured breath. 'I'm ok now,' she said. Her throat felt like she'd scraped it with sandpaper.

Meera handed her a glass of water which Aalo drank gratefully. 'We don't need to talk about this now,' Meera said, stroking Aalo's hair. 'You should rest.'

Aalo shook her head. 'I won't be able to.'

Meera sighed and said, 'Ok, then let's do this slowly. You and Zeb were talking when Zeb got a call. Who had called him?'

It had been Akbar's brother, who lived in Iraqi Kurdistan. He sounded frantic. Aalo couldn't understand what Zeb and he were saying, but she saw Zeb's face lose colour and his body stiffen. From the way he spoke towards the end of the call, Aalo could tell he was trying to calm Akbar's brother down. She watched Zeb move away from her and go into the bedroom. With every step he took to create a distance between them, Aalo felt like her world was losing the gleam and sparkle that had made life feel so magical these past few weeks. She followed Zeb into the bedroom and sat at the edge of the bed, while he stood by the window, speaking softly on the phone. When the call finally ended, Zeb didn't move for a few moments. Aalo was wondering if she should say something, when he looked at her.

'Akbar seems to have been kidnapped while on assignment, and there are confusing reports about what happened, but he can't be reached any more,' he said in a flat voice. 'I need to go.'

'Where are you going?' Aalo asked. She was afraid she knew the answer.

'First Sulaymaniyah, where Akbar's family is. From there, his brother and I will go to where he was last seen. If he has been kidnapped and one of ISIS's cells is behind it, hopefully, we can find a lead. Maybe they'll ask for a ransom.' His eyes finally focused on Aalo. 'I need to go,' he repeated.

'How will it help for you to go there?' Aalo asked, an edge of panic in her voice. 'What if they get you too?'

He ignored her questions. 'Do you want to stay on here? Your flight's next week right? I've paid for this place till then, so you're welcome to stay.' Zeb walked quickly to the closet and started taking out his clothes.

Aalo watched him like an automaton. 'I don't want to be here alone,' she said finally.

Zeb paused in the middle of folding a shirt and nodded. 'I understand. I'm going to leave tomorrow morning. I'll get your ticket changed to whatever flight the airlines can put you on tomorrow. Is that fine?'

'How are you so calm?'

'It's shock. All of us who work in these areas, we know this sort of thing can happen. It's just when it actually happens, it doesn't feel real.'

Aalo took the shirt out of his hands and stepped into his arms. He held her tightly. She did the same.

'Do you think he's alive?' she asked in a small voice.

'He's a photographer. He can edit videos. ISIS can use skills like that. That's what they've done in the past.' Zeb's voice was flat. When he looked at Aalo, his eyes were anguished. 'It'll kill him to do ISIS work.'

'Maybe he's just gone missing and he'll come back,' Aalo said desperately.

Zeb closed his eyes and laughed sadly. 'That's even more of a fantasy than you and me living happily ever after,' he said.

They spent the night packing their bags and waiting for the morning. Zeb worked incessantly at his computer, sending emails and messages. Aalo dozed off on the sofa at one point. When she woke up, Zeb was gone and her neck hurt. He'd left her a note with the details of her new ticket to Mumbai and money for the taxi fare to the airport.

'And now I'm here,' Aalo said to Meera, when she'd finished her recap. A feeling that was thick and heavy sat on her heart and she didn't want to think about it, so Aalo tried for flippancy. 'Somehow, without warning, the rom-com I'd wandered into in London turned into a Kathryn Bigelow film.' She tried to laugh, but what came out was a broken shard of sound.

Meera's voice was steady. 'Did Zeb say anything about when he'd contact you?'

Aalo shook her head. 'He's not going to contact me. I was breaking up with him when that call came. He told his brother that we were having a fling. I'd heard them talking at the garden party in London, so I was prepared. It wasn't a shock. I just wanted to be the one who did it, you know? I didn't want to be the one who gets broken up with yet again. I thought we'd be mature and remain friends. Or something. I don't know. But the call came and he's gone.'

Meera folded Aalo into a hug and held her close. The two friends sat like that, whispering comforting gibberish to one another, while outside the city made space for a million more heartbreaks. Later, they'd step out in the quiet of the night and walk around their neighbourhood, hurrying past the main roads that were dug up, and avoiding that sloping, winding street that partially collapsed last year. They'd linger in narrow, dimly-lit lanes that were just behind the bars that had been loud and buzzing a few hours ago. They'd walk through the market that Meera refused to shop from because even bananas were expensive there, and which Aalo loved because the vendors always welcomed her to their stalls with a smile. At that twilight hour, the market was empty, but for a few street dogs. You could forget at this time of night how manic these streets were during the day and how impossible the neighbourhood was becoming. Instead, you saw the city at its most tired. And in a strange way, it was comforting to know that even if Mumbai didn't sleep, she did get exhausted, and that it was taking everything she had in her to keep herself from falling apart.

But all that would be much later. In the present, when Aalo came home, after she had emptied herself of words and tears, all she and Meera did was sit holding each other in the quiet sanctuary of their home that, for the first time, seemed haunted by sadness.

The first week back in Mumbai was brutal. There was no news of Zeb, and the jet lag made Aalo sleepy at odd hours, which was made worse by the fact that her sleep was the opposite of restful. She threw herself into work at SWETE, hoping that would exhaust her, and it did, but it was weird to be in an office where everyone was so happy and cheerful, while Aalo was gripped by nervous dread. Nightingale Foundation had given SWETE the grant, which made Aalo the resident hero—though, as Rucha pointed out, getting money from a foreign institution was going to be a whole new labyrinth of horrors. Rucha had submitted a mountain of paperwork to the authorities, and a source in the government had cryptically told her to be patient, which everyone interpreted as an assurance that the accounts would soon be unfrozen. Meanwhile, the Nightingale Foundation was brainstorming with legal experts to figure out how to get the funds to SWETE without jeopardizing the fragile peace Rucha had forged with the investigating agency. Unfortunately, each time Aalo heard the words 'Nightingale Foundation', she remembered Zeb, and that would be enough for her to spiral into anxiety and despair.

Aalo messaged Meera incessantly, asking if she'd seen anything about Akbar or Zeb in the news wires, but all Meera found were cryptic tweets. She discovered a thread on Reddit discussing rumours of an Iraqi journalist getting killed after he'd smuggled himself into Syria for a photography assignment, but she didn't tell Aalo about it. Instead, Meera kept repeating that there was no mention of Zeb on any reliable site or news source. 'He's a British resident, he's reasonably famous. If ISIS had him, they'd let the whole damn world know,' she told Aalo. 'When there's nothing about him, it means he's safe.'

After three days, Aalo found Baz online on Facebook, and asked if he had heard from Zeb. Baz wrote back saying Zeb hadn't been in touch. He also asked for Aalo's phone number and they fixed a time for a chat.

When he did call, Baz had the good sense to keep the pleasantries to a bare minimum. 'Look, I know you're worried, and I realize I'm going to sound a bit like a heartless dick, but it isn't abnormal for Zeb to not be in touch when he's working.'

'Do you know about Akbar?' Aalo asked.

'Yeah, he told me.'

'Zeb said he was going where Akbar was when he disappeared. There are internet posts that Akbar's been killed. My friend Meera found one. It didn't say Akbar, but it was about an unnamed journalist who had gone to Syria on an assignment. Meera didn't show it to me, but she took screenshots. I saw them. And Baz, it sounds like they could be talking about Akbar.'

Baz was silent for a bit. 'Your friend was right to not share it. First of all, it's a Reddit thread, not a newspaper report. An unnamed journalist doesn't mean Akbar and it definitely doesn't mean Zeb. Aalo, my brother is careful, he's thorough, and he doesn't have a death wish. And if ISIS had him, we'd know.'

Aalo wanted to point out that ISIS probably had enough of a death wish to make up for whatever Zeb lacked in that department, but she held herself back. Instead, she asked Baz to let her know if he heard from Zeb.

'I'm sure he'll ping you,' Baz said.

'I doubt it.' Aalo sighed. 'We didn't part on a good note.'

'You guys ended things?' Baz sounded surprised.

'I ended things,' Aalo said baldly. She sighed again. 'It wouldn't have worked, Baz. Long-distance, Hindu-Muslim—relationships are difficult enough, without adding all this drama to the mix. But that doesn't mean I can just slide back into my normal life while he's out there, looking for Akbar in ISIS territory. I keep seeing these horrible images and ...' Aalo stopped herself. 'I'm sorry. I don't mean to ramble. I just want to know he's ok.'

'You seem to be doing all the worrying that comes with being Zeb's girlfriend, but without actually being his girlfriend,' Baz said drily. 'As crap deals go, this is topping the list.'

When Baz called two days later, Aalo was in the middle of a workshop, and she was only able to call him back an hour later, but he didn't pick up. Some time later, he messaged to say he'd call

Aalo in four hours. While waiting for Baz's call, Aalo tried to eat dinner, but ended up throwing up instead. Then, she went over to Rebecca and Fatima's, because Meera was at work and Aalo just couldn't handle being alone in the apartment. Baby Jhalkari—the name had stuck, much to Jo's horror—proved to be the only distraction that really worked for Aalo, until the child started bawling for reasons unspecified. Just when Jhalkari's screams reached fever pitch, Baz called again. Aalo pounced on her phone and locked herself in the bathroom, leaving the crying baby to her mothers.

'Baz! I'm so sorry I missed your call. Is everything ok?'

'Hey, he's fine.' Baz's voice was steady and kind. Aalo felt faint with relief. 'Are you still there?' Baz asked. 'If you are, this is not a dream. Zeb is fine. He called my mother last night. He's in Iraq, not Syria. It's all good. Well, not good, but he's doing fine. He even has internet.'

'Is he in Sulaymaniyah? Is it safe? I looked it up online, it seemed ok,' said Aalo.

'It's Akbar's hometown, so Zeb is like an adopted son there. If that's where he is, he'll probably be pampered silly. But I don't know where he is exactly. I don't ask these things. It's best to get these details when you're talking to the guy in person.'

'Any news of Akbar?'

Baz was quiet for a bit. 'Zeb sent me a message saying some people think they saw Akbar getting shot in the neck, and some people say he was taken away on a stretcher. If that happened, he may not be dead.'

'That's good, right?'

'Let's say it holds out a possibility of hope. Zeb's looking into it.'

'Thank god. Baz, thank you so much for letting me know.'

'I also told him you and I had been talking, by the way.'

'What did he say?'

'He said "cool". Pro-tip for the future: when Zeb says "cool", it means he is feeling the exact opposite.'

'I don't think there is a future, but thanks for the tip.'

'Zeb also told me to not "bother you" with any news about him, but here we are. Listen, I'm probably overstepping, but can I tell you something?'

'Of course. Anything.'

'You're right about the odds not being in favour of you and Zeb, but honestly, that's what makes the Shams family. We don't do easy relationships. You've heard my parents' grand romance. Lara's family wasn't exactly thrilled that their bonnie lass wanted to marry a "Paki", and my father was convinced she was, at heart, racist. In fact, when Zeb introduced Meher to the family, my mother was convinced that either Meher had a deep dark secret that would explode in our faces at a future date or the relationship wouldn't work out. What I'm trying to say is that complicated relationships are a good sign, if one of the people in the relationship is a Shams.'

'Cool.'

Baz burst out laughing, and Aalo grudgingly smiled. 'Look, Baz, I love you for this vote of confidence, but it's next level optimistic to think there might be a relationship when Zeb would prefer I don't know he's alive,' she said.

'I don't think that's what he meant, but that's not even the point. Forget what Zeb's thinking. The real question is whether you want to give it a shot.'

Aalo winced. 'Please don't say "shot". I'm still seeing horrific images of dead men and ISIS.'

They chatted for a little longer and then said their goodbyes. Aalo realized she was breathing easy for the first time since she'd left Istanbul. She sent Meera a message, letting her know Zeb had been in touch with Baz. Then, taking a deep breath, she stepped out of the bathroom, ready to cuddle the bejesus out of Baby Jhalkari.

When Aalo came home, she found Meera making herself a cup of tea.

'You're back early,' Aalo said as she dropped her bag and ran to the bathroom.

Meera shook her head, laughing, and yelled, 'You do know Becks and Fatima have two bathrooms in their apartment?'

'I know. I talked to Baz in one of them while Jhalkari screamed the house down. But home is where the bladder bursts,' Aalo yelled back. Afterwards, she came to the kitchen holding a box of condoms. 'I found this in my bathroom, by the way.' Aalo waggled her eyebrows.

'You're in a good mood,' said Meera, ignoring the condoms. 'How's the kid?'

'That munchkin is so cute, she's edible. And I know it makes no sense, but I think she looks like Rebecca. And,' Aalo took a deep breath, 'Baz called to say Zeb had surfaced. I told you, right?'

'Twice,' Meera said smiling, and gave Aalo a hug. 'Feeling better?'

Aalo nodded.

'Good,' Meera said, pulling out another cup to make Aalo some tea. 'What about Akbar?'

'Baz said Akbar might be injured.'

'That's much better than rumours of him being dead.'

Aalo took the cup of tea from Meera and said, 'I have to apologize to you. I did something terrible. A few days ago, I looked in your phone. You really should have a passcode, by the way. But that's no excuse. I just kept getting the feeling that you weren't telling me something, and I saw that Reddit post you'd saved about the nameless journalist who's been killed on assignment in Syria. I didn't see anything else. Honestly. And I shut the phone. Immediately. But I shouldn't have looked in the first place. I'm so sorry, I don't know why I did that, but I just … the point is, I'm really sorry.'

Meera raised her eyebrows. 'So, that explains the frenzy of misery that you've been in of late,' she said mildly.

'I'm so sorry, Meera. Really, I am.'

'Apology accepted.' Meera sighed and looked at her phone. 'And yes, I guess I should set up a passcode. Sorry for not being a better liar. I didn't show you the post because it was so vague. I figured if there was any truth to it, something would show up in a proper news source.'

Aalo nodded. 'You were right. Are we ok? You really do forgive me, right? I promise I will never ever, ever do something like that again.'

Meera pinned Aalo down with her stare for a moment before saying, 'Yes, we're ok.'

The two of them sat quietly for few moments, before Aalo tentatively gave voice once again to the question that had been on her mind ever since she'd returned to Mumbai. 'So can I ask why Jeet left a box of condoms in my bathroom?'

Meera winced. 'Because he's an optimist? I've no clue.'

'If we really are ok and you have actually forgiven for being an idiot who invaded your privacy, you'll talk to me, right? I know my head's been a mess over all this Zeb stuff, but you know I'm here.'

'Well,' Meera said, cradling the teacup in her hands. 'If you really want to know, I think it took about forty-five minutes for me to go from showing Jeet the sofa to tearing his clothes off.'

Aalo's eyes turned into the size of dinner plates. 'You didn't! Omigod!'

'I did and omigod indeed.'

'I get it though,' Aalo said. 'He's updated his photo on Facebook, and holy hell, the hair is gone, the beard is gone, and now I can honestly say I get where you are coming from. Pun intended. So, are you guys, like, dating now?'

Meera laughed. 'Calm down. There's no dating. There's nothing. I told him the whole sex thing was a one-off, he got furious, and then he got drunk, and I had to sweet-talk a traffic cop into not taking him to the thana. Then, he cut off his hair and quit *The Daily*, and is now, I suspect, in Chennai.'

Aalo looked thoroughly confused. 'You should know that made no sense and that I'm going to need more detail. Also, Jo's coming over with a box of wine.'

'A box of wine?'

'Some dude gave it to her, hoping she'd go out with him. She isn't going out with him, but she said the wine is good.'

'I want Jo's life.'

'Me too.'

The three women starfished in different spots of Aalo and Meera's living room. They'd spent hours talking and working through the box of wine that Jo had brought with her. The lights were switched off and candles flickered in the air conditioning while Arooj Aftab sang with her smoky voice about love and longing. Aalo raised her hand as though she were in class. 'I just want to say, I'm totally Team Meera, obviously, but can we take a moment to just give Jeet a little bit of symphathy?'

'No,' said Jo.

Aalo threw the box of condoms Jeet had left behind at Jo, who caught it neatly. 'At least it's not some fruit-flavoured nonsense,' she said after examining the box.

'Feel free to make good use of it,' Meera said, raising her glass to Jo.

'I'm just saying if Jeet didn't feel slightly intimidated by Meera, it would be a miracle. He must have felt like he was being given a gift and then having it taken away two seconds later,' said Aalo.

'By gift, do you mean the multiple orgasms?' Jo asked.

'Multiple!' Aalo looked at Meera.

Meera blushed. 'He's twenty-eight. He recharges quickly.'

'He's not a phone, Meera,' Aalo teased.

'Phones might take more time to recharge,' Meera replied, still blushing.

'I have one question for both of you,' Jo said, pouring herself another glass of wine. 'Why aren't you calling these men who have turned your pubic areas into leaky faucets?'

'That is a terrible image, even if it is somewhat accurate,' Aalo said, wrinkling her nose.

'I'm serious.' Jo tipped the bottle in her hand in Aalo's direction. 'You know Zeb is back in messaging range. You're a sleep-deprived maniac because you're thinking about what's going on with him. He's said he's in love with you and you're obviously in love with him. Why aren't you writing to him?'

Aalo's shoulders slumped. 'To say what?'

'Hello! Just say hello. Say you'd like to chat next time he's near a phone. Work *something* out.'

'It's not going to work, Jo. You think I haven't thought about it?'

'I think you're only thinking about why it won't work. I don't think you're paying enough attention to what you two do have.

And you,' Jo turned to Meera, 'I was totally with you when you said that it was a bad idea to date Jeet while you both were working at *The Daily*. But he's quit. Now what's the problem?'

Aalo sat up. 'He's quit?'

'I told you he's quit hours ago, Aalo. What's going on in that head of yours?' said Meera.

'I'm just a little slow, ok? Bear with me. So Jeet's left *The Daily*?'

'Yeah, without serving his notice period. Faisal is hopping mad,' Meera said. 'Needless to say, I was not invited to his farewell.'

'Is he joining another paper or a website?'

Meera shrugged. 'No idea.'

Jo threw the box of condoms at Meera, who didn't catch it. 'Can we focus here?' Jo said sternly. 'Why aren't you re-establishing contact? If not for anything else, then for the sex, dammit.'

'Because he's really, really young,' said Meera.

Aalo and Jo groaned. 'Now she's going to tell us all over again how she's old enough to be his mother, even though she isn't,' Aalo said.

Meera shook her head. 'That's not what I mean. He's at a different place in his life. He'll want stuff like marriage and kids. I don't want any of it. I'm at a stage in my life where I want my space. I want my freedom and I don't want to earn it by becoming girlfriend material. I don't want to spend every minute with him. I don't want to clean up after him. And I definitely don't want the job of raising a boyfriend. I want the life that I've worked hard to build and I don't want to compromise. I want to go off reporting and not have to babysit his emotions or libido when I come back. I want to work fourteen-hour days when there's a breaking story and I want to be able to go out drinking with you without having to check in with anyone. But that's not fair to him.' Meera shrugged. 'Also I'm not going to apologize for not wanting the drama that would come from everyone knowing I pounced on a deskie. It's been hard enough to get people to look past the whole ex-wife-of-Kapil thing.'

They were all quiet for a moment. It was Jo who broke the silence. 'Ladies, I'm always on your side, but I have to tell you—I'm seeing a lot of ego here. Which is not a bad thing, from where I'm standing. But the fact is, either the two of you are telepathic, or you're making some massive assumptions about these men and I'm not sure that's fair. I'm with you on the underlying points though. Relationships do reduce women to plus-ones and men should grovel.'

'It's not about grovelling, Jo. It's about being realistic,' Aalo said quietly.

15

Ultimately, it took a twenty-one-year-old to convince Sagar that his best interests lay in toeing the line that Meera had drawn. More specifically, it took the threat of a twenty-one-year-old filing a complaint about sexual harassment in the workplace that gave Sagar pause. The complaint hadn't been formalized, but that a situation had escalated to the point where someone was ready to speak up against Sagar was enough to start whispers in corridors. There was speculation about how 'this sort of behaviour' turned people into pariahs and hurt organizations.

That was when the wheels started turning—mostly because Meera and Aishwarya, the two senior-most women in *The Daily*'s pyramid, made it clear that they were in no mood to be either diplomatic or quiet. Upon Meera's insistence, Navin sat down with Aishwarya to apologize for Sagar's behaviour, even while maintaining the 'girl' had perhaps misunderstood Sagar's 'warm personality'. The gossip was that Aishwarya had snorted loudly in Navin's face in response. Half of *The Daily* argued that this was disrespectful on Aishwarya's part. The other half pointed out she could only afford to snub Navin because she headed marketing and didn't actually have to report to him.

At the next edit meeting, Meera bluntly refused to attach any of the women in her team to stories that Navin assigned to Sagar. 'All of you who think this is happening because the political team is being headed by a woman, you're probably right. The fact that I refuse to expose my team to harassment and abuse has everything to do with me being a woman, but in an ideal world, a good boss would protect their team no matter what their gender,' she said and looked straight at Navin. She tipped her head to indicate she'd had her say. Before the next marketing event, Aishwarya sent out a 'request' that if Navin wanted to include Sagar in the guest list, he had to also assign a male chaperone who would ensure Sagar 'maintained decorum'.

For a while, the mood in the newsroom was tense, but little by little, everyone got used to Sagar being aggressively sidelined. When he came to the office, he sat in meetings and glared at Meera, who ignored him completely. She ran the political bureau as though it didn't have Sagar in it, and slowly, his silences started to feel more petulant than threatening. It became clear to everyone that for all the back-slapping camaraderie that Navin showed Sagar, when Meera had made him choose between Sagar and his own reputation as *The Daily*'s editor-in-chief, Navin chose himself, and grudgingly sided with Meera. The crowds of people who would flock around Sagar when he sat at the cafeteria thinned steadily.

The days and weeks settled into a pattern slowly but inexorably. Meera got used to not seeing Jeet at the desk that she still considered his. She made time to go out and speak to people, looking for stories she could report. While commuting, she listened to Jeet's songs on repeat, and then, after a couple of weeks, she asked Fatima to recommend some new music. Instead of a playlist of Jeet's songs, his music became part of a longer, eclectic playlist. Faisal started coming to Meera's cabin rather than her going to his, and Meera cut down on the number of chai breaks she took. There was still at least one every day. The chai break had now become a tradition for the Mumbai bureau, and the chosen hour for what Faisal called 'the OG' came to be 4.30 p.m. Other bureaus in the country nicknamed it 'the exodus' because the chances of getting through to anyone on Mumbai's reporting, photo or desk sections at 4.30 p.m. was practically zero.

Meera started keeping a record of which political stories Navin dropped, which got prime positioning, and which stories were buried in back pages.

'Do you remember why you became a journalist?' Faisal asked Meera one day. 'I thought I was going to speak truth to power, grand crap like that.'

'You do, though,' Meera said with a grateful smile. 'It's why the story on that boarding school for tribal kids is getting a mention on page one. Left to my powers of persuading Navin, it would have probably been buried.'

Faisal made a disgusted face. 'I've barely got it on the page. One seventy-five-word snippet, that's all I could do. Dude, it's a terrifying story. You've got proof that a teacher is a serial child rapist, two victims have killed themselves and named him in their suicide notes, and the guy still holds on to his job. The government is basically using taxpayers' money to pay a paedophile a salary. And Navin doesn't think it's page-one-worthy.'

'It doesn't concern "people like us",' Meera said, imitating Navin.

'And it's depressing, don't forget,' Faisal added. 'Why can't you find happy stories, Meera?' he said sarcastically.

'Which is why Sagar's story about a remote village getting electricity after seventy-five years almost got four whole columns.'

'Anchor slot for electricity, snippet for raped tribal girls.' Faisal stabbed the printout of the next day's page one layout with his pen. 'I wonder if the people who pick up the paper even realize how much we fight to make the front page.'

Meera laughed and said, 'Remember what Karthik used to say? For us, the newspaper is about news. For everyone else, its greatest utility is that it makes a great container for bhel and samosas. So, write and edit those headlines such that the guy reaching for his next bite wants to read the whole article.'

What didn't make it to the newspapers, but felt bigger than headline news to Aalo, was the fact that the CBI and ED cleared Rucha's name, which meant the SWETE bank accounts were finally unfrozen. The call from Rucha's lawyer came on one of those unusual days when everyone was at the office and no one was at a workshop, which meant they could all celebrate at the chai-shop, where a happy Pappu declared all chais were on the house. 'Consider it my contribution to Sweetie,' he said to Rucha, when she insisted on paying. Hema and a couple of volunteers got pakodas, Bombay sandwiches and idli with spicy chutney. It was a proper party, and the first time that Aalo found herself laughing from her heart since she'd returned from Istanbul.

Meanwhile, Rucha had started taking Aalo with her to meetings with donors and potential sponsors. This meant longer working hours for Aalo, which she embraced with gusto because it meant less time and energy to refresh Zeb's Instagram feed, or go through their old conversations, or sit with the whimpering disappointment of knowing he'd returned to London but hadn't contacted her. Determined to focus on work, Aalo signed up for an online course on fundraising, which turned out to be mostly dull, but kept her up at night and gave her some understanding of the kind of strategies expected from an organization like SWETE.

'How do you decide on the amount of money you're asking for from these guys?' Aalo asked Rucha one day when they were coming out of a meeting.

'You can sit with me for one of these budget things. Bores the pants off me, but basically, there's a template that we've got thanks to the BMC proposal, and we tweak that around.'

'Have you thought about asking for more money? Because BMC's pockets and BKC's pockets are not equally deep,' Aalo said, as their cab made its way out of a corporate park in Bandra Kurla Complex.

'How much more do you think we can ask BKC?'

Aalo shrugged. 'Maybe around double.'

Rucha raised her eyebrows. 'You do remember we're a not-for-profit, right?'

'It's just that in some places, I think they'll take you more seriously if you're asking for a bigger number. Aside from the impression it makes, a small amount means you're forced to run after junior executives, who can't really take any decision anyway.'

'Good point,' Rucha agreed. 'Though I think the BMC's pockets may be deeper than BKC's, but it's got less of a conscience and it doesn't need to do charity to make itself look good the way corporates do. Anyway, sit with me on the budget tomorrow. Let's see what we can do.'

One morning, Aalo came to the SWETE office to find it uncharacteristically quiet and empty. Rucha was sitting on a table and talking to Hema, who looked nonplussed. When she saw Aalo, Rucha waved at her to join the conversation.

'Sit,' Rucha said to Aalo. 'There's something I want to talk to you about. That's why I told the others to come in late today. I was just talking about this with Hema. I'm planning to distance myself from SWETE.'

'What?' Aalo squawked. 'That's a terrible idea!' Rucha glared at her and Aalo felt herself shrinking. 'I mean, why?' she asked weakly.

Rucha sighed. 'We can't have the work we do getting disrupted because I won't sit on my hands while this country's politicians go around behaving like nitwits. I'm not saying I'm going to retire. Quite to the contrary, actually. I have many plans, but as far as SWETE is concerned, I'm worried I might be a bit of a liability.'

'I don't think anyone can imagine SWETE without you,' Hema said.

'That's just because I've been running it forever. That's another excellent reason for me to step back. It's about time SWETE got a fresh perspective, and I think you're the person to take charge,' Rucha said to Hema, who shook her head. 'Don't be difficult, Hema. You know you're perfect for this job. So, do me a favour and take over, so that I'm free to go be the angry old lady shaking a fist at the clouds.'

Rucha turned to Aalo. 'As for you, I hear you're not afraid of spreadsheets?' Aalo blinked at Rucha, who smiled and continued, 'Your powers of persuasion are impressive, and you've got a good head for numbers. You read the room well, and foreigners love you. That Markham woman from Nightingale Foundation won't stop gushing about you each time we speak. Also, you seem to have visas for every damn country in the world, which means you can represent SWETE at conferences at the drop of a hat. Basically, I'm telling you to focus on the fundraising. You're better at it than you are at the workshops anyway.'

'Come on! Her workshops are good,' Hema protested.

'Maybe, but her fundraising is better,' Rucha countered. 'Obviously, I won't force you if you want to stay on as an educator, but I really think fundraising is a better fit for you,' she told Aalo. 'What do you think?'

Aalo felt her head spin a little. 'I actually wanted to suggest exactly this to you, but I didn't know how to bring it up.'

Rucha frowned. 'So, you just sat around and hoped I was going to pick that up with what? Telepathy? Next time, bring it up. On your own. By the way, did you meet someone called Henry Whitley during your London trip?'

'I think he's one of the guys on Nightingale Foundation's board. I feel like he was at their office when I made the condensed presentation you'd given me.'

Rucha nodded. 'Sounds likely. His secretary sent me an email asking for your number. I wouldn't be surprised if they offered you a job of some sort. The last time I spoke to Philippa Markham, she asked me a lot of questions about you and mentioned in passing that they're looking to pay a little more attention to India.'

'Wow.' Now Aalo's head was really spinning.

'I might be wrong, of course,' Rucha said with a shrug. 'But if they do offer you a job, figure out the role and the pay in detail. Ask what allowances they will offer, that sort of thing. And don't say yes right away.'

'You seem very sure I'll say yes eventually.'

'You went to London for four days and came back almost a month later,' Rucha said drily. 'It doesn't take a genius to figure out you might be interested in a job that keeps you in London.' Aalo coloured and looked down when Rucha shot a questioning stare at her. 'You've been good for SWETE, and I would like to believe that you and SWETE can grow together,' Rucha said, her voice gentler this time. 'Promise me you'll keep that in mind when you're listening to this Whitley's offer?'

Aalo nodded. There was a lot that she needed to discuss with the girls at their next dinner, she thought to herself, as she sent out a message on the group, telling Rebecca to start planning the menu for the next Not-So-Famous Five dinner, pronto.

On her way back home, in the cab, Aalo couldn't keep herself from checking whether Zeb had posted on Instagram. Ever since he'd come back online, his feed was devoted to reposting photos by and of Akbar. At least once a day, he put out an appeal for information on Akbar's whereabouts. Now and then, he put up photos from Istanbul, which made Aalo wonder if he had returned to London at all. Twice, Aalo had been sure he'd uploaded a photo that he'd taken when she was with him, but then she forced herself to dismiss that thought.

'How crazy is it for me to think he's putting up a photo that I'll recognize in the hope that I'll write to him?' Aalo had asked Rebecca when one such photo popped up on his feed the previous week.

'I hate to sound brutal, but there are easier ways of getting in touch. Like using the phone,' Rebecca had replied bluntly.

As the taxi made its way to Bandra, Aalo looked at Zeb's photos. She couldn't keep herself from imagining what would happen if her paths crossed with Zeb at a dinner or a cafe in London. Did they have a better shot if this wasn't a long-distance relationship? Could Aalo hack it in London?

A horn blared loudly at a traffic signal and Aalo wondered what her girlfriends would have to say about this Whitley development.

Before the grand dinner that Rebecca had planned for the coming week, there was a minor ordeal that awaited Aalo in the form of her parents, who suddenly announced they were going to spend a night with their daughter in Mumbai before heading to their holiday home in Coonoor. Aalo made a dinner reservation at a fancy restaurant in Lower Parel, and booked a car and driver for the day. She told Meera that if she needed help, she'd message.

'I'm literally five minutes away from the restaurant,' Meera assured Aalo. 'Unless an election or war is declared tonight, which seems unlikely. So far.'

As it turned out, dinner was uneventful. The food was good. Her parents were delighted to hear about Rucha's offer to join SWETE's fundraising team. Aalo didn't mention the possibility of a job in London. Somehow, telling her parents about it felt like jinxing her chances. After dinner, they got in the hired car, and Aalo's father, with his atrocious Hindi, struck up a conversation with the driver. The two of them reminisced about how wonderful Mumbai was in the 1990s. Later, Aalo would be struck by the irony of how she'd missed the point at which their conversation turned to the 1993 bombings, because she was distracted by the photographs of a car bomb explosion taken by a photographer who worked for Cameraderie. She was staring with horrified fascination at the photograph, when the phrase 'those Muslims' reached her ear. She looked up from her phone to realize her father and the driver were nodding in agreement while cursing 'those Muslims' for 'destroying' the city in 1993, and because apparently all Indian Muslims supported the Pakistani cricket team.

'If they want to live in India, they should support the Indian cricket team,' pronounced the driver. 'You tell me what's wrong in what I'm saying?'

'Not a thing,' said her father, sitting in the front seat.

'And if they like Pakistan so much, they should just go there, na?' the driver said.

Aalo heard her father laugh. It was a warm, joyous sound that was completely at odds with the toxic conversation. While her mother hissed to her father, telling him in Bengali to stop talking nonsense, Aalo noticed the windshield of the car had a decal of a tiger on it.

'You like the Shiv Sena, sir?' Aalo asked the driver.

He looked at her through the rearview mirror and said, 'Yes, madam.'

'I was just wondering because of that sticker on your windshield,' she said with a smile.

'I've been voting for them since I attended my first rally and heard Balasaheb,' the driver said. 'He was a great leader.'

Aalo made a non-committal noise and wrote a message to the Not-So-Famous Five group.

> —My Bengali father and my Shiv Sainik cabbie are cheering to send Muslims to Pakistan, while I'm in the backseat, breaking my heart over a man named Aurangzeb.

Once they reached home, Aalo's parents got into an argument in the lift that started with her mother asking her father why he had to go around talking of 'such things'. Her father responded with the claim that he was just being friendly with the driver and that Aalo's mother was snooty. The back and forth continued inside the apartment, and at one point, Aalo abruptly said to her father, 'Baba, do you remember the chat you had with me, about how I was free to marry anybody as long as he wasn't a Muslim?'

Her father stilled. 'I don't remember saying that exactly,' he said.

'I do.' Aalo considered him for a moment. 'Are you saying you don't feel that way anymore?'

'Aalo,' her mother interrupted. 'Is there a reason we're having this conversation?'

'Well, he was just having a hearty laugh at the idea of sending Muslims to Pakistan, so that seems like a good reason to have this conversation,' Aalo replied.

'That was a hypothetical conversation,' her father said.

They were all quiet for a moment. Aalo poured herself a glass of water. 'So, coming back to what I asked. How would you react if I told you I wanted to marry a Muslim?'

'Do you?' her father asked.

Aalo shrugged. 'We're just having a hypothetical conversation, right?'

Her father stared at her for a moment and then slowly sat down. 'He'll never fit in. At every point, there will be a difference. He'll always be the outsider, and as long as there is Pakistan, he will always be the enemy. It sounds bad, but it's true.'

Aalo saw her father jut his chin out and wondered if she looked like that when she felt belligerent. 'It's only true because you think this way,' she said to him. 'Because you're looking for the differences.'

'I'm not looking for them. They're already there.'

'There are differences everywhere. There are differences between you and Ma, but you don't focus on them, so they don't end up mattering. What would you do if I married a Muslim, Baba? Disown me? Never talk to me again? Cut me out of your will? What exactly will you do?'

'I'll be heartbroken,' her father replied. 'And I'll be terrified because you won't be safe. He'll have his community, his people, but you'll have nobody. You'll end up belonging nowhere.'

'You should know that what you're saying right now isn't really making feel like I belong in the first place,' Aalo said quietly.

She kissed her mother good night and made her way to her room, saying she had to finish work for the online course she was doing. She didn't look at her phone until she'd come out of the bathroom, after brushing her teeth and washing her face. There was a flurry of messages from Rebecca, Jo and Fatima empathizing with Aalo. Beyond her locked door, she could hear

Meera's voice—she must have left the office as soon as Aalo sent that message about the driver and her father. Now, Meera was sitting outside and calming her father, making him laugh, listening patiently to his lectures, and gently schooling him every now and then. Aalo settled into bed and said a prayer of thanks for her family of choice.

About an hour later, Aalo's parents were settled for the night in Meera's room, and Meera was making herself comfortable for the night on the sofa. That was when Fatima messaged a link to a video.

> —I thought I'd send it to you so that it didn't take you by surprise. I had nothing to do with it. Sarfaraz sent it to me. Warning: contains Jeet. He's very funny.

The YouTube video was an interview with the singer Sarfaraz Aziz, who had a new song called 'Dreaming'. He'd written the lyrics and Jeet had composed the music. In the interview, Sarfaraz said he'd met Jeet at a common friend's birthday party and they'd hit it off immediately. Meera listened to Sarfaraz talk and wondered where the video had been shot. Was Jeet still in Mumbai?

'Jeet writes these incredible melodies, and I just knew that I wanted something like that for my lyrics,' Sarfaraz told the interviewer. A clip of the song followed, and Meera recognized the mellow lilt she'd heard in other compositions that Jeet had shared with her. When the interviewer returned on camera, Jeet was sitting next to Sarfaraz. His hair was still short, but not as close-cropped as when Meera had seen him last, and he was clean-shaven. He kept his head down and Sarfaraz did most of the talking, which made Meera wonder what Fatima had found so amusing. At one point, the interviewer asked Sarfaraz, 'When you wrote "Dreaming", did you get the feeling that it was special?'

'Honestly, I was a little scared,' Sarfaraz said with a laugh. 'After we finished the song, I'd sung it at a couple of small house concerts and people seemed to like it. But I was very scared by all the anger I'd poured into my lyrics. I didn't want anyone calling me anti-national. That's something I've been scared of since the beginning. I live with my parents, they're old, and I didn't want to get into any trouble. If it hadn't been for Fatima Mirza, "Dreaming" would probably have disappeared. But she heard me sing, and she was determined to make a video, to send it around. She kept telling me, "Sarfaraz, how can you write a song like this and be a scaredy-cat?"' He laughed again. 'By the time we got down to making the video, it didn't feel terrifying anymore. When we're performing it, it is incredibly empowering. I sing it as loud as I can, and hearing everyone singing it with me is just the best high.'

'What about you?' the interviewer said to Jeet. 'Did you feel the same way when you started working on "Dreaming"? It sounds slow and easy-going, but, like Sarfaraz said, it's also pretty angry.'

Jeet looked confused. 'I'm not sure I get the question,' he said.

'Did you start off scared by what Sarfaraz had written?'

'I don't think I feel that way about music,' Jeet replied. 'When he shared the lyrics, I felt like I knew the song. It felt like magnets coming together.' He shrugged. 'I don't think of fear when I think of music.'

Sarfaraz grinned. 'But do you feel that way about something else?'

'Terrified but likely to love it?' Jeet asked.

Sarfaraz nodded.

'Sure,' Jeet replied. 'The super-spicy chilli sauce that comes with momos, Korean horror films.' He looked up to stare straight into the camera. 'Nipple clamps.'

Meera almost dropped the phone, while the interviewer and Sarfaraz could be heard laughing uproariously. When she gathered herself and the phone, Sarfaraz was saying he dreamt of peace and harmony in India.

'And you, Jeet?' the interviewer asked. 'What's your dream?'

With a completely straight face, Jeet replied, 'World peace would be nice, but in terms of achievable, personal dreams, I'm holding out for a sugar mama. If anyone out there needs a boy toy who isn't good at much, beyond occasionally making music and lemon rice, hit me up.'

The video ended abruptly, and Meera switched her phone off. Lying on the sofa that had been Jeet's for two weeks, she let herself imagine for a moment how snug a fit it would have been if he'd been here now, pressed against her back, his arms holding her in place. Then Meera turned her phone back on and started scrolling through the Explore page of Instagram.

The Not-So-Famous Five were divided on whether it had been a genius or disastrous move gifting four cookbooks to Rebecca for her birthday, because the dinner spread was now turning into a weapon of mass destruction. It felt wrong to complain that there was too much good food, but that's exactly what Meera did, not just the night they met, but also the next day, when a hangover was added to the mix.

'Don't complain,' Aalo growled. 'You don't have to go into work till noon. I have to deal with a morning meeting with Rucha in thirty minutes.'

'I'm too old for these wild nights,' Meera groaned.

'Mad wild,' Aalo said. 'Five women, one baby and fruit punch.'

'Bloody Jo. My head feels the punch alright. The fruit? Not so much.' Meera popped two Disprins in water and waited for them to dissolve. 'What the hell did she put in that thing?'

'So delicious then, so hangover now,' said Aalo, staring at her cup of tea like she wanted to drown in it.

They'd started the dinner with vows of wrapping up early-ish, and then stayed up till 2 a.m. discussing, among other things, Jeet and Sarfaraz's song, and Aalo's meeting with Whitley.

'It's a beautiful song and it's getting a lot of views,' Fatima said. 'Sarfaraz—who might be in love with your boy, by the way—told me Jeet is working on an EP. Six tracks. Apparently, they're good, which I can believe. But it's hilarious how Jeet hasn't called me once in all this time.'

'Good for Sarfaraz and Jeet, I guess. I can't believe how bone-headed Jeet is though. Why would he not call you?' said Meera.

'Maybe because I'm not a producer.'

'Yeah, but you know producers,' Meera pointed out. 'You could have given him some advice, introduced him to some people. It's just incredible to me that he wouldn't take you up on that.'

Fatima shrugged. 'Maybe he knows who he wants to work with. Maybe he wants to try doing it on his own.' Meera rolled her eyes. 'To give credit where credit is due, he isn't doing too badly. Dominic also mentioned Jeet as one of the people they were considering for the web series that they're doing with some people in LA,' said Fatima.

'Who's Dominic now?' Aalo asked.

'He's a sound engineer. Very well respected. Works with some of the best composers in the country.'

Rebecca and Aalo enthusiastically suggested Meera send Jeet a message, congratulating him on the song with Sarfaraz.

'It's only polite,' Rebecca argued. 'I mean, if you chanced upon a song I'd written, you'd send me a message of congratulations, right?'

'Maybe the song is for you! His version of an olive branch,' Aalo said.

Meera, however, was unshakeable in her conviction that she was absolutely not interested in rekindling anything even close to a romance. 'I'm not invested in the drama. Just let me be the crazy cat lady,' she said.

'You don't have cats,' Jo pointed out pedantically. 'You don't even want pets.'

At which point, the only thing to do was to throw a cushion at Jo. The conversation turned to Aalo, who had, in fact, been offered a job by Whitley, just as Rucha had predicted. The good part was that the job was in London, with the Nightingale Foundation, and Whitley seemed quite confident that getting a work visa wouldn't be a challenge. The bad part was that the role was very vague and the pay was peanuts. As far as Meera and Fatima were concerned, the bad pay packet was a dealbreaker.

'How will you ever survive on this, considering the cost of living in London?' Fatima asked.

'Even if you don't have to pay rent, this is an absurdly low amount,' Meera agreed.

'And I would have to pay rent,' said Aalo. 'My father, sadly, has not bought property in London, in my name. I enjoy that privilege only in Mumbai.'

'Well, obviously the long game is that you stay with Zeb,' Rebecca said. When everyone in the room groaned, Rebecca said, 'What? How am I the only one saying this!'

'Honestly, Becks, I do think that ship has sailed,' said Aalo.

'To be fair, when you've spent forty-five minutes discussing a job offer that is vague as fuck, you're hoping that the ship will do a reverse if you land up in London. Otherwise, this wouldn't be something you'd consider,' Jo said.

Eventually, Aalo said, 'No, boss, I can't go to London. Aside from everything else, I can't abandon SWETE.'

'Maybe you don't need to,' Meera said. 'Couldn't you do both? Tell these guys that you'll continue working for SWETE, and that you'll work with them as a consultant. Especially when they're offering you so little money, they should be fine with you having another job.'

'Probably, but that doesn't actually solve the money issue.' Aalo sighed and stretched her legs. 'I mean, SWETE's salary isn't going to add up to much in London.'

Fatima perked up. 'Maybe you can share a place with Kekoo?' she suggested.

'You know, that could be workable,' Aalo said. 'I might need my dad to help me out a bit in the beginning, but that could work.'

'Your father will jump at the idea of his beloved daughter in his beloved London,' Meera said, grinning. 'Who knows? Maybe he'll sell the Mumbai flat to get you a place in London.'

'No, no. We won't let that happen. I solemnly swear you will not be plunged into house-hunting hell,' Aalo told her.

Everyone laughed, and Meera wryly pointed out that if there was one good thing to be said about being the political editor at *The Daily*, it was that she could afford rent in Mumbai. Later, when Aalo and Meera were going home, they got stuck in a traffic jam on Hill Road even though it was almost 2.30 a.m.

'These are the times when I wish Mumbai would change its tagline to being the city that *does* sleep,' Aalo grumbled, while every vehicle around them honked grumpily.

'I'm just glad I didn't take the car,' Meera said with a sigh, and cast a sympathetic glance at their cabbie, who switched off the engine and settled down to wait for the traffic to un-congeal. Beside her, Aalo tried to find an angle that would let her stretch her legs.

'Don't laugh,' Aalo told Meera. 'Everything in this country is built for people your size.'

'So go to London and enjoy leg space,' Meera teased.

Aalo stuck her tongue out at her.

Meera wondered if this was the right time to bring up a serious topic, and then decided she might as well. 'I thought you'd be jumping on the first flight when the job in London came through, but you're seeming a little circumspect,' she said. 'Having second thoughts?'

'And third, and fourth, and fifth,' Aalo admitted easily. 'At some point in life, I'm going to have to build a habit of thinking about things *before* I do them. When Whitley said Nightingale might have a job for me, I thought, "Perfect. This is a great excuse to be in the same city as Zeb and stalk my way back into his life." Except, that's not exactly how life works, is it? Now, reality is doing its bitey thing.'

'I think it'll be good for you. I don't mean because Zeb is there. I think London will be good for you. It sounds like one of those cities that can become familiar, bring out in you qualities you didn't realize you possessed.'

Aalo sighed. 'Maybe. I don't know. The more I think about it, the less convinced I am. I've never really lived on my own before.'

'Another excellent reason to take the job. What better place to have your big-city adventures than London?'

'Can't you become *The Daily*'s foreign correspondent or something and come with me? It would be a perfect way to put all this nonsense with Jeet behind you … and just think how much fun we'd have in London together!'

Meera, who had been sitting with her legs tucked under her, stretched one leg out to poke Aalo with her toe. 'I'm not your cabin baggage that I'll come everywhere with you. London is your adventure. You should go for it.'

'While the rest of you have food comas thanks to Becks's cooking experiments and watch Baby Jhalkari grow up and forget about me,' Aalo said, only half-joking.

'We're a sisterhood, Aalo. It'll take more than the distance of a continent to break us up.' Meera poked Aalo again. 'Also, I have a confession.'

Aalo raised her eyebrows.

'I think I want my own place. Which is not to say I don't love living with you, but it was really nice to have the apartment to myself when you were away.'

'Damn,' Aalo breathed softly. 'That hurts a little bit.'

'Don't say that,' Meera said, reaching out to hold Aalo's hand. 'It's not about you at all. It's me. I'm just in a different place now, and you know as well as I do that you and I are a lot more than just flatmates.'

Aalo nodded, but her face looked sad.

Meera squeezed Aalo's hand. 'I don't want to hold you back,' she said softly.

'I don't want to hold you back either,' Aalo replied.

In another city, or at another time, this may have been when two friends shed a tear and shared a tender, sentimental moment. Mumbai, however, had little patience for such things. A small and extremely irate woman banged on the windshield of their cab with an umbrella and yelled at the driver to move. It turned out he'd nodded off to sleep, and the traffic had loosened while Aalo and Meera had been talking.

With shrieks of 'Sleep in your bed, you bleddy fool' ringing in their ears, Aalo and Meera's cabbie made the quickest getaway he could. As the taxi bounced its way towards their home, Meera's thoughts wandered back to when Kapil had frozen her out of their joint bank accounts and Meera's parents had refused to let her live with them, insisting she return to Kapil who had moved out to live with his then mistress (now, wife). Without Aalo welcoming her into the flat they made their home, Meera would have had nowhere to go, but she hadn't stayed on as Aalo's roommate because she was destitute. If Meera had wanted to, she could have found her own place within months, thanks to the salary that Sagar had negotiated for her back when he didn't hate her guts. But Meera and Aalo enjoyed having one another around. Maybe they needed each other to heal from the wounds they were carrying at the time.

The next day at work, Meera found herself remembering how Jeet had sneered at her and Aalo living together. 'Maybe she's your security blanket or maybe you're hers,' he'd said. The question of whether she was holding Aalo back buzzed around Meera's mind as she made her way through the workday, glugging mug after mug of coffee. In the afternoon, just as Meera was making a mental note to chat with Aalo's father about renting the flat on her own if Aalo took the job in London, Prateek, who ran *The Daily*'s sales department, knocked on Meera's cabin door.

'May I disturb you for a moment?' Everything about Prateek was slick and oily. It was all Meera could do to contain a shudder of distaste.

'Of course.' She gestured towards the chair opposite her. 'Tell me how I can help you.'

'So you know *The Daily* Hive is next week.'

The Hive was the newspaper's attempt at joining the event bandwagon. The three-day-long 'festival of ideas' had been started four years ago. For obscenely expensive tickets, you could listen to some famous and infamous people talk at *The Daily* Hive, which was, contrary to its title, an annual affair. If you were suitably swish, you could even be invited to the lavish parties that were thrown in the evening.

'We've got confirmation from the chief minister's office that he'll attend the closing night party,' Meera said. 'Has it not come to you formally?'

'That's done. Thank you for your help on that. No, actually, we have a bit of a delicate situation.' Prateek put a sheet of paper on her desk gingerly. 'There are five invitees whose visas have been rejected, it seems. Well, two have been rejected, and the rest are "delayed", according to consular officials.'

Meera looked at the list and schooled her face to not react. One of the names was Zeb Shams.

'We're not quite sure what's happened, why their applications were rejected or delayed,' Prateek said.

Meera looked up. 'Four out of five are Muslims who work in regions known as hotbeds of Islamic terror. The fifth sounds like he's Sikh and from Canada. You do know that we're not on the best terms with Canada right now?'

Prateek looked flustered. 'Look, I'm not involved in selecting the speakers. This isn't really my department, we have an event management group that puts all this stuff together for us, but they're saying they're stuck. So, I was just wondering if there was some way to figure this out. It's very late in the day to get people to replace these guys. All of them have massive social media followings. We'll go viral for all the wrong reasons if we announce this late that they're not coming.'

'Why isn't Delhi doing this?' Meera asked. 'It's not like Maharashtra has anything to do with giving visas.'

'I've spoken to the Delhi team, and they said they'll try, but they didn't seem very helpful, honestly. Aishwarya suggested I ask you.'

Meera nodded and took the list. 'I'll see if there's anything I can do. Give me till tomorrow?'

After thanking her profusely, Prateek left. Meera stared at the list and wondered if she should tell Aalo. Zeb was planning to come to India, for an event being organized by *The Daily*? That seemed like too much of a coincidence. Before talking to Aalo, Meera decided to send Zeb a message saying she'd just found his name in the list of speakers at *The Daily* Hive. Zeb didn't reply. He called her within fifteen seconds of her message getting two ticks.

'Hey Zeb.'

'Hi, how are you?'

'I'm well.' Meera decided to dispense with pleasantries. 'Is it a coincidence that you're part of The Hive? It's organized by the newspaper I work with,' she said.

'A coincidence?' Zeb burst out laughing, but there wasn't much joy in that sound. 'My agent thinks I'm a lunatic because I hounded him to get me any kind of gig that would be a credible excuse to go to India.'

'And why would you want an excuse to come to India?'

'I was hoping to surprise Aalo.'

Meera didn't say anything.

'Meera? You there?'

'Yes, I'm here.'

'Look, this is all a bit odd. I'm not sure how much Aalo's told you, but we didn't finish things well, and I honestly don't know if she wants to see me or have anything to do with me. I don't want to show up and have her slam the door on me or something like that.' He paused. Meera wondered if this was a good time to point out that Aalo had been frantic enough to message his twin brother, but decided against it. 'When my agent said he could get me a speaking gig at this Hive thing, I just thought it was like a sign, you know?'

'A sign?'

She heard Zeb sigh. 'This sounds idiotic.'

'I'm just trying to understand what's going on here,' Meera said, her voice cool and dispassionate. Zeb was quiet. 'There are easier ways to get in touch than flying down to India for a conference,' she added.

'Yes, well, holiday flings aren't supposed to get in touch after the holiday is over, are they?'

'In your experience, do holiday flings practically stalk your brother to find out if you're alive?' There, she finally said it.

'I'm not particularly experienced in the ways of holiday flings, to be honest, but I sort of assumed that had more to do with the possibility of me being kidnapped or killed than anything, well, romantic.'

'This really is a conversation you should be having with Aalo, instead of me.'

'Agreed. That's why I snapped up this chance to come to India. Also, I'll admit it, there's the benefit of me being able to save face and pretend like I flew down for the event if she pulls an Istanbul on me and tells me to fuck off.'

'She did not tell you to fuck off.'

'Effectively, not literally.'

There was silence for a moment. Meera said finally, 'So the reason I found out you were coming is that there's some trouble with your visa application. In that, the Government of India is sitting on it, which usually means they won't clear it. Aside from the obvious stuff, like the name on your passport is Aurangzeb and you've spent a lot of time in ISIS territory, is there anything else that could raise a red flag?'

'Wait, what do you have to do with the visa?' Zeb asked, confused.

'I'm supposed to pull some strings to get you the visa. Now, any other red flags?'

'Wow. You can do that? You're a good woman to know. I don't suppose India cares that my dad is originally from Iran? My mother's Kashmiri. Well, was. She's been a British citizen for years now.'

'Is she in touch with her family?'

'Not at all.'

'Have you been to Kashmir?'

'Never.'

'You should go. You should also be able to get one of those OCI cards.'

'Let's not push my luck. Just get me the visa to come to Mumbai for now.'

Kapil Patil was on his way to a meeting in New Delhi's North Block when his personal phone beeped loudly. A very select few had this number and they knew not to use it unless it was urgent. 'Please go on ahead,' Kapil told the rest of his colleagues. 'I'll just join you.' He took out his phone to find a message from Meera.

—I'm writing to call in a favour. There's a visa application filed by a photographer named Aurangzeb Shams. It's got stuck, probably because his mother's Kashmiri and his work has him travelling in and out of ISIS territory. He is a Muslim. He is not a terrorist. Can I rely upon you to get this pushed through so that he can come to India?

—Visas are not state matter.

—I know. I also know a phone call from you will get this done.

—Do you realize how much of a risk this could be? Can you actually vouch for him and say he's safe given what you've just told me about him?

—Yes.

—If he does anything or is involved in anything, it could ruin my career.

—He isn't and it won't.

—I'll think about it.

—Kapil, you owe me.

Meera finally told Aalo that Zeb was going to be speaking at *The Daily* Hive two days before the event. It took a few moments for the meaning of Meera's words to sink in.

'He's in India?' she asked Meera. 'Zeb. You're saying, Zeb is in India?'

'Not yet, but he should be soon. Unless he gets deplaned on the way or detained at the airport for being named Aurangzeb.'

'Wow. Why is he part of The Hive?'

'He's on a panel about reporting from conflict zones. It should actually be really good. Before that, in the morning, he'll be showing his latest photographs in a solo presentation.' Meera waited for a moment and then said, 'Do you want to come as my plus-one?'

Aalo looked doubtful. 'I'm not sure I should. What if he doesn't want to see me?'

'Do you want to see him?'

'Desperately.'

'So come.'

Aalo didn't say anything. Meera pressed her lips shut to keep herself from wondering out loud how two people who were so bright could also be so stupid.

'How did your call with that Whitley chap go, by the way? Did he agree to the arrangement that Rucha suggested, where you work for both Nightingale and SWETE?' Meera asked. 'You were supposed to talk to him yesterday, right?'

Aalo seemed relieved at the change of subject. 'Yeah, we talked. It went well. I think I've convinced him to take me on as a consultant.'

'What would that mean?'

'To begin with, I can keep working with SWETE and I'll be based in India. For now, I'd just be recommending interesting projects from India and look into possible collaborations for the foundation.'

'That sounds good.' Meera waited for a moment and then asked, 'Any travel?'

'I'd need to check in with the foundation every few months,' Aalo said with studied casualness.

'Aalo? You worked that into your contract, didn't you?' Meera asked softly.

Aalo didn't say anything. Suddenly, the surface of the table consumed all her attention.

Meera tried again. 'You worked out regular trips to London because you want to spend time with Zeb, right?'

'I didn't realize how much it would hurt to not be with him,' Aalo said in a small voice. 'When we were together, all I kept thinking about were the things that would pull us apart and I was so scared. Of my dad, of all this Hindu-Muslim stuff. But when he was gone …' Aalo looked up at Meera, '… all I could think of was being with him. It's not like I can't function. I can and I have, but Meera, we were so happy together and he just makes me feel … more.'

Meera wiped the tears running down Aalo's face. Aalo started. She hadn't realized she was crying. 'You're in love with him,' Meera said gently. 'And I have a feeling I'm going to have to start house-hunting.'

Aalo sniffed and shook her head. 'No, you don't, because my dad said to tell you the flat above ours is empty and the owner is a friend of his. So, if you want to rent it, he can set you up easy-peasy. Also, if you meant you'd move out so that Zeb and I could live together happily ever after, dividing our time between Bandra and Notting Hill, I blew my chances with Zeb. I mean, he isn't even telling me he's coming to India. Not just India, to Mumbai. He obviously hates me.'

Meera cursed herself for having promised Zeb she wouldn't tell Aalo anything of their conversation. 'Just come to The Hive with me, ok?' she said finally. 'We'll sit right at the back so that he can't see you, if you want.'

Aalo sighed. 'Yeah, good idea. If he's wearing one of his black, button-down shirts, I'll probably just tear it off his body if I'm within touching distance of the stage.'

—She's in.

—You. Are. The. Best.

—Safe flight. Try not to get detained by airport security.

—Yes, because that's just the kind of distraction I want while travelling across continents to possibly be rejected by the woman I love.

—The two of you really need to work on your communication.

16

The day of Zeb's events at *The Daily* Hive, Aalo's phone was inundated with hugs and good wishes. From a GIF of an army of Care Bears (from Kekoo) to a long essay of encouragement (from Rebecca), Aalo received messages of all shapes and sizes.

'You'd think I'm the one giving a lecture instead of Zeb,' Aalo grumbled as the cab made its way to the National Centre for the Performing Arts, where *The Daily* Hive was held every year. 'What does this even mean?' She showed Meera a message from Jo. It was a GIF from *Magic Mike*, showing one of the dancers pulling off his pants. 'What am I supposed to do with this? How does this relate in any way to me showing up to ogle the man I'm in love with?'

Meera peered at the screen. 'Judging from the GIF, I'm not sure Jo entirely understands what we mean by lecture demonstration.'

When they reached the NCPA, the complex was full of people and *The Daily*'s banners were everywhere. Zeb's first presentation was at the Experimental Theatre, and the queue for it wound all the way round to the back.

'I'm impressed,' Meera murmured as they made their way to the entry. 'I didn't realize so many people knew Zeb in Mumbai.'

'At this point, I'm kind of glad I know you and can skip the queue, thanks to your fancy gold pass.' Aalo tried not to think about the butterflies in her stomach. It made no sense for her to feel nervous. She wasn't planning to go up to Zeb. She wasn't even planning on him spotting her. She'd figure out whether or not she could work up the courage to speak to Zeb after his second session. This was just about her getting to see him again.

'You do realize there's a downside to gold passes,' Meera said, as they entered the theatre. 'We can only sit on seats marked for gold passes.'

Aalo felt her stomach turn to concrete. 'I can't sit up front, Meera. I just can't.'

Meera steered her inside and said, 'Let's see what our options are first.'

Fortunately, in addition to the front rows, there was a cluster of seats on the first floor that was also reserved for gold pass holders. 'It's a terrible view,' warned one of the ushers.

'That row isn't visible from stage, right?' Aalo asked.

The usher looked confused and mildly relieved when Meera said they'd find their way to the seats without the usher's help and herded Aalo upstairs. Once they'd got seats, Aalo started checking her phone every few seconds.

'Breathe,' Meera whispered.

'I'm trying,' said Aalo.

'Put that phone away or I'm taking it from you.'

'Try it. I'll just pee here out of nervousness, I swear.'

Fifteen minutes later, there was no sign of any presentation starting and there were ripples of restlessness in the audience. Finally, a disembodied voice said the session would be 'a little delayed' because Zeb Shams was running late.

Meera grimaced. 'They're being put up next door at the Oberoi. How can he be delayed?' she said. She checked her phone. The signal inside the theatre was weak. After a few minutes, Meera stood up. 'You sit here,' she said to Aalo. 'I'm just going to check what's going on with Zeb.'

'What do you mean?' Aalo didn't like the tone of Meera's voice.

'Nothing. I just want to check that he landed in Mumbai without any trouble.'

Aalo sat up straighter and literally barred Meera's way by sticking her legs out in front of her. 'What trouble?'

Meera looked around with a tinge of embarrassment. The row was full of people who were quite obviously trying to eavesdrop on the two of them. 'Stop being paranoid and let me through, Aalo,' Meera said in a low voice.

'Tell me what you're not telling me first,' Aalo demanded.

'But if I do that, I'll have told you,' Meera replied, a little smile playing on her lips.

'Dammit Meera, what aren't you telling me? Is he ok?'

'Stop freaking out. He had some trouble getting his visa. That's all. But I know he got it. I also know he got on the flight at London. It's an Emirates flight, so the chances of him being hounded for having been in Syria and Iraq recently are low. Still, I just …'

'How do you know he was in Syria and Iraq?' Aalo's voice was almost a squeak.

'You told me. Are you going to let me through or not?'

Just then the speakers crackled again, and the announcer requested everyone to switch off their phones because they were about to start the lecture demonstration. Zeb walked on stage even while he was being introduced, and considering Meera was still standing, it wasn't surprising that his eye went straight to their row. He was wearing a white shirt, with the top couple of buttons open and the sleeves rolled up. Aalo crouched in her seat, once again cursing her height and desperately hoping that the darkness was obscuring her. Zeb waved. Meera waved back and sat down.

'I'm sorry for being late,' Zeb said after thanking everyone for having come to hear him. 'I was just coming out of the hotel when I got a call. It was from Akbar's brother. Akbar and I started Cameraderie almost three years ago. Right from the very beginning, we described Cameraderie as "a photo agency with branches in London and Sulaymaniyah". The London office was my kitchen. Specifically, my kitchen table. The Sulaymaniyah office was Akbar's brother's garage.'

Everyone laughed. Zeb grinned. Behind him, a photograph of Akbar appeared on the screen. The smile left Zeb's face. 'A little more than two months ago, we got news that Akbar had disappeared after crossing into ISIS-controlled territory. Some people said they'd seen him being shot and falling to the ground. A few people said they saw him being taken away on a stretcher. Akbar is not a foolhardy photographer. His wife is pregnant, so he was definitely not going to take stupid risks while on assignment. But the fact was that we had lost him. Since then, all of us in Cameraderie, Akbar's family—we've all been sending out feelers to anyone who might have any news. We've heard nothing. It's been weeks of dead ends and despair. Until this morning.' Zeb looked up, in the direction of where Aalo and Meera were sitting. 'I was on my way here, when Akbar's brother called to say he'd received a message from someone who is probably a courier for the ISIS. He said that Akbar is alive and that we may be able to get him back.' The entire theatre burst out in applause. Zeb laughed and looked up once more in the direction of Aalo and Meera. He said, 'It feels a bit like India's my lucky charm.'

For the next thirty minutes, Zeb took the audience through a series of photographs he'd taken, as well as photographs by Akbar and other Cameraderie photographers. He talked about what precautions they took, things that went wrong and things that unexpectedly made the images special. He was honest about the hardship he faced, and his passion for his work was evident. When the floor was thrown open to questions, a woman asked him what he considered the most challenging part of his kind of photojournalism.

'Knowing when it's time to carpe diem and also when we should pass the mic, or the camera as the case may be,' Zeb replied, and then he shook his head. 'Actually, as someone who has worked in conflict areas, I actually think it's hardest on the people who love us, those we hold dear. If it's dangerous for us to go to certain places, it's terrifying for our loved ones to be at home and not know what's happening, whether we're safe.' He smiled wryly. 'There's a reason that most of us try to eventually transition towards less sensitive assignments. That said, especially in the times we're in now, it feels more necessary than ever to do whatever we can to ensure photojournalists like Akbar are able to do their work safely and freely.'

For the last question, Zeb pointed at someone who was near the back and it took time for the microphone to reach him. 'What's your policy when it comes to taking photos of people? In terms of getting their permission,' asked a male voice.

'Prickly topic, permissions,' Zeb said with a smile. 'Realistically, it isn't possible for street scenes, but I do my best to get permission from anyone who is the focus of a photo I take. With digital cameras, it's great, because I can show the photo and the subjects know what it looks like. The problem is, a lot of the times, a stranger will not feel comfortable or empowered enough to tell the photographer that they don't like the photo. So, I need to be alert to that. Be aware of my privileges and what effect they have on those around me. Also, I take a lot of photos. With my phone and my camera. Sometimes, I don't realize that I have a shot of a person that works, that sings rather than just speaks, until I see it with fresh eyes. That can be months later, by which time, I've no way of contacting said person. I'll give you an example. I was recently in Istanbul with a friend. I took tonnes of photos, as I always do. It was only later, when I was recovering from a road accident in Syria, that I realized one photo from the Istanbul trip was special.' Zeb squinted and looked up. 'Aalo, can I show these nice people a photo I took of you?' He turned to the person who had asked the question and winked. 'See? I take permission when I can.' He looked back up in Aalo's direction.

Aalo meanwhile found she had lost her voice. Meera nudged Aalo. 'Yes,' Aalo replied hoarsely. 'I think.'

'She said yes,' Meera yelled.

Zeb gave a thumbs up. 'Give me a second while I find it on the laptop.'

Within seconds, the screen was filled with a shot of Aalo laughing with a man who was selling fish sandwiches by the Bosphorus in Istanbul.

'Technically, there's a lot wrong with this photo, but there's an immediacy to it that makes you feel like Aalo is about to step out of the photo and offer you a bite of the sandwich she's holding. I look at it and I can hear Aalo laughing, I can hear the shop owner urging her to eat the sandwich while it's hot, after shaking his head at her claim that Bengalis might love fish more than the Turks. Strictly speaking, the image is a little blurry in parts, the framing isn't perfect, the geometry leaves a lot to be desired, and in real life, Aalo is actually one hundred times lovelier. Despite all this, this photo evokes an emotional reaction in me, and that's transformed an everyday shot into an *amazing* one. Except I didn't get permission from both my subjects to share it. While Aalo just said yes, the fish sandwich man isn't here to give his approval. So, technically, I shouldn't be showing you this photo. The reason I feel comfortable showing it is because I'm confident the photograph doesn't misrepresent him. Obviously, photography is full of people—mostly men. White men, in particular, who say what I've just said. They believe they're representing their subjects when they're actually misrepresenting them. Fortunately, you have critics and the internet. If they do a takedown of your work, I'd advise you to reflect upon the criticism and fight the instinct to dismiss them.'

While he wrapped up the session and the lights came up in the room, Aalo said, 'He's an idiot and he's wrong. I'm nowhere close to being as beautiful as he makes me look in his photos, and holy hell, I'd forgotten how totally hot he is.' She turned to Meera. 'What's this accident in Syria business?'

'How would I know?' Meera asked.

'You seem to be way more in touch with him than I've been.'

Meera ignored that comment and said, 'What I want to know is whether you can walk or if I'll have to carry you to the speakers' lounge. Because that man over there has overcome challenges posed by Islamic terror and right-wing Hindus to come to you, so give him some credit.'

The whole room erupted in applause just then, not because they'd heard Meera, but because Zeb was being given a bouquet by someone.

'At a later point, I will exact revenge for conspiring with Zeb behind my back,' Aalo said unsteadily as she rose to her feet.

On her way to the speakers' lounge, Aalo had a strange sense of déjà vu.

So much was like the night in London when she'd made her presentation on Rucha's behalf, except this time, it was Zeb who had been on stage and Aalo was the one who would surprise him afterwards. Meera kept getting held up by people who wanted to say hello, but eventually, they made it to the lounge. Aalo scanned the room quickly. Zeb wasn't there.

'Are you sure he'll be coming here?' Aalo asked.

'Positive,' Meera replied. 'Do you want a drink?'

Aalo had another vivid flashback of Zeb handing her a glass of red wine at the gala dinner after she'd made her presentation. 'Can you get me two glasses of red wine?' she asked.

'Sure,' Meera replied. 'Stop staring at the door like you're Uri Geller trying to bend a spoon.'

'Uri what?'

Meera rolled her eyes. 'Never mind. I'll be back with your wine.'

Moments later, Zeb walked in with an eager young woman who was probably his assigned handler. He saw Aalo and walked up to her.

'Hey there, Mukherjee,' he said softly.

'I love you,' Aalo blurted out, and Zeb's green eyes flared.

'About fucking time,' he breathed as he took another step closer to her.

'I come bearing wine,' Meera said loudly. Zeb stepped back, a little embarrassed.

The happiness on his face, though, when he saw Meera was adorable. Taking a glass from her, he wrapped Meera in a big hug. 'My fairy godmother!' he said. 'Thank you so much. For everything.'

Meera shook her head. 'Don't mention it. Also, let's be fair, I didn't do it for you. I did it for this one,' she said, handing Aalo the other glass. 'She promised me that she'd rip the clothes off you if you wore a black shirt. But you, sadly, opted for white.'

'I can change and be back in three minutes,' Zeb said, and for a couple of moments, everything and everyone else blurred into the distance. All Aalo and Zeb saw were each other.

Meera cleared her throat loudly, making Aalo and Zeb blink and take half a step back. 'You two, get a grip,' she said, obviously amused.

Aalo's eyes dropped from Zeb's eyes to the region of his belt buckle. 'Don't tempt me,' Aalo muttered.

Both Zeb and Meera choked on their drinks.

'What exactly are the public indecency laws in this country?' Zeb asked Meera.

Meera's phone started ringing. 'I'm going to have to take this, which means the two of you are going to be unchaperoned. Please try to not cause a scandal. Remember, you don't need to get a room. Zeb already has one in the hotel next door. Also, Zeb, your next session is in an hour.' She looked at Aalo, who had eyes only for Zeb. 'I'm guessing we're not going to that dinner that you were dragging me to in the evening. I'll see you in a couple of days?' Meera said, grinning.

Aalo nodded vaguely, and then snapped her head round to look at Meera. 'No!' she yelped. 'Tonight! I'm seeing you tonight. At Ling's. We're throwing a party.'

Meera started. 'We are?'

'Actually, we'll hijack the party that I was going to take you to.'

'We will?' Meera looked thoroughly perplexed. 'Why?'

'Because I want the rest of the gang to meet Zeb. You have to be there.'

'No,' Meera corrected. 'Zeb has to be there, and I'm sure you'll make sure he will be there.'

Aalo took a step towards Meera and glowered at her. 'Meera, so help me god, you are going to be at Ling's by 9 p.m. Is that clear?'

'Okay, calm down. I'll be there.' Meera rolled her eyes. 'Go be hormonal with Zeb,' she said, and after waving bye to Zeb, Meera walked away.

'The way you stared her down, that was great. A little scary, but great,' Zeb said.

'It doesn't work on her though,' Aalo said, her eyes following Meera. Then she took a deep breath and turned to face Zeb. He was smiling at her and Aalo felt like a million lightbulbs had lit up under her skin. 'Ok, since you have a session coming up, a quickie doesn't seem like a viable option. Come for a walk instead?' she said.

'Jesus, Blurty, have some mercy,' Zeb pleaded, while turning pink.

Aalo took his hand in hers and they made their way out of the NCPA, to the paved seaside promenade of Nariman Point.

'Why didn't you message me after Istanbul?' Aalo asked, once they were walking by the sea.

'You gave me the distinct impression that what happens in Istanbul, stays in Istanbul,' Zeb replied.

'Oh, come on, Baz told you I was desperate to find out how you were.'

Zeb stopped abruptly and turned to stand almost nose to nose with Aalo. 'Yeah, about that. Why the hell were you messaging Baz instead of me?'

'I couldn't get through to you, you idiot! You were in bloody Syria!'

'You could have messaged me after Baz told you I was contactable, but no. You were happy to keep chatting with Baz.'

'Aurangzeb Shams, are you seriously telling me that you think I am even remotely interested in your brother?'

'No. What I'm telling you is that I was jealous of my brother because you, Mukherjee, were showering him with calls and texts while giving me the cold shoulder.'

'But you know I love you.'

In a movie, everything would have frozen to a silent stop the moment Aalo said her bit, and the world would have shrunk to just two skittering heartbeats. But no such thing was possible on Marine Drive, where families, lovers, clusters of friends and marathon runners all jostled against each other for space. Everything continued to rush around Aalo and Zeb. The two of them came to a standstill instead.

'Say it again,' he whispered.

Aalo leaned in to put her lips next to his ear. 'You were right. What we have between us is real, and yes, I love you,' she said. She heard her voice. It was steady and ringing with happiness. She loved him, and he'd come all the way to India for her, so he probably was at least halfway in love with her too. Contentment settled on her, as light and magical as fluttering petals. Aalo stepped back and held Zeb's hand. 'This is when you tell me you're a little bit in love with me too,' she told him.

'Nope,' he said, squeezing her hand. 'I'm going to make you wait because you made me wait.'

'Ah. As in, it's a less pleasant take on dick for twat.'

Zeb burst out laughing. 'You remember,' he said.

'How could I forget? I'm a girl in love. I remember everything about you. So quit making me wait.'

'Was I supposed to decode you love me from you telling me we had no future together?'

'No, you were supposed to decode it from the fact that I kept extending my trip till the end of time, as though there was no job or life waiting for me back in India.' Aalo pulled away from Zeb and started walking faster, as though she were leaving him behind.

'I love you too.' Zeb's soft declaration was just one thread in the sonic swirl of traffic and yelling and ringtones, but it was all Aalo could hear in that moment.

She stopped, feeling a little unsteady, and slowly turned to face him again. 'Speaking of jobs, I wangled one at the Nightingale Foundation. I'm going to be a consultant, and while I'm not entirely sure what that means work-wise, I do know they will be flying me to London every other month, for about a week.'

Zeb's eyes flared. 'That's brilliant,' he said.

'The pay is horrifically bad. There's no way I can afford rent.'

'I have a spare room.'

'I don't think I can even afford a room.'

'I'm not asking you for rent.'

Aalo frowned. 'You should know that self-reliance is a big deal for me. Being dependent on someone is not going to sit well.'

'Ok, then you can get one side of the bed, and I'll take payment for it in kind,' Zeb said and then shuddered. 'That sounds way too *Pretty Woman* for me.'

They'd stopped even the pretense of walking by this time. Behind them was the glittering water of the Arabian Sea and the curve of Marine Drive. Zeb took Aalo's face in his hands and said, 'I had a whole speech planned out in which I'd tell you that I was going to change the way I worked …'

Aalo put a finger on his lips. 'Tell me about Akbar. He's alive?'

Zeb nodded. 'It seems like it. They might ask for a ransom, which means that I've got my work cut out. Either way, we're going to need the British and Kurdish governments to help us do this negotiation. But we'll figure it out. It's one of the reasons that I expect I'll be spending more time in London in the immediate future at least.'

'Nice. Now you can go back to your speech.'

'Thanks,' Zeb said wryly. 'It was long and poetic and very persuasive. And right now, I can't remember a damn word of it, because about one quarter of my brain is thinking of all the things we'll do in your week in London, while the other three-quarters is imagining kissing you right now.'

'Probably not advisable at this location, though I've seen others do it,' Aalo said. 'But I've got something that'll do the job of a cold shower. You introduced me to your family, so I feel the need to tell you about mine. There's Meera, whom you already know …'

'And love.'

'Get in line. But yes, Meera. You'll meet Becks and Fatima and Jo this evening. Hema, Farhana and Rucha will be there too. They're my SWETE family.'

'This is one hell of a party you've organized.'

'It's actually my sly attempt at engineering a romantic reunion for Meera. There's this guy, they're not together, but they really should be.'

'Ah. Hence: you staring her down. I get it now.'

Aalo nodded. 'That's why I need her to come. That's also why I'm doing it at Ling's. It's where things got hot and heavy between Meera and her Boy Wonder the first time. You'll like him. But that's not the point.' Aalo paused to take a deep breath. 'So the two people you won't meet tonight are my mother and father. This is partly because they live in Kolkata and are currently on holiday, and partly because my father, in his old age, has turned into a Muslim-hater.' Aalo grimaced. 'It sounds horrible when I say it out loud, but he sounds a whole lot worse when he starts speaking. I can't understand it, but I do love him, and I'm hoping that when it comes down it, his love for me will trump the bigotry, but I don't know whether that will happen. My mum's great though. You'll love her. She's a fan of your photography and your "Pathan" hotness.'

On cue, a group of boys strolled past, loudly singing '*Jhoome Jo Pathaan*' from Shah Rukh Khan's blockbuster film. Aalo giggled and Zeb looked confused.

'I can get hold of one of those Afghan caps, if that helps,' he said. 'But we'll figure out how to win your father over later. There's no rush.'

'Really?'

'Truly.' Zeb scanned the area quickly and then pressed a quick kiss on Aalo's lips.

Aalo pulled his tucked-in shirt out and slid her hand underneath it.

'Seriously?' Zeb raised an eyebrow. 'This was supposed to be a cold shower conversation.'

'I've said my bit. My god, I've missed your skin.'

'You're going to get us arrested. Did you seriously just undo one of your buttons?'

'It's a new bra. It's supposed to 'maximize the cleavage'. Any thoughts?'

'Sweet Jesus.'

'Also, is thirty minutes really too short for a quickie?'

Zeb pulled Aalo's hand out and held it firmly in his. 'Just walk, Mukherjee. And not in the direction of the hotel. We're not beginning the rest of our lives with a quickie.'

'Your hotel and NCPA are in the same direction. What if you look at it as beginning the rest of our lives with an orgasm each?' asked Aalo.

'Blurty, you might just have a point.'

By the time Meera and Faisal finished making the next morning's edition with all the publicity photos from The Hive's opening day, it was almost 1 a.m.

'I hate these events,' Faisal groaned in the lift when they could finally leave the office. 'We could have been done by midnight today if it wasn't for that bloody "red carpet" page. Thanks so much for helping me out today, by the way. I would have probably been here all night if you hadn't stepped in.'

'Glad I could help, but I was slow. My page-making skills are rusty,' Meera said. 'I wish we could leak the news that *The Daily*'s photographers captioned Leo DiCaprio as Prince of Bhutan and put Mammootty down as Muhammad Kutty Panaparambil Ismail.'

'Genius, as usual.'

'Seriously though, you need to do some hires,' Meera told Faisal. 'You can't make the paper with two people on the team.'

'Today was a bad day. Four people couldn't come in for different reasons, and of course, there was The Hive. But yeah, I do need to hire … except, guess what? Freeze on new hires. I'm trying to convince Navin to let me at least replace Jeet, but we'll see.'

Meera tried to ignore how everything inside her revolted at the idea of Jeet being replaced. The lift doors opened on the ground floor. 'That's me,' she said.

'No car tonight?'

'I was at the NCPA in the morning. It's hell trying to get a parking spot there during The Hive.'

'Makes sense. I'll drop you,' Faisal offered.

'Don't be silly. You live in Mazgaon. I live in Bandra. I'll take a cab. There's always a bunch of them at the gate,' she said, and waved to Faisal as the lift doors closed to take him to the basement parking area.

As she walked to the main gate, Meera pulled out her phone to find messages from Aalo and the other girls, asking her where she was. Then there were photos, which were clearly supposed to tempt Meera into coming. They might have worked if she'd had the time to look up from making pages with Faisal. Fatima had sent some videos, which were taking forever to download. It seemed everyone was at this dinner that Aalo had organized, even Rucha Phadke and her husband. Meera sighed and felt stiff around her neck and wrist. It had been years since she'd spent these many hours hunched at a computer screen, making pages for the newspaper.

'You're supposed to be at a party at Ling's.'

Meera's head snapped up at the sound of Jeet's voice. For a second, she thought she was hallucinating—there he was leaning against the black-and-yellow taxi at the gate. He was wearing jeans frayed around his thighs and the slogan of his T-shirt was hidden behind his folded arms. Meera had thought she remembered every detail of Jeet's face and the lean lines of his body, but now that he was in front of her and in the flesh, her brain was frantically storing other details—the way the light fell on the line of his nose and his forearms, the way he stretched out his legs, the bumps that his knuckles made.

Jeet straightened and walked up to her.

'Faisal was short-staffed, so I helped him out,' Meera said. 'What are you doing here?'

'You missed a good party. Aalo's organization was impeccable. Even that old dude at Ling's was impressed by her. Your gang of girls is great, by the way. I met Zeb, who is very cool. I had this elaborate plan of making a grand romantic gesture—which, in my defence, I discussed with Fatima first and she was totally on board—so we cleared tables to do a little concert. Sarfaraz sang a couple of songs, I sang a few. Two of them were for you, and I kept thinking that any moment now, like in the movies, she'll walk in through the door.' Jeet sighed and looked down at Meera, frowning. 'Except you were here, making pages.'

'I'm sorry I missed it. I just thought it was some random dinner that Aalo was calling me for,' Meera said. 'I would have loved to hear you and Sarfaraz.'

Jeet raised an eyebrow. 'That's what you're sorry to have missed? The music?' He sighed again, this time theatrically. 'You're a tough crowd.' Gesturing to a cabbie, he held the door open for her. 'Come on, into the cab. The party's moved to Aalo's place, and I'm your escort service. Aalo's orders.' He put his hand on the small of Meera's back to shepherd her inside. Meera felt every nerve ending in her body spark, and as she stumbled her way into the cab, she hit her head with a loud crack on the door frame.

'Shall I get you some ice, madam?' the cab driver offered, his face full of concern and paan masala.

'No, no, it's ok,' Meera replied. Her head was throbbing, but most of what was inside her head was scrambling as it registered Jeet shuffling inside to sit close to her. While telling the cabbie her address, he put an arm around her shoulders. Then he tugged Meera closer and kissed her temple. She felt him blow on it gently.

'My mum would do that to all my scrapes,' Jeet said, as the cabbie started the car. 'She said the wind would take the hurt away.' They were quiet for a bit. 'I went back home for a couple of days, for my dad's birthday,' Jeet said, as though she'd asked him what he'd been up to. 'My mum got him some weird book on twelfth century Tamil poetry that he's been looking for apparently. In it, she wrote … hold on, let me pull out my phone so I don't get it wrong.' Meera caught a glimpse of his home screen. It had a photo of a bottle of honey. '"Don't ever think I fell for you or fell over you. I didn't fall in love, I rose in it,"' Jeet read out.

'Toni Morrison,' said Meera.

'Yeah, I googled it,' he said. 'I got *Jazz*, too, in case you were going to roll your eyes at how illiterate the youth of the day are.

But the point is, it reminded me of something you told me the night we fought. You told me you chose me. It didn't register when you said it, but when it finally did, I figured I should make some sort of effort to be good enough for you to choose.'

Meera looked up to tell him that she hadn't meant it like that, but he stopped her from saying anything by kissing her. 'Fortunately for me,' Jeet murmured against her lips, 'I have it from reliable sources that you hold jobless singer-songwriters in high regard. Incidentally, I might have an EP coming out next month. Four of the six songs are about you. I almost called one of them "Nipple Clamps".'

Meera lingered over his lower lip. 'You're far more obsessed with those things than I am. I saw that interview.'

Jeet smiled, still kissing her. 'I should warn you, a couple of the songs on the EP are a bit angry at you for being a man-eater who chewed me up and spat me out,' he said.

'I hope to god that's not one of your lyrics.' Meera gave in to temptation and slipped her hand under Jeet's T-shirt and let it settle on his chest. Under her palm, she could feel the soft graze of his body hair and the steady thump of his heart. 'I've missed you desperately,' Meera admitted, as she tucked her head into the crook of his neck. 'But I still don't think this is going to work. We're at different points in our lives. You'll want things from a relationship that I can't give.'

'Give me an example?' His lips moved against her hairline, each word feeling like a hint of a kiss.

Meera started drawing circles on his skin, loving the feel of him. 'There are so many. The hours I keep as a journalist are insane.'

'Not sure if you noticed, but I used to work in the same office as you until very recently. I know your working hours. Intimately,' Jeet said mildly.

'They'll get worse. I want to go back to doing some ground reports.'

'That's amazing! We need more journalists like you doing actual reporting. I promise I'll be there with a lawyer and bail money if and when you get arrested. Or with a dabba if you land in jail.'

'Don't be silly. My point is that I'm not interested in stuff like going out drinking, getting high. You'll obviously want to do that …'

'You're making me sound like an addict in the making, which I'm not, but that's not really the point. If you don't feel like hanging out with us kids, don't. Simple. Just come home to me and let me come home to you.'

'What about marriage?' asked Meera. 'I'm definitely never getting married again, but you'll probably want to at some point, with someone. Have babies.'

'You keep doing what you are with your hand, and there's a good chance that we'll end up making a baby in this cab because I'm not carrying a condom.'

Meera froze and whipped her hand out from under his shirt, awkwardly brushing against the bulge in his pants in the process. Jeet winced. 'Sorry,' Meera said. 'I didn't realize.'

'The veshti is making more and more sense to me with every minute I spend with you.' He breathed out slowly and looked out of the window to figure out where they'd reached. 'What are the chances that you can help me keep it in my pants for about five more minutes till we reach the apartment? Oh god, I forgot everyone's already reached.' He lifted Meera's face. 'When you said you like exhibitionism …?'

Meera burst out laughing and kissed him lightly. 'Seriously, Jeet, how will this work?'

'I'm so glad you asked because I do have a couple of proposals for you,' Jeet replied. 'Don't look so alarmed. None of them involve marriage. My first proposal was to suggest I become a hybrid of flatmate and third wheel to you and Aalo, but Aalo tells me she's going to be dividing her time between London and Mumbai, and you're getting your own place. Which brings me to my second proposal: I'd like to apply for the position of housekeeper. You can leave all the domestic stuff to me, thereby receiving the benefit of a decently-kept home *and* sex on tap, while fighting the good fight for journalism in India.'

'You forget I have Sujata,' Meera told him. 'Are you ready to duel with her for that job?'

'Why would I take on Sujata? She and I make a great team. Or at least we will once you and I have convinced her that she doesn't need to protect you from my smooth-operator moves,' Jeet said, grinning, while Meera burst into laughter. He pulled her closer. 'I also have a third proposal. I hold on to my flat in Dadar, despite my weirdo landlord, and you have your place in Bandra. In this way, we have two places to call our own, in two neighbourhoods of Mumbai. Which is a ridiculous luxury in this mad city, but you deserve nothing less. Neither of us is obliged to hang out with each other's friends, though I do like your gang, and from what I've heard of Rebecca's cooking, I would hugely appreciate a doggy bag from your monthly dinners. Occasionally, we can go wild, and maybe see a movie or attend a concert or step out for dinner together, but no pressure. If—ok, when—I behave badly, you can cast me out to sleep on the sofa. Or in Dadar.' The cab stopped. Jeet cupped Meera's face with one warm hand and lowered his head to bite her lightly on the neck. 'What I'm basically asking is this: that you follow your heart, and I'll follow mine. Because I know, with every cell in my body, that we'll find our way to each other.'

When there was no noise of the door opening or any mention of paying the fare, the cabbie looked into his rearview mirror to check what was going on in the backseat. He found Meera practically straddling Jeet; they didn't so much kiss as eat each other up. Jeet's hands ran over her, bunching the hell out of her sari and pulling her hair out of its bun. The cabbie cursed under his breath and looked away. But he couldn't stop himself from looking up at his rearview mirror just once more for one long guilty second, before clearing his throat very loudly.

'I think we've reached,' he announced and added a honk, just in case.

The two in the backseat pulled apart. Meera climbed off Jeet and rearranged her sari into some sort of decorum. Looking at the rearview mirror, her eyes briefly met the driver's.

'This is the right place, isn't it, madam?' the cabbie asked.

Meera locked her fingers with Jeet's. 'Yes,' she said, 'we're home.'

Acknowledgements

I suppose for this book, the biggest thanks should technically go to all the disappointing people who left me with no choice but to imagine better specimens of straight masculinity, and the hopelessly topsy-turvy world in which we find ourselves. The times are so stripped of hope that escapism is starting to feel like a fundamental human right. However, in the spirit of this book, let me focus instead on those who sparked joy and made this novel possible.

Writing is a solitary activity, but for a manuscript to become a book, it takes a fairy tale. *Lightning in a Shot Glass* has had its Cinderella moment because of some amazing godmothers: Bijal, who listened to every rant, read every draft, and each time made life and the manuscript better; Amrita, who effectively paved the way for the book to be published; Saumya, who read the first draft and used the 'track changes' feature to leave love notes for Meera and Aalo; Hemali and Naomi at A Suitable Agency, who have been absolute champions; and Dharini, my editor at HarperCollins India, who somehow turns official emails and messages into shots of dopamine. Thanks also to Samit, one of the few good men and the best person to whinge with about the writing life.

I could concoct love stories like the ones in this novel not from personal experience, but because I'm surrounded by people whose love stories deserve their own books. My parents will celebrate fifty years of being married this year (!). Ma and Baba rarely agree on anything other than mishti being the superior food group and cream biscuits being a) 'health food' and b) mandatory with cha. Yet for all their divergences, they are proof that it's possible to have and be a partner who will do everything in their power to push you to be the best version of yourself. For fifty years and counting. Thank you, both of you, for being the lunatic romantics that you are.

Thanks also to my little family of choice—Neha, Suhani, Hashim, Zee and the rest of the gang; Irma on another continent—for being so full of love, wisdom and silliness. How the hell did I get so lucky as to have such a talented, beautiful bunch to call my own?

And thank you to Mumbai, for raising me to become the woman and writer that I am now; for being home for two decades, and for letting me go with grace.

Once upon a time, life was giving lemons at a rate that would require any sensible person to not just make lemonade, but add generous lashes of vodka to it. However, I did not make (alcoholic) lemonade. Instead, I tried to build another world, one sentence and one fictional brick at a time, so that I could escape into it. To you, dear reader, goes the sincerest thanks for taking a chance with *Lightning in a Shot Glass*. I hope it brings comfort and distraction, if not a giggle and a few happy sighs. Thank you for reading.

About the Author

Deepanjana Pal has been a journalist for two decades and a collector of stories for as long as she can remember. She has written three children's books, one feminist thriller, one biography and too many film reviews to count. She's a columnist with *Hindustan Times*, and has previously worked with *TimeOut Mumbai*, *Newslaundry* and *Film Companion*. She runs a books newsletter titled *Dear Reader* and may be found posting photos of clouds and lightning on Instagram (@dpanjana).

HarperCollins *Publishers* India

At HarperCollins India, we believe in telling the best stories and finding the widest readership for our books in every format possible. We started publishing in 1992; a great deal has changed since then, but what has remained constant is the passion with which our authors write their books, the love with which readers receive them, and the sheer joy and excitement that we as publishers feel in being a part of the publishing process.

Over the years, we've had the pleasure of publishing some of the finest writing from the subcontinent and around the world, including several award-winning titles and some of the biggest bestsellers in India's publishing history. But nothing has meant more to us than the fact that millions of people have read the books we published, and that somewhere, a book of ours might have made a difference.

As we look to the future, we go back to that one word—
a word which has been a driving force for us all these years.

Read.

Harper Collins · 4th · HARPER FICTION · HARPER NON-FICTION · HARPER BUSINESS · HCCB HARPERCOLLINS CHILDREN'S BOOKS

HARPER DESIGN · Harper Sport · HARPER PERENNIAL · HARPER VANTAGE · हार्पर हिन्दी · BOOKTOPUS